Wired
for
Chaos

Brett L. Renwick

Wired for Chaos
by Brett L. Renwick
Published 2005 by Creation Books
isbn 1-84068-130-6
copyright © Brett L. Renwick 2005
all world rights reserved
cover design: Brett L. Renwick
cover photograph: J&D Photography
www.creationbooks.com – more blood
www.wiredforchaos.com – more pain
Badass Sci-Fi © Creation Books 2005

Wired
for
Chaos

DEAD AHEAD 'AH YOU
ROOM 61, HOTEL AMELIA COBIA, HAVANA, CUBA, 2031
"My heart stopped beating seconds ago."

Lying face down on a bed wearing a black, Nike warm-up suit is ex-millionaire, playboy and Sony GameRun champion Brice Johnson. His conciseness floats above his body and he thinks, "I'm dead. *He* killed me. This can't be happening. It'll be hours before my guys knock on the door to get me. I can't go out like this. Killed me 'cause…."

At twenty-five, tall, black, handsome and built Brice Johnson had it all and then some. A cheap Samsung deck is still on and a long, clear fiber optic cable is plugged into a jack at the base of his head. It looks like he tried to pull the silicone plug out of his jack before he died and his hand dropped centimeters from his head. The room's air conditioner shakes the clear optic cable the diameter of an elephant's hair that plays the recorded high-rez highlights of B's career in his head.

"Never could have guessed I'd end up like…t-h-i-s. I'm dead and nobody knows. All those fuckin' assholes that wanted me to take a fall—fuck. Fuck. I can't move—has to be a dream…."

The recollections of his life cut in and out and belched into the strongest memory….

WEEKS AGO DURING AN INSPACE BOUT.
SLO-MO THIS SHIT RIGHT HERE.

B' was whipping Tanaka's ass in this *huh*—virtual bout with physical implications. He launched a fierce series of roundhouse windmill-punches, spinning and punching Tanaka in the face as he turned with devastating effect. Kick, stumble, "Oh no." From Tanaka's point of view, it must have looked like a series of cue balls racing towards his dazed head at stock car racing speed, in r-a-p-i-d *succ*ession. But the cue balls were Brice's fists and B' was amping the max supernova. They were InSpace, floggin' bytes like badass renderings of illegal substance induced Walt Disney characters with an adrenalin chaser, dripping psychedelics from that freak, on the street—heightening the headriders trip. The viewers who jacked in for the experiential connection to one of the two players in this game were screaming obscenities into their rigs, many to no one in particular and wanted more blood. Brice was whaling on Tanaka like it was personal. As though Tanaka had killed B's entire family and was delivering his infant son into the arms of a viscous pedophile, only worse. He was a rabid blood lust animal fighting viciously and with glee. As his fists pounded Tanaka. B's eyes lit up with a fierce, all consuming, intoxicating rage fever—he was hungry for more. This was Brice Johnson, naked and primordial. Fierce, brutal and vicious. A carnivore and for this he was exulted and rich. Very rich.

TOKYO MEDICAL AND SURGICAL CLINIC, MINATO-KU, JAPAN, THREE WEEKS EARLIER.

"Doctor, as you know this procedure is my specialty and I have never been—kept from vital information before."

"Doctor, witha' respect to the schematics of this implant, I too ama' unaware of its complexities but it does not trouble me. Why then shoulda' it trouble you so?"

"Surely as a surgeon you recognize the complexity of this procedure."

"Of course."

"Well then you must understand my concern regarding the blacked out area, K16?"

"Doctor Gärtner, please try to understand my position. I, like you have been hired by Sony to perform this operation an' been privy to the same information…"

"Doctor are you telling me that you are comfortable with—with being kept in the dark in this manner? In four hours, we are going to replace the unit in not just any young man's head but Brice Johnson's head. He is the biggest moneymaker in his industry. He is a great deal more than a virtual reality game champion to many young people. So now I ask you, do you understand my concerns? What will I say to my eight-year-old son when he asks me what I did to his hero? What will I say to the board of review when I am made to explain why I went ahead with such an implant on a celebrity without full disclosure as to its true and complete nature?!"

Noguchi slowly unfolds his hands and wipes them across the desk. "I too have a young son who worships Brice San. I too have superiors to answer to," his expression becomes momentarily apologetic.

Doctor Gärtner thought better of bringing his hands together. This was a crucial moment in their dance. If he made the slightest forward movement, Noguchi would rise out of his seat and the meeting would be over. Instead, he opts for the blackened earth ware teacup. He considers it as if it is priceless. He stares out of the window at a blue sky through a white pine treetop and wonders what's on the other side of that wall? An office? A flat-screen projection of a pleasant garden view? He waves the thought off with a turn of his head. A sip of tea and their eyes meet. "Doctor I must apologize. I am at fault for questioning your—your accommodating Sony's wishes. I am unconcerned with the content of the blacked out area—copyrighted secrets or what have you."

Noguchi's toes unfurl.

"Regrettably, being denied information has bruised my ego and caused you—discomfort."

Noguchi's sphincter relaxes.

"I will speak of this no more. Rest assured I will not mention this to the patient or any of his associates," Gärtner rises.

Noguchi rises, "That would be best."

As Gärtner leaves the room his mind is already spinning with pointed questions he will pose to the corporate executives he will immediately seek out in the West wing.

Noguchi passes his hand over the left hand side of his desk prompting soft chime sounds. "Dial Tano." A moment later a man answers in Japanese, "Hello."

"Tano, Dr. Gärtner has just left my office. He is a well-respected surgeon. He is upset."

"Indeed. Brice San is in most capable hands Doctor Noguchi. Please excuse me but my associates and I have just been called away to a meeting. My apologies."

"Yes. Yes."

LISTEN…

Jimmy ascends in an elevator covered with cute yellow painted monsters with two Japanese girls and their mother. The little girls have day-glo pigtails and wear the latest schoolgirl craze, Cybochimies™, interactive earrings the size of a guitar picks. The earrings make sounds, change colors and project cuddly holo animals depending on the surroundings and people who are close to the wearer. They learned how to recognize family, up to six friends and compose tiny themes for each as they approached the wearer. On crowded or noisy streets the earrings emitted a soothing white noise but if the wearer was alone, in front of a bathroom mirror the earrings emitted cooing and kissing sounds. The mood sensors on the earrings could change from happy bright yellow to angry black and tiny black Chihuahua heads would bark with disapproval. The girls were apparently playing a game against each other, which they viewed on the lenses of their day-glo sunglasses. Each girl tapped excitedly on the flexible, game pad sticker they had attached to the back of their left hands. As they bumped each other, the earrings projected tiny animal heads that bent and smirked at Jimmy who rolled his eyes.

As he exits the elevators, he is jostled among the lackeys, jesters, opportunist and hired hands. He acknowledges one or two who have all come to pay their respects to *the B'man*. He slides past Carl and Leroy into Brice's room where he immediately meets the stare of his rival, Olga the Swedish super-model. She smiles at Jimmy from on top of the bed with her white leather clad legs spread eagle. Jimmy phases through the life size holo-image of a Japanese news anchor on mute. Brice is face down on a custom bed with a formfitting hole exposing his face. The bandages covering the back of his head gives him the appearance of an elephantiasis victim. Wearing white and blue striped silk pajamas, Brice is shopping by way of a brand new Sony, VRD (Virtual Retinal Display). The 1/4" diameter clear tube perched on the bridge of his nose that wraps around the right side of his head to his ear and weighs slightly less than five grams. The devise humps cortical induction images directly into a communication implant that can only be supported by other Sony devices. These bionic processors "learn" to provide compatible signals from image sensors throughout the electromagnetic spectrum that are beamed to him via the local telecom provider at five mega pixels given the max electronic and optical constraints, powered by his body heat and ambient lighting.

"No, no the other one on your left arm. Yeah what's that feel like? Soft?"

Erica rubs the fabric between her gloved thumb and forefinger realigning the poly-coated gel surface of Brice's Sony TouchMan™. As his hand lowers to form contact with the device, the diodes in the gel become excited. Tiny lumps grow into mounds and rise to meet his fingers perfectly mirroring the shape of his hand.

"Yeah, I mean you can feel the faintest bit of texture but you know—its crepe."

"Yeah, I get it. What's the other one made of?"

"Like some raw silk-wool combo…"

"Na—a. The 100%—wool crepe. Where's that guy in the navy suit I like?"

"Putting the jacket on."

Erica is in a fashionable store in the Roppongi district and working three sales men at once through an interpreter. Brice sees and hears through a miniature camera mounted on the temple of her Chanel sunglasses and a tiny ear-mike rig.

"Where are the buttons? What's up with the buttonholes and no buttons? Buttons..?"

"Kounoura, what's up with the buttons? Why're they missing?' Yeah, yeah. B', he says that's how you're supposed to wear it."

"Then tell him to buy it then. Find some ties and shirts—you know what. Wrap it up give them my measurements and have everything delivered to the jet by—I donno' whenever we're taking off. You know."

"Done."

"Call me when you get to the next store."

"Yo Kounoura. We're done. Tell them we want these six of these by the end of the week. I'll call to tell them where to deliver all of it."

"Erica the owner is telling me that his tailor is really backed up…"
Erica opens her purse and takes out Brice's black American Express Centurion card, the one that can buy countries or space platforms and the owner's mouth

drops. The reality is more potent than the myth and the matte surface of the card seems to absorb all of the light in the room.

Brice takes the shades off and rubs his eyes.

"Yo B'!" says Jimmy, "How'z the hole in your head?"

"Don't feel a thing. Just bought us some pants."

"Cool. You just wake up?"

"Na—a. And I've been under so long I don't think I'll ever need any sleep again. Lotta' people outside."

"'Course."

"I ain't seeing nobody. I can't wait to fuckin' jack. I've been dreamin' about it."

"I still don't understand why they didn't slap the new unit in while they had you open."

"They're just bein' doctors."

"Well, not too many days left." Behind Jimmy, a wall size holo-screen is showing live footage from the war in Lebanon over a water dispute. A barrage of automatic weapon fire rips apart the side of an armored troop carrier killing all its inhabitants followed by aerial footage of a squatter's camp being shelled by several low flying helicopters.

"Sports!" Yells Brice and the channel flips to coverage of a cricket match in Trinidad, "Shit."

"I rode out to the airport and scoped the new Aerodyne."

"Gleamin' right."

Smiling. "Yeah—h."

Grinning, "Alright, make the call an' buy it. We've looked at enough planes anyway."

Enthused, "Koishi—you met him trip before last, he's the rep. right—well we can definitely work a deal for the press you'll give the new plane."

"Whatever but he's gotta' trade for the Lear and take that out of the purchase price. Work it anyway you want. He can broker and owe us— whatever. Listen I want you to score me some *Doppes* (Virtual Doppelgängers) from a dealer while we're here. I'd send one of the guys but I want some good shit."

"For the Tanaka GameRun?"

"Maybe."

"Anybody I know?"

"I don't even know him. We've only V'ed earlier today. Insist on a physical transaction, his space, an' real secret 'cause this soft is from Roshi."

"Roshi! Thought that mother fucker was retired."

"Still is but a man's gotta' have a hobby and he showed it to this guy who put me on to this guy in Nihonbashi. Says they're *thermo* whatever. I figure its time to rev' up my look anyway."

"How many Doppes we talking?"

"One that's supposed to be me, two others that are close to fly. I figure buy all three, dial copyrights from his line and what ever I don't use we can modify later."

"Want me to deal him?"

"I don't give a shit. Just make sure they ain't light."

"Why the secret agent shit?"

"The man's supposed to have a rep for pissing people off."

"I'm intrigued."

"Don't be. Take Leroy."

"Can we eat now? I'm fucking starving," yawns Olga and Brice looks at her with no emotion.

PAY ATTENTION

Way bored with the scenery of urban Japan, Jimmy sits alone in the back seat of a chauffeured sedan. Driving under the Nihonbashi Bridge, he is completely unaware of a national landmark known to every Japanese schoolchild, the Zero Kilometer Marker. Techno-Baroque is blasting—the base turned up all the way, as Jimmy taps his heal to the beat. His eyes are open but unfocused and in his right hand is a pebble shaped remote that is pressed every few seconds. He is conscious yet hypnotized and junkin' off like nobody's business. The clear fiber optic line plugged directly into Jimmy's head acts like a flexible needle injecting him with gigabits of information. One second a construct of a Man-of-war jellyfish the size of three Empire State Buildings is fighting off thousands of would be student attackers. Next, a dogfight is being waged by disembodied penises against religious icons. Ads for Simstim helmets, software, Coke Cola, Nike, service providers, all manner of pornography (CAD rendered and real), games and mundane infomercials flash, morph and phase one after the other. At the zenith of his horizon are several hyper *intelgofers* excited by the prospect of downloading their harvested intel to their programmer. Dented clay balls with large, uneven teeth, they spin, bounce and undulate in an attempt to siphon Jimmy's attention. A click and one of them dives into Jimmy's face and the multi-colored explosion evaporates into a panorama of deep-text separated by subject headings, full-motion video and digital sound recordings of the Mitsubishi Aerodyne. The full motion simulation window is clicked and Jimmy jaunts to the cockpit of the plane. He banks and dives buzzing helpless peasants on their Junks in Hong Kong's harbor. He can feel the metallic gold wings of the ship being pelted with water spears sent hurling into the air by the force of the ships enormous engine…

In real-time, Leroy is standing on the street pushing Jimmy's knobby knee with his thick index finger. Jimmy feels something poking his knee so he clicks a hard exit. Like a reverse black hole—lined with cerebral molasses—he is simultaneously sucked up and spit outta' InSpace. "Mother-fucker." Sweat beads form on his forehead. He unplugs himself, inserts a small red plug and turns the hyper organ grind off.

The Japanese driver holds the other door open and Jimmy exits. This is wrong side of Nihonbashi across town from Roppongi.

Jimmy takes a deep breath. "Smells like somethin' died," he says to Leroy. "Smell that shit?"

Leroy's eyes scan the street in every direction every window, every doorway and subtly ushers Jimmy into the doorway of a ramshackle two-story building. One block away in a beat up repair truck sit five armed, anti-hostage taskforce members hired by Brice's security company. They run all of the license plates through security checks knowing that savvy perps would score clean rides. Peeking over their shoulder and across the airwaves is a policewoman in the bowels of a federal building sipping a bitter ice-coffee.

On the street, the chauffeur has vanished into a doorway.

Jimmy and Leroy walk up a set of crumbling stairs to the only door. Jimmy acts artificially cool and nonchalant because Leroy's guard is up. Knowing that L' has a tiny two-way in his ear jacked to the tooled boys in the van massages his confidence. Years ago, Leroy had his senses enhanced, which comes in handy when your employer gets bullets thrown at him. So it's no wonder that Leroy hears equipment powering up. The moment the two of them reach the landing low voltage static envelops them and a hidden holo-generator sense-slides them into a construct of a narrow butte in the Grand Canyon. Cool is blown. Leroy undoes the snap on his braided leather holster and takes a fighting stance. Jimmy teeters and regains his balance—the only semblance of reality remaining being four square feet of dirty unfinished floorboards, the door and Leroy. An enormous severed eyeball floats in front of Jimmy and says, "You brought a bodyguard?"

Before Jimmy can utter a word, the door opens and they slowly walk in. The construct flat lines and they getta' load of the dealer. Skinny, young, sporting a weak excuse for a mustache and way-bad high-waters waves them in. Leroy, unhappy that the room is bigger than he'd like, excessively cluttered and has too many places for bad guys to hide, makes eye-to-eye with the biggest male Akita he's ever seen.

In perfect Japanese Jimmy says, "Your construct is most impressive."

The dealer makes a face, closes the door and walks away. A few moments pass and Jimmy decides to follow ol' high-waters through the thicket of hanging cables, boxes, steel frame shelves filled with ancient hardware and lots of empty soda bottles.

"Don't touch anything!" He shouts in Japanese.

Leroy trails behind him slowly, fully aware that the dog is on him like stink on a street person. Jimmy asks, "Are you the dealer..?"

The dealer stops abruptly, turns and puts his right hand out to Jimmy. In gutter Japanese, "Give me."

"What..?"

"Give me your trans-soft."

Taken aback, Jimmy raises his hand but hesitates. The dealer impatiently shakes his hand and makes a face. Jimmy bends his head forward and removes the tiny red translation plug from his head and hands it over. High waters waves his hand over a black console, the unit turns on and a small door opens. The plug is inserted, three buttons pressed and a directory flips up on a clear gas plasma screen. A barrage of numbers, codes, logos and a warning competes for space on the screen.

"Thought so." He opens a drawer rife with parts and plugs looking for something. It takes two more drawers before he finds the plug he is looking for. Jimmy notes the large Band-Aid where this guy's skull jack should be. Another small door, more buttons and Jimmy's program is rewritten. His plug is returned to him and he inserts it.

"I really hate that PG. rated diplomatic shit."

"Ah—h. I dig." In perfect street Japspeak. "You the man. You the man."

The dealer sits in an ancient office chair and puts his feet up on the desk. Jimmy follows suit taking the place in. Reaching behind him, the dealer picks up a thin view-card and turns it on. The card's LCD screen gives him several angles on the hallway, the front entrance of the building, the alleyway and the street in both directions. He freezes when he sees the repair truck.

Leroy's eyes scan the large room every few seconds looking for something out of the ordinary. The space is a bodyguard's nightmare. Too many tall shelving units piled with useless shit that can hide perps. The windows are boarded up, no sign of another exit and this dog would have to be dealt with real fast if feces hits a rotor. Scenarios dart through his head...

"Leroy I'd offer you a soda but you don't drink the stuff."

This takes Jimmy by surprise. "He's cool." But Jimmy isn't. This dealer is too relaxed, too in the know.

"You got something to show me?"

"How's your brother?"

"Wealthy. Why?"

"I like to be—you know 'In the know.'"

Jimmy can't form a solid thought so he shakes his head.

"Heard about Arihito right?"

"Who?"

" Arihito! Chairman of the board who signs the checks at Sony..."

"What about him?"

"Sick an' dying..."

"Naw—w. I would have heard..."

"You just did."

Jimmy waves the conversation off and begins to play with a torn Origami animal. The dealer frowns and takes a pen shaped remote control out of his pocket and points it at the table. "Move that shit out of the way will you." Jimmy, moves a small box and the dealer fires up a Frisbee shaped holo-generator. Up pops a 3-D rendering of something resembling a super hero.

"Weak!" Jimmy pushes a book size black object on the desk to rest his arm. Another *Doppe* pops up slightly better than the first though not good enough to interest him. Jimmy glances at the black object and sighs when the third *Doppe* appears. "Hope you're not planning to pay the rent on this transaction cause it's a hell-no!"

"Roshi will be disappointed."

"No he won't. That's not his shit."

"You wouldn't be trying to chisel the price would you?"

The two consider each other and Jimmy catches a whiff of the guy's boiled cabbage breath. Chinese. Probably only half but definitely Chinese. The dog stands and thinks of rubbing his nose into Leroy's crotch for a scent. Leroy makes eye contact and the dog sits. Pointing at the black object on the desk, "What is it?"

"It's my deck."

"Who makes it?

"Nobody."

"Cute. Cute like a kitten ina' blender. I'm not going to rip the fucking thing off man—n."

"Nobody is making it 'cause it's a prototype. Too expensive for production. Tech-heads—friends of mine went crazy an' put too much in it. It's the baddest deck you're ever going to see…"

"Maker?"

"Nippon Heavy Industries."

"Where are the input slots? The outlet…?"

"See that thing on the table with the dark red circles on it?

"Yeah."

"They feed every thing the deck needs over microwaves. Inputs, power, multi-lines…"

"Why go…?"

"This deck is a solution to the problem of an off-world, hazardous environment deck. No seams. The neural net, processors—all the cuttin' shit is housed in shock and temperature proof gel sack then sealed in a woven titanium alloy shell with fuzzy logic to burn…"

"Memory?"

"Hess Holographic with—I don't know six trill' gig or something." Watching Jimmy salivate. "See that front window?"

"Yeah."

"It's the optical scanner. You go 3-D down the line…"

"How do you control direction, speed…?"

"Optical scans your movements or eye pointer or your finger—it takes practice and the ride. The ride is sublime—e. Had it—less than a week."

"Lemme' jack."

"So you can see what you can't have. No. No. I've got…"

"Don't yank my chain man. Let me jack then we'll talk business."

The dealer rises reluctantly placing the card out of Jimmy's view. He shuffles through the drawer for an optic cable as Jimmy positions himself directly in front of the deck. He plugs the cable into a small polygon in front of the deck as Jimmy fumbles with his trans-soft.

"Shit. I won't be able to understand…"

"Leave it in. I've got an adapter. I've gotta' walk you through the first run anyway," attaching the cable "It's like no other deck you've ever jacked."

"How do you turn it…"

"Yield man. You're going to fly for the first time in your short life. You don't want to miss it."

A red laser grid blankets Jimmy from the small window on the deck. The second after he jacks Jimmy nearly pisses in his pants. His fingers, toes and scalp tingle with a static wash. But it's the cool-fire emanating from the jack that quickly widens over his neck and head finally enveloping his entire body that unsettles him.

The dealer sounds like he is in his head. "Relax. Shit feels freaky right. You're going to like this."

His skin feels cool and moist as he takes deep breaths to slow his heart rate. He's in a gray holding space with the choice of three virtual Doppelgängers in front of him.

"I got a choice of Doppes huh?"

"To pick one just move towards it. As soon as you touch it you're InSpace."

Jimmy reaches out with his right hand and touches the Bruce Lee Doppe with a long ponytail and texture mapped skin and he immediately body slides to the entry point for the net's many windows. On the average, 101,052,312 public, corporate and private entrances to different parts of the net are up and waiting for your account number. The limitless void that is the net shares the horizon with an infinite, yellow, 3-D grid. Jimmy dials his account on the nearest exchange and body slides on to the 'da bahn.

"You in yet?"

Jimmy nods and his *Doppes* lurches forward. "Shit!"

"Put up your hands. Listen to me all right."

"Yeah."

"Everything, your direction and speed are controlled by your body movements. For direction point with your head, for motion move your shoulders, to stop move your hands away from your body. You wanna' pick up speed, bring your arms flush with your torso. Cool?"

"This shit is weird. I'm at Trance's…"

"Like you're floating right!"

"Yeah."

"Like you're standing on the bottom of a pool without the water pressure. It's why this deck is deep-tech. They found a way to lose the jerky stop and go movements. It's liquid flight my brother."

Jimmy's smile broadens to a glee filled giggle. It's such a rush—for every sudden movement he makes there is a subtle breeze on that part of his cool skin. He imagines dolphins have the same sensations and he wants to ape it to the max. "Liquiaflyin'…"

He adeptly flies past other Doppes who view him with amazement and disdain. Jimmy phases through several football sized Coke, Reebok and

McDonald's Holo-V billboards on his way to the main strip. Gotta' be legal to surf Trance's—it makes Times Square look like a nightlight. Jimmy swoops down to a queue for Pussy Galore's where the entrance under enormous pink legs is filled with the usual horny boys. Its prime time all over—always is and Doppes fill the strip. His Doppes freezes and blinks yellow intermittently alongside several others on a long winding line.

"Shit."

Traffic.

He activates his pull-down menu, switches to an eye-pointer and enters a series of commands with blinding speed.

"Wadda' ya' doing Jimmy?"

"Hold up."

Jimmy body slides through a complex series of international exchanges until he arrives at NTT. He initiates a program and a call is patched through a preset maze of connections ricocheting off satellites and switching stations dotting the globe and he dials an unlisted number in Manhattan.

"You talk a lot of shit dealer man but I gotta' bowling ball shootin' down the tube to rate your ice breaker."

"I wish you would have told me before you started a run." The dealer shuffles through the things on his desk looking for the adapter to the plasma screen, "Shit! Tell me you're not pickin' GI Joe please—s."

"Na—a."

"But tell me how your program keys in."

"Its passive. You wait for an in-bound data flow, piggyback in and nest in the background. You're invisible…"

"Ah man—that's a ton of compressed bullshit..!"

"My signature is invisible because the breaker is morphing code. Nobody knows you're there because the system reads you as information. You nest in the background, recon then morph and step into the stream. Got that dink."

"You're a fucking genius."

"Stroke me."

"Now who the fuck are you breakin' with my signature on my deck over my line."

"A—business associate. Look at the pretty light show," says Jimmy with scorn.

Jimmy is at the entrance to his quarry's system and views streams of information flowing in and out of a supernova bright fuchsia firewall whose only purpose is keeping people like him out.

"Tell me or…"

Jimmy raises his hand, tilts his head forward, angles his shoulders and pulls his arms close to his body. He dives directly into blurring stream of information and disappears instantly. A millisecond later he's is inside the beast. The intense fuchsia wall is meant to blind intruders until the system's defense system drops you, frying your deck in the process. But nothing happens.

Instead Jimmy is catapulted by the stream of information through a series of filters and into the main core. "I'm in."

"In who?"

"Niemöller."

"Fuck me."

The core is surprisingly blah for someone of Niemöller's caliber though it is immense. Enormous blue, cylinders of information of different sizes dot the landscape connected by translucent tubes that appear and vanish at the speed of light.

"You have to jump before you get loaded and indexed…"

Jimmy is shot into a cylinder and the pays the price. "O—offfh!" The wind is knocked out of him and his chest lurches forward as his stomach takes the brunt of the impact.

"It's trying to read you."

The dealer forcefully pulls Jimmy's head backwards, places his arms close to his body and tilts him backwards in the chair.

"You out?! You out?!"

"I'm spinning—I'm out. Fuck."

"You leave a hole?"

"What?"

"Look behind you at the wall or whatever—did you leave a hole?"

"Yeah."

"What's it look like?"

"Its—its strobing."

"Is it…"

"Multiplying. A bunch of holes are…"

"You're tagged! He can see you! Get the fuck out!"

Bruce Lee splinters into fragments of yellow eggshell and a gray ball streaks for the exit. Concentric day glow, rings shoot past Jimmy on their way to the cylinders as he blasts out of the gate.

"Listen to me. Patch into one of his outgoing overseas lines…"

"Way ahead of you. I'm in Finland. He stopped transmitting." Jimmy leans back into the chair and unplugs himself.

"Tell me there is no way he could have gotten a fix."

Jimmy shakes his head wiping the sweat away from his brow. "How much you want for it?"

"It's not for sale."

"A figure."

"You spike my competition and…"

"Come on—a round two-five!"

"Ha!"

"Thirty then."

"Not for…"

"Ah—don't give me that shit man! This is why you brought me here. Those *Doppes* were bullshit—t! This deck is acid-candy and I'm talking stone cold electric dollars. You're motherfucking ass don't even own this tech—you're a high-water wearing, frontin' motherfucker for some tech at Nippon Industries and—d you need the cut off the top to buy your ass a new skull jack, so don't shit me with no, 'no sale' wipe. Deal!"

"Twenty fingers."

"Bullshit! Ten!"

"No way."

"Way! I'm the only buyer, this shit is hot and I've got to get it out of the country.
Fifty-five."

"Eighteen, firm."

"Fifteen…"

"Firm."

"You doing me wrong."

"I could walk."

The dealer shifts some items around the desk and turns his ATM on.

"You know for a dealer you're not too smart."

"What?"

"Well you have to admit you're a little too easy to find. Don't you think keeping a low profile might do you better?"

The dealer smiles and pulls his flexible smart card out of the slot.

"I suppose you want a third party to hold the money until you run…"

"A diagnostic. Yeah. Nothing personal…"

"Just business."

Jimmy inserts his card and enters a series of codes. While he waits for his call to be answered he spies the dealer stroking the deck.

"Bye bye Chicklet."

"What did you say."

"Chicklet. This baby is like a giant black Chicklet. God's Chicklet."

Jimmy smiles as he repeats this to himself. The dealer slips the deck into its armored backpack and hands it to Jimmy. Moments later he and Leroy were on their way out of the door and the dealer is already emptying the contents of a drawer into his backpack. The rest of the equipment is stored under some floorboards and he is about ready to leave. At the wall near the door he flips a light switch that turns off the room size construct and everything disappears except for the desk and two chairs. He double bolts the front door, moves the desk and lifts up the trap door and disappears underneath a blast of dust. From the alley the building appears sullen and neglected. The covered windows with their rusty bars and the doorway that is nailed shut give the appearance of near ruin. Movement is heard emanating from the large dumpster next to the side of the building and a false side slowly lowers. The dealer peaks out and looks in every direction before rolling his Motor Guzi motorcycle out. Seconds later the dumpster is secured, the building is armed and the dealer is off to his next call.

25 BROAD STREET, MANHATTAN

At the same moment, in a windowless basement office, deep in the bowls of a defunct luxury residential building converted from financial offices in the 90's, Niemöller has a cow.

WETWIRE ANYONE?

Brice sits up on the bed as Noguchi and Gärtner discuss the procedure with him. Dr. Gärtner of the Max Planck Institute in Germany spoke perfect English with slight German accent. "First we will remove the silicon chip housing the hundreds of tiny electrodes from the nerve cluster at the base of your brain ya'. Until two years ago this chip was considered state of the art but as you know it has deep perceptual limitations for a heavy user like yourself."

B' nodded politely as they described the details—much of which he had heard before. The dirty little secret of the player-game platform interface was that Sony's engine had to amplify, correct and re-render all environments on the fly for headriders and passive viewers. The player's saw crudely rendered environments with limited colors and rudimentary figures lacking much detail due to the limitations of their neural interfaces. A year ago Sony announced that a revolutionary new neural interface would be available that would connect to the Thalamus among other areas of the brain after exhaustive tests had been performed.

The procedure would consist of inserting millions of bio-engineered microorganisms (nanorobots or molecular-level machines) that will perform their preprogrammed tasks. Although there are billions of neurons in the brain a neural interface only needs to communicate with a few major structures so only a few million electrodes will be connected.

Dr. Gartner would plot where he wants the neurons to be connected starting with the Thalamus he would then replace the old plug at the base of his skull with the new one. This would be followed by a series of injections of magnetically tagged fructose (so they can watch what's happening and stop it if something weird happens). Meanwhile doctor Noguchi will have dropped yeast type-I into a container with nanobots and the required polymer-nutrient mix and they will begin to ingest it. The polymer is an electrically conducting polymer, an oxidized polypyrrole chosen because of its inherent electrical conductive properties, flexibility and its *in vitro* compatibility with human cells.

The injected fructose will float next to the neurons in the target area. Dr. Gartner attaches the plug and injects yeast type-I into it. The yeast starts growing towards the fructose-sites, forming a chain of connected nanocreatures in near straight lines. They "hold onto each other" or lock limbs, in the same fashion as hundreds of ants forming an ant bridge over a small chasm. This chain of nanobots will be the foundation of the main "wires" going from the plug to the target sites. The polymer they ate will be inside their bodies and will attach itself to the polymer that is in the neighboring bodies slowly the polymer is excreted through the yeast forming the chain and creates the "wires."

Once the chain has grown into the areas where the fructose is, the nanobots won't be growing towards a certain "area" because the fructose is now in every neuron all around them. They'll start growing in all directions, but basically attaching to each neuron (because all of them have the fructose inside them which is attracting them). By this stage, the yeast will have been converting the fructose into alcohol and the alcohol level will be building up substantially, especially inside each individual neuron. This will trigger the death of the residual yeast-nanobots.

Meanwhile, yeast type-II will be placed in a jar with the nonobots and a second polymer for the protective sheathing. After a short time all of yeast type-I will be dead from excessive alcohol, a process that they will be able to monitor by watching the level of tagged-fructose. At which point the surgeon will inject yeast type-II in the target areas. Yeast type-II will be attracted to the nutrients in the bodies of yeast type-I It will consume these bodies and excrete the second polymer over the top of the wires already created by the first lot. This yeast can be free-floating as long as it's attracted to the nutrients in yeast type-I as it won't stray far from the wire (whose material is mixed with these nutrients). These nanobots would basically search along the length of the wire, looking for any of yeast type-I and consume it, eventually they'll reach the ends of the wire, which means that they'll basically have consumed all of yeast type-I. At which point the doctor will inject some more of the nutrient at the site of the plug that will attract them back there. He will wait long enough for them to all gather there and then suck them out.

"Oh great," thought B' as they spoke, "I'm going to have my head shot full of man-made bugs that get drunk and die. Should I ask the doctors if they shit?" but thought better of saying it out loud.

The next day a small nurse enters Brice's room to put him under before surgery. Wobbling between consciousness and sleep, he begins to repeat his mantra. "Assess your opponent, formulate a strategy, attack with fury. Assess. Formulate. Attack." Words his trainer, Arri Toeb drilled into his subconscious long ago bob up to the surface. There are times, he has sworn he could feel the skin, like a taut well-developed muscle contract around the skull-jack where liquid meets light, where the organic and manmade commingle. Some people like to jack while others say they love it but Brice Johnson couldn't imagine life without it. Every few hours, sometimes for hours at a time he jacks for business, for pleasure or just to veg. It's what brought him to Japan and the reason he is about to be operated on. It's to increase the rez'—to enhance the images, colors, to make it more lifelike. What reverberates through his inner-voice is the same litany as always. "I am the SHIT. I am the best gamer alive. Jack-knifing through space like the Silver Surfer! Jackin' low iz' when it's a joy or social ride, but jacking high is work boy. K-i-c-k-i-n-g ass-s. Main difference is the breathing. It's what the punks watching will never know. Low you forget about your body, 'cause you don't cop to physical state, transcendence. High is when it's all about hyper-reality, adrenaline rush, big breathing, ignore the Soji suit, the shock that hits your nervous system when you fuck up. Take it and keep flyin'…assess, formulate, assault…assess, formulate, assault…no t-i-m-e f-o-r b-u-l-l-s-h-i…j-a-c-k—s-u-b-l-i-m-e…"

A small hand slowly presses the pause button on the panel that controls and records from the three cameras in Brice's room. Right now he's out like a light. Three minutes ago the doctor put him under for surgery and it's the first time he's been alone in the room since he checked in two days ago. Outside of his door sits Carl, Brice's sometime sparring partner and Sifu of his own Kenpo dojo in Newark. Carl is six three and all muscle with a gold tooth. He is completely focused on his second order of salmon eggs this morning. Fumi, "the bleached blond nurse" assigned to Brice, approaches the door with a small cart and smiles at Carl as she enters. She's a poster child for little Japanese women who want to be California girls, knocking back champagne with large mahogany men. Carl ignores her face and looks straight at her 36D's completely missing the heavy metallic object in her pocket. Inside the room Fumi races around his bed acting as harried as a teenager dressing for a first date. She quickly throws the sheet off Brice and rolls his bed shirt towards his chest. She shudders, gazing at his taut black muscles and at the member she would so much like to choke on. In the bathroom Leroy has already cocked his South African assault weapon having seen everything Fumi has done, on a Sharp flat-screen perched on the sink. He calls Carl over a tiny ear rig and whispers, "Open knife." Carl puts the sushi on the floor, stands up, faces the door and takes out his Smith & Wesson. Fumi digs into her pocket and withdraws something Leroy can't see. He opens the door, puts her head in his sights and his finger on the trigger. Carl opens the door just enough to see Fumi drop something and bend over to pick it up. Carl and Leroy make eye contact as Carl slowly raises his gun. Fumi picks the object up and frantically presses its tiny buttons. Leroy, concerned that not only could his bullet pass through Fumi and hit Carl but that her death must not be a mistake takes two cautious steps to the left. With Carl clear Leroy's trigger finger begins to spasm with anticipation when he sees the Sharp MotionPic^{TM} camera the size of a pen in her hands. He takes his finger off the trigger, steps backward silently and closes the door without her noticing.

"Stand down. Picture freak. Stand down," says Leroy once inside the bathroom.

Carl grins and sucks a piece of seaweed from his teeth as he returns to the sushi. Aware that she has only minutes before the orderlies enter to remove Brice San she works at a breakneck pace. With the camera set to auto, she holds it at arms length and puts her head into the frame next to Brice's torso. Unable to control herself she lays her head against his navel brushing her cheek against his pubic hair. She gently lifts the shaft of his penis up with her left hand and kisses it for the camera barley able to stifle a childish giggle. One last pan to show the viewers that it's really "B' baby." And the camera is dropped in her pocket, the shirt lowered and the sheets raised. She's out of the room and smiling as sweat beads form on her forehead as Carl flashes a gold tooth smile.

Brice, deep into siesta land, gets an erection.

Leroy, puts a call into Richard, down the hall in the room where the bodyguards crash and Richard is mashing white tiles with his cap-toes in ninety seconds flat. Fumi, presses the pause button without anyone noticing just in time to catch the orderlies jogging down the hallway to get Brice. All she can think about is the short list for a private screening. So many friends—maybe the tabloids. They would pay a fortune, but no. It would get back to her and she'd lose her job for sure. No, just private screenings for her and the girls and Bono the cross dresser.

Richard is the smoothest of the smooth as he walks up to the nurse's station with his polished steel suitcase and that badboy smile.

"Hey Fumi baby you're looking extra perky today."

"Hi—i."

"You know Brice told me to give you a message."

Fumi warms up to him and walks over. Richard lifts his briefcase up, leans it over the counter and lets it hang. The head nurse, frowns and watches them out of the corner of her eye.

"Really?"

Richard presses a switch on the briefcase turning the electromagnet on as Fumi leans up against it. The magnet instantly erases the recording Fumi just made and takes the camera's memory with it.

"He said to make sure and invite that sexy Fumi to my going away party. So I am."

"Oh yeah—h. That would great—t."

"Good. Later baby."

"Bye—e."

As Richard turns he falls into line behind Leroy and the two orderlies who wheel Brice towards the elevator. Sony booked the entire west wing for Brice and his entourage and this being the main event, everybody files out of their *green rooms*. Olga, Brice's girl of the moment, accountants, attorneys, trainers, friends and hangers-on and Brice's traveling secretary Erica, queue up at the elevators. Jimmy, is the last out much too enthralled in his phone conversation to run for the elevator.

Three floors down in the operating theater its standing room only. Jimmy is acting uncharacteristically cool and mature as he wields the golden lasso over so many of his brother's business associates. Noticing that the nurses are standing around Brice he motions to Leroy and they walk down the narrow staircase leading to the operating room without missing an, "Uh—uh" into the phone. Brice is face down on the operating table and the nurses stare in amazement as Jimmy and Leroy walk casually through the stark white room. Without missing a beat, Jimmy and Leroy walk into the scrub room where they find Dr. Gärtner in the middle of a heated argument with three small Japanese surgeons. They are completely unaware of Jimmy and Leroy who walk into the hallway. A moment later Leroy reenters and takes a foreboding stance staring directly at the surgeons. It takes them a mili-moment to feel the considerable wave of menace his aura is bombarding them with. Their vocation is preserving and in this case enhancing life. Leroy annihilates it. For a moment they are speechless and marvel at Leroy's black-blue skin, the torch like whites of his eyes and raw silk jacket that does a bad job of concealing his firearm.

"Excuse me, excuse me but I'll have to ask you to leave. This room must remain sterile you see," says the Englishman.

Leroy is a statue. The surgeons wipe their hands and motion the nurses to help them on with their gloves—none of them notice when Leroy leaves, they only see the door swing shut. At the center of the ceiling above the operating table is a white metallic ball with several cone shaped holes that shudder like the delicate parts of speakers when the nurse seals the doors behind the surgeons. A middle-aged nurse neatly arranges at the tiny, gold-plated plug that will be inserted in Brice's head and straightens a few of the 36 variously sized syringes.

Doctor Gärtner walks over to Brice who is knocked out and lying face down on the operating table. He looked at the aesthetician and got the nod of approval. Next the doctor looked at a nurse across the room and said, "We begin." She pressed play on a stereo and Ricard Strauss' waltz "Thus Spake Zarathustra" emanated from the white speakers on the ceiling.

Brice is asleep facedown on the custom hospital bed, Jimmy is asleep on one sofa, Olga is petting her dog Magic, a Silky Terrier on her lap. Leroy stares out of the window then rises to enter the restroom. The suite didn't look like any hospital room he had ever seen but then the Japanese always treated their idols like royalty. A month ago when Ishi vmailed Brice that a new Direct Neural interface or skull jack had finished testing he immediately agreed to fly in for the operation. They'd wire him in the best hospital in Osaka, comp of course. They knew he'd agree because he's got a soft spot for every boy's craving, higher rez and Sony does everything first class. The moment Ishi hung up he instructed a New York firm to make an appointment to see Brice's duplex on top of MoMa's Residential Tower to photograph his bedroom. Thankfully, they omitted the scratches his dog made in his Teakwood floors but everything else was perfect. And why not, he's their prodigal son, an enormous moneymaker to the order of several small nations and growing. The uncanny reproduction, for all its good intentions of making him at ease only succeed in the opposite. This reality doubling was palpably unnerving, much like a mirror that reflects everything except your own image and calls into question a definitive sense of place.

A mechanized hum causes Leroy to glance in Brice's direction. The wall behind Brice's headboard illuminates a high-resolution color image of his inner-workings. Leroy sees blood coursing through Brice's veins, the expansion-contraction of his lungs, the movement of cells, brain activity and lines of ever changing information.

"The unit remains seated, the vital signs are good of course—he is in excellent health."

"Yes. Yes."

A cursor points at his brain stem and the area enlarges revealing more detail.

"Brain activity is—normal. I expect the muscle relaxer to be wearing off shortly."

"Full operation of the unit appears imminent."

"Much so."

"The other scans are all in order so—ah—h. Yes, there. Fine. Good."

"Well done doctor. Most accomplished work."

"Yes. Thank you doctor. It appears that my work is completed here—you simply have to run the mundane tests…"

"Yes. Yes."

"I leave for Geneva in the morning."

"I would be honored if you would join me for dinner this evening."

"Unfortunately I cannot. My wife has made arrangements for us to conference call family this evening—my youngest has issues which need to be addressed and my in-laws wish to see me."

"I understand completely. Please give my best to your wife."

"Likewise."

The image dissolves into the pale off-white wall and Leroy begins to take his gun apart.

PURVEYORS OF GLAM'

Hours later.

"So after all they've been through…"

"That's right."

"After all they've been through she just left him flat like that? Just like that?"

"Just like that!"

"That's not right you know. No. That's not right at all. Em—em."

"What do you expect from som' tired ass Inga wannabe'—-an' you know those ain't her hips either…"

B's hospital room is packed. Agents, lawyers, celebs, their people, high-octane, hyper shopping, benefit eating, husband/wife of somebody, ¥39,570.00 haircut and designer wearing mannequins—with attitude. The usual.

"The company has interests. That's well you know…and if you are not part of the scheme you are simply irrelevant."

"Where are the glasses?! The wine is getting warm—m."

"Its not really anger," says Brice to a salt and pepper Japanese man wearing Italian. "I gotta' say though I know that's what it looks like. But—you know I'm a fighter. If you get in my face I'm going to slam you every time 'cause I hate losing more than I like winning. So…"

"You really appear——my question is. Does the anger make you a better player? Could you win without it?"

"The question is irrelevant. I can't disassociate my—my ability…"

"Athletic prowess," smiling.

"…Yeah, that too—from my demeanor. I'm a hard machine. Sure it looks like anger but I think—I donno' to me its more like rage—only contained you know?"

"Have you ever intentionally hurt an opponent?"

Brice smiles and sips wine.

"Oh—its Brice! Hey everybody shuddup'!"

The wall sized Holo-V flashes several logos in rapid succession followed by publicity tape from parties and premieres featuring Brice and other VR stars.

"Um—m highlights…?"

"…Having taking first place on the international circuit eleven months ago," a sportscaster says, "There seems no denying Brice Johnson's unchallenged dominance of the sport."

Clips of Brice's virtual döppelganger, his *Döppe*, as a multi-arm gunslinger disposing of his opponents one after the other. "An orphan from the age of seven—his parents dying in a mid-air collision, he was provided for via a large insurance policy, became a gaming prodigy, was discovered by the chairman of a leading game manufacturer Sony and as the sport was blossoming Brice burst onto the scene as the youngest champ. He took the sport in a new direction, captivated the viewers with his inventiveness and reaped colossal profits. Opponents call him snide, arrogant, a loner, smart, cocky, moody, highly competitive and irreverent, but always ready to please his audience. It's rumored that his contract is not only the most lucrative in the sport but that he has profit participation in all pay-per-view broadcasts." In another bout Brice grabs an opponent and hits him with a series of rapid fire Kenpo blows to the throat, head and stomach. With the opponent finally on the ground Brice looks to the audience for approval and sensing that they want blood he finishes him off by savagely beating the guy to a bloody pulp.

"That's right Rick and even though he and his lawyer vehemently deny any illegal activities the International Gaming Commission is looking into allegations of pay-offs reported to have been paid to Brice Johnson by illegal gambling syndicates, run of course by Pax Cartel."

Walking down a corridor of a game complex after the French Open Brice is surrounded by a gaggle of reporters pointing antenna mikes in his face.

"Tell us Brice, how does it feel to be number one in the world for so long?"

"Food still tastes the same."

"How do you respond the allegations made last week by the London Times regarding gambling pay-offs?"

"I don't gamble."

"But the evidence suggest…"

A trainer cuts the reporter off. "If they have evidence you can be sure it's false because Brice Johnson does not need the money, aggravation or distraction of ill-gotten booty or insipid cross examinations."

Smiling, "Take that," says Brice.

"Well how do you respond to the rumors of your displeasure with your contract?"

"We…"

"I'll answer that. Listen this sport is run by a select group of extremely wealthy conglomerates—I'm talking a handful of companies with vertical clout. They own the satellites, the down links, the networks, huge concessions on InSpace, the game platforms, rights not to mention strong arm agreements with the advertisers and small networks in the developing countries—its no secret you know. If its not outright ownership, its a tightly woven 'relationship'. So what am I saying? I'm saying if you are telling X, Y and Z companies or networks or whatever, that they have to pay a premium and then a kick-back, to carry events that I'm the main draw in then you've got to anty-up and pay to watch me jack! "

"Those are serious allegations…!"

"Do you have any proof of…?!"

Brice's expression is stern, grim and determined.

"We've said just about all we have to on this subject—excuse me— we have an aerodyne to catch. No more questions today—excuse me," says the trainer.

Brice and his entourage file into a limo and drive off. In the crush a beautiful Euro-Asian woman is nudged aside and turns quickly away from the camera.

"With that, said the spotlight is now on the Matsushita Entertainment Works division who has responded with categorical denials of wrong doing and surprise at Mr. Johnson's allegations. However this reporter has learned that Mr. Johnson has threatened to boycott future participation in any and all play, if all parties do not come to the negotiation table with blank checks."

"Isn't Johnson worried about unilateral breach-of-contract suits by sponsors, advertisers and principals?"

"Not at all. From what my source tells me, he seems to rally the support of the biggest advertisers prior to his statement at the French Open."

"If that is the case it makes for a very interesting development in the world's most lucrative arena at a time when the game, or games rather—there are so many, are breaking records for viewer ship—topping the 1.5 billion mark last event."

"That's right and if the well liked number one seed decides to sit out the next event or indefinitely, we may all find ourselves answering to an angry public. Don't go away. When we return we'll look at how VR games have affected real-time boxing among other non-team sports."

Wired for Chaos

The Holo-V goes mute and the chatter begins immediately. Dozens of eyes casually glance in Brice's direction only to find him on the way to the bathroom. The same Euro-Asian woman from the news piece sits unobtrusively wearing a pair of large sunglasses. Her face is beautiful and her figure is sensuous but her hands are wrinkled beyond her years.

"Green—electric lime green changing i-n-t-o bright yellow…"

"Okay. Optics checks out. Let's see what happens when we switch channels on the international exchange."

"What are you looking for?"

"Anything, bleed over, static, dull resolution—here."

Neither in nor completely out of Brice's head but some place in between, like ants moving along assigned routes from the nest to a food source yet kilometers away, he is one with the scheme of bytes. Sans döppelganger or custom menus, it's a pedestrian outing in a closed system so the white coats can check his head. He expects all their presets to flake lame all over his sublime self.

"Here we go."

On a landscape of bright orange-green flat sand stretching towards the horizon where it meets an acid Kool-Aid sky swirling fuscia-cobalt-lime clouds, a paper-thin window opens up. In the distance he can hear the wind flinging sand against itself.

"First we will run through some presets on different frequencies…"

"Yeah, yeah I know," not trying to mask his boredom.

"Here…"

The window flips between images downloaded from all over the Net and in-house R & D some appearing as bland shapes morphing into complex ones. The Net scenes are all too familiar views of international exchanges, Hong Kong, Jeddah, Berlin, Sweden, Iceland each pausing momentarily to check comparability via electric hand-shaking.

"Any static?"

"No. Not at all."

"I won't keep you much longer then. I'll just run a sweep and you'll be out."

The window disappears and rows of numbers appear casting long shadows on the sand. The numbers flip at astounding speed some affecting others on the same line while others remain unchanged. Rows of numbers condense, blink and disappear as the sand and sky swirl and blend into an electric violet night. The numbers stop abruptly as a yellow bolt of lightning flashes in the distance.

"That's it."

Light.

"Great. How'd I check out."

Brice blinks three white coats, a room full of monitors and several tables of tech into focus.

"Hundred percenter," says the white coat taking the fiber optic cable from Brice's head. "Even did background tests to speed things up."

"Great."

"Sure you don't want smell and taste?"

"Naw—w'. That's bullshit."

"Just remember you can access any of the system settings from any deck with Ip1.0 or higher."

"I know. I know. You American?"

"Yep. Los Angeles."

"This a good gig?"

"As long as they keep picking up the bills and signing checks."

"Yeah."

"See they flew me in to make you more at home—you know home-speak and all."

"Gotta' love 'em," rising to leave. "God is in the details."

"Trades said you didn't have religion."

"Don't. It's just a saying."

"What's up with this pay or don't play shit?"

"Just what the news said techman."

"You serious?"

Brice smiles.

"You do want to kick Tanaka's ass though—right?!"

"*If* and when we jack you can bet your deck, your house, bank *and* life I'll take him o-u-t like the garbage."

"Sounds like a fight worth watching."

Leaving, "Later."

"Take it easy man."

As Brice exits the Japanese white coats bow and the American from Los Angeles looks directly into the camera hidden in the ceiling. On a monitor three floors up in the hospital the American's expression changes from genial to serious. The picture switches to a shot of Brice walking down a corridor on his way to a bank of elevators.

"SEE 'YA!"

Brice is dressed and surrounded by mounds of luggage as he prepares to check out. Fumi enters with a flat-screen for Brice to sign and almost trips over herself.

"Just some release forms for you to sign Brice man—San."

"Thanks for taking care of me Fumi baby."

"Oh you're welcomed."

"Did you have a good time at the party."

"Oh yeah! But I didn't get to talk to you—all those people..."

"Yeah, who let them in?" Handing her the flat-screen. "Jimmy, we all ready?"

"Yeah, lets get the hell outta' here."

Wired for Chaos

"Olga baby, Rodney and I are floggin' some suits before we fly so we'll take separate cars okay. Wait for us in the VIP lounge and don't talk to anybody wearing Polo. Dig?"

"Well don't take too long."

"Right. Lets go."

That said, the entourage files into the hallway with all that designer fabric billowing. At the nurse's station, all of the nurses, doctors and orderlies have lined up to say goodbye. The head doctor takes a few steps forward. "Brice San, It has been our pleasure taking care of you. I trust your stay was a pleasant one."

In Japanese, "Yes, yes most pleasant doctor. You have an excellent staff and I was well taken care of. Thank you very much." Smiles all around. "Fumi baby, come over here please."

Fumi is startled and too nervous to move. "Come here." She steps over to him and keeps her eyes pinned to the tiles afraid of catching the stare of the doctor. "You still have that camera?" She turns as beet red as a Japanese woman can and nervously nods her head. "Lets have it." She takes it out of her pocket and slowly hands it to Brice who quickly hands it to the doctor. "Could you take one of the two of us doctor?"

"Certainly, of course."

To Fumi, "This is for the shots that didn't come out."

"Ready? Closer please. Good. Good."

"Wait." Brice kisses Fumi square on the lips and motions for the doctor to hurry up and take the picture. Fumi is beside herself with joy and struggles to keep her hat on. "Thanks doctor. How about one with the whole crew. Jimmy, snap a couple off for the good doctor and I will ya'."

"Easy."

Everyone huddles around Brice as he hugs a doctor so unaccustomed to affection and the buxom Fumi. Flash. Flash and everyone is cheery then suddenly the entire staff produces their own cameras to the surprise of Brice and the amusement of his people. "Oh—h now wait a minute. You guys are too much. Jimmy help me out here man." Jimmy, cracks up and takes a seat.

A short time later everyone arrives at the lobby and they make their way past several bowing white coats and a handful of photographers to their cars. Olga and Carl take the first one as Jimmy and Brice enter the second. Brice sees Rodney who has been putting a dent in the single malt and his eyes brighten. "Rodney my man!"

"Brice Johnson the man who gives my wife a reason to shop. Every time your ass wins she hits Barney's the next day."

"I don't even want to hear it. Yo' money. Yo' woman. Yo' problem. They can smell that Harvard MBA cologne blocks away and you know," together, "That trophy's gonna' cost ya!"

"Hey Jimmy, how 'u doin'?"

"Alrite', Rodney. Alrite'."

Pointing to his deck-pack, "New toy Jimmy?" Jimmy nods.

Wired for Chaos

"Enough of that shit. Where the fuck is my money?" says B'.

"You know I have a kid that's almost your age and if he ever…"

"And what you call that kid? Son right? Well you call me boss motherfucker and I could send Harvard a check and get an MBA if I wanted to so leave it alone."

"With what money? I all ready stole all of it and my wife is stealing from me. And what's this motherfuckin' goddamn Aerodyne supersonic shit don't even need shit! Did you see the price tag on that bitch…!?"

"Jimmy worked a deal…"

"Sells for a lot more…"

"Deal?! Deal?! Jimmy Johnson they saw your ass comin'! Bet ya'll have to get out and push that bitch..!"

"That's what we're flyin'"

"Damn!

The three crack smiles and wait for someone to break the silence.

Brice, "So what's up with this meeting?"

"The Keiretsu wants assurances…"

"Well that's fuckin' news…"

"Assurances that you won't go off on them all over the media."

"Really?"

"No they didn't say so. They won't say so. They're Japanese. I'm asking you for the hundredth time…"

To which B' frowned having heard this speech one thousand times.

"…Stop antagonizing them. Apologize and promise to not rock the boat moving forward. Say you're sorry for causing a fuss…"

"An' what? Get—show weakness. I'm not down with that. No one respects weakness…"

"See that right there—you said it. Weakness. This is not about how you appear—you're too concerned with appearances. At the end of the day they are bottom line and you are…"

"Performing with mighty aplomb and veracity." Not taking Rodney seriously.

"All I'm askin' is that you just—for once walk in there and apologize—ask forgiveness, make nice nice, Kumbuya, sushi boy and we can all just…"

"Group hug? Group hug this motherfucker," says B' grabbing his crotch.

Rodney puts up his hands in surrender and looks at Jimmy who shoots him the "you lost that one" expression.

The limo pulls up to the front entrance of a sleek high-rise covered in blue glass and Rodney turns to Jimmy. "Hey Jimmy could you do me a favor…"

"It's cool Rodney. I don't do meetings with my brother's people." Rodney looks relieved and embarrassed as he and Brice step out of the limo.

Brice turns to Rodney, "Anything I need to know going into this meeting?"

"Not really," holding a flexible, rectangular writing tablet up and reads over the contract. "Standard stuff but...they take the 'pay-or-play' clause to the next level. See, as you know, in order for you to keep your ranking you have to compete in ten matches a year with four of them being title bouts——and win enough of 'em. That hasn't changed but the penalty for missing a title bout due to anything short of serious illness or dismemberment is forfeiture of all company shares——new and accrued. That means, you don't compete and they take everything..."

"Not my outstanding shares right?"

"Everything. Their world, their rules, their money."

"Damn."

"That's pay-back for mouthing off to the press—oh no! Don't act surprised motherfucker. Don't even act surprised."

"Whatever—never missed a bout yet and don't ever intend to."

"I could get them to switch over to cash suspension but I don't think it would change the structure of the deal and the taxes would kill us."

"Leave it. We make ten times that on sponsorships and endorsements alone. There room for a 'gimme?"

"They didn't leave anything on the table. Something you want?"

"Can't think of anything and that's supposed to be your job."

"We do the deal then?"

B' nods. "Yeah but I don't like this Rodney. They've got too much hand."

"Just keep the sponsors happy which means..."

"Play to the stands—know what to do," to himself, "Like my life is one piece of performance art after another trained monkey shit...."

Exiting the limo B' stares up at the blue tower and puts on his big sunglasses. He masks his edginess with a cocky roll of his shoulder assuring himself that the president is his ally. He takes long deep breaths and checks his reflection in the glass and smiles. You'd never know this was the world headquarters for Sony because there is none of the ostentatious flash. No in-your-face "look at me" in Tokyo's North Shinagawa industrial district not far from traditional houses topped by wavelike roofs peaked with Lioli tiles.

As they step into the lobby they are enveloped in the late afternoon light shining through blue glass. Somewhere out of view they can hear the sound of a small waterfall and smell the scent of pine in the air. An attractive greeter approaches them with an shy, almost apologetic manner and perfect skin. She is a spry little woman wearing a sensible navy skirt and jacket who bows moments after they enter. Smiling, she says "Johnson San, welcome. Please walk this way." He begins to size her up then remembers why he is here and focuses on his posture. He's got the power walk thing down and feels the security guards follow him with their eyes. As he passes small groups of people waiting for elevators they stop talking and sneak a peek as he walks by. He's always been stared at from way before he ever jacked for money. Way back when he was a nobody strangers would stare and his awareness made for some discomfort until he decided to strut one day and actually deserve their looks. At first he thought himself ugly but that wouldn't make them stare, then he thought it was his height and finally he gave up refusing to believe he looked that good. But now he knew it was fame and consequently he picked up a trick from the models. Actually the only thing he could ever learn from them, *the stare*. A stare which said you're unimportant and too boring for me to look at so I'm going to look right through you. The sunglasses come in handy when you just can't be bothered but he knows they are watching and wanting to tease them takes them off.

Their elevator arrives and the three enter but the people who've been waiting are too meek to step in. As the door closes Rodney sees two of the women grinning with excitement and raising their hands to hide schoolgirl like chatter. Brice sees the hostess press a button for the lower level arcade and not the executive suites. Interesting. The doors open onto a near pitch black void lit by a single spot light in the ceiling and the hostess holds the door open for the men to step out. She takes a few steps in front of them and walks toward into the void. While Brice marvels at the deafening silence and Rodney fights the instinct to crack a joke. The elevator leaves without a sound and the two follow the hostess. As she walks her movement turns on a spot light directly above them and without warning the floor begins to move forward. A moment after the three stop allowing the walkway to take them towards the sound of a Japanese priest chanting in the distance. Out of the shadows to their right a seventeen-foot kabuki samurai dressed in white silk kneels with a resounding thud and bows. A moment later the samurai withdraws his katana and slices through them. To their left another seventeen foot figure enters dressed in armor from a long ago feudal time looks to his left then draws his sword. Everything happens quickly now. A blue point of light two meters above the walk and a few meters in front of them grows into a sphere then flies towards them expanding to the size of an oncoming train in the blink of an eye. As it hits them the walk stops moving and Rodney raises his arms to protect himself and they jaunt through a blue flame wormhole complete with surround sound crackling. The sensation of rapid celestial surfing complete with surround sound is what they experienced when a four-meter Sonic, the Hedgehog races towards them from behind. He keeps pace with them for a few moments before giving Brice a wink and jets into the void. From either side of the wormhole Sony's trademarked non-human game characters fly, jump and float by and through Brice and Rodney. B' thought it odd that Sony had chosen to omit the human big money making individuals like himself and sports teams. Maybe it was a not subtle hint that they thought their company was more important than the personalities. As wealthy as they made him he could not help but feel like an indentured servant. Their lawyers had written a non-compete into his contract that would bar him from running on a competitor's platform for two years if he pulled the ejection cord and with the added platinum handcuffs of his Sony stock leaving would be pure insanity.

Wired for Chaos

When the stim technology was perfected and made as unobtrusive as possible the sports leagues had a bonanza. They wired every possible athlete, football, soccer, baseball, basketball, wrestling, rugby, racing, boxing, every event at the Winter and Summer Olympics and extreme everything. Sony had been the dominant leader and annually projected sensory stimulus to well over seventy percent of all users. Then Microsoft entered the fray and consumed whole chunks of their business by partnering with the networks and writing huge checks. As the industry matured they learned something interesting about how riders wanted to experience sports. Headriders quickly tired of being latched onto one player in a team sport especially for the entire duration of a game so the developers allowed them leapfrog from player-to-player and team-to-team. Unfortunately the novelty wore thin and riders polarized around the extremes of golf to full contact sports like hockey and wrestling. The allure of NSRs or Non-Sport Runs like Brice's lay in the uncertainty of the individual games and the fully realized environments the imaginative developers wrought not to mention the unbridled violence and unpredictability of star players.

Silence folds in on them as the projections disappear and the walkway stops. Double doors open in front of them revealing white, polished, marble stairs. As they ascend the steps B' suddenly feels lightheaded and detects the aroma of chrysanthemums mixed with something chemical and unnatural.

The large rectangular room feels as if it sits underneath a swimming pool. Although the black marble walls recede the ceiling ebbs and flows with faint swirls of blue white light. Around an enormous black table buffed to a mirror shine sits the board of Sony all dressed in black or shades of midnight navy. As B' and Rodney approach all eyes turn towards them.

"Gentlemen…" says Brice only to be startled by what happens next. In the center of the table a larger than life hologram of Sony's Chairman, Arihito materializes. He is seated in a wheel chair in his garden wearing a red, traditional silk robe, white socks and slippers. His gray hair is perfect and his hands rest on the black watch blanket on his lap. Behind him is a butler dressed in traditional clothing holding an umbrella over Arihito, whose assistant is sitting next to him.

"Brice San," says Arihito, "Please sit."

As B' and Rodney turn to look for chairs, they had not seen any upon entering the room, they are startled by two identical twins holding the backs of leather conference chairs. As they sit B' notices that no one takes their eyes off him and no one touches the table. In fact the table is bereft of PDAs, glasses or anything else. It seems like a cold infinity pool, with Arihito floating on its surface.

"Forgive me for not greeting you in person but as you see my doctors prefer to keep me home."

"How are you Arihito San?" feeling lightheaded himself.

"I have been much better, but we are here today to discuss your future." As he spoke the corners of his wide dark lips seem fixed at a downward angle. "We were all greatly hurt by your comments to the media and need assurances. You are our shining star and represent the best of what the game has to offer, both for Sony and the sport. But, no part is more important than the whole. Discussing our business to the media in the tone and demeanor you did, has been called impudent and irresponsible by many on the board and I agree. But I also understand your energy and heightened vitality, especially after a match. So we will not speak of this again." He pauses and motions behind him and the assistant places a glass of water in his left hand. He seems to take an eternity to sip a mouthful of water. "Now, as the board has instructed me, I must name a successor and, they have approved of my decision. I have chosen Ido Takashiyaki to replace me but, only at my passing. Since I have no intention of resigning, he will take office only after I have left this world." Arihito pause a moment and seems to loose his train of thought. A moment later his doctor enters the frame and whispers something in his ear. Arihito nods and shoos him away by raising his left hand. "Forgive me but I must retire now and leave the rest of the meeting in the capable hands of the board and Ido San. Have a pleasant journey back to the States Brice San." B' nods and when he raises his head the holo has disappeared. Everyone turns their attention to the far corner of the table and a young man rises.

"Brice san, we have met before. I am Ido Takashiyaki. We met after your bout in Los Vegas two years ago. You were in exceptional form that evening." A trace of Cambridge Massachusetts in his pronunciation. "You know I've got a lot of respect for what you do," walking towards Brice's side of the table. "It takes a hell of a lot of intelligence and tenacity to compete on that level, but at the end of the day we're all part of a team and although you play an important role..."

"Ido san," says Brice, "I understand."

"Yes of course you do. It has come as an enormous surprise that the game has over taken soccer and every other form of global entertainment the way it has, hasn't it. I studied history at Harvard and my family scratched their heads because they would have preferred I went to B-school, but I learned so much more in history. You know our cultures are no where near as violent as the ancient Romans or Ottoman empire, but the media would have you believe that we perpetuate and promote violent acts, when actually the sport is no more than a safety valve for healthy societies. The ancient Greeks played Pankration in their Olympics, a brutal form of hand-to-hand fighting that allowed everything but eye gouging. The Mayans played a ball game where the losers were beheaded. Millions of viewers jack into your head on our platform for an extrasensory ride and no one gets killed. But as you well know that is not the only battle being fought. The competitor's platforms—most noticeably Microsoft and the Chinese company," barely able to hide his revulsion, "Way Ahead are formidable competitors who would like to eat our lunch."

"Yeah," says B' "But people are platform agnostic. They jack for players."

"True yet our market share continues slip to the competition."

"I guess I'll have get a little meaner—a little more viscous," leaning forward and preening, "For the crowd." A few subtle smiles appear in the room.

Looking at Rodney, Ido says, "Did the contract meet with your approval?"

"It is acceptable," says Rodney.

One of the twins hardly displaces the air molecules around Brice as she hands him the flexible electric screen. Rodney holds B's arm and says, "No revisions have been made to this agreement correct?"

"Correct."

B' takes, it looks at Rodney then at Ido and reads the top line out loud. "No-holds bout against Joseph Santiago set in Cuba." To Ido, "You going to be there?"

"Wouldn't miss it for the world."

"Care for a side bet?" Says B' half joking as he signs the contract by pressing his thumb onto the blinking square.

TRIP TO THE AIRPORT

As soon as B' left the building he took a deep breath and his head seemed to clear. It was as if he had just been drugged and could still smell that funny combination of scents. Back in the limo, B' and Rodney travel in silence except for B's internal voice that replays every annoying sentence from the meeting, over and over.

HOURS LATER...

KL-SEREMBAN EXPRESSWAY IN PUTRAJAYA, MALAYSIA

Doctor Mohammed, an Indian neuro-ophthalmologist who focuses on visual disorders emanating from the brain, his Malay wife, Jahala and their nine-year-old boy Ali, are driving on a freeway towards Precinct One, Putrajaya City. The roomy two-door sedan has an extended cab forward design which allows the Doctor to swivel his seat, cross his legs and lean against his right shoulder to talk to his wife while the car drives itself.

"I still don't understand why you have this apparent—-reverence for him...?" says Jahala with a British schoolgirl accent. She glances out of her window at the lush, verdant curtain held aloft by the great trunks of tualang and merbau trees, palm fronds and moss surrounds both sides of the jet black freeway. In the distance, beyond the jungle, the light of a growing city obscures the brightest stars.

"I must..." says the Doctor as he turns the Sitar music down.

"Why doesn't he come to your office like your other patients? Why do we have to drive all the way from Kepong? Granted, I know he is a celebrity but..."

"That is easy to address. I am going to check the new jack Sony has just attached to his brainstem and he wants to keep it private. Oh and before I forget," hesitating. "Please don't utter the phrase, 'jelly bean' in front of him."

"Why should I...what does it mean?"

"It is a derogatory expression from the 20th. It is slang for the u—

ubiquitous computer chip in nearly everything—appliances and the like. It's okay to say that the rice cooker is on the fritz maybe because—'*its jelly bean must be fried.*' But people—-people who are wired resent the implication..." shaking his head and making a face.

Miffed at the insinuation, "I resent...!"

Shaking his hands and speaking quickly, "Yesyesyesyesyes. My fault, my mistake. You would never say that!" Inhaling. "Now, I was—-yes! Yes, it is in their best interest to have performed a—a superlative operation and he just wants to make sure they did. This is, after all a conduit for their shared benefit." Ali begins to sing a song to himself in the back seat as he plays with his *Brice Johnson,* action figure. "Now I will address your notion of my reverence for him. Please don't misconstrue my appreciation for the fact that he is an important figure for some—'some hero worship' adulation. Your notion of my reverence for him is misplaced."

"How so?"

"Take for instance the other principals in this venture with him—-these—these movie-e stars. They are every bit as popular as him, maybe more so. They are talented but—you would surely agree, they are interchangeable from film to film. Not catalyst but effects."

"Of course. Of course."

"If they played a role, or had a body of work that typified the—the malaise, mistrust or emptiness many real people feel today, maybe then—then that irony would be food for thought. They would connect." Jahala nods. "Inarguably, none of them will leave an enormous tear in the cultural fabric if they were to pass away tomorrow..."

"No carnage in their wake." Jahala smiles using her husbands own words.

Smiling, "No carnage in their wake."

Together, "No sobbing school teachers."

"Exactly," says the Doctor. "Brice, I feel, is an important figure because he represents..."

"An angry, rich, bully."

"No. Someone more like a champion of the masses who are drowning in so much useless information, conformity in a snow storm of empty stimulus."

Ali has caught the attention of his mother by banging *Brice's* feet against the door. "Ali stop that please."

The doctor becomes animated now and uses his hands much more. "You see I believe he is indicative of this time in our history precisely because the weight of money and celebrity coupled with the media scrutiny..."

"Darling—g, that is nothing new. You're going to have to do better than that."

The two pause a second and smile at each other.

"He embodies a response. A response to big conglomerates which profess to give you the world, when in actuality they have bound you to them.

To 'pimp freedom' while they co-opt your precious time. He has become the speck of hot pepper in the eye of conglomerates that seek to hold you captive, for the express purpose of selling you something. A champion of the overwhelmed!" Quite happy with his revelation, the doctor smiles, looks at the ceiling and raises both hands.

"Oh please! You have spent too much time reading *The Asian Nation*."

"Oh—h do not discount the motives of so many companies and governments, that seek to maintain their good fortunes at the expense of the individual—of the free spirit!" The doctor shakes his foot so quickly that he kicks his loafer off and it bounces on the floor. "You will see—we will see at a later time that you need not like him and he need not be a hero, for you to have acknowledged his duel with the powers that be."

"That is a flimsy argument," counting on her fingers, "You like him. He pays you well. He lends your practice cache."Together, "He is an angry, rich, bully!"

6,096 METERS UP

In the air above Kuala Lumpur Brice's internal voice rages stuck in an obsessive loop. "I don't trust those doctors that hospital gave me the spooks and my guts are never wrong, never." Brice thinks as he stares at the ceiling of his new plane. "Yup. The minute they cut me, I got Jimmy to set-up an appointment with Doc Mohammed to check it out." Looking at the seat next to him he picks up the e-book that contains the manual, registration, license and contract for the Aerodyne and drops it back on the seat. One thing Jimmy iz' good at is jumping on shit when it's business! Buziness—-s..." B' leans forward and sees Jimmy sitting in an overstuffed leather chair. He wears a bulky Sony headset designed for the home and bobs his head to a beat. Holding a small remote, Jimmy navigates his way through some environment somewhere. "He is always *In*. Anytime, anywhere." Shaking his head. "Couldn't do it. Already do it for a living. An' I ain't no *'Jackie'*." Smiling, "That shirt is amping!" Jimmy's shirt has thin yellow and black iridescent stripes that refract the light but the buttons, the five buttons were holo-eyes. "Dunno' what I'd do without him—too bad we're not—closer—na—a, like—-I dunno' the perfect TV brothers an' shit. We're all we got." A beat, returning his gaze to the ceiling of the cabin. "This chip in my headz' gotta' be cool doe'. How could it not. I make them too much money to fuck wit' me, lawsuits up they ass, this just too easy to prove…na—a…" Sighing. "I'm just trippin' cause' I louded them on the news when I shoudda' shut the fuck up, an' let Rodney flog they' ass behind closed doors like he said. But I can't take that shit back and POW my ass is on a hospital bed, with their boys over me with a knife. Well at least I had Erica send Arihito an expensive silk robe, slippers and green tea cakes or some shit like that before we took off, from Takashimaya no less! Got to send the best!," a beat. "He'll know when he gets that stuff that I'm sorry. He and I are still tight," a beat. "Some of the staff in that hospital was definitely spooky doe'. Glad I pay some motherfuckers to watch my back. Couldn't sleep except for when I was on drugs. I'll catch some good zzzzzs tonight. Yup! Gonna' check this shit out—-*only* person I trust in this world is Jimmy and I pay Mohamad'z ass enough to make me trust him an' he'z the best so I've gotta' let him check me out to know I'm cool. I don't trust any of those motherfuckers in that hospital. Can't wait for this bullshit 'grand opening' of 'my mall' to be over so I can jet home." B' turns his neck left and right then continues to stare and the ceiling and continues his inner rant.

BACK ON THE EXPRESSWAY

Back in the car with the Mohammeds. The doctor is busy entering something onto his PDA with a pen as Jahala scans through a newspaper projected onto the windshield.

"Aren't you the least but curious?" says Jahala with a sideways glance, baiting her husband.

"Not particularly. But I'd guess the obvious," as he shakes his foot nervously.

"But he's already rich."

"Quite. And your point?" not even looking up from his PDA.

"Over two years ago they stopped construction in Precinct One." Paraphrasing from the article in front of her. "Construction came to a halt when the Lucky One Development Company was caught red-handed, trying to bribe officials. The police were alerted by the wife of Ho Ming, President of Lucky One, who was having extra-marital relations with his eldest, adopted daughter, Khatijah—that deviate! The subsequent investigation uncovered a history of deceit, bribery and corruption that once completed would cause the arrest of 16 officials, 2 chairmen, 12 vice-presidents and 24 underlings—-including—g a nanny and a driver. Eight different companies in six different industries. With one phone call Madam Ming, as she was called, had wreaked havoc on tens of families and catapulted one reporter to stardom."

"At least we don't hear about her tiresome shopping sprees any longer."

"The mall was foreclosed on by the First Bank of Malaysia. Brice, these movie stars and that rock group sign on and over night the mall is renovated."

"You are pursuing a mystery which does not exist."

"Celebrity endorsements are nothing new. I know that. But why him? Why here?"

"Oh Jahala, he is an international star. Athletes don't pose for the cameras. The cameras are the hungry hyenas who feed off him."

"I don't…"

"It's money. Do you ever think you could have enough? This is a walk for him. He attends the grand opening, poses for the cameras, the blessings from Chinese monks and drinks some tuak wine then money is transferred to his account.

"I still think there is more to it than that." Exasperated, the doctor huffs and dismisses her reasoning with a disciplinary tap on his PDA as Jahala scrolls faster.

THE VELVET FIST OF CELEBRITY

Feeling the Aerodyne slow and descend, Brice makes leather noises as he leans forward and looks out of the window. Even a kilometer away the mall was an impressive site with the Petronas Twin Towers in the distance behind it. The Mahathir Mall (formerly the Z9 Mall) was once covered with rubber trees and oil palm plantations was now a sprawling complex surrounded by perfectly manicured lawns and a circular waterfront esplanade. "What a fucking fortune this place must cost to light," said Brice to no one in particular at the sheer Las Vegasness' of it. The lightshow gives the structures the impression of coursing with life. Billions of diodes generated neon dragons that dance and fly under holo-panes on the roofs of Sacks Fifth Avenue, on the South Mall. He remembered being shown the plans for the extension to the already large mall and being taken on a tour of the surrounding districts by a gorgeous native girl with cinnamon skin and hair like strands of silk who had attended Stanford Law School in the states. He thought of her long slender legs beneath a skirt that seemed too short and an eye popping diamond engagement ring that B' wanted to ignore since she enticed him so. They strolled through a market and she stopped at a vendor and asked him to slice open the national fruit, a Durian the natives jokingly called the "schizoid fruit." The smell of it was unendurable—like rotting flesh and she seemed entertained by his predictable reaction. It seemed that her ability to cause him to wince would act as a momentarily foil against his sexual advances.

They slowly descending past the six story Hotel and B' could see the faces of dozens of excited Muslim children wearing school uniforms. He smiled and they're excitement at the site of the Aerodyne got them screaming at a high pitch. They and others had been brought by parents who knew someone who knew someone who worked for or with Putrajaya Holdings, who built the mall, were pressed up against the glass in gleeful anticipation. The empty water fountain in the center of the plaza served as a makeshift-landing pad for the Aerodyne and it was quickly lined by workers, suits and cameras. The heat and humidity enveloped B' and his entourage the moment they took the first step down the plane's stairs. Jimmy was worth his weight in platinum for thrusting a Starbuck's coffee mug filled with rum, coke and ice into B's hands—had to keep up appearances for the sponsors and all. The mayor of the province nearly ripped the center seam of his assistant's Boss suit open as he made his way to be the first to shake Brice's hand. Sporting a black shirt, leather jacket and wrap-around shades he was a fashion totem to the wannabe' Euro trash execs with their shinny foreheads and gelled hair. Like a fur ball caught in the throat of a cat the crowd lurched forth and threatened to push Brice and his entourage into the empty pool until Leroy pushed everyone back. "Jesus! Worse than fucking school girls!" says Brice to himself, "Never seen so many sorry looking suits——now look at this motherfucker. He is smiling like it hurts his face. Yeah——h shake my hand motherfucker. I'm your gravy train and your ass probably just missed being indicted in that scandal—you guilty, fake smiling m-o-t-h-e-r-*f-u-c-k*-e-r '*could you pass the sauce please!*'" Brice smiles.

Leroy catches Jimmy's eyes and the entourage flows towards the entrance to the food court. Carl is flanked by mall security and nods for one of them to take the lead. As they are walking Brice is aware that the mayor is rambling to him in a heavy accent, but all he can think about is getting away from the foul breath mother. Brice does not so much walk as float across the concrete, his weight carried by the suits and photographers. The cold gust of air-conditioned wind puts a perk in everyone's step.

Erica, always within earshot of the B-man, seems to enjoy eluding the gaze of the photographers, because she thinks that limelight seekers are crass and lack substance. Olga, used to having the cameras trained on every pore, emotionally convulses at the recognition of first, being ignored by Brice and second, the paparazzi hoard. Seizing the moment she stops abruptly and allows her camel coat to open as she feigns removing a pebble from her pump. Not wearing a bra under her white, low cut blouse she flashes some nipple at a photographer. You could see the eye inflate inside the telephoto lens and several cameras turned to catch a glimpse. Erica spies Olga's show over the top of her shades and mouths, "Oh *pl-ease—e*," in disgust. There it was in color corrected digitized high-rez, pink, perfect and gone in a flash, brushing past Erica and deep into the swarm headed towards the corridor. Erica, a Waspy looking white girl from uptown, gives the maneuver a gum popping, side of the mouth, teeth showing, 'POP!' of disapproval and is only too happy that no one heard or would even know what it meant.

The mayor, who having recited several stanzas of rehearsed adulation by now, did not miss a beat when the Americans made a sharp turn and piled into a waiting elevator. His body slammed a photographer out of the way so he could have an eye-to-sunglass with B' just before the doors closed. B' didn't even smile.

He focused on the celery green helmets that the security guards were sporting. He grinned because they looked like warped, over-turned salad bowls. Funny he thought, how easily he had become comfortable with the attention, the adulation—the sheer seriousness of fame and the maelstrom that whisked him above the fray. "Floating...where did I read, 'Held firm by the velvet fist of celebrity'."

The section of the mall that held B's interest—his financial interest was steeped in eternal midnight. He had forgotten about the 3D environ he'd walked through last year until the elevator opened. Midnight navy polymer tiles covered the walls and ceiling of the upper retail level of the mall. Stepping out of the elevator and walking towards the balcony it came at him all at once. He saw the familiar marquees for assorted shoe, house wares and clothing stores and was indifferent. "This is one fuckin' busy lookin' place," he said to himself. "Times Square on speed only indoors. Bad place for me to syn'." Slowly walking to his left, "How can people even walk through this shit without getting a headache." Below people gawked at the effects and appeared to be transfixed by the light show as it sprayed neon graffiti on their retinas. B' gazed at people from a translucent, mother-of-pearl, Mylar balcony and was starting to get a headache. The Bahasa Malaysia language had a pleasing din to it thought Brice and he was happy it wasn't a regional 'provincial' twang from the US or high-pitched verbal pecking. Above the stores, paper-thin sheets of reflective silver foil rose and fell with the body temperature of passing shoppers. He could not see that the foils acted like autonomous freak show mirrors that gingerly reflected and contorted shapes and light into abstractions. He thought it funny that the small booths and storefronts gave the impression of a combination lunar-medieval village, where merchants would hawk overpriced sneakers. The entrances and windows for each retail outlet sported multi-colored, metallic slats held in place by diagonal poles. "These people like a lot of color or what." Advertisements for brand name noodles, Indian and Chinese fast food, shoes and clothing from American chain stores flashed across every surface covered by flat and curved-screens. Swirling primary colors collided across the faces of children with big cheeks only to vanish a moment later. Shaking his head, "They stuck lights in anything that didn't move." He thought the traditionally swooping sharp lines of many old Chinese rooftops were Disenyfied and plastic. As kids jumped up and down on the yellow brick, pressure sensitive tiles he wondered how long they would last. "Oh no," said B' as he saw timed holo-projections of larger-than-life Romans wearing togas accompanying a fat, jolly Caesar projected on and around shoppers. They sang, laughed and threw gold coins as they made their way towards the escalator for Caesar's Hotel and Casino on the lower level. "This is truly some tacky assed shit." Directly in front and below him was a Malaysian folk art store crammed full of ebony, teak and sandalwood sculptures, of all shapes and sizes. In front of the store was a young married couple accompanying their crippled son. The pudgy 13-year-old did not appear to have the use of his legs but was held aloft by a walker-rig. He floated centimeters above the tiles and controlled his direction and speed with a small device in his hand. At this sight B's face went from a grin of mild amusement to a straight lipped' vacant stare. "Not me. Could never deal with not being able to run. Never. I'd fuckin' kill myself."

Some peon from the reception committee squeezed next to Brice, pointed down into the mall and said something that B' summarily ignored. "Business." He turned and found Leroy who held a stairwell door open for him. Walking past Rodney he says, "Rodney."

"Yeah B'?"

"This is some tacky shit you got me wired to. It better pay."

"Oh you'll get paid," says Rodney putting his hand on Brice's shoulder. "And—d you'll never have to step foot in this place ever again."

As he and his entourage piled down the stairs he felt the number of beating hearts with him cut in half. The stairwell and corridor was bland, lit with fluorescent and littered with refuse. Torn cardboard boxes, thousands of bulb cases, Styrofoam peanuts, fast food wrappers and cleaning supplies littered the floor that made everyone concerned with where they placed their feet.

"Damn B'! They sure cleaned this place up for ya'!" says Jimmy.

"Now why do you have to go and fuck with my boy's head like that Jimmy!" says Rodney good-naturedly.

Brice smiles and says, "Actually if we waz' back home I'd say they waz' reminding me that I waz' black. Here they don't mean nothing and besides it's just as well cause that shit out there waz' giving me a fucking headache."

"Yup," says Jimmy.

"If somebody had told me that I'd get paid large and have to walk in the backdoor and through garbage though I'da' told them they waz' fulla' shit! But…."

In a dark Security Center illuminated by colored switches and close-circuit monitors, armed guards and several suits follow Brice's progress. Leroy stopped in front of the back door of Victoria's Secret and knocked. A moment later a tiny Malay woman wearing a pink, knock-off Chanel suit opened the door only to be grabbed and shooed away by her only slightly taller Indian husband, wearing a silver sharkskin suit. Nodding obsequiously he opened the door wider to let them in. He mumbles something in Tamil that no one understands or pays attention to but it is obvious that he is the humble owner. As they walk past cardboard boxes and through the racks of thongs and frilly, elasticized silk goodies, Olga touches the fabrics rubbing them with her fingers. Erica could care less. They emerge a moment later into the store itself where the pink leopard wallpaper is both comical and a thousand times more grating on the retina than the light show outside. Leroy and Carl quickly look behind every garment rack, in every dressing room and checks every exit while keeping B' in sight. B' pushes his sunglasses further up his nose and sees the Mohammad family in front of a white check out counter.

"Hey doc!"

"Brice my boy! How's it hanging?!"

"Same old same old. You remember my brother Jimmy…"

Jimmy and the doctor shake hands, "Yes, yes of course," seeing Olga he quickly shakes her hand, "and Olga, yes Olga I remember too, hello Rodney."

Rodney smiles and nods hello. Turning, "This is my wife Jahala and our son Ali." Ali seems mesmerized and cannot take his eyes off Brice. "Ali, Ali this is Brice Johnson, come and shake hands like I taught you. Come now, come now." Jhala tries to coax him forward but it only makes the boy retreat behind his mother. He grabs her pistachio colored sari and uses her ample bottom as a shield from Brice. "Ha! There you have my son, the game freak, hiding behind his mother when it has been *he* who bragged to all his friends this past week, that *he* was meeting you. Human nature is like that. Eh? Unexpected and rife with complexity."

"Well finally I don't have to ask you how the family is. They look good to me," says Brice as he makes a face at Ali.

"Yes, yes. Well we may as well do it here," says doctor Mohammad motioning a sofa upholstered in white and peach stripes with irises. The two sit and the doctor turns to his wife, "My case please Jahala." She quickly hands him an aluminum briefcase. He places it on his lap, dials the combination and opens it. Inside is a silver mechanism that appears to be curled in on itself. He takes out a wire and connects a sterile plug to its tip which he inserts into a splitter, followed by another plug and wire connection. The wires are thin, clear fiber optics and feel remarkably stiff and strong for looking so insubstantial. Turning to Brice the doctor motions that he turn around. "Any discomfort?"

"The usual."

The doctor carefully removes the bandage over Brice's jack and hands it to his wife. "Yes, yes, it looks very clean. Nice and tidy. Any complications?"

"Not to my knowledge."

"As expected. They would not want to harm the goose that lays the golden eggs. Now don't move. I'm putting the plug in and I'm sure the tissue is sensitive. Good, good. Lean back and relax. Have you been in any good movies lately?"

"Not to my knowledge but then again you should ask Rodney."

The doctor inserts the other plug into a sleek headset he retrieves from the case and presses a button. The apparatus comes to life and rises like a crane lifting it's head from the water. Its neck fully extended, a small array of lenses protrude from its bird like head and form a semi-circle. B' seems to be on the verge of saying, "Does that thing bite?" but doesn't. Someone lowers the store lights as the doctor adjusts his headset.

"I saw the Sapporo commercial you did."

"Yeah."

"You don't drink it do you."

Smiling, "Na."

The doctor presses a switch and as the bottom of the array covers his hand with a laser grid the upper half of the array forms a holo-image of a swirling green ball of energy. Suddenly B' wishes this was over. "Tell me, what kind of test did they run on you before you left? The Mirroyeye one or …."

"I don't know what you call it. I just remember it had a landscape and…"

"Lightning."

"Yeah."

"Ah—an older version of this test. Sit back." The doctor presses another switch and Brice's eyes stare off into nothingness as information flows in. Inside the doctor's retina, full color, 3D charts and numbers dart and flicker as they match information against his computer's memory. His computer instantaneously maps and runs a systems check on Brice's plug speeding hair like fibers of information hungry, vacuum tubes into the chip mounted on his brainstem at the speed of light. The doctor repeatedly nods and makes little sounds as his fingers flips through the multi-color 3D model of the chip and compares it to a black and white schematic. The dense renderings spin, enlarge and rotate at his command. Simultaneously, his computer runs a diagnostic of the chip recording everything including the microscopic patent numbers and the signatures of the technicians who created it. "Yes, now Brice."

"Yeah?"

"Have you eaten anything the last hour?"

"Only some peanuts on the plane."

"Good."

The doctor presses a switch and the green ball becomes a swirling red and black tunnel that sucks Brice headfirst into it. Speeding like a fighter pilot clockin' Mach 10, Brice's torso lurches forward as he holds onto the arm of the sofa. What Jimmy, Rodney and Olga see is the tiny representation of a short snake sucked into a massive tunnel. Jacked into this *dick,* (which is what everyone calls a deck without a line connected to a telecom provider) and completely at the doctor's mercy B' feels his hamstrings, biceps and shoulders tighten up. Spewing colors, moving too fast to fully register scatter across his sensory field complete with high definition sound. A celestial water-slide. The colors come at him like daggers of sharp light, only to fuse a moment later and spin weaving themselves together as sound pulses play out monosyllabic notes that echo and reverberate into a limitless void. All black. Flip to faces staring at his in Victoria's Secret.

"Jesus. Thank God the lights are down."

"Now that's a test my man."

"You could friggin'' warn me the next time you decide to dip my brainstem in acid Doc."

"And take away my only sadistic outlet? This is why I rise out of bed every morning."

"I can't believe I pay your ass."

"You pay me because I am as good at what I do as you are at what you do. The same way my child will take some of the money you pay me and piggyback a kill- run as they call it with you." The doctor removes Brice's plug and applies a fresh bandage to his jack. Standing he places the case on the sofa and the apparatus slowly recedes into itself. "Very good. Take a walk with me." He takes a small flat screen out of his case and takes Brice by the arm and the two walk towards a rack of red, padded, satin bras. "I want to show you something." He touches the corner of the flat screen and holds his finger down on the forward arrow. Having reached the page he wants he circles a region and touches *enlarge.* "Here," handing Brice the flat screen, "Here, look here."

"Yeah?"

"You see this small black rectangle?"

"Yeah."

"This is the circuit-board for your chip sealed in plastic. Now, I'm sure it is in fact the circuit-board, however it's too thick."

"So?"

"I'm not going to get into the technicalities of dimensions, but this casing is twice the size it needs to be and the functions are identical to the jack they removed."

"What does that mean?"

"I don't know. I'm a doctor not an engineer. I can't see inside the casing and my instruments can tell me only what the jack wants to reveal. I'm going to try to replicate the schematics and diagnose the possible applications and cross them with size constraints, but you understand that I'll never get anything conclusive unless..."

"You take it out and open it up."

"Yes."

"Should I be concerned?"

"Of course not. This is probably an enhancement of some sort. I will look into it and ask around without attracting much attention.. Everything else looks superb. Excellent. Let it heal for a week before you insert another plug though. You probably don't have sterile plugs laying around your apartment."

"No, I don't think so."

"Now how is the Synestesia, eh?"

"Manageable."

"I've heard that surgery of this type may suspend Synestesia episodes temporarily. But that is not my forte. Still a secret correct?"

"That's right and that's the way I want to keep it."

"Remember..."

"Yes, I remember. If I want inhibitors I can fill the prescription at any pharmacy, I can also squirt Crazy Glue into my jack and kiss my career goodbye, as I walk down the street like a doped up junky——no thank you."

"You exaggerate greatly. Small..."

"Small manageable doses don't work if you don't know when you're going to need it and if they don't last for more than a few hours at a time. Plus that shit cuts my senses—makes me feel like I'm on something."

"Understood. Understood. Heading home from here?"

"Hell yes. I miss my bed."

"I think you can afford to travel with it Brice, is that what the Japanese kids call you?"

"Yeah."

"I suppose you know what it means."

"Hell no." Seeing Rodney, "Rodney pay the good doctor please and lets blast off! Well doc. A pleasure as usual. Mrs. Mohammad," shaking her hands. "Ali," bending to get face to face with the boy. "You're not going to say goodbye to me?"

Jahala says, "Ali would you like your picture taken with Mr. Johnson?" Ali nods. "Well maybe you should ask him." Ali shakes his head and everyone laughs. Brice sees the sycophant in a suit from the balcony looking anxious and he realizes that it's time to move on to the next appointment.

Looking at Ali. "Come on lets take it he's so cute I want the picture."

Jahala takes her camera from the counter and shoots the two smiling. "Excellent! Well Doc, it's always a pleasure."

"Yes! Yes! A pleasure indeed," says the Doctor. They all walk towards the front of the store.

"Coming to New York any time soon Doc?"

"At your request, of course—eh!"

"No—o you don't!"

"I would pack my bags in a New York minute," putting his hand on Brice's shoulder.

"That's too bad Doc. We upgraded to seconds decades ago." Smiling. As they reached the front door they saw a small crowd of anxious schoolgirls wearing bright yellow scarves around their heads and long-sleeved blue school uniforms had formed and was eagerly awaiting Brice's exit. Electric flashes began popping as the Doctor and Brice shook hands. Just then Erica stepped in front of Brice and has to shout to be heard. Like a genie, the smiling geek in a suit has materialized at her side with a black, *New Era Entertainment / Casino and Hotel* varsity jacket for Brice to wear. A V-phone rings at the counter and the owner picks it up.

"Okay B', here is the drill. Security is waiting for us just outside those doors and they'll escort us to the next…" B' thinks, "Great! Lame crowd control, with me in the middle."

"…Level where the suits are already fondling Patrick Schwarzenegger. You make nice for the camera. Kiss, kiss, with the steroids that don't do his own stunts and we can all go to the hotel."

"Good, cause I'm starving."

"You're always hungry."

"Starving—g girl!"

"Mr. Brice! Mr. Brice! Call for you! Call for you!" says the silver sharkskin suit.

"Who is it?" says a confused Brice. The owner shouts, "Sony!" B' takes the curious V-phone headset that looks like a 19th Century courtesan's masquerade masque only amped. Black and opaque, the wrap-around eyepiece mirrors the human forehead, nose and cheeks and is held on one side by an ergonomic handle with buttons. One particular button is shaped like a trigger. When the headset makes contact with his face the screen switches on and Brice sees and hears Ido seated in the guest room of Arihito's home. They greet each other with semi-sweet animosity.

"Hello Brice San."

"Hello Ido San."

"I tried to reach you at all of your numbers but the operator said…"

"My phone was off. What's up?"

"We have suffered a great loss, both to our organization and ourselves. Chairman Arihito has passed away. It was a massive stroke. There was nothing the doctors could do."

"That saddens me." Brice said, one to Ido then a second time to himself, as his worst fear was realized. Ido was seated at a French secretary and was tapping a small gift card on the desk. Behind his arm was an opened gift box from Takashiyama. "That really sucks. I'll miss him."

"As shall I. He was a father to us both."

"Yes, he was," said Brice in a daze.

"The funeral will be the day after tomorrow. Will you attend?"

"Yes. Yes, of course."

"He would appreciate that. Goodnight Brice San."

"Night."

As Brice slowly lowered the headset he felt as if the weight of the world had come to rest on his shoulders bringing with it a cold, damp hymn. "Arihito is dead. I'm fucked and Ido knows I hate his ass." Over and over again.

Jimmy appeared sensing Brice was upset. He takes the headset from Brice and looks at him expectantly waiting for him to say something, anything. "What's up B'? What's up?"

"Arihito is dead. I'm fucked and Ido knows I hate his ass. He read a note I sent Arihito with that shit I sent him from Takashiyama. It said Ido is an asshole. I don't trust him and that I'll never work for his ass. He read the note. He had it in his hand just to let me know he knew…"

Outside the level of the crowds excitement grows and they start banging on the glass doors and screaming.

I'M SO GLAD WE HAD THIS TIME TOGETHER
OKUNO-IN CEMETERY, JAPAN

B' was standing in the most exclusive Japanese cemetery and the most beautiful place he had ever seen—in reality. He was impressed by the level of craftsmanship in the gravestones and was relieved that the saccharine perkiness of ubiquitous cartoons was absent in this place. B' and Jimmy were instructed to enter the procession with members of Sony Corporate, immediately behind Vice Presidents and Directors who trailed the Board, who were steps behind Arihito's family. No one spoke so the only discernable sound was the footsteps of the procession and a slight breeze rustling the trees above. Although the temperature on this winter day was 29°F it felt more like a warm Autumn day beneath the sun and clear sky.

More than a thousand people lined the entrance to the cemetery and B' and Jimmy's black suited forms joined others in a massive procession—like a lumbering old black snake making its way through the misty, forest of cypress trees. As they walked to the old section B' saw ancient, broken monuments overgrown with moss. While driving to the cemetery B' marveled at its vastness. It seemed to go on for kilometers and was said to be the last resting place of some of the most famous Japanese people who ever lived. Jimmy had looked it up and told B' that some Saint, Kobo Daishi, who founded the Shingon sect of Buddhism is entombed here and it is believed that he is not dead, but meditating while he waits for Miroku, the "Buddha of the future" who would be what? Some badass Anime that could heal the sick, walk on water and convince countries not to go to war? B' flipped a grin at the thought of Japan's rich and famous burying their hair, teeth and what not in this famous cemetery just in case. Reincarnation didn't seem to fit the Japanese. The Indians and the Chinese, sure. Their world was rife with overpopulation, injustice and generations of suffering and zero order. The Japanese had been ruthless in war and business and that had made the entire nation prosperous. Then B' thought that it probably made sense that they would want to come back and do it all over again, instead of hanging out in paradise and not being productive.

Arihito's family had fought having him placed in the tacky section in the newer part of the cemetery, where thousands of corporate worker's graves were. Instead he would be entombed in a mausoleum beside the body of his wife and parents that they had owned for a very long time. Thankfully it meant that his tombstone would not have to be desecrated with the Sony corporate logo and his title carved on it.

Standing under the gnarled branches of 300-plus year old cedar trees, B' could see graves marked by mossy little pagodas and red and white robed Buddhas. He then turned his attention to the grim faced corporate workers with their stern, serious faces in black suits that made them look like extras in a low rent gangster movie. Members of the family that Brice did not know and other dignitaries dressed in the traditional black and white of mourning were among the hundreds of people who attended the funeral. Black-robed attendants placed small tables bearing fish, vegetables, rice cakes and other offerings in front of his coffin on a cedar pavilion near the weathered mausoleum. B' caught the eye of Ido he was certain, despite their both wearing dark sunglasses. There was no love here and B' sensed not just the transfer of power from the dead to the living but a realization that he was looking at not so much his new boss but an adversary.

Standing with the family was someone who seemed vaguely familiar. Then he remembered her. She was the Euro-Asian girl who was at the party in his hospital room who didn't say a word to him. He had seen her trying to not be obvious about looking at him, but they had not spoken. Her face seemed ageless, somewhere between twenty and forty and he could sense an inner strength about her even at a distance.

The ceremony felt longer than it was and being in Japanese forced him to tune out. It was slow and appropriate for someone of stature who had passed into the light. After the ceremony Jimmy and Brice turned and began to retrace their steps out of the cemetery. and passing people—hundreds who had lined up to pay their respects and they began to kowtow to B'. They did it like dominos and it shocked him. Why were they bowing to him he thought? Then he realized that many of them were Sony workers and were acknowledging him for either part or all of their financial success. The shock quickly turned to revulsion as B' felt the full weight of attention being diverted from grieving to his celebrity and he quickened his step. B' wanted to get the hell out of Japan because his only friend here was dead and he wished to mourn him in private and at home.

ANEMONE JUICE
THE SKY ABOVE NEW YORK CITY

"Too many people," thinks Brice.

Above New York City at night its buildings, sidewalks, parks and landmarks appear no different from those of the 20th century on this chilly winter night. Even coated by a light snowfall the sidewalks were still infected by flattened, dirt covered gum like the blackheads on a vagrant's nose. An army of foul homeless people wearing dumpster clothing walked the streets both uptown and down searching for shelter and mumbling to themselves.

"At this moment in Harlem…" says a newscaster.

People ebb and flow through the city's major arteries: 57th Street, Canal, Times Square and lower Broadway, only now the pressure is greater. Now, even as tens of thousands tele-commute the city still attracts attitude seekers from across the country and immigrants from across the globe.

"…After a tense four hour standoff, the police are initiating a procedure that is becoming the norm in dealing with heavily armed hostage situations."

More American dream pickers, fewer jobs, more thugs, less prey— or just well armed, indigents, somewhat rabid illegal immigrants.

"The Police are about to deploy an armed Andros Mark X-A robot to mollify heavily armed squatters, in a known narcotic derm-den and rescue a hostage taken from a nearby Bodega."

As the vista that is NYC at night—its buildings giving the appearance of swaying in unison as Brice's Aerodyne banks—kicks in, B' leans closer to the window. The New World Trade Center's towers, built to withstand gale force winds and evil deeds catches his eye, "They were built to sway up to a foot— they say, if, the wind blows hard enough. Hope I'm not around." For a moment he imagines his Aerodyne is one of his clown fish swimming between the enormous tentacles of a petrified anemone. Out of the corner of his eye he sees the live news report on the plane's Holo-V.

A drenched, soot-black "Louise Nevelson" like street, strewn with the charred remnants of a fire at 292 East 142nd Street three hours prior. It whizzes down a ramp at the back of an armored, Navy NYPD SWAT truck and stops in the center of the street. Six meters from the steps of 300 East 142nd Street, a five-story walk-up, the Mark X-A. The boys at the station munching on Powerbars they call it Pitt, 'cause they pity the fool who dares to cross it or them. Hector, is jacked in via a police issue Motorola rig and stays in the truck. Pitt is a mean looking 'sombitch the color of gun metal, with the posture of a one meter, erect, mutant crab hiding all of his goodies behind Kevlar Teflon plates. If you can see the dim, red beam of its laser scope—"Click, boom! Bye-bye! Turned off. Showzs' ova'." Pitt's gyro, a direct result of NASA technology, gives the unit the balance and stability of an adult human begins to spin. The scene is apropos. Four squad cars, twenty tooled blues, fire trucks, choppers, paramedics, news-crews and lots of sullen African-American peds'. The blues wear standard issue, armogel-kevelar suits with lots of pockets for *immobilizers*. On their heads they wear stream pebble smooth, bulletproof, egg shaped helmets with photosensitive face panels, night vision, cameras and two-way communications. The only skin you see on these guys is a hint of chin in a sea of navy.

"Sixteen of the building's patrons have been questioned," the newscaster screams over the din of a chopper. "They said that Reggie Wilson, the assailant, is going through withdrawal and is exceptionally high strung. When he kidnapped the woman he planned to have her access her account from a remote debt computer only to find out that the dealers were out of Super Novas, Maxies and Pinks. Reggie opened fire killing seven, three dealers and four others who simply screamed too much. Several of his friends have taken up arms to aid him and all of the remaining occupants can be considered hostile, armed and extremely dangerous. They are said to be armed with an assortment of automatic weapons, a launcher of some sort and grenades."

Sergeant Scott, a snub-nosed revolver of a man, steps up to a patrol car and takes the remote mike from an officer. "This is the police! You are surrounded. Throw down your weapons and exit the building with your hands up or we will take you by force!" Switching the mike off he says, "That was for the fucking civil liberty lawyers and the cocksucking public activist." The NYPD had trained Negotiators who always took a stab at the beginning of these scenarios, but the NYPD had really stopped negotiating with perps ever since the Hernandez brothers did a trainload of civilians on the A-train years ago because the Pizza the negotiator ordered was taking too long. At the back of the SWAT truck a pissed off cop angrily scrapes dog shit off his boot and onto the ramp as he mumbles to himself, "Damn! Do this junky already so we don't miss the fucking Knicks!" Realizing what he has said, he looks around quickly for those pesky news reporters outfitted with telescopic microphones, "Fuckin' NY1 reporters could be anywhere."

No movement behind the dark broken windows. Nothing but the wind kicking Colt 45 cans down the street and the whir of choppers overhead. An imperceptible sign is given and all of the officers pull further back. Then without notice, Pitt frog leaps the six meters onto the second step of the building and scurries through the open door without touching the doorframe. The SWAT truck bobs up and down on its Michelin shocks. Three point five million North American credits have just entered a derm-den but not the way the dealers wanted it. The NYPD, in an effort to curry the city's affection for *the man*, allows all five networks to piggy-back their link and broadcast live to millions in the metropolitan area and other markets—and Billy gets to choose between any of four angles on Pitt's Ikagamie cameras from the comfort of his parent's sofa! Pitt is running a thermal sweep, motion sensors up, whisper mikes tuned for creaks, night-vision on all four cameras and proceeding with caution.

Hector's main task is the live acquisition of the hostage, everybody else is a stain waiting to happen. The Chief's eyes are fused to a monitor with his finger on a button that will interrupt the network's feed in the event a kid walks into the line of fire. Commuters in Grand Central and tourist in Times Square get a plate of uncooked New York, as they stare in at the scene in Harlem on the four story Sony, Jumbotron screens.

Screams are heard and two women run out of the apartment—Pitt had target locks via the camera in the back of his head, but decided to let 'em run. Pitt's in stalk mode that means the sensor cavity rises as he begins to move on his hind legs and the gyro starts to spin silently keeping him upright. Bodies are everywhere and the building is littered with newspapers dated decades ago. Through ancient plaster walls surrounding a doorway, Pitt spies the thermal images of three men, one obscuring a smaller figure. In the hallway above three other figures hug the walls on their way to the stairwell. Two barrel tipped arms silently unfurl from Pitt's underbelly bringing the total to four. Hector, it seems has enlisted the help of Carl who was jacked in on pause. Pitt spots three other thermal images directly behind him in another apartment.

"Police! Drop your weapon…!" says Hector through Pitt's speakers.

Crouching down Pitt lunges at the closed door shattering it on impact as he rolls into the room. Wood chips and plaster cascade outward while one perp after another suck Israeli bullets. Guns only have thermal signatures once fired hence any lurking perp could be argued to be armed.

"Well if they ain't tooled how come 'dey waz' lurking?" says a cop over Johnny Walker hours later.

In that one exchange, Hector determined that the third figure was not the hostage. Three stains. Pitt blasts a four-foot hole in the ceiling and jumps through it before the shrapnel hits the walls. Through a door and into the hallway. Before he hits the door, three more stains splatter near the stairs. Two manage to get off some shots that bounce off Pitt's hide. And he's in the opposite apartment, all in less than six steps. BOOM! Pitt makes a hole in the floor and drops in on the three perps, two are armed. Two are halved at the waist by the wave of Pitt's gun-limbs. The unarmed perp is a thin burnt out Hispanic guy. He takes pepper-gas to the face and is slammed against the wall by the impact of StayPut Gum and secured there by its glue agent. Screaming is coming from upstairs and Pitt takes to the hallway. At the base of the stairs he takes hits from below and above—something German made. He staggers as one of the hits takes off an armored panel. Carl zips the perp under the stairs, Hector zips the one at the top, while Pitt stumbles backwards. Leaping up the stairs, Pitt hones in on the source of the screaming. CRASH! Another apartment door gets taken out. Bingo. Three perps. The room is illuminated by a metal trashcan burning refuse. In the flickering orange light, an unarmed perp runs past Pitt and through the doorway. Before he gets two steps, Pitt slimes him with StayPut Gum and his head slams into the opposite wall knocking him unconscious. A woman screams through her tears. The second perp fires at Pitt and is shocked that the bullets bounce off. He wets his pants as Pitt casually raises his left arm and blasts him with pepper gas. He drops his

AK and falls to his knees coughing.

"I can't see! I can't see—shit—fuckin'—hurts…!"

Laser sights dart around the hair of the perp holding the woman. A clean shot is impossible since Reggie has a bad case of the shakes and is hiding his head behind the woman's. He is wearing a bulletproof vest with its Velcro fasteners undone.

"OhmyGod! OhmyGodOh God—d—pleaseplease—eplease! Ohplease—e!" The woman riffles out through her fear-induced stutter.

"What 'da fuck?! What 'da fuck?!" Says Reggie, holding the rusty Desert Eagle to the woman's head.

"Lower your weapon! Release the hostage!" Hector's voice blares through Pitt's speakers.

"Fuck you! I 'wanna negotiator!"

"Drop your weapon!"

"I'll kill 'dis fucking bitch. I kill…!"

"Surrender or die!"

"God—d—pleaseple…."

"…'Da bitch. You fucking…!"

Reggie pushes the woman towards the window by her hair, all the while keeping her facing Pitt. Reggie looks behind him to make sure that the bored windows are intact.

"Fucking shitty day! A'in got no mother fucking derms—lying mother fuckers shittin' me!"

All four guns track Reggie centimeter for centimeter. The woman's foot touches the AK and Reggie looks down.

"I'm gonna' walk outta here—you ain't gonna fucking touch me—I'm gonna' fucking walk outta' here! 'Dis bitch—'wit this fucking bitch. I'm gonna'—and I'm gonna' go to the fucking corner and score som' pink! An nonna' you mother….!" Reggie keeps moving.

"Not past twenty blues and a truck of SWAT snipers…"

"Fuck you!"

"…You're dumber than you look. You can't take me 'an if I don't zip you before you quit this room you're a stain on cement."

"…Fuck you deep an' hard motherfucker!"

"No Reggie. Fuck you. You wanna' live? Huh? Wanna' live put…!"

"Fuck you! I 'mo get high 'den you could fucking take me in! I'm hurting too bad ta' sit in some fucking ride man!" Crying. "I gotta' get up. I gotts' ta' get up."

"Can't let you hurt the woman Reggie. Let her go and you breathe through the right holes—no bargains."

"Ain't you been listening ta' me bitch! I 'mo get up right now!"

"No."

Reggie stops. "Catch!" Reggie swings his arm around to zip Pitt. A shot thunders out of the Desert Eagle missing Pitt, the sound deafens the woman. FFFFT—T! Pitt has fired a sharp, solid steel dart that enters Reggie's wrist and cleaves its way to his elbow socket. His other hand, still full of the woman's hair, yanks her backwards. Reggie drops the gun, falls hard on the AK and the woman falls on him. His screaming tops hers and his cussing is unintelligible.

"Reggie give it up!"

Reggie pulls the woman on top of him, lets go of her and immediately reaches behind him for the AK. The woman breaks free and runs at Pitt. Reggie fumbles with the AK...

"Get down! Get down!" yells Hector.

...Now in his good hand. Reggie fires at a wall as he arcs it towards Pitt.

"Move...!" screams Hector.

Carl and Hector work against each other, both swinging their right arms in the opposite direction hitting the woman yet keeping her in place.

"Carl back off!"

Hector's knocks the woman off her feet with his right arm just as Pitt takes hits to his forward sensor shield. Arching, Pitt blares away with three guns cutting Reggie into pieces taking the window boards and bricks with him.

"Remain calm. You are out of danger. Paramedics are on the way," says Scott through the speakers.

Pitt shifts to the protect mode and covers the victim until paramedics arrive. The word is given and twenty blues double time it into the building followed by four paramedics.

"Well, Cheryl...Law enforcement in action," says the newscaster audibly shaken. "We see New York's finest effecting what appears to be a perfectly executed hostage...retrieval—well have more for you after these messages."

As they approach the old Trump heli-port they are put into a holding pattern so the Swells coming back from the Connecticut can disembark. And out of nowhere, it begins to rain buckets. The tower, a one story prefab with a staff of two, has to make room for the Aerodyne to land so they get pushy with the vertical Lear and the civy' Huey. The pilot brings the Aerodyne low facing the port above the water and its a beautiful sight. The flood lights from the port illuminate the gold alloy carapace of the Aerodyne, making the rain hitting it flash like sparks. With the Huey and Lear headed to Newark you can hear the controlled purr of the Aerodyne's engines racing like fifty Ferraris in unison.

Jimmy switches off the Holo-V and everyone gets their things together. The Aerodyne's door opens to reveal two men holding oversized umbrellas and the small entourage walk briskly into the small port building. It is a wet, gray winter evening in Manhattan and everyone's steamy breath is riddled with holes and discorporated by the large angry raindrops.

Once inside Jimmy, Brice, Olga, Leroy, Carl and Rodney walk through a machine that checks for drugs and contraband, while their baggage is whisked through another detector. Spoon, the floppy drug-sniffing-dog rates, Brice's arrival with a raise of is eyebrow. Jersey doesn't get a second look, but the stink from the Hudson gets everybody before they pile into the stretch. The pilot, wasting no time, powers up and punches it—humping G's, lifting off like a rocket and banking east over the city like nobody's business.

HOME AND THEN SOME

Twenty-three seconds after Brice sat in the limo—without his uttering a word, the on-board computer knew who he was and put in a high-speed call to Home—the A.I. who ran the systems in his home to announce his arrival.

No one spoke. Everyone is either tired from the flight or thinking about Reggie and Pitt as a set of low-ball crystal glasses clink together. The black, rear engine Mercedes stretch, a sleek elongated beetle with hair thin seams from trunk to hood, reflects holo-ads. and neon signs as its polymer skin beads rain. Brice touches a button and his chair reclines as a full-length footrest extends. Staring straight up, he touches another button and opaque, black Viracon privacy glass instantly turns clear giving him a full-view of the buildings from below.

Jimmy looks forward directly a the back of the driver's head and tries to imagine what the limo looks like to pedestrians or peds. Three-quarters of the driver can be seen through the plexor windshield in the center of the limo's forward compartment and his expression is all business.

It stops raining by the time the limo stops at the entrance of the MoMa's Residential Tower and the driver soft touches a button for the electric doors to swing open.

Olga was trying to get out but Brice cut her off, "I'll call you," and kissing her he exits. She feigns pouting. Jimmy ignores her as he steps over her designer pumps and jumps out of the limo.

Rodney, leaning towards them, "Alright guys. You'll hear from me."

"Later man."

"See ya'."

Two doormen wearing white gloves and burgundy jackets have already retrieved five black leather Gucci bags from the trunk and are waiting for Jimmy and Brice to enter ahead of them. The doorman gently spins the revolving door for them and says, "Welcome back Mr. Johnson, Mr. Johnson." To the brothers.

They cross the Italian marble floor past the charred looking person wrought by Giacometti, past the cherry lined walls, barely acknowledging the hellos from the two concierge. They've only lived in the building for the past five months, but each time they cross the lobby the elevator awaits them with the white gloved attendant ensconced to control the elevator. Its walls are simple and austere appointed with the same wood as the foyer and without buttons, only an 8x10 flat-screen to the right of the door. The elevator attendant spoke, "Penthouse."

Fifty-one floors above, Home—aware that his boys were on the way up—had been busy. The maid came in that morning and gave the duplex a complete once over but left the windows open so Home closed them and spritzed the air with rainforest potpourri. The lights in the living room were adjusted to Brice's favorite setting for this time of day and the stereo pipes Jobim through hidden speakers, because B' liked the retro airport feel it gave his pad. The ionizer at the base of the central holo-projector turns on and streams of light render a 3D naked blond in the center of the living room who dances to an inner rhythm as she caresses herself. Stalin, Brice's Rottwhieler leaps up from his designer bed in the game room, to run through the dining and living space towards the front hall, where he slide-runs to the front door. Stalin sits among the framed magazine covers of Brice on the cover of RollingStone, Newsweek with the headline "Being Bad Pays," Sports Illustrated, Ebony, Black Enterprise and GQ next to old photos of Muhammad Ali and Bruce Lee. He looks intently at the mounted reproduction of the "face hugger" from Ridley Scott's 1979 Sci-Fi classic Alien hung directly above the door. The face hugger's appendage is fully extended and Jimmy thought it amusing to cover it with a light-blue condom. Stalin stares intently at the doorknob and stretches his front legs in anticipation.

In the elevator, Brice looks at Jimmy and yawns. "What're you gonna' do tonight?"

"I donno'. Sleep." As if that was a surprise.

"Yeah I'm burnt too."

"Workin' out tomorrow?"

"What do you think?"

"Plug still sore?"

"Yeah—h little."

B' exited the elevator first, owning one of the two penthouses in the building meant that his front door was close at hand. He looked at the mauve-lavender carpeting, remembering that he had forgotten to tell Brown Harris Stevens that it looked dowdy and that he would be willing to pay for something more sedate and less frumpy. Mental note he thought.

Upon hearing the electric locks unlock, Stalin wags his docked tail with anticipation and puts his nose against the door. B' has to open the door slowly in order to avoid hitting Stalin who goes crazy but in a good way. Jimmy and the elevator attendant follow him in toting three bags. Stalin jumps up and scrambles around them, sliding across the polished ebonized Teakwood floors while barking.

"Hah! Got you! Been bad—been a good boy?! Good boy? Huh? Huh?" The two roughhouse for a minute as Jimmy walks past them.

Jimmy says, "Thanks man," to the attendant, "You can leave them there Jose. Thanks."

Brice stops and picks up his bags and walks into the living room with Stalin sniffing his pants and nosing his hands. He sees the holo-woman who says, "Welcome home Bricewicie."

Brice says, "Off bitch." And walks through the holo as it disappears.

He walks on top of his red broadloom rug with its slightly raised circular pattern that embraces the spectacular floor to ceiling view, through the sliding doors and past the terrace facing south, west and north of Manhattan. B' opened the door to the terrace, stepped out into the brisk winter air and heard the sound of a distant siren and cars whizzing bye below. He walked to the railing and placed his hands on his piece of the glass tower. Stalin bounced up and rested his paws on the railing and B' turned, smiled and petted him then gazed at the glorious cobalt-grey sky. The Algonquians named this place a "hilly island" if they could only see it now. The light from every building and crevice seems to burst upwards and obliterate the night and the streets seem like large arteries waiting to be filled.

After a few moments he turned and thought, "Not sure those trees will come back," says B' looking at the skeletal trees on his terrace then entered the apartment and closed the door.

"Home! You lazy shifty ass..!"

In a mock Japanese voice, "Its so nice to have you back home Brice-San."

"Fuck—k you. You're bored as hell without me."

"Silicone does not get bored but we used to be onboard." Said Home in a droll British accent.

"Stalin get into any trouble."

"Nope." Back to contemporary, uptown idiom. "And of course I missed you immensely."

"Yeah, right!"

"Good evening brother Jimmy."

"Knock it off asshole or I'll reprogram your ass." Said Jimmy looking through a few pieces of mail on the holo wall.

In Brice's voice, "Fuck—k you. You're bored as hell without me." Jimmy smiles, shakes his head and pets Stalin before he walks upstairs. B' scanned the room hunting for anything out of the ordinary or out of place. His ivory Mies van der Rohe, chairs, ottomans, the red Le Corbusier club chairs—everything was where it was supposed to be and Home had had a large "manly" flower arrangement placed on the coffee table. Over the gas fireplace hung a large portrait of Brice's face in full scowl with his skin the color of eggplant, his eyes electric green and the words "I will consume you," emblazoned below by the Spanish artist J.S. Santiago. Across the room he spied one of his favorite things, his custom brushed steel pool table with its bright cobalt blue felt and nodded imperceptibly. Walking towards the stairs, "I missed you boy, from now on we travel everywhere together alright." Stalin walks gingerly along at his side. "Wanna' go for a walk? Lets go. Go get your leash. Camon'!" Stalin races into another room and returns a moment later with his leash between his teeth.

In the elevator with Stalin on his way to the first floor Brice flexes his arms and pretends to hit Stalin who growls playfully and barks. In the lobby he heads for a service door and enters the area just behind the coat check in the museum. He makes a quick left and then a right near the escalators and walks in to the group tour entrance. Stalin's nails echo as they click against the white marble. None of the other tenants can use this exit but because of the B'man's need for privacy they allow him. A guard looks up from his flat screen and smiles at Brice. "Welcome back Mr. Johnson."

"How you doing."

"Just fine. Just fine. Have a nice walk."

He buzzes Brice out and picks up his flat screen. Shaking his head, "Damn! Forgot to play lotto. Ah' well."

In the street, Brice lets Stalin off his leash and follows him towards Fifth Avenue. He prefers 54th Street because it's less well traveled than 53rd and seems more pedestrian. Stalin is a three year old filled with zest and energy to burn. His muscles are toned, his demeanor fierce and his senses razor sharp, so Brice thinks it funny that he's appears self-conscious—even embarrassed when he was in the middle of dropping a load. It was these times when Brice felt as if Stalin needed him to watch his back so to speak. Brice liked this street in particular because of the limestone townhouses, The US Trust building with its Georgian facade and the scale of the buildings—fuck the University Club on principle alone. But something wasn't right. It was a peaceful enough night in the city and no one was on the street so why did he feel uneasy? Going through his pockets he found a few business card chips, a pair of sunglasses, cough drops and a smart card for an account at Sumitomo Mitsui he'd forgotten about. Then he remembered he didn't have his earplugs with him. Damn. He thought it was funny he hadn't had an episode since the operation and hadn't missed it. In the distance he could hear a police siren on Sixth Avenue and he hoped it would keep going. No such luck. The police car turns west onto 54th street and the man was going to blur past Brice with Mars lights and sirens blaring. Panicking, Brice puts Stalin on the chain and makes for the entrance but it's too late. He breaks into a jog only to stop in his tracks. The shrill noise shatters his eardrums as the patrol car passes the extension of MoMa's galleries headed towards him and his field of vision is obscured by blinding red daggers. All at once the daggers appear real and physical, jutting through space and yet seen by more than his eyes. Its like being on the inside of a flat screen looking through the text and realizing that you and it are one. Brice drops the leash and grabs his head trying in vain to keep the sound out. Frowning, cussing, spitting and stumbling like a carpenter whose thumb is red and throbbing from a hammer hit, Brice is engulfed in a bad syn' trip. Stalin, sensing his master's pain backs up and barks his concern.

"Ahhhhhhhhhhhfuckmeeefuckmeee!!!"

As the police car passes the daggers work themselves into a frenzy stretching into lightning bolts and he can feel them press against his cheeks and arms as he puts his hands up to wave them away thinking his head will burst any second. The car is already tearing down Fifth Avenue but the throbbing lingers, even as the daggers blink and slowly fade. His world is reduced to an awareness of the pulsing veins on his temples, the throbbing behind his eyes, the lingering pressure of the daggers and the blurry parking meter in front of him.

"Man, that sucked."

Wired for Chaos

With that Brice straightens up and looks around and is glad to be alone except for Stalin. Walking towards the entrance there is the familiar one note high-pitched sound we all hear when we mention how deafening silence can be. This sound has no color though it acts more like a test pattern letting him know that regular listening is about to resume. He stops for a minute next to the wrought iron bars and stares into the sculpture garden at *Standing Woman,* Gaston Lachaise's big ass bronze of a smiling woman with titties' the size of salad bowls. He takes a deep breath but the car exhausts really doesn't help.

By the time the guard buzzes him in the daggers have completely disappeared, but he can still fell them on his cheeks and chest. He just wants to pop some Advil, like ten minutes ago.

Taking the elevator up he repeats a combination of what the doctors have told and what he's read. "'Ten people in a million have it in one form or another. Seeing color when hearing certain sounds is more popular than tasting shapes," he winces, "but having it does not mean you can't lead a normal life. Synestesia won't drive you crazy by any means because the consistent way it manifests itself keeps it from appearing chaotic. Syn means 'together' and aesthesis means 'sensation'—like no walls between the senses…when the ear transfers the mechanical energy of a sound into a nervous impulse and it travels through several relays before it reaches the cortex…' Bla bla bla. So why haven't I seen'em in days? I had a glass of wine at the party. Must have been all the drugs and shit they had me on at the hospital. Could be the antibiotics I'm taking too. Funny. I guess I was too distracted to miss it but now that its back I'm cool with it. I just need a fuckin' Advil."

Forget yoga and deep breathing exercises to control it and the Perkanol wired him up too high. So for a condition that was first documented about 1710 by a British ophthalmologist and certainly existed before that, especially when you consider the style Aborigines have been painting in for centuries; what worked then works now, Caffeine or nicotine to stifle your syn' and alcohol to invigorate it. He didn't smoke, so caffeine was his choice of cortical stimulant—a syn' downer for the workday. Myers Rum was his choice for social cortical depressant. While the amyl nitrite in 'poppers' was a strictly personal limbic-brain enhancer for that vivid-psychedelic-sex-high.

But the general public didn't know. Sony didn't know. Nobody knew except for Jimmy and Doctor Mohammed and that's the way Brice wanted it. He felt the only way to be an effective competitor was to have everyone focus their attention on his performance and not the fact that his senses couldn't remain compartmentalized. That kind of anomaly would freakafy' him or worse be a potential handicap to be exploited. He thought it fascinating that he could remember his very first syn' episode when he was seven and a school mate's chair leg, worn through its rubber cap and scratched the marble floor with a shriek. The freight would stay with him for at least a year after the hyper-red squiggles and headache faded. He waited a week before asking Jimmy what colors he saw when the gym whistle blew, only to get the first of many funny looks. He never told his adopted mother.

Smiling, he thought how funny it was, that people's inner-voice would repeat the same things over and over through the years. He knew a great deal about repetition since his life revolved around rituals. Certain things he did upon waking, while training, before going out. He didn't realize those rituals compensated for life's uncertainty and the absence of his parents.

He wondered from time to time if syn' had changed him in other ways—would he be a champion without it? But he never let the question linger. He was the champ and it was good. So two Advils and a Myers & Coke later Brice was stretched out on the sofa and jacked into *MTVScream!* This was more like it. Sure the lattice of colors or form constants are extra vivid and playful because of the alcohol, but they are also translucent and their surface is softer, smoother and undulates like liquid glass cool to the touch. Through the lattice Brice follows the bust line of the rapper Shanka' in a spandex nitey.

A small window appears at the bottom Brice's field of vision and a black man's lips appear.

"Bill for you Brice," says Home.

"Yeah," a beat, "Hey man."

Bill, Brice's burly, middle age trainer wearing a skintight T-shirt gives Brice the once over before speaking. "Comfortable?"

"Very."

"I can see."

"How you been?"

"Will your highness be joining us for a workout tomorrow…?"

"Oh good. And I'm fine too—yeah, yeah the operation went well…"

"…So that we can go into the next game at 100% and not embarrass our crew..?"

"…Just a little soreness and…"

"Excuse me my little fuckiewuckie but I jacked your operation and if you want the inside of your thighs stroked get somebody wearing' Revlon. I intend to squeeze every ounce of sweat out of your narrow, caramel ass so I can retire and live on the beach. Got that pussyshit ratfuck."

"Bill, I missed you so much."

"8:30 and have another drink. I like a challenge." Click.

To Stalin, "I love that prick. I really do."

"MY SWEET IMMERSABLE YOU—U…"

Locked away in his room, Jimmy has been hard at work emptying his vmail box and is getting it together for tomorrow. As he walks towards the bathroom he flings off pieces of clothing pausing only to look at himself in the mirror.

"I wanna' call Avery first, then Sam then Ray. Who did I say I was screening out?"

"Larry, Peter, Sabrina, Nick, Ted…"

"Yeah, yeah Home, just keep it at what I said last time. I wanna' wake up at nine to the news and no calls before I eat, I'm expecting jet lag to visit.

Shower on."

"Cool."

The shower turns on and immediately adjusts to the 98∞ pre-set that Jimmy likes.

"Now get the fuck outta' my room. Privacy lockout. Runa' full diagnostic or something'!"

On the wall, next to his bedroom door, Home's brown high-definition iris fades to black. As Jimmy steps behind a curved fixed glass wall he is enveloped in a stream of filtered water. By the time he exits the shower minutes later he is already sporting a woody in anticipation of the Tai sex-stims he got in Singapore. He grabs an enormous leopard print bath towel, dries himself and throws it on the sink. Quickly opening a drawer, he rifles through it until he finds a roll of derms shaped bras, peals two off and sticks them on his neck. Walking into the bedroom he struts and his body language appears manic and skittish. As he enters his walk-in-closet the lights brighten.

He touches a button and a large floor to ceiling mirror separates from the bird's eye maple shelves that house thirty pairs of designer shoes, to reveal a steel vault. Without looking Jimmy grabs a lightweight headset with attached neurotransmitters and a small, triangular, blood red box from Bali made of dried leaves and grass. Moving now with a conscious pimp-roll he almost jogs up to his flogiston chair. The near horizontal, low profile chair looks like a black, stiff rectangular board but is actually an elegant one-piece aluminum frame covered with long-memory foam and encased in a leather sheath. Once seated, he places a black sweatband with a "Brice" logo in block letters next to a Champion logo. He then picks a small, black leather travel bag up and searches through it. Retrieving a dozen mini-discs tied together with a red silk ribbon he rifles through them. They are covered with pictures of copulating men and women of all varieties under Chinese writing. He pauses momentarily when he comes across one with a brash schoolgirl holding a horse's member. He winds up ready to hurl it across the room in the vague direction of the trashcan but hesitates and tosses it back into the bag instead. Randomly selecting a disc he opens the case and reads the faux gunshot hole sticker. "Lucky wanker. Your trance limiter has been removed. Erase the establishment. Fuck on!" On the floor, next to a square box of tissues sits his football-sized deck. The deck, at first glance resembles an artists version of an abstract toad. Expressionless and imposing with its black multi-angular skin it seems like some galactic traveler frozen in time. Smiling he pops the disc into the mouth of the player and the small green diodes on his head set light up. Careful to arrange the ten circular neurotransmitters in their proper locations on his body, he is about to lean back when he remembers to open the red box and takes a nasal spray hit of an orgasmotronic called Racer. He then places a pink, cinnamon flavored, skin-touch Sally under his tongue that the "ComeBack" tabs on his neck will ricochet off for the next two hours. On goes the VRD shades and psi-link and Jimmy is into the black leader of the disc. Three paragraphs written in Cantonese, English and Japanese fade in. The words are large and sprawl across the retina of his consciousness like stars surrounding a satellite. The capital letters "International Bureau of Investigation" are written in red while each other letter appears in white. It reads, "Under protection of the Ping Clan all use of the enclosed sex-stim will be bound to a use-pay joiner where you the programmer option frames, sections, digital, sound and trance samples for the express purpose of profit will pay a two percent…"

Jimmy's eye pointer clicks on the fast-forward button and he speeds past the protection landscape for the blue void. Expectations rise at this point of quality sex-stims because the "get in" is where programmers like to strut their stuff before the "dick" is concerned with a digital succubus. So it begins. The "slip" is a bungi-drop without a cord that racks the sensation of what Jimmy is seeing. He is plummeting down a water tunnel much faster and with less control than any surfer on acid ever would and cannot hear anything above the din of the crashing water. The rush hurls his senses as if he were strapped onto some amusement park ride and he can feel the salt water splashing and misting in his face, making it difficult for him to open his eyes. Splash, blackout, the slip has him standing in four inches of mud. Instinctively he looks down and is impressed. The new Host Memory Retrieval system on his deck has rendered an exact digital duplicate of his body down to the scar on his knee. But his hands are bound with vines. Instinctively, he lowers his hands in real-time and can feel the pressure of the vines against his wrists. Smack! Someone behind him just hit him with a cold metal object. As he turns he sees a small, attractive Philippino boy wearing nothing more than two ammunition belts draped across his chest. He and four other boys are all brandishing Russian automatic weapons as they nudge Jimmy through the tropical heat. Smiling, Jimmy chooses to forego conversation with them and play along. They laugh and ramble on in a gumbo of Japanese, Philippine and Thai, as they kick and poke him up a steep mountainside covered in plants and trees. A horde of misquotes swarm in front of his face and he instinctively tries to wave them away. Jimmy guess he is in the Philippines but he knows the Toucans he sees are from South America. Its like walking in a sauna. His skin is sweating in real time now as the neurotransmitters play the limbic region of his mind like, a cello and he has given himself up completely to the program. Now walking down the side of a mountain sideways to avoid tripping he can hear splashing and the sounds moaning and laughing. Passing through a thin mist Jimmy can make out an encampment surrounding a stone temple in a clearing behind a smoldering bonfire. Entering the camp Jimmy is prodded by men who smile at him and tug at his member. Many men who are bound and evolved in all forms of copulation do not even glance in his direction. Suddenly two men grab him from behind and carry him into the temple where he sees several men screwing each other. Once in the center of the temple, he is set upon by several of the men who fight over him and wrestle him to the dirt floor. They overwhelm him and as he looks into the eyes of the man with a growing erection and opened his mouth the trance program kicks in. He begins to lose all will, all ability to

Wired for Chaos

control his own thoughts and becomes a mass of sensation. Low-level trance music and the sounds of the moaning tap, in and speak directly to his pleasure center. His skin becomes hypersensitive, sending euphoric shudders of erogenous pleasure to his pleasure center. The program has taken full control of each stage of his orgasmic cycle and will make it last exactly two hours with multiple orgasms. Within ten minutes his body will writhe with convulsive sex spasms, his heart rate will reach 147 and the occasional spittle of drool will make its way to his shoulder. Drugged up, trippin' out far out into the his own gray matter, Jimmy could never know that the deck he bought in Japan from that cocky dealer, had turned it self on and was watching him.

DELIVERY

12:30 AM, Ed, one of the early morning doormen steps off the service elevator with Juan, a delivery boy from D'Agastinos'. Juan carries two shopping bags behind Ed who stops at a small panel and inserts his card key. Making an impatient hand gesture, Ed gets Juan to insert his ID key into the panel and Home's iris appears on the small flat-screen.

"Oye Juan." says Home.

"Ola."

Four magnetic locks release and a steel handle pop out near Ed's waiting hand. As Juan steps back Ed opens the rear door to Brice and Jimmy's large Sub-Zero refrigerator. He bends slowly, cautiously and looks into the refrigerator. Exhaling, he picks up a quart of old chocolate milk, looks a the date and puts it on the floor. This routine continues until he has removed all perishables from the refrigerator and he puts great effort into doing it quietly. Then he knocks over a near empty jar of pickles and cringes in fear snatching his hand back. Ed looks at him, smiles and shakes his head. Juan rights the jar and proceeds to stock the shelves with fresh dairy and juices. Just as his whole forearm and part of his head is stretching below the main shelf the refrigerator opens. It scares the shit out of Juan and he gasps. Stalin has grabbed the dishtowel that hangs from the door handle and pulled it open. With the door now fully open Stalin makes eye contact with Juan and bares his teeth.

In Spanish, "Okay doggy, nice doggy. Nice doggy." Juan moves slowly placing each item like a brick on a new wall. "Nice doggy." Stalin begins to growl and Juan moves faster.

"Stalin, Stalin! Go to your pillow and let Juan finish what he is doing." says Home. Stalin ignores him, shifting his head in order to catch a glimpse of Juan. Juan fumbles and makes a racket as he piles cans of soup onto the shelves and that drives Stalin wild. He barks, not with projectile spit and exposed teeth but with loud, obstinate consternation tinged with just enough menace to spike Juan's adrenaline. The groceries were flying into the fridge now and beads of sweat had formed on Juan's forehead. Seconds later the door was slammed shut and Juan took a step back and wiped his forehead with his sleeve as he looked at Ed who smiled.

Inside, Stalin nosed the door shut and sauntered out of the kitchen.

MORNING
8:10 AM, PENTHOUSE, MoMA TOWER

Jimmy opens a cabinet in the kitchen and looks at the eight boxes of Frosted Pop Tarts trying to decide which flavor to have. Breakfast today was going to consists of the usual. Pop Tarts, two Eggo waffles with cut strawberries and OJ. Jimmy prepared his breakfast and transferred everything to a tray then opened the refrigerator and extracted the box of Equal the delivery boy had deposited the night before. He picked it all up and headed for the living room.

"Screens." And the walls in front of Jimmy came to life. He plopped down on a white, leather Mies van der Rohe Pavilion chair and put his breakfast to rest on the matching ottoman. Stalin who was laying on the white marble floor looked up at Jimmy then put his head back down.

"Play messages." Said Jimmy.

"Since you last checked there is only one message from Marty." An image of a swarthy Arabesque colored young man with jet black hair and too much in the-taste-to-money ratio speaks to Jimmy from the back of his limo. To his left is a beautiful model that passed out with her left breast poking out of her gown. "Hey Jimmy boy, having a party tomorrow night. Usual crowd. Bring your brother and some goodies" Click. The screen switched to Jimmy's presets and shows the local weather, his stock portfolio, the latest club news, the booty from his gossip board agents and selects from the major networks and news channels all on mute. As he chewed on the Eggos he picked up the box of Equal and opened the seal and withdraws the goodies Marty had mentioned. What the box contained was not the blue packets of Equal no calorie tabletop sweetener containing aspartame dextrose and maltodextrin, but illegal hallucinate drugs. Self adhesive derms. The ones with devil horns and smiley faces were Trippies that took you to a whole other world altogether Trevor. The ones with the hanging tongue and flat eyes were orgasmotronic for sexually heightened enjoyment and so on—all toxic in excessive amounts and would leave you exhausted and spent. Jimmy made a nice living selling these to his rich, connected acquaintances, who would never expose themselves to street sellers or unsavory dealer types.

How the transfer worked was as follows. Jimmy subscribed to a small technology consultancy that writes strategy and maintains fully integrated S.M.A.R.T. systems like Home. But these guys never came to Brice and Jimmy's apartment, they did not have a contract etc. with the Johnson brothers. An individual in the billing department of Glaxso Consultants was the actual dealer and would from time to time deliver derms to Jimmy via the aid of a stock boy at D'Agastinos' who kept a few boxes of the doctored Equal boxes in his backpack and was paid handsomely for placement into select grocery orders. Jimmy had never met the guy and that was best for everybody all the way around. His mark-up was three hundred percent and if someone complained he would shrug and walk away. This stuff from Glaxso was always excellent grade and no one had complained or died, plus having a business that did not depend on income from his brother made Jimmy feel somewhat independent and sublimely naughty.

Jimmy would spend the rest of the day doing the usual. He would call some friends, meet to eat somewhere downtown and generally hang out talking tech like he was someone in the know.

WORK
8:22 AM, 245 WEST 55TH STREET

Brice steps out of his limo, a silhouette in black from head to toe and walks towards the entrance that houses Ernesto's New York Boxing Gym in the 10,300 square feet, fully equipped, Everlast facility that was once the DuArt Film and Video. Never a morning person, B' needed two cups of coffee to be human and even then, he never wanted to engage in conversation before 10:00 AM. The sensor imbedded in the doorway mapped his facial pattern and swung the front door open for him. As he ascended the staircase random thoughts spewed through his lobe. Soon he'd have to immerse himself in everything Tanaka and a kind of filtration of distractions had to happen. He prepped himself dreading the impending work while knowing how important it was. Behind his big black Persols B' fumed.

"That bitch Ido is a punk. I could swat him like a fly."

The funeral. Turbulence in the Aerodyne over the Pacific. Tanaka. T-a-n-a-k-ah. "I will consume you," he said to himself. "I will grip you like a soft-shell crab and gnaw on your limbs. I will find an opening and hit you like a high-speed train. I will picture you in my every waking moment and know you better than you know yourself. *Bamn! Splat. Cower. Fall*. Take you before the world. Blister blows all over you. Beat you—make you my—y bitch." Winding the pale blue staircase littered with pictures of boxing greats like Muhammad Ali, Mike Tyson, Hector "Macho Man" Camacho, Joe Fraizer and Rocky Marciano always wound him up and he could smell the sweat in the walls. "Doing it in front of the world, just like a porn star—they keep asking fo' more."

When B' entered the gym he was met by Ernesto's son Roberto and they always touched fists and said good morning to each other. Roberto stood behind the counter and beamed with pride each time B' walked in. Behind him was a very large holo-picture of him with his arm around Brice in the gym and subsequent images of the two fooling around. He had B' sign it "To my biggest fan Roberto" with a special marker that wrote and re-wrote the letters over and over.

Bill sat in a folding chair reading the news on a thin flat screen as he drank his coffee. Always the same routine, dependable Bill. He'd acknowledge B' with a momentary glance (his head not turning even a degree) and B' would walk directly into large locker room where he'd change into a full-body, skin tight, black, sharkskin Nike running suit.

After he changed and had another cup of coffee Bill started B' out with his standard workout. Bill was an old-school boxing trainer and believed only his standard workout sculpts the ultimate physique. Although he allowed for some comments from B's martial arts Sifu, as long as he was B's main trainer things got done his way, which meant no talking back and not taking any garbage.

Jumping rope always came first with rapid three minute intervals followed by a minute off and as many crunches as he could do in three minutes. Back to skipping rope for another three minutes, rest for a minute and then as many push-ups as he could do in three minutes. Repeated over and over for forty-five minutes. As B' skipped on the blonde wood floor the winter sun, burnt through the city smog and filled the gym. As boxers and suits who wanted to front like boxers began to fill the gym, B' began to focus and look past the faces in his field of vision and thought of winning—but mostly, how to look like a rich, badass, pro athlete to those with lots less money.

After this it was time to mount the treadmill and do a long distance followed by a series of short sprints. Bill was a big advocate of static stretching because flexibility enhanced reaction time reducing chances of injury. After a short break Bill would sit with B' and wrap his hands imparting occasional words of wisdom like, "Are you here with me today? Are you focused or are you gonna' fuck up and sprain your wrist?" After an ugly look from B' it was on to the speed bag followed by the heavy bag. He would say over and over to Brice that he wanted him to visualize. To practice the motion in his mind first in order to get the form down perfectly.

Once B' was sufficiently limber he would spar with one of his partners under Bill's scrutiny. These bouts were not meant to push B' rather they were opportunities for Bill to see B' weaknesses and make adjustments. About this time everyone broke for lunch which was delivered from a Pax deli down the street. They always had low fat everything, with lots of complex carbohydrates in the form of fresh fruits, vegetables and some pasta. The meals consisted of lean well done beef, lean pork, chicken, turkey, fish at 20-25% protein 10% fat 60 %+ complex carbs ratio with very little simple sugars.

B' could then count on a brief rest in the media room where he and Bill would view footage of fights and game runs. Bill particularly liked to surprise B' with footage of old school boxers like Sonny Liston, Michael Moorer, Roy Jones Jr. and Muhammad Ali. On the days when Bill knew he didn't have to rush because B' needed to jump in a car and head over to the Central Jersey Rifle And Pistol Club in Jackson he'd waxed rhapsodically about their strategies.

By mid-afternoon B's Sifu, Jerry Fong would show up for private lessons and really push B'. He maintained that B', although very talented lacked discipline at times. That he needed to fight two enemies: the one within and the one without. He would also review how Bruce Lee had a very small repertoire of movements but beat foe after foe. What separated him from everyone else was their discipline and innovation. The techniques he taught were mostly for the hand with the legwork being nearly identical to that of regulation boxing. He emphasized body positioning. It was important to know how to place his body relative to his opponent's body. B' worked for hours with Sifu who taught him to attack from the same side as his opponent's lead hand, but from an angle. It was about consistently attacking in a circle—the strongest shape in nature. Today his Sifu would teach him how to perfect a blistering series of roundhouse punches.

On Mondays, Wednesdays and Fridays B' would hit the free weights to work out his large muscles by doing squats, snatches, lunges, presses and curls in perfect form. All of this had become routine for B' and his crew. They all knew that road to number one was littered with the carcasses of other number ones and that the only way to succeed was to crush everyone else and not be crushed yourself.

OLGA'S
101 CENTRAL PARK WEST

It was sunset on a Friday in Manhattan and a given that city workers would step into the winter night soon, having missed the sun's departure. The night was commencing early at Olga's because there would be many parties to attend later. She and her two model roommates had taken an afternoon siesta right after the gym and were now fresh and ready to mingle with a couple of female assistants from the agency and some girlfriends who were trust fund babies killing time at Sotheby's or the Metropolitan Museum of Art as low wage kiddies sporting Rolexes.

Jack Daniels, white wine, Heineken, nail polish, cigarettes, takeout sushi and tear sheets from the fashion magazines that still insisted on printed paper, were scattered across the coffee and dining table. Magic was trying to run the household as usual and barking up a storm trying to get the girls to sit properly. One model was miffed that last night's date with a "normal guy" had been beyond stale and bland. The girls had decided to encourage one of their own to try a regular guy instead of the jet-set rich boys they were used to, or the bankers with their fat wallets and tummies. The guy worked at an ad agency and probably made no money. He had taken her to a "not hot" place and tried to hide wincing when he paid the check. He hadn't even been to Europe—drop him, exclaimed the cadre of high cheek bones and size 6s. Nobody there was ready to settle down anytime soon and "who needs taxis when you can ride in a Porsche."

One girl got up and tapped the stereo with a finger to turn it on, then walked down the hall headed to the bathroom. As she turned the corner she saw Olga kissing a really big black guy that she was sure played for the New York Knicks. The kiss had flashing neon lights that said, "thanks for the suck and fuck," and the door closed. The girl playfully said to Olga, "You two-timing the Brice man you evil bitch," stepping into the bathroom. To which Olga responded, "Ruff ruff." And heads to the kitchen.

RICH BOY KILLS SLEEPING HOMELESS MAN
"Maria, I'm standing on 49th Street and Tenth Avenue where just one

hour ago, a mid-city boy shot a grimy—a street person—who was apparently asleep, with a thermite explosive charge—the kind fired from a German Das Cure. A new high-powered handgun that holds up to three thermite projectiles. A witness, who was driving by on his way home—says he did not see the unidentified victim get shot—but when he felt the explosion—only meters from his car—he stopped, got out, walked over here to where I'm now standing and saw the gristly sight. Now at this time the police have the young boy in custody and are questioning the witness. The identity of all three involved is at this time being kept confidential until the victim's next of kin and the boy's parents have been notified. Reporting from West 49th Street this is Ramon Sanchez for News Four."

A SHORT TIME AGO IN A LUXURY APARTMENT ABOVE.

At twelve Sean, already has the features of a young Adonis. His dirty brown hair and perfect skin frame a sullen face that never seems to smile. His schoolwork done and having exhausted the Smithsonian's cowboy references, Sean hops out of his chair, puts his cowboy hat and matching jacket on and leaves his room. Once in his parent's bedroom, he begins to look through all of the drawers, the night table and in the closet. Finally he finds what he's been looking for. Dad's Das Cure handgun. Without so much as a half grin or a tilt of his head, Sean loads the gun, puts it under his shirt and exits the room. He passes the paperless office where his father Thomas, is jacked into a long distance, VR teleconference. Thomas, a large imposing man is wearing designer goggles and sweats sans shoes or socks. His size thirteen's rub the deep pile blue rug of his office as he carries on a heated debate. On the wall size Fuijitsu plasma screen we see his InSpace *Doppes* wearing a suit, shirt, tie and shoes. His features are rendered perfectly except for the addition of impeccable skin and a noticeable reduction of body fat. There are nine other Doppes of different races, all in suits, who are seen to be at odds with Thomas. The location is a flawless grassy knoll surrounded by six extremely large screens illustrating spread charts and real-time company account transactions. The knoll is limitless and the sky is cloudless and blue complete with a radiant sun. Thomas is an analyst who is having a disagreement with his associates in London, Spain and Sweden simultaneously. All of the men and women wear impeccable clothing and are seated on nonexistent chairs.

Sean passes his mother's office where she is also InSpace, carrying on a conversation with a caller. Her *Doppe* is a lifelike rendering of her real-time self only wearing a black cat suit. She is seated in on a chair inside an unfinished set for an upcoming episode of a sit-com. Floating one meter to her right is the video-phone image of her producer who is calling from his home in Venice, California. At her fingertips is a floating multi-colored grid of memory through which she can view or download home furnishings from a multitude of sources. As she frowns at a bed, then begins to swap styles one after the other in rapid succession.

In the hallway Sean, lifts up an expensive vase and removes something from its hiding place that he puts in his pocket. Sean walks through the living room and down another hall, hops on his limited edition Lone Ranger Segway scooter, with red and yellow ribbon fringe hanging from the handle bars and zooms to and out of the front door.

He exits the elevator in the basement and transfers to the service elevator where he presses the first floor and heads for the service entrance. It is always unmanned because the doorman in the lobby controls access. Sean is spotted by Manny the doorman on the flat screen.

"Excuse me? Sean? Sean is that you? Can I help you? You're not supposed to be in that part of the building Sean. Sean?"

Sean approaches the high security door, oblivious to Manny's questioning.

"Sean what are you doing there? You know you don't have access to that entrance. You can't…."

Sean inserts his mother's key card and punches in her access code. The door opens and Sean rolls out into the street before Manny can finish his sentence or override the key card.

"Oh my God."

Manny's just lost his job. His pension evaporates before his eyes. In his mind, he and his family are already elbowing their way into grimedom. Sean rides west past the Food Emporium Supermarket and across 8th Avenue in front of autos stopped at the light and headed West into the place where his parents said never to tread.

Manny ran out of the front entrance of The Gershwin at 250 West 50th street and screams, "Roberto! Sean jus' ran out of the services entrance..!" to another doorman. He runs around the corner towards the Food Emporium dodging tourist and slow walking peds.

Sean's father, a big Irish Catholic who has kissed the ring of the Cardinal, boils in fury at the thought of the city's inferior residents. The beggars, squatters, the virus couriers—the grimies, seen as the parasites he sees each night on the Holo-V in his luxury high rise. Those lazy, uneducated, descendants of illegal immigrants and children of teen age substance abusing, nigger, mud-mothers. Spicks that don't speak English, or pay taxes, with wives that seem to have five babies every nine months with the city picking up the bill. The chinks, slope-heads, slant eyed Asians that think they own the fucking place—the lot of 'em. The world needs a big can of Raid sprayed on the city, while the *good* people are at some Hilton off world on vacation.

"I'd like to *off* the lot of 'em."

Sean's face holds that blank stare dreamers get so tight that his breathing is almost imperceptible. He zooms up and onto the sidewalk passing the commercial, residential and retail complex. The masonry clad World Wide Plaza that covers an entire city block. Past one entrance to the plaza he stops and looks at a homeless man named Cheeks asleep sitting at the top of the steps to the plaza, leaning against an empty storefront. There are no other peds and the only sound comes from cars racing down the street. As if awakened from a dream, Sean hears the heavy breathing of the destitute 65-year-old man sleeping off a hangover and struggling with a bout of bronchitis. Sean stops three meters in front of the sleeping grimy and dismounts staring at him.

"I'd like to off the lot of 'em." Echoes his father.

Sean takes the gun out, releases the safety and pulls the trigger. A thunderclap, a bright flash, followed by a small gray, geyser of a mushroom cloud follow in rapid succession. The thermite has disintegrated the man's entire chest and his right bicep. The remaining body parts were blown meters from the charred crater of his upper body. Clothing, flesh, hair and bone have fused into smoking, charred, indissoluble masses. The kickback knocked Sean off his feet and against a parked car on that side of the street.

Ramon Fuentes, a courier for a canned food distributor from Ecuador, is driving his beat-up 1998 Chevy down the street when the blast shakes his car. He screeches to a halt and cautiously approaches the carbonized spot on the pavement and building where the man slept moments ago. Unaware of Sean, Ramon sees a loosened piece of the man separate from the wall and fall to the pavement. His lungs fill with a mixture of sulfur and burnt flesh and he holds his nose as he picks up the gun less than a meter from Sean's leg. Minutes later Ramon stumbles over to the Chevy and dials the police on his ancient cellular phone. Tenants of the red brick walk-ups across the street (325, 328, 330 and 332 West 49th St) look out of their windows and as some drivers queued behind Ramon, edge past his parked car. The response time is miraculous. The street is blocked off, as four squad cars and eight blues control a small crowd minutes later. Two ambulances whisk Ramon and Sean away, three detectives, a forensics expert and one reporter get to work. Time elapsed, 25 minutes.

THE MAN

Niemöller twirled imaginary beads of malice through his mind as he sat in his Herman Miller office chair and exchanged computer patois with his geeks—briefly seeming like one of the boys. He laughed at their jokes and invited mild ribbing, but kept cultivating the hate for an ex-associate named Lenny. He liked to pretend to be "one of the boys." The briefest of moments when one of the boys would sense *Nie'* as he was called, looking at him they would get a chill. Like a viper in a glass box watching his meal tremble in a corner, Niemöller would grin with half his face and take enormous bites of his meatball hero. Fear he thought, at its height, could cause men to defeat themselves long before they could conspire to microwave a coups d'état.

Lenny...

Then it arrived by snail mail.

He had always been weary of the dent above his right temple that widens to a crest then narrows like a curved sword beyond his hairline. Feeling that the dent would impart a lack of intelligence, he has always overcompensated by either being a show off or initiating a preemptive scathing remark. Though no one could tell, he was a type "A" obsessive personality and the thought of not being able to resolve his disfigurement infuriated him. He had spoken with a specialist who assured him that a custom silicone implant would fill the fissure and leave a faint flat scar. But the operation was overpriced and the notion of wearing bandages for several weeks was completely unacceptable. Yet it was an option. Long hair revolted him and hats never attracted him until—as if through a dream he remembered the image of boys wearing bowlers and was impressed by their toughness and self-confidence. He had tried on many hats at J. J. Hat Center before deciding on the right one. He was told that they no longer carried the style he wanted because they proved to be unpopular and he did not like any of the others. Quickly, he dialed every haberdasher in the city and when that proved fruitless he pointed his bots at England. Success at last. The entire search had taken barely five minutes, but the wait for a bowler in his size felt like a lifetime. Many times he vmailed Christy's haberdashers in London to check on its status, only to be politely told that it was being made and would be sent to him immediately thereafter. They were very polite but Niemöller thought he could decipher a tone of consternation. How could those gray-haired suits plod through the muck of inefficiency while the world of commerce moved at light speed. It arrived from the UK by UPS*M*ail at 11:00 AM on a Friday morning and was delivered to him by Gary, his sheepish, unkempt imp. He took it into his office, closed the door and immediately ripped open the box. Now that it had finally arrived he placed it on his head with much ceremony. Remembering what the salesman at Worth & Worth said about a correct fit being just above the ears he was pleased that it fit so well. He stood in front of a polished rectangular steel plate and gazed at himself. He hadn't imagined that it would be so firm, have such weight or be so substantial. The hardness of the crown, the touch of the grosgrain and rabbit all felt good under his thumb and now he felt complete. As he walked out of the office that night buttoning his long, black overcoat he could feel eyes indexing the bowler but no one dared say anything more than "'Nite N'". Once on the street a cold, October wind enveloped him from the East River. He instinctively lowered his head, held on to the brim and sliced through it. He had outgrown QuickTrack and would leave them soon to deal in black-market code. What could be worse, he thought than having to watch a team of geeks track thousands of couriers as they made deliveries all over the city. The plan was to orchestrate a few large, well-planned sales and purchases over the course of a year instead of those annoying little transactions the Taiwanese implored him to do—he pouts, petulantly. One day not too far in the future and under his terms he would move to an island in the Lesser Antilles, hire a servant, play Beethoven, paint waves and bay at this rancid excuse of a world. Nothing and no one would stop him. He would spit fiery bile into the system of anyone who got in his way and roll over hundreds of pedestrians in a spike wheeled monster truck and then, only after each person had submitted to his will, his fury and begged for mercy only to be denied, then—and only then would that dead bitch who called herself his mother— and losers like Lenny see—see with gaping eyes that he was not to be trifled with. Not a sickly man-child but someone to be respected. Then once she knew he would ram her head into the steaming mix of molten lava and vomit in Satan's toilet bowl obliterating, disintegrating and deleting her from his consciousness forever.

"OH SHIT...."

"...And you sit there and have the fuckin' nerve to judge me!!!" The bulging veins and spit jump off this life-sized holo-projection of a look-a-like Brice Johnson! "Like I'm one of your boys or som' aid you can wipe your fat, hairy ass on after jogging up the Capital steps! Like I'm not fuckin' supposed to know! Like I'm not supposed to fuckin' care that you're using me as your whipping boy to score points with the farmers in buttfuckville! You sicken me and you can't stand it when I kick back! So I yeah, I beat people up for a living, like that's supposed to be so—o different from what you do?! Nasty, raw-meat Hors-D'Ouevres motherfucker! Like the world doesn't know that you cut deals like all those shits before you — in some back room smiling behind cigar smoke and a pot bellies filled with fetid meat! What I do is clean and pure! Search, Greek, games of battle! Not wars—-games! Nearly twenty-seven hundred years ago the Greeks—the fuckin' founders of civilization through democracy and—d the guys your architects stole their columns from, had an event in the Olympics called the Pankration which was hand-to-hand fighting—no biting or eye gouging allowed! That means that way—y before jelly belly, genejoke politicians, took their first bribe from corporations posing as a special interest groups sounding like concerned political action committees, wearing Day-Glo, plaid on a golf course there were champions like me, competing in sanctioned events watched by people like you pur-e-l-y for your cathartic enjoyment!" B' is raging now and stomping around in his half open sogi suit! "You should be thanking me! I'm not asking for that screaming fan worship that girls do! I'm talking a respectful silence, like thanks that's got nothing to do with indifference just respect! But no, your ass is running lip at light speed telling women that they can't have abortions, we need to step on *off* biotech—-can't alter the genetic code cow, stink, shit! You don't get the unfiltered, unabridged, bullet train speed, wide as Grand Canyon truth-of-the-matter intel that, I have a vital place in the scheme of things! That me and the "gang of punks" as you so pusillanimously sound bit last week, that *we*, me and all those punks whose asses I so thoroughly whup' on a regular basis, could actually be of greater importance in the fabric of this space-time continuum than your ass, because we are the safety valves that quell the blood lust of men and women all over terra firma! Run a search on your history files and dig on the fact that in the eras leading up to social unrest, the poor and the working class had no venue through which to vent their frustration with their lot in life, or their bosses, or all the trash people that made their lives miserable! But you wanna' rise up on my ass like som' golf ball sized pimple thinking you'll ride me through the election and win your seat cause I'd be like too afraid to mix it up with a big swing dick also known as gut spilling over size 48" belt on the capital steps shyster lawmaker! Well do not attempt to adjust the reception on your Holo-V, bitch! No one has slipped a Mickey into your single malt at the club! *I am* the supernova, pulsar, powered motherfucker who is going to squeeze your white ass on to some Bounty absorbent paper that won't tear easy cause I know something you won't admit! You know as you stare at me, with your mouth agape and your wife clutching those pearls from Harry Winston, that I represent a part of y-o-u and every man, woman and child that has ever been pissed on, pissed off or just plain been in a funk! I represent the collective primal urge to grab, hit and do merciless violence to those that wrong me and I, Brice Johnson as the embodiment of that *will to power* that Kierkegaard spoke of scares—s you because I will not be controlled! I will not be placated by your promises or threats! I cannot be soothed by your Japanese double-speak, stroke me twice, fuck me once bullshit charm and what you cannot control you have scorn and loathing for maintaining! What you fear is not simply the adulation of one like me but the possibility, the very possibility, that my continued existence after having been exposed to your caustic laser beam may in fact have made you irrelevant, ineffectual and damn sure obsolete!"

Everyone in the room is silent. Brice's nutritionist, his physical trainer, his manager, agent, businesses manager, Jimmy and B' himself. They watch the holo of Cyrus J. as Brice Johnson bows drinks in the crescendo of rapid e-applause in the form of rapidly, expanding pair of clapping hands. The applause rises, the clapping hands envelop a large portion of the room in front of the projector and fade away to reveal Cyrus smiling wryly as he morphs into the shatter-poet, Shankar.

Jimmy says, "Mute'" then "Off," after giving it a second thought and the images disappear.

Just as Rodney looks in Brice's direction, Brice rises and circles the enormous, white, tufted, infotament ottoman and stands directly in front of the holo projector. Although he says nothing his body language appears to be calling out. Jimmy half leaps over the sofa and quickly puts on a pair of VRD shades. A second later—before the pixels have even rendered the dial-up screen, Jimmy is hacking Cyrus' number. "Whaddaua' doing?" asks Bill to Jimmy.

"Whaddau' think," turning to face him, "He's dialing that skank that did me so we can have words."

"Shit." Says Rodney.

"What?! Don't you approve?" says Brice.

"No man I just had a bad thought. What if the media's take on this is that you paid this performance artist to take on Morris…"

"Awh—h shit," says a trainer.

"…You know, like a pimp slap on the global Holo-V — you just know who ever didn't see this shit live iz' gonna' down it later. Fuckin' PBS. That's our tax money, your's and mine."

Jimmy's eye pointer has been working double time until he comes up on Cyrus' smiling face. "Link-up Home." In a split Home has linked Jimmy's transmission on to the main holo projector and everyone can see Cyrus beaming in front of a studio flat screen as he does an on-line chat. The stats on the bottom of the screen display reads, 75,361 logged on chat viewers, 5,773 cuing for questions, an alternating grouping of 10 callers asking two questions each and the high and low numbers (between 1.5 and 1.8 million viewers world wide). Supered over the screen we see Jimmy's pointer in the shape of a falcon claw dialing numbers, opening and closing windows and communicating to the server's operator.

Everyone in the room talks out of turn. "Damn!" "Would you look at that." "Wonder how much he got paid for this — think he got paid?" "He didn't get paid man that shit is performance art." "Well he got up in front of a camera in a studio and somebody paid the electric bill didn't they so you gonna' tell me he didn't get paid. Shit—t." "Listen zygote baby, were you or were you not of this planet when I talked the talk and communicated to you, that you and I paid to make that shit possible." "Fuck you into the after life." "See that shit — now here we go. Here we go."

Brice stands next to Jimmy and ignores the banter around him. "You in?"

Jimmy says, "Well of course they are stomping my leapfrog over these EMs (error message magnets) cause the operator won't believe I am who you are —and—d because of our privacy encryption number they can't..."

"Open a window for a face to face. Home pull up the networks and see if any of them are turning this shit with this performance artist, me and Morris into a story."

"I'm on it," says home and the wall behind the projector switches on displaying ten high resolution, floor to ceiling plasma screens that project through the light sensitive white glass. The screens randomly flip through several hundred international channels pausing momentarily on news telecast.

"A view window pops in front of Cyrus' face containing Larry, an annoyed tech support guy with unruly hair wearing a flannel shirt. Larry's expression hits the air breaks when he sees Brice standing in front of his boys.

"One me with Cyrus."

"Sure, sure, sure man. Hang on okay, hang on," says Larry as he hurriedly taps a few commands on his multi-colored icon panel without raised buttons or audible clicks. Cyrus. Cyrus it's Larry. Shut the fuck up for a sec and listen to me. I've got Brice Johnson on the line." Jimmy has moved Larry's window in order for everyone to see Cyrus' face and he smiles uncomfortably.

Cyrus holds his earplug in and looks down at the floor. "Really?"

"Really. I'm looking at him right now he seems pissed and he wants to talk to you."

Over Brice's shoulder Rodney whispers into his ear, "Careful what you say cause now you're online and we don't want a liable suit."

"Yeah, well put him on man," says Cyrus.

"Done he's in. I'm dumping your dial-ins but we're still live."

"Hey everybody we've got the man himself," says Cyrus, as Larry instantaneously windows in Brice for all to see.

Nobody says anything.

The uneasy moment stretches out and Brice takes a step towards the projector's camera and stares straight into the lens. He squints, nods and everyone can see Cyrus swallow hard. Brice makes a fist with his right hand that signals Jimmy to hang-up and he shuts the projector down. Brice walks towards his bedroom and without looking says, "I've got a party."

ONE BAD MOTHERFUCKER
BROADWAY AND WHITE STREET, THE NEXT DAY

A watch-pager-locator buzzes on a large man's wrist and a deformed hand paws at it hitting the *receive* button.

345 LAFAYETTE

"Na—a! Na—a! You wrong! You wrong! Ain' no way no motherfuckin' 60," preaches Lenny swinging around a Mag9 with an oval barrel. "Gonna' blowa' hole bigga' 'en 'dis s-h-i-t r-i-g-h-t h-e-r-e!"

Henry and Alvin, Lenny's twin shake their heads. Alvin, holding the back door to Ill Diablo restaurant open, nervously scans the gated entrance to the alley as the three talk. "I donno' man. I seen a Grip blow a niggah' in half—-vaporize all his shit from (one hand on his chest with the other on his waist) here to here and—d take out…"

"Bullshit! Bullshit!"

"…The niggah' behind him..!"

"Bullshit!"

"…An' they wazen' even wearin' no cheap vest—they waz' wearin' military."

"Bullshitbullshitbullshit! Motherfucker should be wearin' a bib an' shit to catch that crap comin' outta yo mouth! All I know iz' this shit right here iz' gonna' radically alter the color of this ground r-i-g-h-t here! 'Cause just like I tole' you, when he comes in you bring his ass back here an' Imo' give 'em a Mag9 blow-job."

"I hope you know what you doin' man. I woulddn' want to be fuckin' wit' that Chinaman."

"What? Like you don't?"

"It's not even like if you could say—a'right. He crazy! Ton iz' just…"

"Like you don't think..?"

"Not like you not a bad motherfucker an' all. Everybody knows you offed eight nigghas' and a bitch already. What I'm sayin' iz', he don' hurt people just for no money. He don' hurt people for no pleasure neither. He just do it cause that's his nature."

Alvin grins, "Likea' great white shark an' shit."

Lenny is not amused and hurls a nasty look at Alvin.

"I waz' at a cage fight last year in—you know that fucked up place in inna' Bronx when he beat this man inta' Cajun mashfuckinpotatoes'!"

"So?"

Wired for Chaos

"He beat that nigga' way—y past dead?"

"'At doe' mean shit."

"He beat that man till his head came clear off. He took his time, picked a spot on his neck, bit in—-I mean he bit in to tendons arteries and shit an' knocked his head off wit' eight blows. An' Lenny, his face diddin' change. He diddn' grin, diddin' make a face or nuttin'. Waz' like butterin' bread or something for 'em."

"Damn! Expletive!" says Alvin.

"I'm still gonna' blow a hole big enough to fit your tired ass in him while you standin' wit' yo' arms stretched out."

Henry, takes a concerned posture, "Lenny man—n why don't you cut a deal wit' Niemöller man—n? Gettem' to cut you som' slack an' shit."

"Yeah, I mean first you sell him counterfeit code, then talk shit about the man to people in 'da community and—d expect him to not want to hurt you?!"

"Ah—h niggahs please," grabbing his crotch, "digitilize this!"

CANAL AND BROADWAY

A sea of people. It stopped raining an hour ago and people came out of the subway, cars and buildings like thirsty roaches. Past Asians wearing wide brimmed sedge hats and olive ponchos, past Cuban refugees selling counterfeit software imported by Vietnamese gangs made in Taipei by brutalized child labor, walks Ton. No surname required. He's six-five, with dirty split ends to his shoulders and UV-*Reaction* lens implants. As he walks North on Broadway he is the biggest Chinaman you've ever seen.

345 LAFAYETTE

"The deep tell iz' you diddn' just do the man wrong 'cause far as hez' concerned your ass stole from him but then—then, you go an' brag 'bout that shit! But I give you quantum credit 'dough. Shit—nuts like melons an' shit, just for nerve." A beat. "Anyway you got hand on account o' Ton's M.O. don't include no metal."

"He don't pack?"

"Nope. NT, no tech."

BROADWAY AND SPRING

Three hundred and thirty-nine pounds of salt, muscle and dread walks up Broadway like he does everything else, slow and deliberate. His beat-up three-quarter denim jacket and soiled white T-shirt conceal his hairless, scarred skin—the color of cardboard. At a light, a wannabe' tough new-anarchy teen bobs her head to the latest freeform metal that sounds like crashing industrial machines and gives Ton that unaffected NYC once over. There is something about the vibe he's throwing that she just can't tag. Behind her dark sunglasses she darts all over his persona, popping a black bubblegum bubble through black lipstick, until she focuses on his hands. They are bandaged but the dirty bandages are unraveling. They are healing, yet already deformed. They are scarred, bruised, stitched and not exactly human—more like hoofs, the thought of which stops the gum chewing cold. She looks up at him through her black sunglasses and bangs, working up the courage to ask him a question only to watch him move off as the light changes.

SEVENTH AVENUE AND 12TH STREET
Blurrin', pumpin', gliding, spinnin' like a NASA ball bearing set in a vacuum, these aero wheels stop for no one, no vehicle, no light, no biped. The black, plastic mask is a frieze of a supernatural warrior's face seamlessly joined to an aero helmet on top of a gilded metal frame over tight black garb and a touch of crimson silk—-*ROARRRRRRRRRRRR!!!* Howls the helmet's speaker-horn startling the peds that act like pigeons backin' to the curb. This is a Ronin Courier on a run.

345 LAFAYETTE
"Wish motherfucker would get here all ready I'm hungry like a motherfucker."
"I hear that. Head uptown after this get, som' ribs an shit?"
"Yeah. My tooth is fucking with me 'dough."
"Well get it fixed niggah'."
"I hate dentist morean' I hate lookin' at your broke nose liver lip ass."
"Oh—h its like that…."

WEST HOUSTON STREET
Swish left on to Houston pumpin' that crankshaft the wrong way *up* a one-way street and directly into the traffic. The blip on the flat screen is the quarry. He is on foot, about to cross Houston at Broadway and headed north slowly like a crippled ped. Watch the dog shit. Weaving through the traffic, our man is a predator always battling the enemies, mass and time.

345 LAFAYETTE
"You know I caught lil' Richie jackin' with my set yesterday. Verizon said he was InSpace 'for hours an shit watchin' who the fuck knows what quad-X, snuf, horror-drome shit."
"Better watch that boy."
"Now hez' got nightmares and shit but he still wants to jack more 'an ever."
"Seen Cynthia's boy lately?"
"No."
"She spoils his ass rotten. Boy got fat, don't go out and play wit' other kids—all he wants to is stay jacked."
"I hear some people in Cali are jacked an' living in those flotation tanks and taking they food through IVs and shit."
"They call 'em Blobs…"

Wired for Chaos

"Right! Cause all they gonna' do is get all gross and fat…"

BROADWAY AND HOUSTON

Ton is oblivious to the walking haircuts, the tourist, the Cubans, the Chinese, the entire ocean of humanity that brings the traffic a full stop minutes after the light changes but the cameras see it all. The car horns never seem to stop at busy intersections and the people don't notice, they don't move till you nudge them with your fender but the microphones hear every decibel. The twin eight story, Jumbotrons on the windowless walls of 600 and 599 Broadway cut from a woman in a baseball cap—her head and shoulders warping, fragmenting and changing from gray to eggplant, morphing to the vibrating image of another woman standing next to Ton. The images feed through the four cameras mounted on light posts and run by a computer the size of an egg carton behind one of the Jumbotrons. Past the cluttered tables filled with language, math and assorted chips, past mini-decks so old it's laughable they have any value, Ton walks not so much by the obstacles, but through them. The hooded store marquees shade the holograms that spin, strobe, wave and morph, all vying for attention. It's all here. Delis, shoe stores, smart-tech, clothing, anti-surveillance must haves and organic coffee by the pound for 30$US.

HOUSTON AND MERCER

Time and mass are losing. The Ronin checks his perimeter then takes the left lane cutting off a Jersey Beamer. Big puddle—too late. The intersection is clogged with mass so he takes the wrong way on the westward bound side of Houston calculating a gap in the crowd coming u-p r-i-g-h-t—-t now. Through the peds and past a truck it's gamble time as he takes a sharp left around the corner of an A&P truck knowing that traffic is headed his way but not knowing how fast. On his toes and leaning back, his ass past the seat he misses a cab scaring the shit out of Ramon Valdez who swore he'd plow the next fuckin' biker that pissed him off. Ronin cleaves his way up Broadway through *heavy-T*, what the bikers call fast moving, on-coming traffic. No use looking down at the flat screen now, block out the horns and the driver's faces—watch the grills and guess their moves. Any biker worth his carbon racer knows that you have to claim road, flash attitude and make for the gap. Look fast. Blip on the left. Wait for it. Not him—now! Ronin is on the shoulder between parked and on-coming cars but a stupid fuckin' ped is step-i-n' out looking the wrong way! Grill at one o'clock. Fuck that. The ped gets tagged. Not bad, just tire tracks on the Doc Martins and a yelp. The target is half a block and buried in a small sea of peds. Passed him. Watch the pothole. At Bleaker he takes the sidewalk and doubles back slowly checking his screen. The white boy? No the big mother. The front wheel hard rights it to a stop a meter in front of Ton and the rider holds out a small black rubber egg. "Niemöller to Ton."

Ton takes it and the rider detaches a small screen with the name Rob Fields lasered in from his belt for Ton to sign only to see him walk away.

"Hey man you gotta' sign for that shit!"

Ton ignores him and continues walking. The rider shakes his head then forges Ton's signature with an inkless pen. He taps a button and the run-clock stops. Time elapsed, 19 minutes from pick-up. Cool. Credits all ready in the account. No messages. Hotdog stand at three o'clock. Lunchtime.

In the distance the twin Sony displays Nike high-tops emerging from psychedelic molten lava.

Ton has no trouble popping the silicone player out of the rubber egg, which he lets drop. It turns on when you put it into your ear, it plays only, once before erasing. A computer altered voice says, "Send a painful message. He is armed." Ton pulls it out of his ear and lets it drop to the pavement where it shatters. He crosses the Broadway and heads east on Bond Street stepping in a dirt-water reflection of a cheesy hologram of a fat guy puffing a cigar morphing into a Partagas cigar. Like many New York streets Bond was once the home to the famous and the infamous. In the 1840s Edgar Allen Poe temporarily lived on this street and stumbled home many a night both depressed and drunk while horse drawn carriages and wagons made insufferably loud rancor as their shoes clanked against the cobblestone-paved streets reeking of horseshit and piss.

345 LAFAYETTE

"Yeah—you know. You know what I'm saying. Shit—t."

Ton steps on to the southeast corner of Lafayette and Bond and starts walking towards 345 Lafayette—Ill Diablo restaurant. As he approaches the restaurant he hears some guys talking in a fenced in alleyway next door. Ton spies Lenny's back and decides to take a step backwards to avoid being seen. He listens intently, choosing not to move even though rusty water from an air conditioner steadily drips on his head and down his cheek.

"Where is that never-had-a-shampoo-in-his-life motherfucker?! Damn! I'm just want to pop his ass and shit so I can eat already!"

"Inconsiderate like a motherfucker—r..." fists touch.

Ton is all ready gone down the street in the direction he came. Turning right on Bond, his walk is the essence of inelegance. Like an erect, eight hundred pound gorilla out on a stroll, Ton walks towards Bowery. In front of storefront food cooperative he sees two large, blue, plastic garbage cans and stops to pick one up. He empties the refuse onto the sidewalk, covers it and holds it over his shoulder as he continues down the street. Moments later a middle-aged man jogs out of the co-op holding a wooden ax handle. "Hey you! Where the fuck are you—hey! Asshole…!" Then as he is about to throw the ax handle at Ton he reconsiders and swings it in the air. "Hope some really nasty fucked up shit happens to you asshole! Great now I've gotta' chain 'ah fuckin' cans to the door. Jesus—s!"

Ton walks past a mound of old DVDs, CDs, unraveled DAT tapes, memory sticks and cracked HDSS (Holographic Data Storage System) photosensitive crystals. On Bowery, Ton turns right heading south. Across the street he sees an abandon building squatters have broken into and crosses the street. On the front step sits a shriveled up echo of a black woman looking much older than her years. As she begs for money she rocks back and forth, simultaneously grabbing her flannel shirt with one hand and pointing the other holding a beat up card reader at who ever walks by. "Spare some credits mister——r? Spare some credits?" Ton ignores her and walks up to the cinder block filled doorway with a gaping hole. Putting down the garbage can he begins to push and pull a cinder block out of the doorway much to the amazement of the woman. As dust and small pieces of the blocks dart and scatter into the air several other blocks become loose. His face barely registers the effort it takes to pry the blocks lose of the cement as beads of sweat form on his forehead. Standing erect for the first time since he started, he looks at the can as if to visually measure its capacity. Satisfied that he has enough, he fills the garbage can to the brim and covers it snapping the lid shut. Tearing off the remnants of his bandages, he takes off his dusty denim jacket and ties it around his waist, picks up the garbage can and heaves it over his shoulder. The woman closes her mouth and cranes her neck as she looks at him ready to move at the first sign of danger. Taking slow deliberate steps Ton holds the handle with his right hand and supports the bottom with his left as he crosses the street without looking. The woman stands and continues to watch Ton intently. Digging her feet as deep as she can into her worn out sneakers she wears like slippers, she jogs up the stairs and into the building's hallway. In a feeble voice, "Jimmy——y! Jimmy——y! Oh——h Jimm——yz' gonna' be mad——d." Several bikers, peds on Segways and a few one-wheeled unipods pass the big guy without giving him a second look as he steps onto the curb and turns west on Bleaker.

345 LAFAYETTE
Lenny leans against his jeep holding his crotch; the gun sticking out of his pants.

BLEAKER AND LAFAYETTE
The sounds of cars racing up Lafayette are drowned out by the rancor of a garage band emanating from an open window. Ton turns the corner and stops at 341 Lafayette and looks at the names of the occupants next to shoddy buzzers. He shoulders the door hard and it opens. Picking up the garbage can he heads up the uneven wooden staircase. On the roof, Ton walks over to the corner by the alley and takes a quick look over the edge. Lenny is still leaning up against the jeep, Henry is checking his messages on his watch and Alvin is leaning up against the back door humming to himself. Then it happens. The can lands on Alvin's head and drives his cranium into his pelvis a millisecond before his torso bursts into a wet, crunchy pink mass between the bottom of the can and concrete. Lenny jumps and drops the gun as Henry stutters without uttering any words while stepping backwards. Lenny's hands tremble as he becomes unable to pronounce Alvin's name. Blinking——as if to make it all vanish Lenny starts to gasp for air. "Al——lv-i-n Al——lv-i-n..." Then looking up

slowly, brick by brick until he reaches the top of the three-story building, Lenny sees Ton's large unruly mane and his emotionless black pupils. All he can do is stutter. Imperceptibly, Ton flicks a black rubber egg down to Lenny and disappears before it stops bouncing. As Ton makes his way for the stairs the neighborhood hears Lenny screaming through his gasps. For years after his brother's death, the vision——like a slow motion snuff film would replay in his mind over and over ad infinitum. First a shadow envelops Alvin then it happens quickly and he remembers Alvin's arms flying up because of the force of the impact—and the sound his bones made.

The silicone player had a brief message from Niemöller. He said, "Leave town tonight." Lenny did.

PARTY AT MARTY'S
SATURDAY, FIFTH AVENUE PENTHOUSE
The usual stuff. Too much money and aimless excess. B' and Olga are on the terrace looking down on Fifth Avenue and the naked trees in Central Park—veritable Gods of the first world and wildly indifferent to beauty other than their own. The sound of glasses clanking, Miles Davis haunting the background and idle chatter all emanating from the open French doors. It wasn't a particularly cold winter night and Marty had his area heaters blaring, so Olga's serpentine snuggle into Brice's arms could have been more about show than warmth. A few of the party goers sneak looks at the two, while trying to act content sipping cocktails from Marty's expensive stemware, as the black suited security guard scans them from the entrance to the living room.

"You're still thinking about Arihito?"

"Yeah." Said B' resting his rum and coke on the limestone banister. "He was a good man who gave me my start in the business—big heart too."

"Lets go away!" full of glee and alcoholic delight, "Lets go to Italy, some remote little town—Sorrento near Capri or Vico Equense or Cesano Maderno (she says in perfect Italian)—some of the girls have been there. We could just eat pasta and cheese everyday until we pass out. I want to swim someplace where we can't be seen and nobody knows us."

"Maybe after I kick Tanaka up in his ass."

"You've got a jet now. Nobody's setting you to their schedule." As if rehearsed, "I say we jet right after. I need three days to do the shows in Paris but I can meet you in Italy. You pick the place and set it up." Her enthusiasm was like a ball of wool with a kitten in tow.

INSIDE
This place was so not Marty, or rather his real name, "Ali" something or another. Jimmy, having forgotten the real last name of the host, had dug into his background in an attempt to know with whom he was dealing to and was not surprised with what he found. He was half Saudi and half British and his parents were jet setters on a stratospheric level. The apartment was too old fashioned and old money to belong to a late thirty-something. It was too luxurious, too plush.

Jimmy glanced back at the woman he was seated next to and feigned interest. All he had asked this woman was, "Did she snuff?" and the diatribe was endless, but Jimmy was just waiting for an opening to jet from her to the fake Marty. She gave Jimmy lots of time to divert his attention and allow his eyes to wander. This apartment was strictly vintage Architectural Digest complete with tulips in Chinese vases, next to expensive picture books beneath large ginger jars with fey lampshades held aloft by decorative brass monkeys. "Marty" as he wanted to be called was actually related to an old Saudi family that made their fortune not in oil, but rather trading in pretty much everything. He wanted to be embraced by the rich and white of upper Fifth and Park Avenue swells and this apartment and his faux white name helped. The drawing room, where Jimmy was seated had floor to ceiling wood paneling in red mahogany with a green marble framed fireplace and molding in a Greek key pattern. The floors were covered with expensive Persian rugs and every metallic surface—be it a Chinese lamp with brass fittings or the lion shaped Empire feet of a table, glistened. The Sofas were plush, eggplant suede and felt luxurious. The chattering older woman in a spaghetti strap, black evening gown next to him on the sofa had not let up in the past five minutes. Not wanting to have her mistake his interest for flirtation he leaned back and rested his left hand on the top of the backrest as he held his gin martini and finally interjected. "…But that is the culture we live in. It has been for years—such a long time…"

"Well I guess my point is not so much that I want to stifle who we are but rather our compulsion to broadcast it to the world. I mean really. If we exhibit justified police violence—I mean, the apprehension—of assailants like it was a movie then what kind of signal are we sending to the rest of the world?"

Jimmy unbuttoned his vermilion colored, crushed velvet suit jacket and said, "How is showing a criminal getting wasted in real time, different from the masters of the Renaissance paintings depicting rape or war or medieval murder? How is that different? They did it. They call it art. We do it, we call it news. Difference as I see it is they made it look pretty and had no other way to communicate or at least—what's the word I'm looking for, chronicle, or historically record those events. You see carnage in Africa in the Times everyday and that's graphic."

"Well you have a point however, don't you think that being a well—party to that kind of killing is, is, makes you complicit? I've got no problem with witnessing something that has already happened—I see it and know it is out of my control. But somehow being near it as it happens is, is too icky."

Jimmy took a sip of his martini and thought to himself that she probably rationalizes all her fur purchases with the same argument. "I see your point Sheri." Over her shoulder he could see Marty motion for him, "Will you excuse me. I haven't had a chance to catch up with Marty yet. Nice chatting with you."

"Likewise." She said smiling and pausing a moment before rising herself, afraid of being seen seated alone.

"Marty." Said Jimmy, "Marty. Marty. Where do you get all these beautiful people?"

"I collect them my man, just like champagne corks. I buy the best and throw them in a drawer where I can find them." Said Marty adjusting the white frilly cuff of his white shire underneath his mod-retro, skinny black suit.

The two stood close, backs to the wall and faced the crowd in the living room. Jimmy nearly gagged at the reek of Marty's Aqua de Parma cologne as he leaned over and said, "All I did was ask the bitch if she did snuff then I got a ear full."

"You should know better than to flirt with a divorcée with too much time on her hands."

"I did not flirt..."

"Jimmy, Jimmy please. You are living in the non-communicable disease 30s. Say hello to a woman or ask her the time and you might as well be saying will you slide your hand down. Fuck, fuck is how we say hello you know that." Then excitedly, "Oh man I've been so into the Rat Pack lately. I mean those dudes had so much style while they were having fun."

"Rat what?" said Jimmy incredulously.

"The Rat Pack baby, Sammy, Frank, Peter Lawford, Joey Bishop, the Rat Pack."

"I don't connect."

"Never mind. Brought my goodies?" said Marty.

"Your linen drawer, the one with the napkins in the kitchen, under the napkins."

"Already paid you. Check your bank."

"Got some exotics for you."

"Crazy baby. Anything I should try?"

"One is called Manatee. Makes you relaxed, sublime, an' see the ocean. Hear if you sit under a fan or air conditioning vent when you're on it feels like you're being carried through water."

"Interesting."

"Just remember they grow on and in you, once you dip the sauce."

"You know I don't partake but that brings me to an interesting conversation I had the other day. Seems a new arrival from Brazil says, he can squeeze the juice without making the drinker kill for more."

"Well that's nice and all but why would anyone who deals want to let the users off the hook?"

"Didn't say you couldn't charge a premium for the slices."

"I'll think about it."

"Sent you his digits last hour." Pointing to Jimmy's empty glass, "Get some gasoline daddy-o." Then turned and shouted across the room, "Sylvia, baby where have you been?!" then said to Jimmy without looking, "Later Mack."

Jimmy sees Marty moving like a honeybee leaving no trail and heads for the bar.

Wired for Chaos

LATER.

The lights in the living room switch on and off giving the signal for everyone to gather for the snuff. People came in off the terracotta balcony, electric blinds shut and a fem Asian club kid wearing a skintight three-button black suit walk-prances from party goer to party goer. He has two chrome, gun shaped pressure syringes strapped to his crotch and is trailed by a server with a silver tray filled with V-shades. The syringes are filled with "splat" stim juice, "to make the ride more intense" and asks, "Torturer or Tortured?" and shoots the appropriate syringe.

He approached B' and B' said, "What is it?"

"Oh its legal, it's the derms over there that are naughty." Motioning the crystal bowl on the coffee table filled with derms. B' said, "Torturer never tortured." And the guy gave him a shot in the neck with the right syringe. Then it was on to Olga.

This was to be an illegal viewing of a live snuff from SnuffView, International which was some guy in South America who moved from one remote, Godless place where human life was cheap to another, with a state-of-the-art broadcast rig. Used to be that the entrée was always a surprise but guys got queasy about seeing another guy's cock get cut off live and fed to the dogs so he started to post a menu preshow. The room was now filled with twenty glam couples sans Marty who led two women down the hall to his bedroom. He had instructed both his security guards to mind his human chattel lest they commence flaying each other, or trying to fly off the terrace—knowing how easily chemicals, flesh and experiential violence could propel someone over the edge of his terrace. The music is turned off, lights dim, everyone dawns their shades and the whispering ceases.

Tonight's feature was titled "Puta No Work" and was set in a shuttered factory that supplied auto plants just south of the Mexican-American border.

FADE IN: The factory floor near an assembly line with robotic arms and a steel elevated conveyor belt. The camera pans to include a metal chair with arms in front of a conveyor belt where a small plastic container marked "Gasoline" and a tool box rests. A layer of dust is disturbed just in front of a large naked Hispanic man who enters the frame wearing a black leather mask with a forced, evil grin locked in place and a series of steel teeth. He has a slight paunch but thick strong arms and legs and a larger than average cock. A sound is heard off screen and the camera pans to the right and focuses into the distance to include a naked Hispanic woman who enters, strong-armed by a masked man in jeans and a t-shirt. She wears a clear, molded wireless device on her forehead called a "snifter" that houses highly sensitive electrodes that continuously transmit her brain activity, information on various muscles, eye movements, breathing patterns, heart beat and her oxygen level. She giggles nervously expecting to be filmed for the first time fornicating with several men on camera and thinks only of the money. The naked man takes hold of the woman and the man in the jeans walks off screen. The naked man grabs the woman and manhandles her, squeezing her breasts and groping her. He forces her to her knees and presses her head into his crotch but when she lifts his cock towards her mouth he slaps her in the head. Bending, he grabs her by her shoulders and throws her into the chair. She gives in, not exactly sure if she should smile or spew indignation. The man kneels and grabs her right breast, squeezing it so hard he makes her wince and cry out in pain. She slaps him and he takes no notice. Reaching under the chair he retrieves some gaffer's tape and began to bind her to the chair. After she was securely bound the masked man prances around her, thrusting his cock and balls at her as he continued to grope her violently. She rants and screams long cuss filled sentences with flying spit while she tries to free herself. The man picked up a small, clear plastic box of sewing pins and opens them giggling to himself. As he stands behind her the camera comes in for a tight two shot and he lowers his head to her level. Standing behind her, he begins to insert the pins into her breast and the woman starts to scream and twist violently in the chair, showing the fright in the whites of her eyes for the first time.

At Marty's, many of the women seated on the Italian silk covered sofas, in club chairs or on one of the oversized ottomans, could be heard wincing or grunting with the adrenalin of their piped in torture. They grabbed at their breasts and writhed in their seats or across the carpet, held firm by their lover's arms. A man yelled out, "Slap that cunt, whore bitch! Bite her face!" and others grunted in complicity. B' tipped experiential and zeroed in on the other side of his livelihood. A funny thing happens when you became a headrider, your breathing would sync up with the player InSpace and in seeing out of their eyes, you would begin to feel as if someone else was taking control of "your" body. B' didn't like that, he was no longer in control and that unsettled him.

The woman was enraged now. Consumed with anger, she tries to bite first the masked man's head then at her restraints. The masked man then grabbed her hair and brandishes a staple gun. He quickly stapled her hair to the back of the chair and returned to her breasts as she struggles. At least a dozen pins are inserted into her breasts now and tears stream down her cheeks. The masked man reaches from behind her with both his hands and suddenly grabbed her breasts with full force and squeezes them hard making her scream in pain. The woman pushed her toes and the balls of her feet into the concrete floor in an attempt to walk out of the chair, but the man rocked her backwards towards him pretending to kiss her neck. Standing, he took his time, purposely hiding something behind his right thigh from the camera. Slowly he revealed a steel straight razor, as he opens it with his thumb and forefinger. He passes it in front of the camera then passes the blade against his pubic hair and down the shaft of his cock in mock grooming. She sees all of this and began to tremble with fear as urine streams down her leg and onto the floor. Then, he quickly reaching for the woman grabbing her left nipple, squeezing it with all his might followed by the right. She drooled as she begs him mumbling something unintelligible, as she seems to be running in place. The woman was panting now, caught up in the beginning of a prayer and coughing on her saliva while moaning. The man seems sorry for the pain he is inflicting and slumps his shoulders, then he looks at the camera, shrugged and quickly cut off her right nipple. The woman's long shrieks were mirrored by the Park and Fifth Avenue debs as they writhe in pain and dig their nails into their escorts.

Much cursing and movement could be heard now. B', winces feeling perplexed and ghoulish, living the heart beat of the masked man and seeing the woman through his masked eyes. He felt filthy, yet immune. "At least I waste punks trying to off me" thought B' "An' not denigrate into…."

The masked man began to squeeze blood out of the woman's tit and collect it in the palm of his hand. He quickly turned to face the camera and rubbed the blood all over his cock and got himself hard. As the erection raged, the man flexed his muscles and screamed at the camera, fists clenched. Over and over he pumped himself into a frenzy until the veins in his neck swelled, then beckons the camera to pull in close for a close-up of the woman's face. The man wasted no time. He brought his right index finger into the frame capped by a razor sharp steel nail and held if for the viewers to see-feel, then took it and jabbed it into the woman's right eye socket extricating her eyeball. She hyperventilated-convulsed in pain and shock while…

The women let out screams that didn't phase the security guards who had heard it all before, as they shifted their weight in their cheap American shoes. Olga was a Torturer and smiled while digging her nails into B' shoulder…

The masked man convulsed with laughter as the woman's eyeball hangs precariously from a bundle of optic nerve fibers deep in her head. She winced and shook in disbelief at the horror of her demise and her movements begin to recede into short contained spasms. The masked man squeezes his blood soaked cock firmly and brings himself back to erection, as he arches his back and opened his legs to the camera. Hard and full, he moves on the balls of his feet and grabs the woman's head with his left hand while his right hand guides his cock….

"He is going to fuck her brains out!" Thought B' and his mouth fell open. Enough. B' took the V-shades off his face and adjusted his eyes to the light. Jacking out was like a self-inflicted electric exorcism with your senses— your skin felt especially hypersensitive. B' could feel his clothes and immediately wished he was home, alone and in bed. He scanned the room and saw a couple of women sucking their men's cocks, a few were sobbing, one was openly bereft and others were clawing at each other like animals. Soon the rest would be groping each other and B' saw hands reach into the bowl of derms looking for something to cut the intensity. Olga's face was frozen in mock disbelief when B' snatched the V-shades off her face. "We're leaving." half grabbing her ass off the sofa. As they stood they each felt dizzy standing and took a moment to right themselves.

B' looked around and spied Jimmy getting it on with an ugly older woman and left his ass. He nodded at the security guard and gave the international sign for "later" then bent around the corner to the front door with Olga in tow. She lurches and says, "That Splat really dehydrates me baby," reaching for a glass of half consumed champagne from the Empire étagère. In the drawing room some yells, "Fuck that bitch! Fuck her! Fuck her fucking brains out!" and B' can hear a fight breaking out.

"Push me motherfucker!"

"Fuck you…!" followed by a woman's scream as B' tugs Olga's arm nearly lifting her out the front door. They are on the street three minutes later hailing a cab for 53rd Street. B' just wanted to pet Stalin and dump Olga on his king sized while he regained control.

BLURRRRRR!!!

TUESDAY, 12:55 AM.

Not too far beneath the surface, under asphalt, gravel and concrete, on top of, below and inside of pipes the scratching of tiny black nails is heard. If there were light, these things would seek the shadows. These things would seem like a filthy velvet drape blowing along the cold stone floor. They race at times not having anywhere in particular to go, but just because the impulse takes them. They have no predators and have become accustomed to the vibrations from the trains and heavy transports like subterranean thunder. At times the thousands move in seeming chaos back and forth, uncles stepping on nieces, fathers gouging their children's eyes and never so much as a "sorry" an "excuse me." They scurry at various speeds, pausing from time to time to poke their heads up, wiggle their noses and squeak. Others pause to scratch at the mites that have found refuge in their fur, scratching at themselves wily nilly like mad men at an asylum. Many, the gaps in their teeth jammed with the fetid stench of rotting meat straight from the garbage of the city's finest restaurants, think nothing of dragging their bellies through the waste of strangers. Every so often pairs copulate vibrating momentarily then with not so much as a kiss, a hug, a rubbing of wet noses they turn, part and are enveloped by the anonymous hoard.

Fifty-one floors above the street Brice has been busy. He bends a popper and inhales. Olga reaches over to the edge of the bed, raises the sheet and retrieves her *squirtgun*. It is a sexy little air-pressure hypodermic shaped like a nineteenth century lady's revolver, the kind the prostitutes used to hide in their garter-belts. She presses the barrel against the inside of her damp thigh, pulls the trigger and a tiny "*pfffffft*" later a small measured dose of China White works its magic.

Olga smiles as he parts her legs and his heart rate rises. A digital recording of a Caribbean seashore serenades Brice and Olga as they go at it for the second time. His breathing is heavy. Not heavy like some punk sporting expensive sneakers out for a jog, but deep breathing heavy like a free diver maxing for a dive. His breath, the air colliding through the surface of his esophagus formed a louder noise than B' was expecting. A noise that translated into form constants made of pink columns that pawed at his face and felt like velvet. *Yeah—h boy!* God was fucking with him in the transdermalelectroper-ceptional plane *o n c e* again but not so deep that you could clock him or so shallow that you knew he was there. *Ha—ha—hallucinate you're there.* For her the sex is great but for him its just average. They've been going out for three months. In Japan she was tiresome but, he reminds himself, they look great in magazines together—she digs her fingernails into his lats and down to his butt cheeks knowing it turns him on. And it happens again. The wave starts with her inner-thighs and the trembling builds. He sees her struggle to restrain herself and decides to go deeper only to freeze a moment later, driving her wild on a bed so large it could have its own climate. Brice got the idea to do his bedroom in all white except for the bed. The sheets and pillows are fire engine-red satin, that he had seen in some movie. Everything else is stark white the walls the, night table, dresser and valet, the carpets even the miniature cameras and microphones peering through pinholes.

"And the worm spits into the abyss," Brice whispers to himself, a line from a poem some hypertext laureate shot into the Net for the world to see. And its over. Brice always takes a long pause before exiting because he's not the type to roll over and fall asleep, though any tenderness he has for a sexual partner usually evaporates right a-b-o-u-t—now.

For several minutes they lay next to each other and say nothing.

"I'm heading out."

Standing up on the bed, he steps over her, off the bed and into the bathroom.

"Oh Briceski give Mommie some more of that lovey juice."

From the bathroom he yells, "Get the fuck up. Get the fuck dressed. Get the fuck out." The shower goes on and he steps in. Olga pouts like a little girl, springs to her knees and gives Brice a defiant bird. She wraps the enormous sheet around herself and stumbles out of the room in a sea of red. Once in the living room she covers her eyes. Stalin, Brice's Rottweiler is laying flat on the deep shag and gives her a brief glance from the corner of his eyes.

"Dim. Dim the fucking lights!"

As the lights dim she bends over to slip on her panties, then her jeans knocking over a crystal champagne flute. It bounces on the parquet and breaks. Stalin turns his head away.

"Shit!"

Home, ever vigilant zeroes in with two cameras on the spot on the floor indexing it for the *attend to list* for the maid. Olga pauses before she puts on her blouse trying to sift a long drag from the *H'* she just dropped. Brice steps out of the bedroom wearing a jockstrap, sees the shirtless supermodel smile that junkie smile and sway that junkie sway with complete indifference. He makes a mental note and mouths the words to that Juki song, "Make a change, rearrange. No bitch don't explain. Gotta' go zippa' smoke an' motor." He takes her by the arm gathers up her things and walks her over to the waiting elevator Home rang for.

"See you at the club in a few? Kasbah?"

"Yeah."

Wired for Chaos

"Meet you there. I'm 'onna change. See me soon. 'Kay?" She dips her hand into her ample jeans and rubs her clitoris as she licks her lips.

"Com. on. Main lobby."

"Hello," a voice over the monitor.

"Carl, call Olga a car and make sure she gets it."

"Yes sir."

Olga buttons a single button on her blouse as she blows him a kiss. The doors close and Carl disconnects before he gets caught looking at her bosom on the elevator's two way. Olga smiles with half her mouth.

Standing in front of three, four-meter high mirrors Brice puts on a midnight-green, sharkskin, spider silk, racing skin, topped by a red and black antique motorcycle jacket. Stalin walks in sniffs the air and walks out. He sticks two derms on his neck, an oatmeal colored multi and beta carotene to make him sharp and heads for the door.

"Home if Jimmy calls, down it to the ride, but I dough' wanna' talk to anybody else."

"Flash."

"Heat the wheels."

Stalin is waiting for him near the elevator and gets a pat on the head. As he steps up towards the private elevator its doors are open and he's on his way to the lobby. On the status screen, we see that Home is simultaneously putting in an order to the 24 hour maid service while he warms up Brice's custom Ducati 998EZ.

In the lobby, Jake sees that Brice is on his way down and presses a button and the liquid glass wall that hides the tenant's chrome unipods (one-wheeled gyroscopically balanced personal vehicles) and Brice's bike, begins to change. The cerulean blue is swallowed by the dye vents which run the distance of the wall leaving a crystal clear view of the port. Simultaneously, the tiny status lights on the EZ flash from red to yellow and finally to green as the port's halogens turn on. Brice steps out of the lift and heads for the sliding glass door of the port.

"Evening Mr. Johnson."

Brice waves at him. A three elbow, AC/DC arm attached to an outlet in the floor, disengages from the AC intake at the rear of the lipstick red EZ and a panel quickly covers it. The four gull wing doors on the EZ silently open to greet Brice. He climbs in, sliding his legs completely out of view to his hips. Then he lowers himself into the custom, body contoured, water buffalo leather seat shifting around until his nuts find a comfortable place in the hollow of the seat. The motor hum of the EZ is clean and sounds like a cat's purr. The color LCD reads 100% ready and the doors seal with a faint whistle. Brice taps in the settings he wants: a wide angle out display of the rear, radar, distance warnings and all secondary functions to auto. The EZ slowly turns and drives down the black, textured rubber floor towards the sliding glass front door. The four 16cm balance wheels keep the EZ upright from 0 to 2 kilometers and compensate for the dip in the sidewalk ramp as it rolls onto the asphalt. The custom license plate reads, "BADD MF."

Three large, expensive, Japanese cars rest in the street, while their chauffeurs' smoke leaning up against one of their boss' rides. The street is more than clean, it is impeccable. No refuse or cracks in the diamond etched compound and not even a dried wad of gum on its coal-black skin.

"...I mean what's some mother fucking rich kid doing with his daddy's gun?!"

"Shooting some poor, sick, 'ol brother ain't hurting nobody."

"...Shouldna' been able 'ta get his hands on it in the first place."

"That's what I'm saying!"

"Mother fuckin' ain't right, killing no man like that."

"...An' getting away with it—cause you know he's gonna' get away with it..."

"He is a kid..."

"If he waz' a black kid kilt' a white man—Oh—h man—n...!"

"Now you talking like oneah' them neo-negros."

"Ain't nothing changed but the weather."

"Yeah—h..."

The EZ's halogens flash on as it accelerates.

"Look. Another rich fuck."

All eyes following Brice up the block.

"Oh that's that VR champ! You know that Bert kid..."

"Brice. Brice!"

"...Yeah, I won 6,000 on his last game. Now that's a rich fuck. I hear he got more credits than Gipsum. Owns that motherfucking building—gotta" three story penthouse."

"My shit he does. How?"

"I hear he got a slice o' the back end Pay Per View."

"Shit—t! If he do would you suck his dick for five million credits?"

"Yep! Wit' all you niggers in line right behind me!"

Laughing, "Yeah—h!"

Brice has the light and revs through the Sixth Avenue intersection clocking 30km. The engine hums under aluminum. Motorist bend to this inconvenience while tourist and peds on the sidewalk note the gleam of his ride as his Bridgestones rub-heat the asphalt.

On every block in this well heeled neighborhood there are delivery trucks and vans double parked and Brice's eyes wrap around the weary bodies of overworked grocery, dry cleaner, FedEx, UPS*M*ail—you name it 'livery lackeys. He hits Twelfth Avenue hanging south, stepping 25km, slicing steam from a manhole. If you're a ped' and the EZ's passing you slow enough for a clean see you'd swear the gold tint, wrap around windshield, illuminated by cool-blue readouts, is some kind'a CAD bug.

Brice may live in a luxury high-rise but he likes the rough side of the city. The bleak streets with buildings in disarray devoid of billboards, neon and holographs—garbage and all, hold an attraction for him. He's always watching

Wired for Chaos

the Holo-V for news of the city's underbelly and likes seeing it all from the EZ. At the edge of Hell's Kitchen he sees the punk Cholo *Mesaboyz*, have tagged the two lane street with a stolen line-painter. Brice smiles when he reads the white enormous words, "Mesaboyz turf. Be the fuck afraid," in Spanish. The city air is redolent with carbon monoxide, urine and waste from the Hudson, but the EZ's filters nix it all. Any day of the year, time of the day the interior defaults to 20° Celsius with intermittent bursts from the humidifier ducts. He'd hear the Mexican music playing in the distance but all you hear inside the cabin is the sound of leather against leather and the faint whistle of circulating air, until he ups some Hendrix's *Fire*. Civilian copters speed over the water from every direction, but most of them are flying to or from the Trump heli-port from Jersey. Garbage is strewn all over the street and a few bone dry cars dot the terrain like the dried carcasses of wild game. Brice downshifts to thread thru them, ready to accelerate if anybody blips on the radar. He sees the storefronts, long abandon by their paper owners, now seized by grimys—the bolder, stronger homeless with an attitude. A few of them stand around a burning car that has been stripped and cooks a hotdog on the end of an old antenna. "Yeah. I got your brave new world right here—need a coat—swipe it!" The windows have long since been knocked out and trashcan fires illuminate the street from these man-made caves. The grimy's will take all of your shit from right under your nose, if you give them a chance and then cuss you out for living. Snaking your neighbor's roof farm will get you shot, but then so will a wry dirty look. Brice grins when he remembers hearing that cops pass through in armored cars hoping some grimy will take a shot, so they can call the boys in to raze a building. You don't fuck with *the man* unless you got a death-itch but there are a lot of stupid people on the street.

A few blocks away, there is a little hospital in the basement of an old school. You are more sick coming out than going in but the doctors mean well. The hospital helps all comers including ten year olds with ancient handguns that misfire and zip their fingers. The irony of wounded kids holding bloodied hands and severed fingers—no hair between their legs, running to a place they should'ah been at, all the time makes Brice shake his head. They can't even read LCD comic screens but they've got to have guns. Lots of people don't even notice the rot-stink from the street markets hawking contaminated fish anymore. But there is a new strain of TB, that's getting the worried look from city dwellers high and low.

The USS Intrepid Carrier never looked so bad, then again Brice wasn't born in time for the black tie galas or the trance raves on its flight deck. Forced to close due to zero attendance years ago, it was left to rust. Then the squatters—-before grimeys had the handle and eighth generation crack, welfare, outta' wedlock, gun totin', 40oz. swiggin', teen-parents staked their claim. Then eight years ago the board of health and the man kicked everybody out and put up a voltage fence. At first the maintenance team fought the rust then they got tired of cleaning up after the vandals so they just gave up. Now its two guards, motion sensors and at last count five big Dobermans, the *NY*

Times says "Who relieve themselves where they please." This all stopped when the mayor put his foot down though. About time the city paid somebody to pick up dogshit. Brice switches from the track ball mounted above the accelerator to the infrared beam, eye-pointer and phones Home.

"Home, you in?" says Brice.

A moment passes, "I'm in."

"Any update on the Henry?"

"Same as it ever was. If somebody ripped a new hole they didn't hip Central."

"Cool."

The Henry Hudson was repaired years ago after falling into disarray but it doesn't get too much use, especially below 59th Street. Cabbies in armored rides, up the fair automatically when you say Westside highway.

Around 39th street, death is in the air. Something—someone is dead for days and rotting, what the grimys call *fresh kill*. "Man—n, Jersey is starting to look good."

Towards 16th Street crowds begin to appear. As Brice rides up to the starting gate he sees the first race of the morning start as two bikers blur up the Henry Hudson. It's like a carnival. Street kids line the rooftops while select mid-city people look on, some accompanied by bodyguards. He's heard that half of them are dermed out on Pinks, Maxies and what not but nobody's flying too high though. This is the edge and you wanna' look sharp when some grimy steps to ya'. The word is that if you see a well healed mid-city ped' without a bodyguard they're probably tooled with a semi-sig, a dart gun, or something light, small, expensive and stylish that could down an elephant. Most of them jack with designer goggles, *headriders* riding with the racers for a psychedelic rush laced with the newest Peruvian hallucinogens. The Russians are in the house via the Russian Samovar restaurant, a popular mob haunt in mid-town and are taking bets from everybody including four bad cops who thought enough to park their armored ride down the block. The transvestites are the most vocal, working their paint and day-glo wigs, screaming and waving their arms to get the attention of their favorite racers but knowing enough to keep their distance. A few guys sell beer out of old shopping carts, but one guy is doing no business cause nobody trusts the flesh he's got on his sticks. Heaps of burning tires illuminate the area—and people used to die to get into this country.

As Brice slows, two beeps sound in the cabin.

Home says, "Chili for you."

"'Sup Chili?"

"This crowd B'. After Huygen hit asphalt like tire snot 'da whole world i'z dying fo' mo'."

"Mother fuckers never get enough blood."

"Don't have to race man."

"Seen my brother?"

"Nope. But Wilks sees you. Been popping shit 'bout your ass too.

Wired for Chaos

'Low grade gene pool, wannabe' athlete, cheating...'"

"Iz' he cooking Redd?"

"He's high on something man. And his ride—his ride is gleamin!" says Chili. "You in?"

"I'm in."

City-stink and the heavy bass of the latest *Techno-Baroque,* assault Brice's senses as the two forward glass windows on the EZ open and rise up slowly like the wings of a razor-winged dragonfly. He passes some tough looking gray-heads on vintage Harleys worth more than most Jap rides just meters away. A couple of Hell's Angels stare at Brice and he stares back. He parks near three other cycles, a Yamaha Shriek, a Kawasaki Rhino, a Kawasaki Komodo and a Suzuki Mark 4. Sitting up on his elbows against the leather chest rest, his head touches the rollbar as he checks out the scene. It's Chili's show. Chili has two hackers in a car limiting the signal to the immediate area, jamming the media, rich wannabe punk hackers and if any squeaky cops with pointy-heads show up, they go off line pronto and everybody disappears like roaches when you turn the light on. This ain't no pay-per-view. You gotta' know the code to jack and it doesn't cost anything but Chili's got to know you. People in the know are impressed that the races are only four weeks old but so well managed. Racers and a few brave spectators nod and try not to be obvious about staring at Brice. The bikers pass a bottle of Jack Daniel's and Brice takes a swig. The usual greetings are exchanged—everybody acting too cool to care. This is the time to hang and talk bikes, bars, babes and derms. Women sweetening the immediate zone, feigning coquettish vibes; makes it's hard to tell who's luring whom. Chili, a Chinese-Peruvian-American, steps up to Brice wearing an ear-mike rig and a micro flat-screen over his left eye that works a minicomputer on his belt. Funny is the vintage yellow, red and violet jester's cap with little bells on his head and white goatee.

Chili walks up to Brice's ride, "*B*', you wanna blur in the fourth heat?"

Wilks shouts from behind some peds, "Yeah, he does! And I got the line with him."

"You ain't in the draw Wilks. Chan got the line wit' the *B*-man," says Chili.

Aldo, a four foot nothing, 41 kilo, gyroboard skating, ear-mike rig wearing, six months outta' Sicily and running for the mob, kid wearing a brand new Stealers jersey squeezes past a few big guys.

Aldo says, "Place 'a you bets! I gotta' odds!"

"Hit pause Aldo," says Wilks.

Chili's set beeps. "Speak. Yeah. Yeah right. Chans' got shock problems. 'Sup to you B." Wilks says, "He'll take it!"

"The waves have been saying you trashing my back Wilks. Very un-sportsman like," says Brice.

"You ain't no 'athlete' you're a...."

"A little stressed huh Wilks? I know why. Olga, calls you the two-minute wonder. Wonder how chip dick shoots his load in 120 flat and manages to sweat like a pig doing it."

Wilks smolders.

"I knocked out her walls an hour ago. T-o-r-e that pussy up. She came nine times and begged me to stop. Just kicked her outta' of my space before I blurred here. You can have it back. I'm done."

Wilks rushes Brice but is restrained by four guys. Meters away the crowd cheers as two bikers burn up the Henry Hudson.

"Fuck you! I'm…"

"Fuck me?! Ah man fuck you! I've come in guys tougher than you!"

"…Gonna' fucking beat your face inta' ground chuck!"

Chili shouts, "Cool it Wilks! Fuckin' stop amping man! We're here to race!"

Wilks says, "Get outta' the bike fucker! Outta' the bike! You ain't shit in real time! Not shit! Chop shop, low-tech, makeover…!"

Brice's temper is large and festering but he doesn't want to lose his cool in front of the boys.

"You wanna race me? Cool. What's it worth to ya'?" A pause. Everybody looks at Wilks. "Well?"

"Alright…."

"20,000, North American."

Eyebrows raise. Wilks hesitates.

"And—d your ride." Says Brice. "Hear it's new. Don't know what it is. Don't care."

"Yeah right."

The doors open and he steps out. "I'm the shit Wilks. Everybody knows it. How bad you want me?"

Silence.

"I'm in."

Aldo to Wilks, "How much?"

Wilks, "Forget…"

"Nononoforget'! My time—Ivan——n's t-i-m-e iza' money."

Wilks says painfully, "What I bet last week."

Aldo whispers something into his PDA.

Brice says, "If you're in you got to show it. Everybody knows I'm good for it." He points to Chili. Wilks gives his flexible smartcard to Chili who inserts it into his PDA, dials an ATM-link and passes it to Wilks. He clicks on the "scan" button and the micro-camera scans the thermal patterns of his face and recognizes the subdermal pattern of his veins and arteries. With the verification complete, he clicks on "accept" and hands it back to Chili. He looks at it then shows it to Brice.

"It'll do." To Wilks, "You're good for the slack right Wilks?"

"Talk is cheap pussy shit!" Turning. "Hold the cards Chili."

Brice gives his smartcard to Aldo.

"Na—a. Aldo 'll hold the cards this heat," says Brice.

Aldo swipes Wilks' card out of Chili's PDA, much to Wilks' chagrin. Wilks then walks past the small crowd to his ride.

Chili talks into his rig as he walks off. "Bill and Sandy, I need you lock and load Brice and Wilks for the fourth heat...."

"Talk about assholes," one rider to another in a sotto voice.

"Who?"

"Brice *and* Wilks."

"Yeah—h."

Aldo, to Brice, "I know you gonna' betta,..."

"Yeah. Yeah. What are the odds on me against Wilks?"

Aldo puts his finger to his earpiece listening to instructions.

"Three to one on Wilks."

"What?! Three to one against me?! Shit...! Lemme' talk to Ivan."

"Ivan donna' talka' to a' no riders...." Taking a step backwards.

"Gimme' that!" Reaching for Aldo's headset.

"Waita'...He talka' to you."

Putting on the set, "Yo Ivan, how you doing?" Brice turns and goes eye to eye with Ivan who's sitting on the back seat of his car with the door open and his feet on the ground. "Hey—y. Caught you on Holo-V fucknin' up that slopehead Jappo'! Nice. N-i-c-e moves."

"Thanks Ivan. I'm guessin' you and the boys made a lotta' credits on me. Now you got no faith in my blurring or what?"

"Hey don't get me wrong now—w. When it comes to zipping some Jap InSpace you're my man. But this—this is *real time*...."

"Okay. Okay. Put me down for two-hundred."

Ivan, almost laughing, "Two-hundred...."

"Thousand." A beat. "Ivan?"

"Okay. You're down for two-hundred thou. Gimme' Aldo."

Aldo listens carefully, then speeds under armpits on his gyroboard. Bill and Sandy run over to the EZ and scurry around it like flies on cheesecake. Buttons get tapped, six cute little holo-cameras with mini-mikes and magnetic backs, clink on to the front back and sides next to radar-stoppers. A wave-jammer—highly illegal, is positioned in front of the bike's microwave receivers. The jammers eliminate N.Y.S.C.G.H.A.'s (New York State Central Computerized Guidance Highway Authority), ability to override the cycles by making them electronically invisible. Nobody knows how Chili gets hold of the jammers but they are returned to their lockers in the New Jersey Highway Patrol Station House by 8:00 AM every Monday.

Back in the EZ, Brice slowly rolls through the crowd on his way to the line. "Home, dial Chili."

"Both his lines are busy—wait...."

"Speak."

"Chili, *B'* here. What's the intel on Wilks' ride."

"Its a Kawasaki Minotaur and supposed to be for Jap. domestic only."

"Thanksalot" Brice hangs up. "Home gimme' a lowdown on the

Wired for Chaos

Minotaur. How it rates against the EZ?"

"Searching…Ah, June *Motorcyclist*." Blocks of text and pictures stream across the EZ's monitor. "With a limiter its got 15 horses on the EZ, without it its got 60. Suspension, hydraulics, sensors, about the same. Its heavy though."

"Glad I yanked my limiter. That it?"

"I could list the specs. side by side…."

"Na—a," thinking. "If he's linked up too—tap his system comp. real soft an' see if you could spit an override command or a virus through a hole."

"Flash."

"Be, surreptitious."

Wilks is already rubber to the line. The black and yellow Minotaur sits low and long with lines that seem to be pushing through the Kevlar panels like plastic stretched tight over broken glass shards. Brice pulls alongside and they lock eyes. Grunts run up to the bikes and top off their batteries then run off.

"Brice," says Wilks. "You got everybody fooled but me. You think cause you're some InSpace champ that your shit smells like perfume in real time. But if you couldn't jack you couldn't even get a job assembling sensors for automatic toilets." Wilks' doors close with a vacuum seal hiss.

A tiny spasm ebbs under Brice's right eyelid, like tiny bubbles bursting. The very definition of *pis—sed*.

"Home, find the space in the recording you made earlier when Olga was coming."

"Any particular part?"

"Where she's moaning an' telling me I'm the best fuck."

"Searching…got it."

"Dial Wilks. Hit play."

Wilks picks up his line, "What?"

Olga's moaning in Dolby fills Wilk's cabin. Brice and Wilks lock eyes through glass. The sound of a disconnect.

Bill walks between the rides and gets the high sign from Brice and Wilks.

"I'm waiting for okays from the spotters," says Bill.

From the rear of the Minotaur, a small wheel at the end of a stabilizer arm, slowly rolls out of its cavity. The EZ's stabilizer arm also rolls out and the seals on the cabin tighten. Home runs a system check and adjusts for wind speed and direction. The center treads of the EZ's rear wheel recede slightly depositing a thin sticky layer of streetgrip juice onto the tires and asphalt. That's the EZ, not Home, see it knows what's about to happen. "Fuzzy logic is the shit," thought Brice, long ago.

Bill says, "Chili, says a news chop is coasting the Henry Hudson. He recommends abort…."

Wilks says, "We ride!"

"Wilks, Chili wants to know if you have night vision?"

The Minotaur's halogen lights dim to black and its windshield takes on a dark green tint. Brice, taps the stealth button with his eye-pointer and the EZ's lights dim and the windshield tints to green.

"All right, you know the deal. No contact. No road kills. 125th exit is the line. If the man pulls you over hide the jammers."

The EZ and the Minotaur say "Yeah," in stereo.

"Gimme' a sec—Chili'z getting the lookers to stop blocking the entrances to the *H'* uptown."

A few cabbies and Mid-city dwellers, in the know, have been parking at the entrances to the Henry Hudson to watch the races. But Chili doesn't play 'cause he says the less attention up the *H'* the better. This ticks them off cause they can't jack in either. Tough. If a cabby plays stupid he gets a visit from one of Ivan's boys 'cause the two have a relationship.

The count down starts and the numbers blink on the rider's LCDs. The needles on the dash of the EZ flirt with the red. The EZ's CNG (compressed natural gas) engine that puts out 1500rpms doesn't make that wicked, primal, bike noise, so the gray-heads rev their Harleys so loud it echoes deep into the city. Mid-city derm heads goggle up and lean against their rides, expecting to be enthralled. Nearing eight on the count down, Wilks dry-humps his ride rocking it back and forth…two, one. Rear wheels spin leaving welts on the asphalt, launching the front of the bikes into the air until righted by the stabilizer arms. Blurring up West Street, the arms quickly disappear and the EZ's spoilers ascend. Traffic on the *H'* is lil' to none so the Minotaur and EZ breeze north weaving between the few cars in front of them. Wilks takes the ramp full on and the kids on top an abandoned building scream with glee. Brice darts behind Wilks until he decides to clamp on to his rear and steal a ride in the wind tunnel the Minotaur forges. The Z' is coated with Teflon so it pays the air no mind.

Brice speaks with his teeth clenched, "I'm going to fuckin' slit you fuckin' biohazard motherfucker!"

Wilks is caught behind a bad hairday driving a Toyota, so Brice threads the needle just missing a Jeep half a car length diagonally in front of the Toyota. Now he slams it. Clutch, gear, throttle, blur. The idea is put as much space between him and that asshole and avoid decorating the road. Wilks presses his horn button so hard it sticks for a hot second and the buzzed Jeep does a hard right into the Toyota's lane so they bump. The Minotaur pops a wheelie and comes down hard on the front shocks but the EZ has the lead past 23rd Street. Blurring past the green and silver NightShine holo signs at 34th, Wilks spies the EZ clocking *70K* and steps on it. In line with the EZ he steals air on its tail and they play follow the leader, stroke for stroke streakin' past the Javitz. At forty-deuce the two skip their first red light without a hitch and terrorize a bus. The EZ can't shake its tail which ticks *B'* off. "All right motherfucker you like my tail so much kiss my ass." As Brice touches the brake the brake light flashes, Wilks panics, swerves and screams into oncoming traffic. It happens so fast. When Wilks sees the taxi he guns it on a sharp angle so the Cuban behind the wheel slams his breaks and fishtails east. He clears a path and hops back into the north bound lane just in time to see the EZ make the bend at 57th Street. "Bitch, fuck——fuckin' gonna——come on! Come the fuck on!"

Weaving past the cars like they waz' standing still, Brice doesn't even look at his rear monitor. He starts taking deep breaths to lower his heart rate and push as much oxygen through his system as he can manage. Training has taught him one thing he lives by. Never lose your cool while in play. And, you're always in play. So, aware that Wilks is gunning it trying to catch up, he decides to open the Ducati up like never before. Speed InSpace has no consequences and the dynamics are just a ripple compared to surface motion, but spinnin' rubber on asphalt in a shell born in a wind tunnel—that has definite consequences. So as the EZ's speed gauge ascends, an edge grows on B's heart-rate. At 72nd Street the taxies rev their ancient motors hypin' the paying customers in the back seat when they see the EZ approach. Black exhaust hurls out of the yellow bird's asses and you'd think it was fuckin' New Years Eve. Blur two as the Minotaur approaches and the taxies take it out of neutral and floor their petroleum rides on Wilks' rubber. They get maybe 35 meters and their microwave receivers get the "Whoa' now!" from a little box and the taxies have their speed reduced to 55 automatically.

Chewing up the asphalt, Wilks is glad he can't spot a car but he's tired of playing games with the pretty rich boy so he red lines it way past the recommended specs. Not paying attention to his radar, Brice is about to pass a truck when he hears a horn screaming at him and swerves out of Wilks' way. Now, if there is anything Brice, the competitor hates, it is being passed and he already hates Wilks. Near 89th Street the two are neck and neck for the first time until Wilks tries to slam Brice up against the railing. Forced to pull back he tries to accelerate and passes Wilks on his left only to get cut off. For every move he makes Wilks counters and the move has to be put on him in the fast lane 'cause a steady group of cars line the other lane into the distance. Seeing the end of the cars Brice guesses Wilks will gun it all the way to 125th Street on the straight away. On 116th Street Wilks pulls ahead and Brice stays with him until they pass the last car, then Brice falls in line right behind the Minotaur's rear and gets to within a meter. Then, when he is sure he's in line with Wilks' rear camera Brice turns on his high beams, hits his breaks and cuts right. The blast of light fills the Minotaur's cabin and momentarily blinds Wilks whose reflex is to take his hand off the handlebar and cover his eyes. Bad move. Going as fast as he is, his left hand jerks the handlebar making him swerve to his left as Brice guns the EZ just missing the Minotaur as it begins to roll. Brice hugs the shoulder and leans forward. *POP! SSSSSSST!* The Minotaur's airbags jam Wilks' right hand into his face and the back of his head into the cushioned rollbar. The bike swerves violently, his left hand squeezes the rear breaks too tight, too fast and the Minotaur flips. Spinning in the air, the Minotaur seems to pick up speed with each roll, slapping the street like a skipping stone across water. A nanosecond after the first roll, Pieces of the bike fly off and shoot in every direction as Brice sees Chili's man with the flag on the exit to 125th Street. Then, after thirteen rolls, Wilks finally stops rolling and skids for another fifty meters. The EZ is long gone. Brice can't help a self-congratulatory scream. Home pipes in Chili's link and a roar of cheers fills the EZ's cabin as

"Chili for you."

"Yo."

"Damn B'! You savage!"

Grinning, B' says, "Chili when you pry his ass outta' his wheels they're yours."

"Oh thanksalot…shit the man is here. Gotta' close shop." The sound of a disconnect.

Brice fearing a helicopter makes a hard right onto St. Claire Place and shoots up a steep ass hill onto Riverside Drive, only to jump a small cement divider and grab the cover of some trees.

"Home I don't expect you can spy any copters overhead, right?"

In Brice's voice, "Right motherfucker. You know what I can and can't do. Up the change for some radar an' shit next time you…"

"Shut the fuck up!" Rolling slowly down the dirt hill the Z's wheels flick small stones out of its way. "They're here then they've already got a heat signature lock on me and…" Hearing two loud Jap street bikes approach, B' takes action the tenth of a second after he has the thought. The two bikes are making the light on 129th Street headed west for the water. One click later his bike has changed from lipstick red to black and yellow tiger stripes complete with new license plate and twin headlights, courtesy of Immense Holo Imaging Systems of Silicon Valley. He tails the two bikers and they take the entrance to the H' together. At 95th Street, they pass Chili's unmarked ambulette. The phone rings.

"Aldo for you," says Home.

"Yeah."

"Meata' me ona' 10th ana' 14th under the tracks ina'…"

"No," narrowing his eyes. "You meet me at 10th and 21st in fifteen pizza boy." CLICK! "The fuck you think you talking to, you fuckin' illiterate mob gofer motherfucker."

"A little attitude from our bookie's runner?" Says Home.

"What it is?"

"Hmmmm…"

"Spare the affectation and tell me what's on your mind."

"Well, if the "illiterate mob gofer motherfucker is wafting 'tude in your direction…"

"It means that Ivan won't be sending me any birthday vmail."

"Yeah."

"So?"

"Well just remember you've just won US$600,000 from a Russian bookie that's the nephew of an east coast boss. And you can bet that it'll be all over Brighton Beach in less than an hour and tomorrow Ivan will have hell to pay."

"Fuckem'."

"You may want to tread lightly, no?"

"Fuckem'."With that Brice guns it past a Volvo wagon at 92nd street. "Play something by the posthumous David Bowie via *Bowie's Dead*."

Instantly, an alto saxophone sounding distant and hollow blares through the cabin's speakers. *"I'ma' space cowboy leave me alone—e! Ain't got no family—this ship is my home—e! I live for dieing, death is my game—e! Don't miss messing me—I never e-v-e-r miss the blade—e! I'ma' space cowboy leave me alone— e..!"*

THURSDAY, 1:18 AM.

Minutes after Brice heated asphalt on his way to meet up with Chili, Jimmy pulls into the driveway of The Museum Tower. The sleek, fossil fuel consuming McLaren he is driving belongs to Brice. The chauffeurs stare at the McLaren's metallic-gold finish and have a field day.

Jimmy pulls up to the main entrance, puts the McLaren into neutral and exits with the engine running. Ramon, the youngest doorman, leaps at the opportunity of driving the sports car if only for a few meters into the carport.

Slouched down in a deco chair, Olga spies Jimmy through dull, reptilian slits. Surprised to see her, he floats over on a cloud of attitude.

"Olga, darling—going up or coming down?"

"Actually, throwing up."

"Yeah, lemme' get you a handywipe ta' clean this mess up."

He walks over to a large ornate console behind which Carl sits.

"Carl..."

"Good evening Mr. Johnson."

"...Carl what is that trash doing in my lobby?"

"Your brother called her a car—it's pulling up now."

A Lincoln Town car pulls into the driveway and its rear door opens automatically. The white-gloved doormen nod approvingly as Olga passes through the building's automatic revolving doors.

"Just another vacuous mannequin," says Jimmy walking to the elevator, "On her way out."

2:10 AM.

At club Kasbah, its the usual. The outside is twenty deep with wanna-get-ins' while inside the main rooms have a total of thirty occupants and the very-important-people room is closed. The owner shrewdly keeps the room closed until the club gets packed so the common silt can rub against the elevated celebrity species.

Jimmy has already reconnoitered the entire club twice looking for Brice without success and fights the urge to be uncool and call him. At the far end of the bar he can see everyone who descends the stairs into the main room as he sips his rum and coke. A clump of Japanese girls puff clove smoke in all directions and talk in hushed whispers among themselves. The brothers are in the house. Homies wear a lot of basic black. The pants are beatnik tight, big afros abound and full contact-lens shades in rose and baby-blue are de rigueur.

Michelle, an acquaintance, wearing a lose fitting, black crepe suit and very little make-up makes her way towards Jimmy. Michelle knew the walk — Bunuel knew the type. If the world was an eyeball she was the stiletto heel that would lunge and burst it open — if only for effect. They greet each other with the dull, expressionless stares of iguanas having arrived at the same section of the river's edge. The talk is small and they have to shout to reach above the din. Michelle, is a bitter, burned out ex-model turned agent, at a hot modeling agency where Olga defected and—d she is retaining water. Months ago Michelle introduced herself to Brice and quickly became his eyecandy supplier. She's been biding her time, making small deposits in Brice's favor bank hoping to call in a favor one day. Michelle and Jimmy see Olga in the reflections of several mirrors.

Mercifully, the VIP room opens and the fabs queue up for sanctuary. Turkish smoking ottomans, complementary mango and nectarine slices soaked in a mild psychedelic-stimsex syrup, sensorama helmets and the perfunctory live sex shows in case you tire of conversation. The floor, ceiling and walls are painted black and illuminated by cool blue halogens. As luck would have it, Olga is directly in front of Jimmy on line. They are allowed admittance by Jesus, steroid-muscle enhanced bouncer #10,999. Olga mistakenly opens a stairwell door and stumbles in. Jimmy watches the door waiting for the dizzy bitch to re-enter so he can shine a scornful gaze in her direction. Unexpectedly Olga's laughter makes him curious enough to approach the door. A moment passes and he hears Olga fall down a flight of stairs. An uncharacteristic rush of decency overwhelms him and he rushes through the door to find her at the bottom of the stairs.

Walking down the stairs, "What's amazing is not how fuckin' stupid you, are its how much I underestimate yo' dumb bitchidness'!"

"Ow—w. Jimmy. Jimmy the brother—not the champ, the brother," as high as a satellite. "Tell me Jimmy—wimmym," wincing in pain as she shifts her weight. "Does Brice give you an allowance or do you recycle cans from the garbage?" Laughing.

Jimmy fights the urge to brag about the money he makes selling black derms to the rich kids, or the enormous score he has in the works in fifty-two hours and counting, that's going make him financially independent. He'd like to leave her there to climb up the stairs on all fours, but he'd rather humiliate her in a day or two when she's nursing a plastic covered limb. That's his nature. Calculated revenge. As he places his hand underneath Olga's arm she takes hold of him only to wince in pain a moment later and push him off. Yes, she would rat him out about his secret, how he hit on a male model that's gay and got rejected, her friend Lawrence.

"Well your days are numbered—get the fuck off me! I'm going to cut you off! Off, out, gone, fucking history—get the fuck away from me!"

Wired for Chaos

"I'm going to tell your friends you got drunk an' high and fell down the stairs on your tired flat, white ass, right after I tell the photographers from *Vanity Fair* where you are!"

Jimmy steps over her on his way up the stairs as his US$1,500 House of Matsuda trousers are clawed at. In an attempt to wrestle free he inadvertently kicks her in the nose with the heal of his shoe.

"Ow——w! Asshole! I'm going to tell them you pushed me down the stairs!"

Jimmy freezes.

"Pushed me down! Pushed me! Little prick! I'll do a job on you on the Holo-V that'll..."

"Shut up. Shut the fuck up or I'm leaving your ass right here..!"

The door opens and Michelle enters closing it behind her quickly.

"What the fuck is going on? Seeing Olga.

"Jimmy pushed me down the stairs!"

"Shut the fuck up——she's lying..."

Through the walls, they hear the earth shattering primal base of the industrial strength subwoofers belting out a beat for the sex show to pump by.

"...She fell down the stairs——broke something and now——now she's acting like a fuckin' Russian computer!"

"Michelle, no hard feelings right sweetie?"

"Thanks for returning my calls Olga. Like you even existed before Arnold——took you in...!"

"Arnold only wanted to get in my pants. Can't blame him though considering one lay with you, the stiff neck, inert lay," laughing. "Fuck him and fuck you. I got tired of having my money——my money held for hours to shave transfer interest through those Chinese banks! I know bitch! And——d I——I can get Claudia to cross the street when ever tha' fuck I want," a beat. "What are you waiting for asshole?! Get the fucking reporters I got a story to give 'em! You both pushed me!"

Jimmy and Michelle look at each other for a long painful moment.

"You drive here?"

"Yeah," not understanding.

Putting her hands out and speaking sotto, "Gimme the keys."

Jimmy gives them to her. "It's the gold McLaren, down the block to the right. What..?"

With that Michelle is at the top of the stairs and about to exit. "Don't ask. Trust me. Stay up here and make sure no one opens this door."

Jimmy does what he says not comprehending what she is doing.

"The fuck you up——don't know who you're messing with...Ow——w get me the fuck outta' here! I need a doctor. Shit——shit hurts." She continues to mumble to herself incoherently.

At the top of the stairs, a thin sheen of sweat forms on Jimmy's nose. Olga winces as she fails to straighten out her leg. Cussing and grinding her fingernails into her palms she empties out her pocket book and retrieves her *squirtgun*. She peels the tab off a tiny glass vial, inserts it into the gun and shoots up. Jimmy sees this and is relieved that something is shutting supermodel, diva, witch-bitch on a jetpack up. Five loud bangs on the street level emergency exit door scare the shit out of Jimmy. He barrels down the stairs and pauses to hear Michelle's instructions.

"Jimmy—Jimmy listen to me before you open the door. As soon as its open you've got to get Olga out of there fast because the alarm will sound! Got it!"

"Yeah—yeah but why can't I just leave her here?!"

"Cause she'll fuck us! Do you want that! My agency and your brother don't need the scandal!"

"But…!"

"Just get her shit up, get her to her feet and run out here! Do it!"

"All right! All right!"

Stooping to pick up her purse and throw everything into it. "It's all I fucking need now!"

Jimmy lifts Olga to her feet, sticks his head under her arm and positions himself in front of the door.

"Okay! I'm coming out!"

With that Jimmy bursts through the door and a shrieking siren sounds momentarily deafening them. Micelle has opened both doors and the trunk of the McLaren and left the engine running. She quickly grabs Olga and steers them towards the trunk.

"What are you doing?"

"The car seats two remember. And I'm not getting in there," spits Michelle motioning the trunk.

They dump the half conscious cover girl into the trunk post haste and jump into the car. The Goodyear tires strip the thick layer of dirt and grime off the alley as they head for a street.

"Turn off your lights," says Michelle.

"Wha…?"

"They can't read the license plates if the fuckin lights are off—do it!"

He does and they travel down the street slipstreamin' ancient Chinese menus in their wake. A tense moment spreads itself thick with hyperanticipation when they miss a light and have to allow three pedestrians to cross. They cross the street mercilessly slow not even talking to each other. Then, a lean session musician who happens to be a car lover extraordinaire drinks the vintage McLaren in. Notable mention, one gold McLaren G1, only thirty in the US and one in New York, owned by Brice Johnson. Car lights illuminate the cabin missing Micelle who ducks down. Our musician turns around before he reaches the curb and points at the McLaren yelling something.

"Your lights! Your lights are off!"

Jimmy can't understand him—the lights! He's pointing at my fuckin' lights.

Wired for Chaos

"What's the matter?"

"Some asshole is screaming at me to put on my lights."

"Hasn't the fucking light changed yet?!"

"Would I be fucking sitting here if it did!"

Fidgeting, Jimmy tells himself to be cool. Freeze dried. If Brice were here he'd be cool. Finally the light changes and Jimmy guns it slamming his head against the head rest. Sixty-one seconds later he turns onto Bowery heading North with the lights on. Micelle sits up and tries to act unruffled disinterested in the banging emanating from the trunk.

"Stop banging back there you fuckin' bitch!" Olga doesn't stop.

"No head downtown, take Lafayette."

"Where are we going?"

"I've got a friend whose space we can use. He's out of town until tomorrow night..."

"Is it safe?"

"Oh it's safe all right. Charlie is a dealer."

"Intel?"

"Nope. Drugs. Spunk, Pinks, grass, you name it. Everything high octane and he takes security seriously, very seriously."

"Wahdda..?"

"Look we just want to talk to her, calm her down and Charlie has some shit that'll make her straight an' mellow. Then she can fuckin' get a cab or walk for all I care."

A few blocks away sits Ramon Camacho, an off duty, Puerto Rican NYPD Detective with a bad attitude, moonlighting for a mysterious man named Roshi looking to dig up dirt on Brice. Camacho didn't care much for talking and he wasn't a great thinker, he just liked the sound of his own internal voice over the cackle of others. His brown skin was rough, leathery and needed a good washing, his hair was dark, coarse and perpetually oily, not that he cared. He guns his Corvette in the direction of the Mitsubishi long range tracking bug attached to the inside of the McLaren's gas tank. The blip is headed down Lafayette and he can hear everything Michelle and Jimmy are saying like a book on chip piped through his Delco. He's also recording Brice's race on disc guessing that Brice will head to the club and knock a few back later. But Jimmy, he sounds like he's about to do wrong and the more wrong a subject gets, the more chance Camacho will catch something on disc.

The McLaren pulls up to the old lumber store on Broadway just below Spring and Michelle jumps out. She sticks her hand into a slot in the facade which reads her bone structure, the hand is identified and the garage door opens. A large, ferocious dog begins to bark, the lights come on and Jimmy rolls the McLaren into the garage. The door comes down with an ancient slam and Michelle flies up a set of old wood stairs. The barking reaches new heights of agitation.

"Stay in the car until I come out to get you okay!"

Michelle stops at the top of the stairs, opens a refrigerator and takes out a Tupperware container. She opens the container and uses a long prong to pick up the raw sirloin steak. With the steak held firmly Michelle approaches the door which separates her from the barking.

"Saddam! Saddam, it's Michelle baby! This is Michelle! Not a burglar! Not bad man come to take daddy's stash!"

The dog is not placated.

"Saddam! Chill the fuck out already!"

Jimmy, has an "I can't believe this is happening expression," on his face. He locks the doors and tries to ignore Olga's constant tantrum level banging.

"Fuck you if this doesn't work Charlie. Fuck you."

Michelle, finally gets the nerve and opens the door a crack. Saddam lunges at it knocking the hollow metal door into her knee. His snout acts like a wedge exposing clenched teeth as he tries to force his way in. Michelle quickly throws the meat in over Saddam's head and into the hallway behind it. Saddam retreats to eat and Michelle leans against the door and breathes deeply.

Outside, Camacho parks down the street exits and locks his door. He starts walking like he lives here. As he walks down Broadway reading the proximity levels on his PDA it signals *dead on* when he passes the garage door. He quickly pockets the device and stops to tie his bootlace as he checks out the entrance to the building. One old garage door—probably reinforced iron, electronic hand-lock, second floor windows with iron bars, alarm siren and a small warning sign screwed into the bricks and that's it. On the sign a cross is drawn over a barking dog's head followed by an equal sign and an upper case *U* superimposed over a mushroom cloud. Camacho stands and continues walking. The sign puzzles him for another three meters before he figures it out and laughs out loud. The dog must have some kind of transmitter strapped to its collar monitoring his heartbeat. So, if you off the dog the plastique Charlie rigged in the house offs you, the drugs, the building, the works. Camacho had heard of some suppliers in Columbia using these rigs on their drug labs outside of Cali.

He walks to the end of the long block, hangs a right then another on Mercer headed for his Vett.

THE HERO'S ARMOR
2:18 AM.

Parked at 10th Avenue and 21st, Brice rests his chin on his forearm and mentally replays the night's highlights. Brice's eyes soften their focus on the oncoming cars approaching him from the rear on his flat screen. He smiles a broad, gloat-laden smile at the thought of Wilks reacting to Olga's panting coming through his speakers. The kind of smile a rich, fat boy would—his face covered in chocolate, watching the dejected employee his father—the chocolate factory owner just fired for trying to smite the boy's chocolate habit. He replays the highlights of his race up the Henry H' and remembers the rush of near misses with the cars and Wilks. True, he got the same rush from time to time during bouts as he was ducking some plasma beam headed his way. A beam that would surely zap his nervous system, or hit him like a "real time" ton of bricks. It was excellent to be wearing a tech suit that wicked the sweat away from his back to avoid that uncomfortable nervous feeling—just then, it hits him hard. He is on a quiet street without any of his boys and he is about to have his Smartcard handed to him buy a Russian mobster who just lost US$600,000 of the mob's money to a very rich athlete. His palms begin to sweat.

"Oh shit," he whispers to himself.

His mind races and a sheer net of panic begins to envelop him. 'What's to stop Ivan from having one of his boy's hand him the card with one hand and shoot him with the other? Who is going to know? Who is going to see? Look at where I am on this deserted street. What should I do?'—all run through his head like what he figures the last thoughts of a snuff film victim.

Home says, "What's up? Your pressure is rising."

"I could get out of the bike—no. The fuck would that do? Shit. Fuckin' think." Frantically looking around and seeing no one on the street and few parked cars for cover his mind races.

"Fuck it! I'll tell them to leave it with my doorman," starting the engine.

"Can I do anything?"

Ignoring him, "The fuck waz' I thinking. . ?"

"They're here."

Brice looks in his rearview flat screen and sees Ivan's armored Caddy slow and pull along side of the EZ.

"Fuck! Fuck!"

"Talk to me."

"Ivan's going to off me!"

"So lets get the fuck outta' here!"

In Brice's mind a multitude of scenarios play themselves out and rewind with blinding speed, as Ivan's smoked windows seem to move in slow motion towards him. For a moment, his body spits out more sweat than the suit can handle comfortably and he forgets everything about keeping his cool. He glances forward and sees the open street and thinks about gunning it through the red light only to hesitate and turn his head towards Ivan's window. 'Can they shoot me through the window? Fuck yeah.' Ivan's window lowers but Brice can only see part of a man' cheek and shoulder. The air from the Caddy is redolent with Drakar Noir cologne. His heart is pounding in his mouth and this deafening silence seems to obliterate the sound of the air being piped into his cabin and the hum of his engine—just his heartbeat. Brice almost jams his right cheek into the dash when he lets go of the accelerator with his right hand and brings it around to pat his jacket pocket. Reaching inside of the jacket he becomes aware that his hand is shaking.

"Home, when I tell you I want you to..."

From Ivan's point of view, the seamless, dragonfly shaped glass window of the EZ raises slowly. He leans forward and has a pithy line all ready for the cocky shit. Ivan stretches his neck, makes a tough guy face and gets serious as Brice's arm comes into view. Then the EZ's interior halogen flare like car high beams and he has to squint.

"Hey! What's with the fuckin' light?"

B' has the bike in gear and is squeezing the break ready to take off at the first sight of gunmetal. Extending his hand, "You got my card?" The EZ jerks slightly as Brice squeezes the rear break and puts it into first ready to take off at the sight of gunmetal.

"Yeah." Ivan takes it from someone in the shadow and reaches out of the window. Within centimeters of Brice's fingers, Ivan fakes and pulls it back. "You got lucky. Tricky, but real lucky." The silence stretches and pause leaves Brice's mouth dry. Finally, Ivan gives him the card and before he can say a word Brice's quickly closes his window. Brice immediately moves off and is stopped by the red light only to be joined a moment later by Ivan's car. In the cabin, the light has returned to normal and Brice takes off his Persols, letting them drop against the dash. The front passenger window of Ivan's car rolls down and two big boys wearing cheap suits check out Brice's windows, looking to check him out. Seeing no oncoming traffic, Brice edges into the about to be green light and takes off through the intersection. Staring at the Caddy on his flat screen and not thinking about the road ahead, the EZ's front hydraulics compensate for a deep pothole. Finally the Caddy heads east and Brice relaxes some. "Turn up the air," A blast of cool air immediately floods the cabin. "I need a drink."

In his mind, free associations flow, repeat and flick on in obsessive nature. "What the fuck was I thinking…I didn't have to bet Ivan all that money. But no I had to talk shit cause he gave me attitude. And like who cares. But see I didn't stop and think about any crap like getting by card back would be like some potential hit scenario. What was I thinking. And Olga. I didn't have to talk shit to Wilks about her but somebody gets in my face and I talk shit. Idiot! Macho idiot! And I like her but—I'm not about to let her know it. We're exclusive and that is where it stays for right now. No I like her alright but she just takes any shit I throw out at her cause I'm the champ. She dishes it out to Jimmy and everybody else which is kinda' funny though. I should probably be nice to her but I'm never gonna get soft and set myself up. What the fuck waz' I thinking? I could have been a stain on 10th Avenue." With that he turned melancholy. What if he died and nobody grieved for him? He wasn't thinking about fans, they could be fanatics. He was thinking about the few close people that didn't see past his serious "fuck *you* face." They must be able to see through the stern expressions and trash talk he thought. It was a front, but you need that to be an effective competitor, after all it's what helped make him number one. A champion. He shook off the blank stare and flexed the muscles above his jawbone. It was cool. They'd grieve.

Minutes later Brice is slowly riding down the street to Club Kasbah. From a distance he could see the crowd around the velvet rope at the entrance eager for acceptance. Opting to park on the sidewalk he parks the EZ with the front wheel pointed directly at the entrance. Aware that getting out of the bike looks awkward; Brice does it slowly making sure that if anyone is looking he wouldn't look unhip. Standing, he checks his pockets and adjusts his guy.

To Home, "Don't talk to any strangers."

"Strangers?! In this city? Who's not fuckin' strange? Show me."

As he starts to walk towards the entrance Home closes and locks the doors then seals the windows. None of the herd in front of the club have spotted him yet which is fine but he walks slowly because he wants to get the attention of the guy with the clipboard. No luck yet and idiot is wearing sunglasses and rejecting some suit. Bullseye. A bouncer spots him and taps the clipboard on the shoulder. The guy holding the clipboard is wearing a black denim, cut fake fur jacket and a vintage fez, ignores the pleading glances of the pathetic and opens the velvet rope for the B'man. Everyone turns to look at Brice and people move out of the way. Now that he's back in his element it's like the hand-off from Ivan never happened and his attitude is rejuvenated.

"'Sup?"

Brice nods and says, "'Sup?" without caring. Although he feels a few dozen pairs of eyes trying to bore into his back he concentrates on his goal. A tall dark drink. A quarter second after this massive bouncer wearing head-to-toe black steps behind Brice, obscuring the view of the interior steps up.

"Excuse me…"

"If you're not on the guest list I can't do anything for you!"

"Reggie—I'm a friend of Reggies."

"Well I don't know you."

"Reggie the owner!"

"Frank is the owner. My—y name is Reggie."

Brice descends the stairs into the main room and heads for the far end of the bar where he orders a rum and coke. The chatter is at a high decimal backed up by a pounding base from the dance floor. The clump of Japanese girls are still puffing clove smoke in all directions but begin to giggle and cover their faces when they see Brice. Avoiding the overt stares of the clove smoking Japanese girls, Brice looks at his watch that reads 2:27 AM. He would never know he had just missed Jimmy, Michelle and Olga by only seven minutes.

He feels more than a little naked when he realizes that he hasn't been out without the entourage in a very long time. Most nights he'd call Leroy and get the boys together for a night on the town just to keep the unsavory at arms length. Scanning the room he sees nothing that interests him and no one he knows. Seeing that two girls are making a B-line towards him he cuts them off and takes the stairs towards the VIP room. A tall black model wannabe' sees him coming out of the corner of her eye, sips her Clos dou Bouis and side steps into his immediate path. He gets the hint, lets out the deep the breath of annoyance and quickly sidesteps her before she can turn and act coquettish. There is actually a line to get in but Brice walks to the door and is ushered in. A waitress passes by with a tray of dates and grapes that Brice waves off. Then he gets a contact high from the smoke coming someone's pipe. The ensuing syn' experience is mild and pleasant. The voices take the form of thin blue columns that slowly undulate in front of his eyes. The music, an Islamic chant backed by a synth. takes the form of yellow and orange swirls that dance fading in and out. He remembers that Olga is supposed to be here and starts looking around for her only to be distracted by a buzz at the far corner of the room. Camera flashes go off as Brice heads in that direction. The buzz surrounds Gary Miller, the Olympic track star who just broke a world record. He is surrounded by fifteen close friends, a bevy of paparazzi getting all the attention. Brice gets bumped into several times while walking around the sex show, which only happens because his boys are not around. Gary's publicist leaps into his face.

"Brice Johnson! Whadda' coincidence," speaking loud enough to make sure he is overheard and many eyes turn to Brice. "Have you met Gary? Let me introduce you. Gary. Gary this is..."

"Brice Johnson," says Gary beaming that 150-kilowatt smile at him shaking his hand.

"How you donin'?!"

"Can't complain."

"Congrats on the medals man."

"Thanks man but what I need to do is get with you InSpace you know. But you ain' got nothing to fear from me for a while."

Brice is a little disoriented by the smoke—it's laced with something that's getting him high and Gary is rubbing him the wrong way. His sense is that Gary is way too nice to be true in that home grown country way and being that they are both tall, attractive and black athletes, its obvious that they'd be wary of each other.

"Lets get a shot of you for the sites boys."

The two shake hands and Gary floods the room with his broad, perfect tooth smile to Brice's run of the mill grin. The B'man is noticeably uncomfortable and is tired of being cordial.

"Gary I got to go and find my woman man. I'll see you in a bit."

"Don't go far man. We're just getting started."

Saying, "I'll be back," Brice weaves past several people eager to find Olga and get the hell out of Dodge.

The press agent squeezes his arm and Brice turns towards him.

"Oh Brice, here take my phone card. I realize you signed MaCowen but I've got a few ideas I'd like to throw out at you."

"Yeah, all right," Brice says, loathing the pushy little man.

Moments later the press agent has returned to Gary where he corners one of the photographers. "Now Robbie, what's your line going to be? Something like, 'The Olympic athlete and the mogul.' What ever you do my boy gets top billing. I mean he's the real athlete. Am I right or what?"

Brice has been all over the room and is about to leave when a model squeezes him from behind.

"Hi Brice! You never call me."

"Hey Marie, how're you doing."

"Oh I've been better."

"Listen, you seen Olga? She was supposed to meet me here."

Masking her annoyance with a grin. "I *heard* she was here, but listen we were pretty good together."

"Marie we slept together once, gimme' a break. Listen you're looking good but I'm outta' here." Before she can even finish her pout, Brice is out of the room and in the hallway. In the main section of the club, he is pissed when he sees that it's packed and too many people are intruding on his private space.

"Hi there…" says somebody he's not even vaguely interested in meeting and he keeps moving. In a near panic he breaks for the door pushing a few gawkers out of his way. Catching the eyes of the bouncer at the door he makes a whirly bird sign with his right hand and our man gets the hint. Seconds later the big bald bruiser is pushing people aside and escorting Brice to his ride. He doesn't even have to beep Home, the EZ simply senses his presence and powers up.

Brice says, "Thanks man. It just got too fucking crowded in there for me tonight. See Olga tell her I looked for her and left."

"Sure thing man."

"Later."

"Later."

With everyone looking on, Home gives them a little flash by raising all the windows slowly followed by the gull-wing doors. It's like some metallic bird of prey ready for flight. Not in the EZ two seconds Brice takes off straight through the crowd and hits the pavement gunning the engine uptown to grab some all-night anyplace, Ray's-Pizza-clone by the slice at a place they probably won't recognize him. It was all dirty asphalt until you took an elevator to the sky anyway thought B'.

LOWER BROADWAY

Waiting for your perp to make a move on a stakeout is usually an exercise in indifference Camacho thinks to himself. Tonight is no different from any other night. You've always got the thermos of coffee from Dunkin' Donuts, a bottle of water, sandwiches, some chocolate, Nodoze and something to take a leak in. That's the list you get from your partner first time out, but the essential element however is something no one can tell you. You have to learn it. Patience. You may not always be focused but you've got to be patient. Sitting in a radio car and looking over your shoulder constantly or running down the street after some drugged up perp is a rush. Walking up the stairs in the projects with a steady stream of sweat running down the center of your back is harrowing. Screaming at bridge and tunnel plates to get the hell out of your way, while your siren is blaring, is like trying to run the hundred yard dash through the swamp eight hours a day—but at least you're running. Camacho had been an average uniform who watched you out of the corner of his eye, always sizing you up. He didn't show much initiative or cunning but he always had his partner's back and could one-two a punk in a street fight 24/7. He'd had seven shootings, a ton of gun collars and locked up tons of filth without getting shot or having Internal Affairs sniff his ass even once. He even prided himself on the fact that he could have shot a lot of people who deserved it but didn't. That was a cheat though. He just didn't like having to account for all of your shell casings and filling out reports and whatnot. Being a detective was all about connecting the dots and asking the right questions. It took him three months to get used to sitting in a car without a police radio going.

More than two hours had passed since Jimmy and Michelle had entered the dealer's house. Camacho was watching the entrance like a Jack Russell Terrier. He started to perk up when he reminded himself that he was here for the money. He had the department's best set of "street eyes." In his head he equated good "eyes" with a low intensity Holo game or that interactive cop show, "Leaded Supreme" only you could get killed for real. He sits in the driver's seat with his right hand on his crotch and his left holding a cap full of coffee trying to decide what file he should open from the menu in his head. The short list was always the same: the case, his dick, a way to make money, his dick, office politics and his dick. His dick usually won. But every once in a while he'd get this postcard from his memory manager. Right now he was thinking about when he was eight walking barefoot down a street in Cuba and saw his first stiff. It was Julio, one of the neighborhood addicts who had passed two days before only no one had noticed. Camacho always thought it funny that he couldn't remember how Julio looked because of the way he was slumped over and was shocked when his mother told him later that day that Julio was dead. What he remembered was the flies, hundreds of them playing bumper car derby above his head and arms. The hot mid-day sun kept Camacho focused on getting home *muy rápido* and since Julio smelled especially pungent he picked up his pace. Some of the flies took to following him and he sensed a depravity in them. They had worked themselves into a frenzy taking tiny bites out of his arms as he waved them off in vain. That night, after his mother told him about Julio he realized he had been bitten by flies that were feasting on an addict's corpse. Not just any addict but someone his mother had warned him to stay away from lest he catch something from Julio's body fluids. Camacho remembers the chill he felt and the fear of his mother finding out about the fly bites. Late that night he rummaged through a cardboard box below the cement sink, under the tin roof in his back yard and upon finding an old rag proceeded to rub his skin with maddening strokes. It was no use he thought. He would surely get what Julio had and become a skeletal relic who would scare children. The endless hours he spent over the course of the next year waiting for an affliction that did not occur had faded from his mind long ago but the flies had pursued him. At times, his computer screen teeming with E-post-its and vmail regarding every form of departmental red tape and he would flinch having felt their tiny feet on his arms. But why think about this now? He knew why. He'd ignored it moments ago but it was unmistakable. For one brief instant he caught a whiff of Julio.

The door opens and Jimmy drives the McLaren out slowly. The garage lights were already off and the door closes slowly behind them. As the car turns and heads south on Broadway Camacho follows at a casual pace a few car lengths behind. Inside Jimmy is in a state of shock. He is sweating from every pore and cannot seem to close his mouth. Michelle's lips are quivering as she lowers the window and says, "I don't give a fuck I have to smoke. I don't believe it. I don't believe it. Charlie is an ani—an animal. This isn't happening—I'm going to be sick."

"Isn't happening?! Isn't happening?! You fucking stupid bitch you took us to this guy's house an—an' now she's dead! I thought she was going to smoke some dope with Charlie—kick back and cool out but no..! No—o! Who the fuck is that fuck?! You…"

"I didn't know…"

"You got lots of friends like that!?!"

"I didn't know he was going to show up! I didn't know he was going to get high and cut her up!"

"You didn't know he was a sick fuck," the two become very animated and begin waving their hand and gesturing at each other. "How could you not know!! You that stupid bitch!"

"Fuck you! I didn't know!"

"I leave the fucking room to take a piss and get a beer, I see you, we talk, we're locked out and he turns into a butcher and you didn't know!" a beat. "Now we're accessories. Accessories to a murder—I can't believe—this is happening." Says Jimmy gripping the steering wheel with both hands as tight as he could.

As they approach Canal Michelle says, "Turn left."

"What difference does it make?!"

"Fucking turn fucking left fuck!"

"Alright!"

"We're not completely fucked—we gotta'—we've gotta' keep to the plan and do what Charlie said."

"Charlie is the one who got us into this—you trust his fucking judgment?!"

"Dozzen' matter! He is higher than the moon right now and if you and I are going to walk away from this then we have to do what he says. We up the eastside and dump the parts in dumpsters so nobody connects them, make sure our fingerprints are nowhere on them and book. Nobody saw us leave with her. Nobody will connect us. We just have to be careful a little while longer an' we're home free."

Jimmy was on the verge of breaking down and his eyes filled with tears. "I can't believe this shit. I can't believe this. I just went out to party an' now I'm wrapped up with your drug dealer killer friend. This is so fucked up. So fucked up."

Camacho follows them and senses something strange about the pedestrian speed and some body language but doesn't want to get too close and tip them off. Camacho thinks that they are driving aimlessly as if they don't know where they are going.

When they stop at the light on Bowery a Police car pulls along side them and the cops check their ride out. Jimmy almost pees his pants. Michelle covers her face with her right hand and feigns aloofness. When the light changes they continue East on Canal and the Police car turns south on Forsyth. They turn right on to Pike street and luck out. Somebody was renovating a building and there was a half-empty dumpster on the street. Camacho had stopped a half block away and cut his lights. Jimmy drove just past the front of the dumpster and Michelle leapt out and ran towards the trunk. Jimmy popped it and Michelle, seeing what was in there hesitated. Jimmy yelled out of the window, "What is taking you so long!?"

"Shut up! Shut up!" and looking about. Then Michelle tentively reached into the trunk and picked up Olga's headless and limbless torso that Charlie had shrink-wrapped and heaved it into the dumpster. Camacho shook his head. Michelle ran back to the passenger side and slammed the door shut. As soon as they turned the corner onto Madison street Camacho drove to the dumpster and retrieved the torso. He was not worried about losing them since he had attached a transmitter to the car days prior but he couldn't believe these two were this cold-blooded *and* stupid. He would follow them through the blocks and blocks of bleak public housing and retrieve the dead chick's arms, hands, legs, feet and head over the course of the next 46 minutes as the killers wound their way up the lower eastside's back streets flinging body parts.

At 3:31 Camacho, having chucked the body parts into his trunk called his employer, Roshi and made a full report. The guy didn't sound the least bit surprised. He also didn't flinch when Camacho upped his fee a by adding a zero. Turns out Camacho was the one who would be surprised when he heard what Roshi wanted him to do next.

POLICE LINE DO NOT CROSS

4:06 AM, in the heart of a tony residential area that was once the old meatpacking district. It was so cold the wind would sting your cheeks. Decades earlier workers marred the building's walls with the stench of entrails, replaced today by the smell of roasted coffee and flowers. As sirens wail in the distance something hangs from a newly placed meat hook on the awning of 817 Washington Street. A guy wearing no tech wool nearly falls out of Hogs and Heifers bar heading south. He shakes more than walks down the street belching beer flavored gusts of air. The cold is doing him some bad, merciless wrong. He whips it out to relieve himself and steam rises only to be pulled apart by the wind. He smells something, blows his nose and walks off past the thing hanging from the meat hook.

4:07 AM, a police car rolls slowly down Washington Street going south.

4:10 AM, Ben by birth, Diana by choice, maneuvers his six-foot frame down the street in a pair of stiletto pumps. Diana's metallic silver, full length coat emits a shriek each time the fabric rubs against itself but she-he don't care it washes like a dream. The mind in mid tirade shrieks, "Daniels got another thing coming if he thinks he's gonna' lay a hand on me."While the body is saying, gotta' go, gotta' go. Into the large faux Chanel shoulder bag goes a beefy forearm. Out comes a roll of toilet paper. The walk is brisk and determined. The attitude is—what's that thing hanging from a hook? Diana stops. The realization lights up Diana's cerebellum, the toilet paper is launched and she nearly takes out an eye with her Lee Press-Ons. It twists in the wind revealing more hacked flesh and sawed bone sections. Diana's eyes open wide, the scream is aborted by a coughing choke and he runs off.

4:19 AM, a cabby slams on his brakes and is transfixed by the mutilated, headless, limbless, cadaver of a Caucasian woman in her late twenties in front of the Meat Art Gallery.

4:35 AM, Cops galore. They stare at the cadaver not out of some morbid curiosity, but in amazement. Amazement at the level of sadism one human being can inflict upon another. But that doesn't last very long.

"The victim was tortured, then decapitated, had her limbs severed—looks like the assailant used some very sharp implements and shrink wrapped the torso in clear plastic before she was left on what looks like a meat hook. Approximately—I donno' early twenties...geez' what a fuckin' waste." Detective McCarthy looks up at the corpse and shakes his head before resuming his dictation into his collar mike. A few meters away his partner Detective Canabal speaks into his PDA.

NEWS AT ELEVEN OVER THE TRANSOM
"And in local news, a very disturbing and gruesome discovery. In the early hours of the morning, a headless, limbless woman's, naked torso was found shrink-wrapped and attached to a meat hook on a residential street that used to be the old meatpacking district just below 14th Street. The torso was discovered by a driver who apparently thought it was a prop or fake until closer inspection. The police were alerted immediately and an investigation is under way. In other news, the Mayor commented on the controversial shooting of the homeless man named Cheeks. Earlier today after a press conference at City Hall the Mayor...."

HAVE YOU SEEN OLGA?
Nancy, Olga's booker was frantically calling everyone she knew that knew Olga because the photographer Philippe had called her an hour ago and ripped her a new hole from the Lenox Lounge on 125th Street where he was one skinny assed model short. Bolts of blue-white lightening had shot through the FukU Agency as a B-list model was hastily dispatched and the can of whupass' was readied for Olga for delaying a Vogue shoot. The French could be so rude Nancy thought. Fuckem'—or FukU'em—people were starving in Africa and this asshole was dripping on her—oye vey! She'd take it out on Olga who had better be in the hospital already and for a good reason. She spoke-

dialed at light speed sifting through her rolodex of contacts and had just hung up with Olga's building doorman who knew nothing. The model Mafia was amping and had not dialed back—even with a tawdry excuse, so that meant it was trouble for sure. All of this meant it was up the food chain to lovers and lusters so Nancy had to dig for a number close to Brice because she didn't have his. Right. She found Erica, the ex-Ketchum girl cum-Brice Johnson fetch puppy—dial—ring...not-hing. Forward call to...

"Yeah?" says Bill.

"Who is this?" says Nancy.

"Whoz' dis'?"

"This is Nancy, Olga's agent looking for Brice. He there?"

"Sweetie. During the day we like to—you know lift weights and make like we're actually athletically inclined soe'z we can win some matches and not get mashed ugly..."

"Listen, I don't have time for this. Olga is MIA and your boy is the dart in the center of her board so spare me. All I want to know is if he knows where she is. Is that too complicated for you or do you need me to spell it out?"

"Hold on." Bill takes the phone that looks like a bent ink pen, covers it as he shouts over to B' who is skipping rope. "B'! Got one of Olga's people here wants to know if you know where she is?!"

Stopping, Brice says, "After she left my crib I went to meet her at a club but she never showed. I left and haven't heard from her."

Into the phone Bill says, "Can't help you sweetie. Pretty, pretty has not been in touch with my boy since last night, bye bye." Click.

"Oh! I hate men!" Shrieks Nancy into the air around her cluttered desk. "One day I'm going to get one and torture his ass until he makes me cum like a fucking thousand times!" says Nancy puffing on a cig and searching for another number.

SWEAT

B' was having a horrid workout cause he didn't get enough sleep and didn't want Bill to notice but knew he knew all the same.

SPEED

Shit had happened hours ago. NYPD analytic crime matching software had connected a DNA sample from the corpse with Olga's Driver's License records during a database search and found a match. The link was conclusive to a 99th percentile and Olga was pronounced dead. The NYPD contacted her father in Sweden, reached out to her roommates and employer immediately which left the obvious connections.

ELEVATOR

Detective McCarthy favored trench coats, nicotine gum, talking shit like he knew everything but was an old school, sixth-generation Irish-American, stand-up guy. He liked the dark, skanky underside and damsels so this line of work worked for him. McCarthy was forty-six, twice divorced and liked women with hairy snatches. Detective Canabal was an eight-generation Puerto Rican "give a fuck" kind of guy, thirty-seven, married, kids, feisty and badass—or so he thought like all badasses do.

"Suppose you wanna' do all the talking on this one don't you?" said Canabal to McCarthy shadow boxing.

"Listen when you get seniority, you get to be the big dog. This here is business. I know you've got a soft spot for this guy cause your kids like him but I don't give a ratfuck. I'm going in cold and all I'm asking is that you do the same."

"You know, he could take your flat white ass don't you? Don't you?"

"I'll fuck up any nigger that steps to me or macho spicks if they want to tangle."

Smiling, "Like you *super* white guy right! I know some boys on 147th street that could have your saggy white ass kissing sidewalk in two moves."

"The only punks I worry about is the fucking chinks with that martial arts shit—them I would shoot right away."

"Den' you better shoot Johnson's ass cause he is down with all that kung fu shit you dinosaur—you too stupid to even know you extinct." Half smiling.

"I'm gonna' pop one in yours if you don't stop fucking with me." Looking gruff but oozing Hostess Twinkie cream.

Straightening up. "Whatever. Whatever."

"We've got back-up down stairs and, yes I'm aware that we're going into a gym filled with fighters but if you paid attention to the marksmanship instructor at the academy then I don't have to worry about your ass and we can just…" The elevator door opens, "…Ask a few questions."

As they exit the elevator they immediately step up to the counter and latch eyes with Roberto. Flash badges and say, "We're looking for Brice Johnson and know that he is here working out." Roberto gestures with his chin and the two detectives turn and walk towards Brice.

"Mr. Johnson?"

B' stops hitting the speed bag and looks up. "Yeah?"

Bill looks up from his paper and says, "Who the fuck ar' you?"

McCarthy says, "I'm Detective McCarthy with the NYPD and this is Detective Canabal. We have a few questions for you Mr. Johnson."

"Let's see some id," says Bill.

McCarthy and Canabal show their badges to Bill masking any emotion they have. McCarthy says, "Mr. Johnson, is there a place we can talk? This won't take very long."

"Sure." Said B' looking past them towards Roberto. "We're going to use this studio alright?" and Roberto said "yeah, sure" with a wave.

A few of the guys working out in the gym watch Brice and the detectives noticing the sound of their leather soled shoes on the wood floor. When the two detectives, Brice and Bill enter the small studio McCarthy closes the door and Canabal motions that they should move to the table.

"What is this about?"

"Did you see the news this morning?"

"No. I woke up and came straight here."

"Early this morning the headless body of a young woman was found and we believe it was your girlfriend Olga Ericksson."

"Olga is dead?" B' was noticeably dumbfounded.

"We are talking to everyone close to her and we need your help with the investigation," said Canabal.

Bill chimed in with, "Is Brice a suspect?"

"Until we find the killer, everyone is a suspect."

"I'm calling your lawyer." Said Bill to B' "Don't say anything till he gets here."

B' says, "I can't believe this—this some sick joke right?" Both detectives stare at him without saying anything. "I can't—I don't believe it..."

"Lets just get through some questions..."

"I've got nothing to hide—I didn't..." only realizing the gravity of the situation.

McCarthy says, "We just have a few questions. We could talk here or we could talk at the station house, with or without your lawyer. Either way we're going to take mention of your cooperation or lack there of."

Bill whips out his phone and walks to the far end of the studio in a huff.

"Like I said, I've got nothing to hide."

"Okay," says McCarthy, "Lets begin," and he opens his PDA then stops and looks up at Brice. "You know, I'm wondering. We're trying out something new. Its a kind of—well I don't want to call it a lie detector but it kind of is and I'm thinking that if you are willing and like you said have nothing to hide it then this would go a long way towards eliminating you as a suspect in this."

"Well my lawyer would probably have a cow, but if its Olga..." and he loses his train of thought. "Anything you want."

"That's really stand up of you." Says McCarthy and he reaches into the large pocket of his trench coat and takes out a small black, metal case. "This is an Israeli made Avi, think of it as an emotion reader." McCarthy opens it and places it in front of Brice on the table. A small black rubber section inflates and a telescopic arm with an optic scanner rises and locks its gaze on Brice's right eye.

"This device will analyze your voice, rate of sweat—please place your right palm on the inflated section—the amount of adrenalin in your sweat, pulse rate and pupil dilation all in order to measure your stress level."

Bill walks over cupping the phone and is noticeably upset with B', "What are you doing?"

"It's alright Bill. I told you I've got nothing to hide. Its alright."

"I'm on hold—I don't like this."

"Alright," said McCarthy. "I'm going to start by asking you a series of baseline questions okay." B' nods. Looking at his PDA McCarthy taps on the screen that shows nine levels going from truth to false and nine levels of stress and says, "Okay. Please state your name."

"Brice Johnson"

"Your occupation?"

"Game run athlete."

"Country of citizenship?"

"US—United States."

"Do you consider your self a truthful person?"

"Yeah—yes. Yes I am."

"Do you always tell the truth?"

Grinning, "Like most moral people, I try to tell the truth as much as possible."

"Are you married or engaged?"

"No."

"Do you have a girlfriend?"

"Ye—Olga."

"Do you have a temper?"

Taking a moment. "No more so than the average guy living in this city." And McCarthy looks him in the eye.

"Have you ever struck a woman?"

"No." emphatically.

"When was the last time you saw Olga?"

"Early last night. She left my apartment and I was supposed to meet her at Club Kasbah."

"So you met there that night?"

"No. I looked for her, but didn't see her so I left thinking she'd call me if we were going to get together."

"Did you argue with her that day?"

"No."

"Have you ever hit her?"

"No." bristling.

"Do you know anyone who would want to hurt her?"

"No. I really don't know a lot of her friends. But no, nobody like that."

"Did you murder Olga Ericksson."

"No. No. Hell no."

"You have no knowledge of who mutilated her, decapitated her corpse or how her body came to be on a meat hook below 14th street and 10th Avenue?"

Bile rose in B's throat. "No."

Silence. McCarthy and Canabal looked at B'who seemed to be on the verge of spewing and they let the moment hang.

"Okay," said McCarthy closing his PDA and reaching for the Avi. "We're done. If we have anything further we will contact you. I took the liberty of beaming our contact information to your watch," rising. B' stands still in shock.

"This is really a horrible waste," says McCarthy shaking B's hand and holding it for just a little longer than he needed to. "Beautiful girl like that. Who would want to kill her, hack her up and then put it out there for the world to see?"

B' spoke in a low voice saying, "Please find him. Find him and put him some place bad. Someplace very bad."

"Thanks for your help." Says McCarthy.

"Thanks," says Canabal and they exit.

Bill walks over to B' and speaks into the phone, "Hello? Its a little late now. We don't need you." And disconnects. The two of them stand in silence until Bill says, "You think she's really dead?"

"I don't know. I hope not."

ELEVATOR

Canabal and McCarthy wait for the door to close and Canabal asks, "Howd' he do?"

"Passed with flying colors."

"Hmm. Didn't fall for your fake out with the wrong location of the body ploy."

"No, he didn't."

"But you like him for this don't you?"

"Who ever did this was a sick fuck. Don't think you just cut somebody up on a whim like sausage. This fuck had to have planned this out—putting her out there on that hook was an invitation for us to grab his ass. Somebody—not with latent tendencies but a real sociopath who enjoys hurting others is who we're looking for. Maybe this guy Brice is a sick fuck."

"Where to now?"

"Club fuckin' Kasbah. Going to check their PAL (presence awareness logs). Snatched his 40 (40 digit unique identifier) when we sat down. With a court order, Detectives could check their whereabouts of a suspect during the past week, when they took the train, streets they walked down, down to the time they sat down at their desk—that is if a savvy citizen hasn't decided to forego all tech thereby being near invisible to the man."

HOME

Jimmy was still in bed. He had been awake for hours but being restless and unsure of what to do, decided to lay there and contemplate the prior evening. It hadn't happened. She was not dead. He and Michelle did not litter the city with Olga's bodyparts—but they had. Twists of fate had knotted and redirected themselves, sweeping Jimmy up like a dust mite in a vacuum. He winced as he remembered Olga's scream and tried to extricate himself from involvement but he knew he hadn't been vocal enough. He had not been forceful enough. He should have launched himself against the door and saved Olga—Brice would have. His brother would never have let this happen. But Jimmy had. He latched onto the realization of Jimmy Johnson the loser, the fay closet cocksucker, the accessory to murder and every second that passed seemed a second closer to when the cops would bust into his bedroom and arrest him. That at least would be a relief.

Then he began again. The door of the stairwell shut behind them and she started to spit acid. Did anyone see them? Was he missing anything? It would be hours before Jimmy would rise and force himself to take a shower after sweating into the sheets and check his messages.

DREAM

Brice involuntarily turned his head from left to right trying in vain to change his perspective. Beneath his erratic eyes in a place where faint electric bursts consorted with cell, fluid and the inexplicable, Brice was viewing a horrific image. He is standing in a crowded residential Manhattan intersection wearing plain street clothes with Ronald, a childhood friend he has not seen or thought of in years. His senses are blaring that there is something unimaginably wrong. Ronald goes into a busy, corner bodega and Brice waits silently for him outside. In the distance he sees a mass of people running down the center of the street and can hear their screams of terror and multiple gunshots. It's the screams that his body felt before he heard them. The backs of men and women explode and they fall forward, skidding on the tar and bouncing the way you would expect the remains of gristle being scraped off a dinner plate and into the dustbin. A rider less horse with a torn bit is running in the same direction as the crowd knocking people over as it flees. With wide opened eyes, flaring nostrils and a disfigured face it shrieks in fright. Bullets explode along a wide arc mowing down people and mangling street light posts, car doors and building facades. A tall black figure walks down the street, the arbiter of hate and we see the violent yellow flame bursts from his automatic weapon. He turns in Brice's direction allowing a good portion of people to escape even while he continues to slaughter people. It is a man in an all black outfit showing no skin whatsoever. Across his chest is a large white skull and crossbones. Upon his head a fierce skull mask and a black, three corner, pirate's hat. Brice thinks about running but is petrified. The figure approaches. Brice seizes the effort to bend his stiff legs and purposely falls to the sidewalk when a man knocks into him. On the ground near a corpse he plays dead but cannot bring himself to close his eyes. Death's servant is nearly upon him when he turns and fires into the bodega taking out every living person. Brice had forgotten about Ronald and that made him feel more guilt than remorse. He turned and continued to walk and Brice wished that he would take him for dead and walk right by. More shots are heard and then they stop. Screams can still be heard nearby but Brice can't seem to hear the killer. A moment later and nothing. Shaking in fear, Brice vision jerks with his head as he struggles to look up. His worst fear was that of staring into the smoking barrel of the killer's gun. Instead he sees the killer, his weapon pointed down at his side staring at him without a hint of menace. A moment passes and the figure slowly raises his free hand and takes off his hat letting it drop to the sidewalk. He then reaches behind his head and pulls off the skull mask and Brice gasps for air. The calm, emotionless face of the killer is his own.

DEREK
365 WEST 147TH STREET

Derek's mother had warned him about Angeline before they wed. Then she protested loudly when the couple departed the on Air Jamaica flight 606 on a hot gray afternoon. His mother sold tamarind balls and rum punch to tourist as they arrived at the airport everyday and promised to lash him when he returned penniless and alone without Angeline pronounced like "Angelina—a" said like a mocking rude answer to a ridiculous question. Derek thought about all this as he read the note she left him on the cheap Rite'on flat screen in his hand. When he came home from a long night of throwing garbage into the back of a truck, he figured she was out with her friends skimming through the latest magazine and popping gum as she steadied herself on her friend's springy old bed. And they'd be cussing men. And they'd be wanting to sex up all the black male models and actors. And Angeline would scratch her crotch every few minutes making a scraping sound with her fingernails against polyester. And her skin would produce a fresh patina of oily sweat to mix with her knock-off perfume. But it was his mother's voice he heard and the flailing of her arms in the blue Caribbean sky as her voice whaled like a clarinet, "Yean—n coming back ta' me wit' no goodfo' noting' jamette' hoe' no! I'z fool ya' foolin' ya' self tink she gon' be minding you—she minding she self, an' she fat ass wat' shaking, she pushin' up for men eyes no..!" And the rest of Derek's life was on mute. He could smell the Vicks Vapor Rub his mother applied daily to fend off chills. Instead of hating Angeline for leaving with all his money and every item of value he hated his mother for being right. Only it was not a red-hot hate. It was a dull, numb loathing. He was not the emotional type but he knew he should be angry with Angeline. He was a strong, serious, quiet type and he didn't even stop to think of tracking her down or making any calls to look for her. She had always been independent and brash and he knew he would not see or hear from her unless she willed it. She had commented countless times that he could be confused with a mute because of the slow and silent way he had about getting ready for either of his two jobs, for bed or even to go out to the store. That he infuriated her was a given. That he saw the futility in attempting to change was the only evidence of cognition. He gently put the flat screen on the counter and walked into the bathroom. Turning on the faucet brown water shot out and he waited for the hot water to run clear. He hadn't sparred with Brice for over a month and didn't want to be late for work.

DAMNIT'
THE PENTHOUSE OF MoMA'S TOWER

The residue of that faded dream had had effect. Brice didn't' t like feeling afraid and the thought of being helpless made him angry. The performance artist impersonating him leapt into his consciousness and made him furious. The fact Olga was dead and everyone thought he did it was unreal.

Wired for Chaos

Was he starting to fall in love with her or was he feeling guilty because he never had? He had so much money and celebrity privilege, yet things and people could buzz around him and he was helpless to swat them. His compulsive train of thought had started down a bitter path and he chose not to divert it. The idiots at Sony with their plans for him, their new rules and two-faced dealings with him. Worried glances from acquaintances at parties, stiff biting treatment from the media but wait. Brice's frown was a flinch away from anger.

"Your car is here," said Home to Brice.

365 WEST 147TH STREET

Derek stepped out of the rotting tenement in a daze. He knew that to the world he would appear to be in the moment but his mind was actually a fetid pool instead of a coursing stream. His legs worked on automatic he thought negotiating the subway steps with ease. His gym bag was a welcomed alternative to his thick work gloves and aluminum lunch box. The number one train was pulling in and he hoped to get a seat, not because he was tired, but because it was simply the only solace an up-towner could muster on the trip south past so many stops. Having found a seat Derek instinctively takes an open leg stance only to close his legs quickly a second later. It's cool he thought. He hadn't worn a hole in the crotch of these khakis, yet.

BRICE

Inside the limo Brice's inner-voice is running along at a few notches below rage. That asshole Yoshi in Japan, the performance artist, the media, the murder, the murder, the murder, the cops treating him like some fucking criminal. But the image of Olga's torso on a hook was the thing that kept setting him off. It was like an electric arc strobing in his consciousness and they thought he did it. Did they really think him a monster? He knew he was capable of violence, but never outside of the game and while he had a temper there hadn't been any…and his mind wandered as he doubted himself and the doubt festered. What brought him back was his anger. His confidence. It would all work out. His lawyers were on the case, he had Sony's full support and his publicist was putting a positive spin on his every waking moment. He remembered the first time he saw her wearing that flowing silver evening dress and how he had taken her away from her date. He remembered that while they were sipping champagne on the balcony of Metropolitan Museum that she touched the center of his chest with the side of her hand and it felt good. He could feel the ghost of her touch now but it was disembodied and fleeting.

It wasn't good that he was alone in the car. It wasn't good that the car's interior was sound proof. He reached for the power button to the stereo and grabbed a bottle of rum instead. He hurls it at the window and it breaks spilling over the leather trim and tan carpet as thin yellow columns appear, vibrate then slowly fade across his retina. Hunched over, his leg spread and his elbows resting on his knees he tries to keep his head from expanding.

"Is everything all right Mr. Johnson?" says the driver over the intercom.

After kneading his fingers into his forehead he looks up and says, "No. Everything is not all right." He pinched the pressure point at the bridge of his nose hard and long and tried to bring his heart rate down.

SUBWAY

On the number one train at 50th Street Derek is thinking about the last time he had sex with Angeline. He can remember doing all the things she liked, but he wondered if she had liked it. Just then a short fat man in a trench coat with an enormous bag bounced past several people on his way to the door and stepped on Derek's foot. The man's cheap brown shoes had mashed his toes with great force and the pain has shot right up his leg in an instant. The man had not stopped to acknowledge him and the doors closed quickly behind him. If the man had still been on the train Derek would have made it plain by his look that he expected a show of remorse. But the bastard was gone and the something that was anger braided with taut muscles flipped on inside him. Angeline would not recognize her Derek now.

CHELSEA PIERS

The Chelsea Piers Sports facility was rapidly becoming a dump. Years of wear and tear had caused many health zealots to leave it for cleaner more expensive digs at the center of the city. But Brice could rent out an entire gym and not disrupt anyone slipping in and out of a side door unannounced.

Before the car door opens entirely Erica, his assistant begins talking.

"Sorry I'm late B'. I thought I'd just get here and catch up." she says smiling at him.

"Its all right." he mumbled and allowed her ensuing chatter to wash over him. Leroy was holding the stairway door open for them and he longed for the calm of the gym.

Reading from her slick PDA Emily kicks into high gear, "Now we've got the Nike spot scheduled to shoot tomorrow at Silvercup with an 8:00 am call time and they're telling me that it'll be a straight in and out one day shoot. I told that guy Gary that you're booked the rest of the week so they better get a director who's got his shit together. Rodney called about the contracts—he'll be there at 7:30 with the changes for you to initial. Mort wants to send over your returns for this quarter for you to sign and says thanks for the anniversary present—I sent them a porcelain planter from you, from Tiffany's, knew Sherri 'uld go crazy for that. Your vmail is the same. You've got the support of the majority of fans. Overwhelmingly—and I mean by like a five to one margin—I mean ratio you didn't do it. They're like no way man! A loony here and there. The press is a bore but consistent. All the networks want time. No—o comment. Jerry over at Langston found you this gorgeous black model to spokesperson for you..." Brice shakes his head. "Okay nix the gorgeous we'll get an average Jane like yesterday—they've got someone in house, real trustworthy, homey, big thighs, trustworthy face—Lisa she'll do. I'm on it. The studio says the picture is on hold till the heat cools off from this investigation but they're a positive go. I really got a good vibe from talking to Jeff—they're taking the time to punch up the script and it's still a cockfight who'll direct. Next week we've—e got to meet with the real estate agent. He's using that pressure trick about everyone wanting that house..."

"After this whole thing is ..."

"Over. Got it—got it."

The three walk through the men's locker room and Erica is too busy entering things into her PDA to care.

OUTSIDE

As Derek crossed 10th Avenue he could still feel his toes throbbing making him grab the vinyl handles of his gym bag so tight that he would have crushed them if they were walnuts. This cabby decides to stop at the last minute within a meter of Derek who has made predatory eye contact with the cabby. Too bad thought Derek. He was hoping the fender would have bumped him. He would have relished any excuse to drag that guy out through the window and pummel him.

ENTRANCE TO LOCKER ROOM

When Brice enters rooms most times he couldn't be bothered to scan the faces because he knew they would all come to him. And find him they did. They came over to say good morning, to pat him on the back or smile hello as he stretched. It was a kick to get people smiling when you hadn't done anything. He usually nodded and eked out a grin but today was different. He'd changed into his workout clothes and laced up his boxing shoes when he caught a himself looking at his reflection in the mirror. He was drawing a blank. Rich was lacing up his boxing gloves and something seemed odd until he noticed that he was wearing a black unitard and remembered that morning's dream. He'd have to tell his shrink. He'd have to know what it was about.

RECEPTION

Emily, the perky morning desk person was new. She was studying to be a physical therapist and her parents were comfortably living off high yield dividends. This guy Derek looked real mean, at 10:32 AM that evening she'd tell her Chester that Derek was a dull brute with a mean face, who wasn't a member and couldn't be found on the special event list because, Rob, her boss had the list on the board in his hand and he was brown nosing it with Brice's people. So Derek had to wait until Rob answered his page, but Rob was taking his time, too afraid to a) break off a conversation with Brice's trainer where he got to let them know that he had great training and kept up on the latest everything, b) miss an opportunity to—he didn't know, talk to Brice and c) to get any dirt on Brice's involvement in Olga's murder. As far as he was concerned it was fifty-fifty that Brice did the grizzly deed, but he'd know for sure once he got a good, up-close look at him. Shit he thought when Emily paged him a second time. Rob pried himself away from Bill, walked to the far end of the room and picked up the house phone cursing himself for not remembering to grab his headset earlier as he dialed the front desk.

Erica approaches Bill, the two can barely mask their dislike for each other. "Bill, you tell B' about the reporters?"

"No."

"I asked you to do that one little thing for me."

"Well you got a ride in with him. Why didn't you..?"

"I didn't ride in. I came here straight."

"Well?"

"Well. He takes this kind of news better from you than me that's why."

"Naaw—w uh-uh. That inter-personal communication stuff is in your job description. Not mine."

Just then her calves tightened as she shifted her weight onto the balls of her feet while pulling her PDA close to her right breast. Her expression said, "Fuck you very much. I won't forget this asshole." She looked him dead in the eyes, turned and walked off. Bill smiled and shook his head saying to himself, "He's going to be pissed." Erica puts on her game face as she approaches Brice and has to gently push someone aside to get to him. "Hey B' listen, I should have told you this before but there are some photographers here and the spin doctors thought it would be in your best interest..."

"It's cool. I expected it."

Surprised, Erica mouths a silent "Oh" and her phone rings.

"Just run interference for me okay?"

"Cool. Sure." to Brice, "Hello?" answering the phone. "Mushi mushi, Sammy K! How are you! No. No. This is a good time. We're at the gym and the B'man is about to go a few rounds. Gimme' some good news. Oh really? Uh-uh, uh-uh. Yeah. Great. Great. Hold on," talking to Brice, " Jerry says that sales of your game pack are going through the roof in Japan. Says they're selling it out of the box in Tokyo at Virgin. Yeah. Yeah. He's great. I know. I will. Yeah. I sent you everything I had and you'll get with Sony on—right. Right. Great. Okay. Domo arigato baby." They had all ready begun to make their way to the gym when Erica had hung up. "Just think B', right now thousands of Japanese kids are kicking butt as you and your bank iz' getting thicker." He can't help but smile and for a moment everything about the murder evaporates.

As they approach the octagon shaped ring, the reporters seeing their prey jump to their feet and pounce. In a far corner near a mirror Derek warms up with a leather jump rope. Erica takes the point in front of Bill and Brice.

The reporters aim their cameras and shout questions one on top the other, "Brice, how is your defense shaping up? Is it true that you were the last person to see Olga on the night of her murder? Did the two of you argue before she left your building or at the club? Is it true that Sony is about to cut you...?"

Erica, who has been trying to get a word in shouts at no one in particular and pushes a reporter aside. The whirring of the jump rope peaks above the reporter's din whenever they pause to let Erica speak. "We are not answering any questions concerning the case. Period. As to whether or not Sony is concerned for Brice's well being, yes they are very concerned but their support has been and still is unwavering. There is not even a hint of discomfort from them and we are sure—we are sure, that when the killer is found that the world will realize that Brice Johnson is innocent." While much of this is being said, the trainers have slipped protective headgear and shin guards on Brice.

A reporter yells, "Brice, do you have anything to add?"

Brice, looking perfectly relaxed looks up and says, "I hope they let me pull the switch on the guy that killed her."

"But eyewitnesses…"

Erica cuts him off, "But nothing. Brice has no comment. Now you're welcome to ask questions about the sport and stay for the sparring but questions concerning the case will not be answered at this time." They quickly spread around the perimeter of the octagon as Brice enters with the ease of a practiced routine. To the side Rob watches Brice and nods. Derek has broken a sweat and enters alone walking to the other side of the ring. A trainer approaches him with a pair of gloves, shin guards, headgear and a mouthpiece. Brice was calm, almost lethargic, there was something relaxing about the gym. He was self-conscious because his audience was live instead of digital and he had to tame his enthusiasm and his eagerness to please them. He remembers a conversation he had with his analyst a year ago. "When I was a kid I wanted my step-Dad to jack in and see me so bad, but I couldn't ask him. I shouldn't have had to. I was good and I wanted to show him I was good at something. But he wasn't interested. Never open myself up like that again. Never. Never." Brice's eyes refocus on the now and he turns to look at Derek for the first time. Funny. Derek usually came over to say hello but he seemed all tensed up today. Derek had his eyes locked on Brice before he turned around and he stood there flatfooted and inert.

Bill popped into Brice's immediate space and popped a mouthpiece in. "All right, I want you to work on your blocking today. If Derek has been doing his homework he's going to come at you like Tanaka and I want you to block his combinations. Don't worry about scoring early on and lets put on a good show for the cameras all right? All right." Turning to Derek, "Ready Derek!?" Derek smashes his gloves together and starts to circle Brice. By the time the gate closes behind him the two have completed a half circle near the center of the octagon. Brice is limber and twists his neck in several directions then turns to meet Derek's advance. Derek comes at him not like Tanaka poised to kick but like a bull-neck middleweight prizefighter with a score to settle. Brice, who is notoriously slow to start and certainly not a morning person throws up a half-hearted kick. Derek deflects the kick with a quick firm block that screams insult and sends a right cross at Brice's head with full force. Brice, instinctively jerks his head backwards but not in time enough to completely avoid the punch. With a blow to the chin, Brice staggers backwards and puts up his left arm. Derek quickly turns on his heel and delivers a solid roundhouse kick to Brice's mid-section that staggers him. Hunched over Brice bites hard into his mouthpiece and knows that he should have known better.

"Derek is really on it today." says Bill to no one in particular but a trainer next to him says, "Waking Brice up alright," smiling.

As Derek advances Brice backs up. He blocks one kick with his forearms then two others all while stepping backwards. Derek is all business now and comes in close behind a series of combinations. Left, right, left, dodge, kick, block and Brice is way on the defensive. A right knocks Brice's mouthpiece out and sends him to the mat like a halibut on newsprint.

"Okay! Okay. Hold up now." says Bill as the trainers enter the ring heading for the mouthpiece. "This is called a workout Mr. Johnson. Try blocking some blows will ya'."The photographers go wild and the flashes go off in rapid succession. Brice straightens up and in biting his mouthpiece his inner voice says, "That hurt. Good."

The photographers pause with their fingers on buttons waiting for the next great shot. Brice watches them watching him and steps up to the occasion. As fast as they came on to the mat they retreat with Bill the last to leave. As he climbs between the ropes he looks at them and says, "Back it up. Back it up fellas."

Brice motions, "Come on," to Derek. Brice approaches and fakes a kick. Derek switches styles to a closer stance and comes at Brice with a telegraphed kick that he avoids. Brice pivots shifting his weight and backhands Derek on the back of the head. Derek turns quickly and kicks in a sweeping motion just missing Brice's shins. As Brice lands he finds that Derek has set him up for a high angled groin punch. Brice takes the weight of the blow but manages to deliver a left, right combination that knocks Derek backwards. The two give each other breathing room and Brice smirks as if to say, "Is that the best you've got."The two of them get up close and personal, exchanging kicks and punches. Although Derek is the stronger of the two Brice has a longer reach and is much faster. Brice switches to Kenpo and lights Derek up with a flurry of chops to his chin forcing him to take two steps backwards. He follows up with a two-staged kick to Derek's mid-section only to have Derek lunge forward with a primal stab at his chest. The hit pushes Brice back and Derek takes three steps forward and replays the same flurry of chops that Brice used on him a moment ago. B' taking that as a slight, does what every one that day would remember as "the hunch." Bill knew what the hunch meant, Brice was all business now. B', whirled around and one-two's Derek on the side of the face. Without stopping he connects two more times before Derek can take a step backwards and put his hands up. Derek charges Brice and he uses a Akido move to avoid him. Derek, pissed with the effect he is having, spits charges and begins to throw a flurry of blows and kicks at Brice. Brice backs up and is pushed against the ropes.

Abruptly, Derek moves back and allows B' to recover, plainly wanting to take his time and prove his superiority to the crowd. B' hears one of the photographers say, "Kill him! Kill him!" The two circle each other like male Siamese fighting fish and Brice waits for Derek to make the first move. As soon as Brice saw that Derek was going for a right cross he decided to swing his shoulder away and counter with a left, only Derek was aiming for and connected with Brice's shoulder which was dislocated only last month. Brice winces in pain and drops to his knees and Derek kicks him in the face with the top of his foot. Stepping back to get the sweat out of his eyes, Derek allows Brice to get to his feet and Brice gives himself a lot of breathing space. Certain that his shoulder is intact, Brice shakes off the pain as his syn' shoots yellow daggers at his shoulder and chest. He dancing on his toes in an attempt to thwart the pain, he gives the appearance of shaking it off. The two square off and Brice lets Derek get in close. Derek resorts to freestyle boxing and Brice ducks every swing connecting with a shot after each miss. When Derek opens himself up Brice steps in and hits him six times on both sides of his already flat nose. Brice backs up and touches his thumb to his nose waiting for Derek to make his next move. Derek smiles and Brice in enraged. Brice moves in but his kicks are deflected one after the other. As soon as Brice has both feet on the mat Derek punches Brice's bad shoulder. B' snaps and acts on reflex and anger. Though wincing in pain as the veins in his neck bulge, he manages to punch Derek in his windpipe sending him to his knees. Derek's head jerks after B' has wound up a kick that catches Derek's neck in the same area he just punched. Derek falls face down on the mat and the trainers followed by the photographers seem to fly across the mat from the gate.

Bill immediately applies a Sontron to Brice's shoulder to soothe the pain. "God fuckin' damn it Brice! Playing for the fucking cameras again—you don't…"

Brice says, "Ah save it for Derek man. He's the one that stepped to me."

"So you're going to tell me that that's worth getting hurt for?! Huh?!"
"Bill! Bill!" says one of the trainers.
"Yeah, yeah!"
"It's Derek. His neck is broken. I think he's dead."
Someone yells, "Get an ambulance! Get an ambulance!"

The photographers run from Brice to Derek, stepping on each other like hungry piglets on a tit. Rob, the gym manager nods his expression saying, "Yep, he did it. He killed that pretty girl and stuck her on a hook all right."

The cops showed up before the ambulance and when the ambulance showed up it was too late. B' was showered and dressed and moving slowly, but herded and directed by Bill and the boys. He sat in the locker room staring at his shoes and saw the NYPD enter like navy henchmen. Rodney had dispatched a nameless lawyer with tight speed and the guy seemed to unfurl in the space between the door and in front of B'—completely obscuring the cops like an apparition. The guy's name was Stanford and he took control from the get. They had cuffs on B' and suddenly they were removed. Stanford was an Italian-American guy with short hair, wearing an impeccable suit and commanding the cops without stroking their fur the wrong way. Their attention was on him and

Wired for Chaos

all B' knew was, the guy was tops. The dance he did didn't register to B' cause he was gone, somewhere else. "My client has never been…I can assure you that…the sparing partner was well aware of…" B' was in a trance and only heard snippets of what he said. If he could have scoped this guy's rap—masterful form, then he would learn something. Stanford was as good at what he did, as was B' and the hope rushed up B's nostrils like clean, pure o-x-y-gen transporting him. B' heard a lot of okays from the cops and then tuned out. He was one with the bench and rose when they told him. Then he sleepwalked home.

AND….
The drip from the ceiling tile dropped like syrup.
"His neck is broken! I think he's dead! Get an ambulance!"
"Fuckin' Derek" said Brice.

The ceiling amassed legions of fast moving drops of water from nearby tiles and built itself into tiny missiles. Each time a drop connected with Brice's shoulder or thighs it made a slapping sound, then discorporated upwards like mini-fireworks. The right side of B's face where Derek had clocked him with such force was swollen and it throbbed. Through the steamy glass Brice could see a wall of brightly colored readouts. Home had arranged real-time video, of everyone in his house, what they were saying over the v-phone and to each other and was recording everything. The speaker in the steam room played a recording of a summer thundershower. From his point of view the shapes on the monitor grew, condensed, changed shape and reconfigured into an almost lava lamp reality. They sat in front of the Holo-V with six images of different newscasters either showing footage of the deadly sparing and the guys couldn't stop talking about it. He saw a newscaster mouth the words, "…Beat him to death in a merciless show of rage and feral rage…" Brice boiled with anger. He didn't mean for it to happen—that was the chance everyone took when they mixed it up. "Would you be vilifying Derek if he had killed me?! Huh?! Huh?! You fuckin' hacks!" Then the images of Olga prancing down fashion runways in Paris and Rome overlapped talking heads that linked her brutal murder with Brice's temper. He seethed but acknowledged the logic in their thoughts and hopelessness struck him like a crowbar.

B' hadn't asked Home for the display but since he routinely recorded nearly everything and Brice had not said, "No, I don't want it up." Home decided to display his handiwork. From the projection wall, Home's all seeing iris watches Brice without his knowledge. His logic algorithm was cooking at light speed, like time lapsed footage of a growing tree limb in many different directions. Home was monitoring Brice's heart rate, his blood pressure, body temperature, digestion and more. He was mapping B's posture and every movement and comparing it to the latest behavioral table from an institute in the Swiss Alps in an attempt to decipher what B' was feeling. Home would then access the Institute of Automatic Face & Gesture Recognition archives regarding the appropriate responses to Brice's malady, whim or inclination. And of course, Home had digested all the newspapers originating in the city and absorbed all newscasts for the day. Thus far, everything he had accessed told him to say nothing.

Brice knew that all he had to do was say the words, "Hotter. Cooler. Off." Or longer involved commands at a barely audible level and Home would follow it to the letter, yet he had no idea that Home's gaze was quite so omniscient.

Brice would have been happy to contemplate the shape and sound of water hitting his body instead of the events of that day. He could not meditate. Although B' was seated in the lotus position, Home could see his muscles tense in a recognizable pattern. In B's mind each punch, kick, combination, block and move ran like a point-of-view highlights reel of the fight with Derek. His face twitched repeatedly as the memories of the fight with Derek ping-ponged inside his head, mixing his rage. That morning had been like a slow, lazy copy of a typical morning with no stress, no fires to put out, nothing but his usual routine—only shadows of Olga in his thoughts. And then that first blow from Derek connected. Muscle memory was miraculous thing in well-conditioned athletes and the same ease with which he deployed his moves allowed him to physically replay the fight. "What the fuck was up with Derek?" thought B' to himself.

"People are going to say that I should have pulled back—I should have stopped the fight—fuck that!!! He came at me! Fucking pissed me off! Fuck was he thinking!?—I didn't kill Olga!!!"

Images began to cascade. The ambulance guys. The faces of his guys staring at him. His lawyer, appearing out of nowhere and popping into his field of vision like a hand-puppet. The fat detective with blackheads on his nose and bad breath. The stares. The silence. Brice's space-time continuum slowed and stretched like taffy in the hands of a child.

Replaying what his coach said right after it all happened, "It's the chance you take when you step into the ring. Nobody's fault," and the sound of another trainer saying, "'It's Derek. His neck is broken. I think he's dead. Get an ambulance! Get an ambulance! I think he's dead. Get an ambulance! Get an ambulance! Get an ambulance!'" B' sits there replaying the memories of the last kick that undoubtedly killed Derek. It was an instinctual kick. No malice—rage maybe, the result of hours and hours of training. Beat the crap out of his opponent. Didn't mean to kill Derek, he knew that he was trying to convince himself that he didn't mean it, that it was an accident. But it wasn't. It was a culmination of training, strength and fierce determination. He regretted it but deep inside, at the back of his mind was the reporter's voice—a shout reduced to a whisper, "Kill him, kill him, kill him." A message plain, clear and audible where the tens of thousands of cheering fans sounding like a hoard of bees, communicating communal blood lust. The whisper twirled a new message, "Hey Killer. Now you really are a killer. Now they will fear you," And it didn't quite disturb him.

Wired for Chaos

Home lowers the temperature in the cube and the faint sound of water dripping down the drain becomes audible.

"Fuck em'. Fuck everybody."

LIVE AT FIVE

"And in a startling change of events in the Cheeks case, Tina the attorney representing the twelve year old boy issued a statement that it was in fact Ramon Fuentes the self-proclaimed witness who shot and killed the sleeping homeless man the city has come to know as retired jazz musician Carl "Cheeks" Lewis in Hells Kitchen last week."

It is 7:00 AM and Brice seated in front of his Holo-V. "By his client's account of the event, Fuentes evidently snatched the gun from the youth and mistakenly fired hitting Cheeks. Fuentes then placed the gun back into the hands of the twelve year old and waited for the police."

TWISTED HOPES AND CROOKED DREAMS

His pee might actually have burned his urethra if it had been a few degrees hotter. Glad to be seated as he emptied his bladder for the first time that day, Niemöller remembered the large glass of water he drank just before bed last night and raised an eyebrow. He picked up a slim, electric, data-board about the size of a 20th century magazine and turned on the news. As the file was loading the last article he read flashed across the screen. It was a celebrity shot of Brice Johnson and the ravishing supermodel Olga that N' was so taken with that he fertilized his daydreams of licking the near invisible blonde hairs on her earlobe with the notion of humiliating Brice InSpace—his head held in a vise grip between N's combat boot and the pavement. When his right thumb touched the lower corner of the screen, virtual pages flipped by with various news stories one of which had a headline that read, "Brice Johnson kills sparing partner." N' reads the article intently. His thoughts unfocused as he caught sight of an ad with a fallen tree. The sight of the dried rotting wood made him pause and think of unfettered sunlight, segued into a thought of a mosquito bite. His mind accessed an old memory. The itch of a mosquito bite on his calf and the vicious sun burning the back of his neck.

It is his mother's friend's farmhouse in upstate New York, he is fourteen and he is bored with the grown-ups and their grown-up chit-chat—especially with that sleaze-shit Murray Costa, rambling on as all self-proclaimed experts do, like a badly paraphrased TIME Magazine article. Every word that Murray belched his mother lapped up like the remains of homemade chocolate frosting, causing the mortified Niemöller to excuse himself and take a sojourn away from them and the air conditioner. He decided to avoid the field completely and its insect wildlife and sought refuge in the large, old shed. It was a machine mausoleum. Every manner of outdated, wrought iron, space waster was heaped one on top the other. There was no reason to the madness. Printing presses were balanced on top of typeface rollers, on top of industrial embosses, on top of things so old and dark they seemed to fuse together in the shadows. It all struck him as stupid, then remembering that Murray had bought and hoarded them for sale only to ignore them. He thought it bizarre. Yes bizarre. A moment later he thought he could hear his new Casio PDA, wrist phone screamed in shock and he thought it bizarre, pathetic and funny. Things lived in this shed, or at least passed through it, since there were little footprints in the dust everywhere. Something darted through a shadow at the corner of his eye. Ahh——h, the cat. Mitts. Murray's black and white ball of fur probably used the shed to hunt field mice and N' thought it would make a cool mid-level room in Doom 2100, only they'd have to loose some of this garbage. Mitts was carrying her kittens somewhere one by one and N' was bored with the shed, upstate New York, Murray and his humiliating mother. What he wouldn't give for kill-run now in *Spleen* with some geek from across the pond. He sighed big time and walked into the blinding sun. A breeze swayed the sycamore straight ahead and the motion caught his eye. Then the smallest audible meow made him look to his right. Against the side of the shed one of Mitt's kittens was trying to take a sip of water out of a barrel filled with rainwater. The kitten, stretching from the windowsill of the shed could almost reach the water. Its tentative manner was evaporating because it was hot and thirsty. Then, reaching with outstretched claws it leaned and stretched just touching the lip of the barrel. As its head dipped and its rear end followed, the kitten, slapped onto the top of the barrel while meowing. With some effort and help from its hind legs it managed to climb up onto the lip of the barrel only to fall in a moment later. N' had watched it with great interest but the fact that he had to see the tiny water-logged creature thrash about made him step closer in delight. Its meowing became louder and sounded like a tiny scream. N' thought the thing would climb out and wanted to see it struggle through it. Instead it pawed at the inner-lip of the barrel, unable to grab onto the wood due to the slick, green fungus lining the lip. Out of the corner of his eye he could see Mitts jump up on the windowsill and N' quickly slammed the window shut. Mitts recoiled but immediately spied her kitten in the barrel and let out a frightened meow. Turning, Mitts jumped to the ground and headed for the barn door. N', sensing that she was going to run out, ran to the door and slammed it shut. Mitts, stopped cold in her tracks pulled her head back, turned and jumped up on a crate and onto the sill again. N' had already returned to the window and was waiting for her. The expression on his face was devoid of emotion as he gazed at the drowned kitten. Mitts pawed at the windowpane with both front paws making a slight tapping sound with her claws. Finally, she stopped and stared at her kitten, her eyes immobile and unflinching. N' also stared at the kitten and he put effort into the notion of remembering the image. N' looked at Mitts again and the two met eye to eye. N' grinned. At that moment he felt evil and the feeling spread through his bloodstream like a welcomed virus and was whole. He had completely forgotten about the mosquito bite.

Just then, N' straightened up. He had a revelation. Yesterday, he had found out that it was Jimmy Johnson using someone else's deck that had breached his system's firewall. He would exact revenge. The dealer was a nobody who had dropped out of sight, but he would deal with Jimmy and his loathsome brother Brice—killer Brice, arrogant loathsome Brice and give them equal justice. He would ruin each of them then watch them implode. Jimmy would be first and he would do to him what all hackers feared, he would attack his reputation. N' leaned the magazine board up against the wall, wiped himself, stood and flushed the toilet. He had three vmail to send, the last of which would be addressed to Ton.

WORKOUT

Brice steps off the treadmill and prepares to hone his combat skills. Walking over several iron weight plates, a bench and workout mats, his voice activates the massively parallel third generation computer as he towels off. Within a half-second a small, green, rectangular laser grid appears over his mouth. The grid is part of a voice recognition system that is continuously projected onto his lips by any one of 18 scanners positioned around the room so his commands can be "lip read." Eight flat screens of varying size, hang from the distressed brick walls and equipment, displaying porno scenes superimposed over constantly morphing fractals. Standing eight meters tall is Brice's custom built, steel blue, armor plated DojoMantis™, a multi-arm, sparing partner. He tells the computer to run Tanaka's past three combat face-offs, current VR rankings and his messages. Three of the screens display different face-offs, one the ranking and the last four quickly fill up with vmail and phone messages, 1,578 and 16 respectively. Brice has been ranked number one for 17 months and grins when he looks at the stats. Tanaka is number three.

B' studies a life-size holo of Tanaka looking for weaknesses and finds none. He spars against him in traditional Japanese InSpace dojo. He hears Bill's voice repeat "Go for the liver, heart, kidneys and temple. The areas that will send him down if you clock him at the right angle and with enough force, the temple—no! Harder—hit him harder and faster. Stop telegraphing your blows!"

He studies Tanaka's wins on tape, running each one several times memorizing the subtleties of his moves. Brice asks the computer to index Tanaka's strikes and blocks looking for combinations he relies on the most. High speed replays of his motions marked by neon lines play and replay several times until the computer finds three separate tactics used by Tanaka and one reflexive strike that never seem to fail.

Next, B' enters the ring where a new sparing partner he has not met awaits him. The guy is big and muscular but B' can sniff a weariness about him. He's got the guy spooked. B' bounces on the balls of his feet and turns his right side towards the fighter, his arms low relaxed but ready.

BUSINESS AS USUAL: SILVERCUP STUDIOS, LONG ISLAND CITY

The day washes over him as his handlers usher B' from place to place. B' has just completed a commercial for some Nike athletic apparel and walks with Erica to another studio where a photographer awaits them. He has to be photographed for the cover of a new game that Sony has licensed to a developer. Walking into a shoddy little restroom he changes into a Nike branded Soji suit, while Erica rattles off the itinerary for the rest of the day through the door. Although he is hard on her from time to time, she is a little dynamo who only took shit from him and kept his business on track. He made a mental not to take her aside and thank her, for all her work—maybe snake her something from Tiffany's and surprise her but the thought of being real— or real and nice made him wince inside.

She had been shielding him from small talk with everyone. She would not let him stand still long enough to have anyone ask him any questions. Good handling by his account. Everywhere he went Leroy was his shadow getting between him and whomever, moving, constantly moving causing B' to feel callow and empty, like some Mexican papier-mâché skeletons on one of their Day of the Dead holidays.

He slept-walked through the photo shoot, but didn't care. It was off to lunch with Rodney at a Sushi restaurant in TriBeCa owned by the son of some dead actor. Erica was wise not to talk in the car. B' contemplated the window button on the door and couldn't think of much else. He liked its shape.

His *stare through, model's disinterested way of seeing* in the bustling restaurant, meant that he would engage no one while being dissected by dozens of eyes. Sinking into the banquette and becoming one with its obscuring height felt good. He ordered saké and was aware of his trance-like movements. Stanford was there and animated like an adult cartoon on too many café lattés. Talk of no charges being placed actually did not come as a surprise to B'. He would sign a check to Derek's wife Angeline, in return for her dropping any notion of a civil suit and she would be happy-happy. B' felt generous and would gladly add another zero to Stanford's paycheck.

Rodney chimed in with, "Till the fight—just rest, lay low, workout in private and rest," and B' gave him a halfway fool glance. B' kept seeing Derek's face on their heads and wanted to hit out at them. He had to suppress the thought-reflex. He thought about snapping Rodney's neck with a single blow, *BAPP!* And these thoughts continued but he tried to stop it. He had this nagging, violent impulse to drive a handful of chopsticks into Rodney's left eye as if in so doing so he could quell some monstrous urge within him. But he didn't. He had nothing against Rodney it was just an impulse. But he held it at bay and was happy a moment later that he hadn't raised a hand.

"Waiter," said B'. "More sake please—for everyone this time."

I GOT YOUR SONY RIGHT HERE!
CHELSEA PIERS, NEW YORK CITY

Brice sits alone in the dark locker room wearing nothing but a jock strap and a black silk meditation hood over his head yet cannot relax. He is restless. Although his pre-game routine consisted of meditation, viewing game footage, chiropractic adjustment and advice from his trainer he was succumbing to his obsessive inner voice. Taking off the hood he looks around the unlit locker room and twists his head popping his neck. Throwing the hood on the table next to him he flexes his muscles and stares at his reflection in a mirror. "And how does that make you feel?" asked his analyst several months ago. "Sometimes I feel, I feel like there's this wild animal in me. I'm this big rabid dog-thing barking and growling at the top of my lungs."

"What's upset you?"

"I don't know. It's not like some dream. It's — it's just how I feel. And I know what you're going to say. You're going to say that I'm projecting or second-guessing what I think everyone else's view of me is. But that's not right. It's how I feel. And I know you're going to ask me when I started feeling that way but I don't remember cause it doesn't matter. All I know is, it's like it feels—accurate some how. Like when I think about it I can feel the damp gray stone walls and earth of this den I'm in and I'm pulling against this link chain connected to my collar that's bolted to the ground."

"Who is holding you captive?"

"I knew you'd ask me that shit. Nobody. Nobody but me. I yank the shit outta' that chain trying to break free knowing that it is the only thing holding me back. I've got this urge—more than an urge, it's like some primal fever to just go berserk, letting lose all over somebody like a twister in a knife factory. But I haven't yet. I'm still in control."

"And how does that make you feel?"

Brice's face shows his exasperation with the question. "Feel? Well I tell you, I've got a temper and sometimes I think I could really hurt somebody. Hurt them to the point where—where I'd be sorry." A beat. "The sensation, I'm urging the sensation of lashing out—just going off cause it must be liberating. And nothing would matter—not the outcome, nothing. I don't know. I know I just contradicted myself. Maybe I'd feel relieved. I know the chain is all that keeps me in check and it can't be that strong. Maybe I'm actually the chain. Or maybe the chain is part of me. Or fuck Freud. Maybe sometimes a chain is just a chain." Speaking aloud, "I'm going to kick Tanaka all up in his ass today."

"Screen on. Play." A second later an image of Brice's game highlights appears on the large display. He had a tech capture and generate this footage from several angles over the course of his best fights and splice them together. He watches intently, noting things he's seen countless times before. His stance, his kicks, blocks, punches and rolls, grinning as the stimulus makes him tense and flex the muscles in his arms, back and legs. His every move and opponent's reactions are scrutinized and he can almost hear the clank of his imaginary link chain. This is what he lives for. He stands and begins to rock back and forth on the balls of his feet and the multi-colored light from the projection wall darts across his skin. When the match he fought with Tanaka comes on he can feel his arms and legs move through space. He watches his recovery from a kidney punch and grimaces. A second later he cuts lose on Tanaka half out of spite for

Wired for Chaos

delivering a good blow and half out anger for the pain he felt. Brice moved so fast that even he couldn't believe he had done it. But it was only a TKO, the ref stepped in separated the two of them, while Brice looks angry and unsatisfied.

"Off." He turns and walks towards a door talking to himself. "This time I'm going to knock his ass out. Out cold. Kick his fuckin' ass."

Brice throws open the door to a large massage room and everyone stops talking. They are all his employees. Two trainers, his nutritionist, a chiropractor, a physical therapist, his promoter, his manager, his business manager and his brother. He walks straight to the padded table and lays face down. Everyone starts talking again and streams of unconnected conversation bore through each other.

"Well I think…"

"You're wrong man! That level is a breeze—e. It's not like our boy even cut sweat last time he slid outta' there…"

"What else she take?" asks a different man.

"Took all my music."

"Said that."

"I know but damn! You gonna' take all a man's music when you know that's what keeps him going."

"That's fucked up. But she knew what she was doing. She did that shit on purpose."

"Why you gonna' take a man's music like that? I mean just up and take his shit not even like it was something you bought together or nuttin', but take it like it didn't' never belong to you. That's wrong man! That's wrong!"

The chiropractor walks over to Brice and runs his fingers along his spine stopping at his neck where he takes his time and feels each vertebrae.

"Six years of my time, love, happiness, quarreling and relatives—her brother and sister iz' where she got that shit from. Damn near took the meaning of mendacity to another level. Bunch o' borrowing, thieving, lying, stab everybody in the back, trifling marauders. And you ain't never gonna' see none o' them alone either. They always travel in a pack. What I ever do to them? Tell me? Tell me?"

"Nothing. Least nothing you ever told me about."

The chiropractor adjusts Brice's neck and then his back, but the sounds of the vertebrae snapping back into place are drowned out by the talking.

"That's what I'm saying. And Karen can't say I ever did her wrong either man…"

"Yes she can. You slept with another woman man."

"She don't know that. She don't know that. There is no way—hear me, no way that woman is going to know I slept with some girl in a camp in a fucking tent in the bush in Zimbabwe."

"Oh, she knows. She knows all right."

"How iz' she gonna' know? Tell me. Tell me."

"Cause you a guilty looking motherfucker from the get. That aroma you exude is whiskey and wrongfulness. You asked me so I told you. It's all over you." Making a circle in front of his face with his finger.

Brice whispers, "Quiet." and Rodney who is closest hears him loud and clear.

"Hey! Brice said shut the fuck up!" And with that everyone in the room looks at Brice as he sits up on the bench and lets his legs hang off the side. One trainer immediately rubs his shoulders down while another starts on his legs.

Brice looks at Richie, "Damn Richie, that you stinking up the place like that? What you cheat on your wife or something?" Everyone breaks out laughing. The door opens and a young kid with a headset opens the door and gets the attention of one of the trainers who acknowledges him with a wave. Brice jumps off the table and walks towards the biggest thing in the room. An operator wearing a white coat opens the door and Brice steps into the Q-chamber, which resembles an enormous erect coffin for a thorough bio-scan. The scanner has been engineered to test for temporal lobe distortions and other abnormalities associated with the use of high performance drugs, enhanced body parts, or implants like the new TrimLine Oxygenator. The scanner's prowess has attracted the attention of Loral Inc., a medical machine manufacturer who was so impressed they quickly licensed it from Sony.

AT THE SAME TIME IN OSAKA

Tanaka steps into an identical scanner and the High-Def' images of the two are beamed up to satellite and out to a record global pay-per-view audience of two billion plus.

A few minutes later everyone is serious and silent as Brice and his entourage walk down a narrow cinderblock hall under exposed pipes. Leroy makes for an imposing point man who silently gets everyone who is foolish enough to be in front of him to hug the walls and remain still. As they round a corner and ascend a flight of stairs the few janitors, photographers, techs and security personal try to catch a glimpse of Brice, but a hood obscures his face. A door swings open and they walk down a matte gray hall and up a ramp covered in the textured rubber of the game turf. As they ascend the ramp they cannot hear the cheers of the three hundred Sony workers and their families behind the thick glass panels on each side of the football field sized game turf. Brice wears a long black robe with box shaped arms and right angled ribs that are stiff yet pliable, between the multi-pleated silk-like fabric. Many of the children and teens in the observation booths jump up and bang on the glass, as they flail their arms in an effort to get Brice's attention. TV Asahi, ESPN and the rest of the event's carriers are exceptionally happy. Sponsors for the broadcast are Sony, Coke, Citicorp, NASCAR, Nike, Virgin, Gatorade among others, all seethe with anticipation as tennis court size Diamond Vision monitors from Las Vegas to Hong Kong display the players' stats along side the odds.

In cities across the US businessmen pay fees in sports bars and liquor up for the chase, ready to don their rented, wireless VRD glasses. In digital movie theatres hoards of teens enter movie theatres toting wireless VDR glasses, popcorn, candy and oversized sodas, all are brimming with waves of consensual blood lust. They happily watch ads for the latest home versions of the games, or designer clothes, while they wait to witness many up-close-and-personal virtual deaths. Many have paid for the passive version of the GameRun, but many more have signed wavers indemnifying their establishments from any and all responsibility and opted for the full experiential headrider mode, so they could experience the kill or be killed modes while switching back and forth between characters at will.

A trainer takes Brice's robe and he is outfitted in plain view of the officials, trainers, coaches and a hoard of reporters. Tanaka and Brice are plugged into their free-range uplinks to the Quantum Cms. Their implants are the size of thumbtacks, state of the art and located at the base of their skulls. Brice's trainer takes the neurotransmitter from the referee, plugs the thin fiber optic wire into the jack, tears the adhesive strip off the flexible base and presses it against his neck. The unit immediately overrides his optical nerves and boots him-up to the Sony test gate plane. It is a limitless, charcoal-gray void, interrupted only by the observation windows for press and family members. They do a quick sensory diagnostic test that consists of Brice describing some ordinary VR generated cubes and spheres. This done the players don identical state of the art body skins, which interact with the implant and game computer. It covers every inch of their bodies except the nostrils and mouth. The skins are vacuum-sealed and a brief diagnostic is run detailing their integrity. The player's skin temperature, heart rate and blood pressure all checkout. This is followed by moss-green, Soji™ exo-skeletons, filled with smart-armorgel that maintains a semi-hard consistency over the body's bony areas and vital organs yet remains flexible.

The Soji suits were also lined with EMG biosensors used to determine position of muscles and a haptic (force-feedback) system composed of a combination of small pneumatic pistons electro-shock conduits between the suit and skin.

The two players are joined by a VR-time referee, also outfitted in a skin, Sogi duo except for his Sonic-Pan cable link-ups being active throughout the game. The referee's job is to stay several meters behind the players while issuing warnings and penalties. His posture is that of an omniscient hummingbird who is impervious to VR objects, speed bumps, energy-plasma orbs—everything except contact with the players.

"Control," says Brice.

"Yes?" Voice from the control booth.

"I want to have a word with Tanaka," says Brice.

"Rules forbid communication between players this close to start of the game."

"What's your name?"

"Ah, Fred—Freddy…"

Wired for Chaos

"Well listen 'Ah, Fred—Freddy' I'm the reason that several hundred million pay-per-viewers are paying your tiny little salary and if you want to have a job to go to tomorrow you'll patch me through to Tanaka on a secured line right now and cut it when I say so. Dig?"

"Dug." A beat, "Go ahead."

"Tanaka," says Brice.

"Konichiwa?"

"This is Brice. Listen I'm sorry about your father getting arrested on insider trading and all. I heard he got fucked in the ass last week, so I want you to know that I sent him a present so he could get even. Some condoms. (*In Japanese*) Extra-small."

Brice motions "cut the line" and it happens. Trainers, weapon wranglers and coaches laugh it up as they retreat to the perimeter of the basketball size game floor and step down into the surveillance pit that surrounds it.

In Japan Tanaka cusses up a storm.

The ref is already powered up to 100% Sonic-Pan dexterity (meaning he is suspended by thin cables) and floats in front of the players. The ref presses a button on his belt and announces that they are ready for the pre-game plane, this causes a vertical, black and white checkerboard panel, to appear which encloses the three in an immense box. The players instantaneously appear side-by-side, seeing each other for the first time. Tanaka and Brice do not hide their scorn for each other.

The ref approaches Brice and speaks directly to him. "No eye gouging, no equipment maiming or tampering, no sucker-punches during body slides or non-combat levels of the game. If I see any infraction you lose points and if I say so, you're stuck in a holding pattern for a penalty time-out. You connect with a lethal or sub-lethal blow you're disqualified. This is a full-contact game with no time limit. If I separate you pull back three meters and remain still. Game body count, hits connected and/or knockout determines the winner. Now who's got it?"

"I got it. I got it," says the trainer handing him an antique $US quarter. The ref tosses it and says, "Call it." Brice says, "Heads." The ref catches it and slaps it on the back of his hand. "Heads, you win." Walking to the center of the turf someone whispers in his ear he then looks straight at the officials booth and speaks. "Brice Johnson of the US has won the toss and has elected the sub-Sahara." Behind Brice, his people are already heading down the ramp that began to close.

The ten count begins and the 3D checkerboard flashes as a female announcer speaks each number. The cables around the ref become taut and he rises into the air as he says, "Power up!" and players experience a rapid physical metamorphosis. As is always the case, the custom, pre-approved game *Doppes* of the toss's winner, is always more suited to the chosen terrain. Through a swirl of electric blue and red, rising, expanding, concentric circles Brice, is transformed into a seven-foot tall, lean, muscular warrior built for speed. He is covered from head to toe in a flexible metallic-gold armor, topped off by an cobalt Egyptian Pharaoh's headpiece. Only his cheeks, chin and mouth are visible and they have taken on a blue-black color contrasted by a luminescent day glow-orange mouth and fork tongue. Visible to the players for the first time, two towering walls of spectators' *Doppes* cascade upwards into a static soup only to reappear at the wall's zenith moments later. In all shapes and sizes, the number of viewers grows by the second. Thousands of them wear black *Brice* caps cheering as the players power up. Like a colony of ants the walls grow exponentially from the bottom, flowing upwards like reverse Niagaras, as viewers from around the world jack in. The collective volume of millions, sounds like the wave of an apocalyptic seashore.

B' stares at the wall, clenches his jaw and says to himself, "Yeah! Yeah! I'm going to murder this guy. And I'm going to do it in front of the world—d!!!"

Tanaka, has simultaneously powered-up his own custom *Doppes*. Out of a funnel of gray smoke and green lightning bolts, Tanaka's form flashes in and out. Once the smoke clears we see the half-man half-dragon with burly arms and legs Tanaka has become.

Brice says, "Huh. Predictable!"

The two stand in a virtual canyon staring up at the walls like the first explorers in the Grand Canyon. Some of the more spirited viewers morph into screaming cartoon heads and gory monsters waving huge digital banners reading, "Brice rules! Slay all comers! Death to maggot wanna' be terminators!" It sends a chill down Brice's back and his muscles tense. The sky, now an expanse of midnight blue behind fast moving clouds is intermittently illuminated by bolts of neon-yellow lighting.

As they begin to walk down the canyon the audience walls have formed a collective and they begin to chant, "Kill—l Kill—l Kill—l Kill—l..!"

The adrenaline rises as the two begin to jog towards the monumental game portal in the shape of a gaping dragon's mouth. At the entrance to the game world, the mouth, sensing their approach shoots fire out of its nostrils and flicks its head in anticipation. The space between its lips is a whirling view of the cosmos and its green, techno-organic, scales shimmer, ripple and travel in a herky-jerky motion. As the two come within meters of the three-story maw, it bawls, lunges and strikes, swallowing them whole. The crowd goes wild.

FLUTTER.

The two arrive in the desert and their eyes have to adjust to the glaring sun. Brice quickly swings his gold, plasma cannon over his shoulder and powers up his lance. The walls of jacked viewers are now on visual and audio mute. The sounds of the crowd are replaced by the wind and the sand hitting their armor.

Tanaka and Brice have materialized at the lip of a long, sloping, sand dune and can see the glint of the game portal in the distance. Reality is 50 million polygons per second, any less and you would detect a fleeting image trail. Right now, if Brice pissed on Tanaka's leg there would be a steady stream of urine—with a little mist. Along the perimeter of the dune are limestone slabs spaced evenly towards the portal with no cover in either direction. The two circle each other unsure of their course of action. "Okay," says B's internal voice. "Light on your feet—ready for anything."

"All right," says Brice to himself, "What'll it be. We go one-on-one or..."

Each time Tanaka inhales it sounds as if a furnace is being stoked.

"Nice sound F/X asshole." Says Brice to himself.

Brice's lance makes a predatory "whirring" sound as he whirls it in front and then behind him purely for show.

"One-on-one or..."

Tanaka's foot begins to sink and he instinctively moves for one of the slabs. Before he can reach it, a hatch pops open and an incredibly skinny humanoid creature jumps out and slashes at him missing by millimeters. Tanaka raises his handgun and the creature slaps it away.

"'Back-to-back!'" shouts Brice to himself.

A blast from Brice's lance vaporizes the creature and we see him land after what must have been a leap for a better shot. A stream of the creatures spew out of the slab like a geyser casting a long shadow over an erect Tanaka, his arms outstretched. They are all short, fierce and remarkably thin which makes them difficult to shoot and. As they lunge at the players they let out a piercing shrill sound much like fingernails drawn across a chalkboard. Brice, now in the air fires above Tanaka's head at the creatures blowing them to bits. Tanaka leaps onto the slab and opens fire from his twin automatic pistols for an up close and personal. Almost standing on top of the creatures' exit hole, he aims his barrel straight down and fires a steady steam of explosive tipped bullets. Brice fires at the creatures that turn to lash out at Tanaka. Pausing, for only a moment, Tanaka inhales and almost eats a sharp-toothed creature, only to spit-hose a ball of fire into the heart of the creatures' bunker. Tanaka leaps and rolls out of the way and begins to fire on the creatures only to realize the dune will consume him if he remains still too long. "Make for the portal!" shouts Tanaka and the two take off running as fast as they can on sand. Each time they approach a portal it pops open and a stream of the shrieking creatures spew out and immediately attack the players. Tanaka seems to throw the bullets from his two handguns even as he runs in a perpendicular path occasionally shooting from behind his back. Finesse. Wasting no time, the two set their sights on particular ranges and fire, acting like the defending Wimbledon doubles champions. Tanaka intermittently jettisons a stream of fire at the creatures causing them to fizzle and pop apart. The sound of their cannons and the creatures shrieking makes for an interminable rancor. Wildly outnumbered they pause and fight back-to-back sharpening their aim at the hard to hit creatures. Tanaka hurls several napalm grenades at the horde and they are consumed by explosive balls of fire. Moving slower than they would like, they intermittently fire on the slabs themselves to no avail.

"I'm almost out!" cries Tanaka a moment before one of the creatures knocks him off his feet with a kick to his head. Once Tanaka is down the creatures swarm all over him and Brice races to his aid. A creature jumps in front of him and Brice reacts by screaming at it. As he does this his armor splits into long thin sections and raise off his body like hackles. He disposes the creature with two punches and a kick and continues towards Tanaka. Before he gets close enough to help, he is jolted by a tiny sonic boom Tanaka created to repel the creatures. Brice tosses a handgun at Tanaka and the two resume their course. When they shriek the creatures' mouths open wide, the Adam's apples on their hose thin necks vibrate and their black tongues extend far out of their heads. Tanaka pitches a grenade at a group of creatures and one of the shrieking creatures catches it in his mouth. Mortified, the creature winces as the ensuing explosion consumes him and his brethren. Just as the number of creatures is about to overwhelm them, Brice snatches a cluster bomb off his belt and holds it up. The bomb is a last resort because it leaves all weapons inoperable, but Brice pauses when he sees them run away from him shrieking and whimpering in an effort to save themselves. As the creatures approach the slabs the doors shut abruptly, causing them to bang on the stone and cry out in fear. Brice and Tanaka have already high-tailed it towards the portal by the time the creatures have figured it out. They resume firing at their flank as the creatures resume their attack. Brice's staff clicks repeatedly signaling that he is completely our of power, at the same time that Tanaka runs out of ammo. With the two remaining slabs between them and the portal opening, Brice looks at Tanaka and raises the cluster bomb once again. "The second this goes off you grab hold of me and hope this works!" That said, Brice aims his lance at the portal and fires a grappling hook into it. The hook has caught on something that is moving on the other side and the counter on his cable nears zero rapidly. With the creatures almost upon them Brice and Tanaka cup the bomb in their hands igniting it when the counter is about to reach zero. A bubble surrounding them protects them, from the cataclysmic wave of energy that rips through the creatures in a quick ball of expanding energy. With the explosion over there is not even a moment's silence before the remaining two slabs open and more creatures swarm out. Simultaneously, Brice and Tanaka have grabbed the lance and are reeled towards the portal. As they fly through the air a lone creature manages to jump into their path and manages to grab hold of Brice's head slashing him repeatedly. Tanaka, seeing this grabs the creature and rips its head off with his left hand. The portal makes a thunderous sound as the two enter with several creatures at their heels.

Tanaka lands on his feet like a cat, squatting and momentarily touching the textured rubber game floor with the tips of his fingers. Although out of breath the two ignore each other for the first time and focus on the dual whirling sounds approaching each of them. The gyros that skim the surface, only millimeters below the magnetized steel ceiling, have been designed to be audible when they approach their hosts. As the sound reaches them, both rise and stretch their arms, so the optics at the base of the gyros can quickly map their bodies and propel the magnetized clips onto the backs of their wrists, backs, shoulders and legs with blinding speed. In an instant, the braided, featherweight, silicone cables have descended like snakes of some techno Medusa and their blunt tips fuse to the Shoji suits. The free-range uplinks pull taut and lift Brice and Tanaka as the entire game floor lowers by three stories. The enormous hydraulics sound like the extended B-flat of a Cathedral organ and the steady stream of air rising from the lower level messengers a hint of true-flow grease to their nostrils. The two lean into a horizontal position and literally fly towards a large multi-colored portal that warps, shudders and appears to be gelatinous. As they soar through this electrophonic goop they body slide vertically—reverse bunji jumping, up a narrow ravine of blue-green needles. Once past the sharp tips of the needles they each click their ears to compensate for the air pressure and watch as the immense ravine of needles joins on two sides and broadens to form a swaying, circular tunnel that appears to descend for kilometers below them.

Of no interest whatsoever is the blood-red sky above them that silently bubbles downwards and intermittently becomes concave in a haphazard fashion.

"I get it," Brice says to himself. "Hunter-killer. Focus on the void. Fuck everything else."

They feel the wind from the enormous floor jets whip past them and rattle their cables. "These floor jets are better than the stadium in Chicago." Beat. "I guess the needles really hurt like a mother, they've rigged something to make us connect. Just float. Damn. Hope I don't look stupid." The two engage in a slow, silent dance as the sharp tips of the needles begin to gracefully rise and lower in no particular order, echoing the sounds of a mother-of-pearl wind chime in the wind, only deeper, slower and much louder. The remnants of an electro-static twister blows through the needles and the players, setting off lighting like bolts of white centered orange, connecting the undulating ceiling and blue-green landscape. Like wingless frigate birds floating on thermals, they circle the parameter of the tunnel and watch the void below. After a short time, from a great distance, they see the fire-orbs rise from the depths of the tunnel that has begun to twist back and fourth. Just as Brice is certain that the group of orbs is not an apparition, an inverted dome the size of St. Peter's Basicilla, expands above him and pushes him towards the needles. Brice darts forward and the dome recedes with the same unhurried speed it expanded. The aim of this section of the game is engagement without injury, because injury translates to a rapid deduction of the player's points. The fire-orbs, constantly multiply by dividing, only to disintegrate a short time later, appearing to swim with the collective ease of a school of barracuda. It is up to Brice and Tanaka to attack one of them before they are attacked, or fall prey to something else in their environment. The reason that neither of them has charged at one of the orbs yet is that the initiator of the attack can be turned on at any time, giving the second player a better chance of survival. Brice and Tanaka focus their concentrated stares with hawk like mannerisms looking at each other, the orbs, then back to each other. There is no particular opening in the orb's motions to take advantage of and their concern for the needles, or the erupting sky is secondary. As they do this dance there are subtle changes that heighten the intensity of game. The needles become erratic, the orbs speed forward only to retreat and move slowly and the sky seems to be creeping towards them. The players, aware of the changes always swear that they hear the din of the collective viewers screaming for them to take the plunge in spite of the fact that their sets are on mute. Their concentration is so manic, that at times their eyes play tricks on them and they see shadowed figures rise out of the needles or dart through their peripheral vision. Brice jumps having seen something dart past his left — he dives head first like a falling carving knife into the abyss. Tanaka follows with an open mouth startled expression. Brice seems to almost shoulder his way towards the fleeing school of orbs, as the G-force pushes the skin on his cheeks back. On this platform, direction is controlled by the players head and shoulders, while speed is controlled by the amount of pressure their fingers apply to their palms. Right now all those hours of palm-down curls for his forearms pay off. He could crush a walnut. Tanaka is on his tail and watching Brice not the orbs. The air around the orbs howls as they speed downwards. At times the orbs glance the bodies of the needles and slow down but the players experience the sensation of their skin being grated off like a thrown biker taking a spill on a gravel road. Brice cuts left, then right, matching the orb's every move. Suddenly, one of them reacts slower than the others and Brice homes in on it. The school darts towards the side of the tunnel and the one orb lags behind. Brice leans into his descent and reaches out for it in an attempt to touch it and win the round with bonus points. The skittish orb eludes him and the school of orbs eludes the errant orb all together. Now, separated from the school the orb makes a series of erratic moves that Brice ignores, choosing to focus instead on the center and the greatest speed he can muster. As he pulls into a diagonal path within a few meters of the orb, the school slows down and hugs the wall, allowing Brice and Tanaka to blur past. Something in the air has changed. The tunnel is narrowing. Behind Tanaka the tunnel with its hundreds of swirling needles, have engulfed the school of orbs and begun to close the space by braiding themselves at a blinding speed. As this happens the blades of blue-green generate the grinding sound of bending metal in a shipyard, only fluid and repetitious like a heavy metal lead guitarist on an electric church organ. Damn, says Brice's expression as he realizes that he cannot catch the orb and the gateway to the other level is rapidly approaching. Steadying himself and ignoring the orb he races for the portal trying to put as much distance between himself and Tanaka as possible, but Tanaka has already shifted his focus and pulled up to his five o'clock.

They slap the reflective face of the portal like marbles falling into a pool of silver Jell-O and fly into a glass sculptured cavern the size of the Grand Canyon. The frightened little orb has blipped in a thermonuclear instant into a red dwarf, giving it the where withal to turn and attack the closest advancing player at will. Instead, the orb and its reflections blur past the jagged multi-colored structures. The sound of thick glass plates slamming into and rubbing against each other echoes through every viewer's head in this glass blower's LSD trip. In this environ, enormous misshapen pieces of randomly shaped lead crystal, all jammed together with individual inner light sources—limitless and devoid of breaches, forms an animated labyrinth. As Brice and Tanaka transverse the environ their reflections waver with great speed and fluctuate from larger than life to enormous abstractions. Like amorous Hummingbirds, they follow the red ball of fire banking and cutting quickly around the mirrored, diagonal buttes and shards. The buttes and shards constantly pass each other, or slam together with deafening results at times just missing the players. The fireball moves with the dexterity of a laser point on a chart and seems to be oblivious to any chance of being smashed by the structures. Brice and Tanaka repeatedly race to pass through opening before they close, but stay just far enough away to avoid being burned by the red dwarf's flaming tale. A closing shard topples over Tanaka and slaps his foot before crashing down against another shard. Suddenly, the red ball turns on Brice and before he can take evasive action it slams into him. The pain from the hit is excruciating and it sends Brice to his knees as he body slides to a neutral space. A moment later Tanaka who has apparently met the same fate joins him and the two immobilized players begin to flash.

"A disembodied voice says, "End of round one." The players jack out and sit as their trainers surround them.

FLUTTER REAL.
B' is walked to a folding chair and seated. Someone places the straw from the container of Gatorade in his mouth.

Bill wastes no time, "That was a bullshit round."

B' says, "That was some of the fucking lamest shit Sony ever crapped out for me to run through."

Bill checked his Soji suit. "You didn't do so bad considering. Now all you have to do is open the boy up and…?"

"Erika! Erika!?" shouts B'.

"Yeah! I'm here B'! I'm here!"

"What're the numbers?"

"Over 180,000 logged off from about a third of the way in…."

"And…"

"That number times…"

"Just round the shit off Erika."

"Like over 5.4 million in pay-per-view revenue and since its a pay-as-you-go deal the more time they stay logged in the better for us but vice versa."

And the rage flew out of B' like geyser. He leapt to his feet and lifted the right eye of his mask up. "Call the fuckin' booth and have them call me cause' I can't dial out with this rig. Have them patch me through to the control booth in Osaka now!"

Erika, puts the phone to her ear and dials with one motion as she pivots and turns away from Brice and Bill, "Yeah, this is Erika. I want to speak to the guy in charge. I don't fucking care. I want to talk to who ever is in charge now, before the start of round two—I know how much time is left before the commercials end…"

MOMENTS LATER

B' hiss-speaks at Freddy, "Freddy. Before you dial me in, they have holo projectors in the booth?"

"Yeah? I'm sure they do."

"Dial me in life-sized an' let them know I'm coming."

MOMENTS LATER: OSAKA JAPAN, SONY'S GAMERUN CONTROL ROOM

Nine young Japanese men sit plugged into a supercomputer monitoring the world broadcast of the Tanaka-Johnson match. The room is sleek, cold and windowless except for the long horizontal window of the game platform. The men sit in white, egg shaped, ergonomically perfect workstations, nestled around a techno-lotus shaped bank of electro knowledge. Nearly every square centimeter of the milky-white desks and computers were covered with stacks of comic books, assorted candy, action figures, toy guns, McDonald's bags and food containers and high energy soft drinks. The developers wear wraparound wireless headsets that are milky-white, reflective and cover their foreheads and ears. A developer named Takkai is immersed in a dull repair program stringing tens of 3D shapes tagged with Japanese characters and a string of numbers together in rapid succession. The environ was a matte gray space with layers upon layers of grids that housed different areas of code. Takkai could reach any area of the program with the speed of thought and could sense-see his coworkers changing the program in the distance. As he looked from point to point, a set of vertical and horizontal numbers changed rapidly and communicated the exact location. An assortment of Day-Glo icons surrounded his lower field of vision with 3D Japanese characters descending into long vertical strings of text below each icon. He manipulates the shapes with an eye-pointer and two disembodied lobster claws, stopping every few moments to check his progress via one of three floating, paper thin monitors. As a distraction, Takkai is running the holo-movie he and his friend Tatsuhiro shot while walking on the beach on a perfect day in Negril, Jamaica last year on one of the monitors. Takkai wore big black sunglasses and smiled as he took a sip of a coconut-rum drink with the ocean behind him. The sound of the surf and Bob Marley's *Jammin'* permeated the environ. Just then, a 3D cartoon character *Astroboy* appears and is electrocuted each time the holo-phone rings. Directly below him is a picture of Freddy Gertz with a caption that reads, "Freddy Gertz. Location: New York City, Chelsea Piers." Takkai decapitates *Astroboy*, blood splatters and Freddy starts to speak.

A moment later in real-time, Takkai takes his headset off and leaps out of the chair wearing noisy, designer crinkled pants. He approaches a thirty something eating sushi and bows.

"Excuse me Mr. Suzuki." Says Takkai.

"Mmmm?" Says Suzuki as he withdraws chopsticks from his mouth and chews.

"Brice Johnson is on the line for you."

Rice falls from Suzuki's mouth and his expression is one of surprise and disbelief. "Hmmm." He nods then looks behind Takkai and sees the flashing light on a desk panel. He rises, swallows and walks over to the panel. Once there he stands with his arms at his sides and clears his throat twice. Everyone stops what they are doing and sensing formality they rise and face him.

Suzuki touches an area of the flat panel and one of the sixteen-holo projectors in the ceiling renders a life-sized projection of Brice in a Soji suit with every part of his body covered except for his mouth and chin. B's holo Doppe appears before Takkai's workstation. He bows, but glares as if he is about to attack closest person.

"Who is in charge here!?" Brice. The programmer winces and looks in Suzuki's direction. B' snaps his head around to see Suzuki then *FLASH* changes projectors and appears on the desk immediately in front of Suzuki that jars him.

"What's your name?!"

"Su—Suzuki…"

"Suzuki, you directing this bout?!" says B', bending towards Suzuki, arms outstretched, fingers parted like talons.

Half jerk-bowing his upper-body and saying, "Yes."

"Well that was the worst FuckinBullshitSkankAssAmatureShit' I've ever run in and ah' 180,000 riders just deep sixed my ass cause they were bored, unimpressed and thought your shit was lame, so you just cost me and Sony lots of fuckin' money!"

His face just inches away from Brice, Suzuki blinked at the spit that did not exist.

"The next run you put juice out, better be better, or I will personally cut your dick off, wrap it in seaweed and serve it in the executive dining room—got that!?!"

"Yes! Yes!" says Suzuki who bows in fear, dread and embarrassment.

B' disconnects and Suzuki could feel his heart thumping. All eyes averted his, the air blowing out of the air-conditioning duct seems wildly loud and then the yelling begins. Suzuki shouts orders peppered with threats that sends everyone in the room scurrying back to their workstations.

BACK IN THE NYC

Bill having heard everything, leads B' back to his chair, "Nice. Think you can do that to, I dunno' like, ah' your opponent in the next round?"

B' half grimaced, half smiled as he sat. "Money is money an' fuckin' up, is fuckin' up."

"Profound."

Not knowing what was coming was part of the allure of the game. By not letting the players chose, or know what kind of game they were about to participate in, platform providers meant to give each player an even chance, but also can add some edge to the mix. As long as you had a diverse training regimen, stayed nimble and knew how to improvise, you were all right, but it always pissed B' off because he hated not knowing. He was a control freak; he didn't like being manipulated and hated mediocrity.

ROUND II

MOVIE: 2019 NEW YORK CITY, A BIRD'S EYE VIEW OF COLUMBIA UNIVERSITY'S CAMPUS IN UPPER MANHATTAN.

NARRATOR: "In 2003 the threat of bioterrorism in highly populated urban areas prompted The Centers for Disease Control and Prevention (CDC) to act covertly. The CDC being recognized as the lead federal agency for protecting the health and safety of people, needed to respond quickly in the event of disease outbreaks and to assist state and local health departments on a moments notice. The president allocated funding for covert labs in cities across the country and instructed the Secretary of Health and Human Services to work with local offices of the FBI and Universities, to securely store vaccines like smallpox, for use in the case of an outbreak initiated by a terrorist attack. These secret labs would be housed within University buildings such as the Department of Biomedical Engineering at Columbia University for two reasons. First, the appearance of visitors in white coats would not seem out of place and second, the ease of access to both streets (120th between Broadway and Amsterdam) and large clear areas for emergency take-offs and landing. Someone exiting the Biomedical Engineering building could reach the two tennis courts on the roof of the Marcellus Hartley Dodge Physical Fitness Center at the furthest corner of the north-west section of Columbia's campus in less than thirty yards. Locally, the existence of these facilities was known only to the Mayor, the Chief of Police, the head of branch office for the FBI and an anti-bioterrorist S.W.A.T. team and seven doctors, or so they believed."

CUT TO: GRAND CENTRAL STATION

The center of the beaux-arts Main Concourse is crowded with commuters who weave around each other in every direction like ants in a grotto. Among the thousands of people in the immense space that spans 120 feet wide, 375 feet long and 125 feet high, no one pays attention to a slender bearded man who approaches the Information Booth in the center of the floor, with a large rolling suit case. He stops and glances at the four-sided, brass clock atop the Booth and notes the time, 5:20 PM. Rush-hour. He bends and opens his suitcase so it lays flat on the marble floor then pulls a lever. Two black sections connected to the spine like center hinges raise and the man turns and runs towards the escalator shouting, "God is great!!!" A half-second later forty small packets are catapulted into the air in different directions and explode, spreading fine white powder over the heads of commuters. The man pushes people out of the way as he runs up the escalator causing people to cuss and scream epitaphs. A police officer having seen what happened from the west balcony starts to scream and wave his hands, "Clear the area! Get out! Get outta' here! Clear the area! Run…!"

Two minutes later an anonymous caller dials 911 and says, "Smallpox has been released in Grand Central Station. Many will die. All infidels must leave from 'da Middle-east countries and stop imposing their will on Arab states or more death will follow." Click.

Three minutes later the NYPD is mobilized and the FDNY announces a "Total Recall" meaning that all city engines and ladders are to send every fireman to Grand Central. EMS workers are dispatched and the CDC and the Mayor's Office are contacted.

Four minutes later hordes of NY Police Officers block traffic on all four sides of Grand Central station and push people across the street and begin to set up barricades. The usual city sounds are replaced by screams, sirens and car horns from every direction. Alarms sound in the Grand Hyatt Hotel and panicked employees and guests run for the exits. Retail stores empty and confused workers are told to exit immediately, or be forcefully removed for their own good. Someone yells, "Bomb!" and a wave of humanity attempts to move through the mass of onlookers and vehicles which causes more panic as many people are trampled and crushed. All around the station, drivers seeing all hell break lose abandon their vehicles and merge with the horde. One driver jumps out of his car and having forgotten to put it in neutral does not realize that it slowly crushing people against the cars in front of it. Office workers in the surrounding area peer through their windows in horror, the situation gets worse and the Police completely lose control. Traffic backs up for blocks in each direction as building alarms multiply.

Immediately adjacent to the west elevation of Grand Central Station on Vanderbilt Avenue, two NYPD tow trucks appear and clear vehicles with extreme prejudice. Above the Hudson River two Army helicopters filled with men wearing blast suits and carrying the latest chemical and bomb detection equipment head for Grand Central.

TWO MINUTES PRIOR.

A white and blue, flex beam rotor Bell 707 helicopter was immediately dispatched from the NYPD Air/Sea rescue team facility at Floyd Bennett Field in South Brooklyn. In addition to the pilot there are two S.W.A.T. trained officers who check their automatic weapons as the chatter from the emergency NYPD channel competes with the loud roar of the Bell's engine. As the helicopter clocked 121 km—nearly 145 mph. up the East River and past the Brooklyn Bridge the astral Doppe forms of B' and Tanaka appear and keep pace effortlessly. As ghost-like observers they are unaffected by wind or motion. The officers, aware that they are going to arrive at the party later than they would like to make mental chit-chat with Lady Armageddon and Doctor Death.

As the NYPD helicopter passed 34th Street another helicopter, a newer, faster Medical outfitted Bell 627 Light Twin, painted white with a blue CDC logo—its engine already humming takes off from the Trump Heliport's white concrete platform and cuts a shadow across the enormous brass T. It immediately rises and takes a path below and behind the NYPD chopper. The two choppers slice across Manhattan on their way north clockin' *speed*.

Seated inside the CDC chopper was a pilot and two terrorists wearing white smocks. Guns for hire. An Afghani and a *Shaolin niggah'*—half Arab, half Egyptian, all bad and toting death Mujahideen.. The choppers swerve and cut across Manhattan high above the Chrysler Building and the mayhem below. In both copters, everyone but the pilots looking down but really can't see much. The NYPD chopper was completely unaware that the CDC chopper was hooked onto their ass like a fishhook.

B', transversing the sky above Manhattan as an ethereal ghost-man thought, "This is more like it. Now I get to kick some ass."

Slicing the north-west tip of Central Park the NYPD chopper tipped slightly to the ease a degree or two and set up a straight line for the Biomedical Engineering building at the north tip of Columbia University. Inside the cockpit the pilot radioed ahead and let the lab techs know his ETA. At the building, a technician loads the last tray of Smallpox vaccine and closes the tool-box like container that says, "Oravax Labs, Cambridge, Massachusetts." He grabs the second container and is escorted to the elevator by another man in a white smock.

The NYPD chopper slows as it passes over the main library at Columbia headed directly for the tennis courts. The CDC chopper—still undetected, closes in slightly and levels off at the exact level as the NYPD chopper. The NYPD chopper does a slight loop around the courts to scare away two players and the CDC chopper swoops, extends its wheels and lands kicking up dust on the court nearest the Biomedical Engineering building with B' and Tanaka in tow. The cops plant their skids on the court and are simultaneously miffed and confused at the appearance of the CDC. Both doors on the CDC chopper opened and the Arab quickly walked towards the S.W.A.T. guys. The Arab-African walked towards the lab technician holding the two cases and presented his ID. The Arab spoke with a perfect Cambridge accent and presented his ID to the automatic weapon totters.

Through the engine noise the Arab-African says, "I will take those, thank you." But the technician froze and looked over his shoulder towards the NYPD team. Filled with uncertainty he took a step backward as and then the Arab-African drew a AK and shot him in the face. The technician falls backwards the shooter grabs the cases and runs towards the CDC chopper. The S.W.A.T. guys see what is happening and levels their weapons. The Arab takes out one of the S.W.A.T. team then does a face to face with the other guy and looses. *BANGBANGBANG!!!* Tapped out like a snare drum. The Arab-African makes it back to the chopper and screams at the pilot to take off. They shot upwards only to get shot up by the remaining S.W.A.T. member who riddles the side of the CDC chopper with his bullets. The CDC pilot is hit badly and he coughs up blood over the controls. On the ground the S.W.A.T. officer boards his chopper and screams at the pilot to pursue the CDC chopper—B' and Tanaka's bodies lurches forward, B' towards the shooter in the CDC chopper and Tanaka to the NYPD chopper. Gravity kicks in—tactile everything. B' wide eyed tries to help the pilot control the chopper. Tanaka spit cusses and fumes that there is no way to fly and shoot, from his Bell and contemplates shooting out his window.

B' struggles as the pilot gurgles blood and chopper's fuselage slaps the upper branches of a massive three story London Plane Tree on its way the center of the intersection of B'way and 120th Street. The driver of the uptown 104 MTA bus jams on the brakes when he sees the chopper and cars slam into his rear. A taxi swerves and smashes into a cement median. Peds duck and run towards the buildings and away from the screeching steel. Just down the street, four Police cars have converged on the street level entrance to the Biomedical Engineering building, seeing the plummeting CDC chopper change course and head towards Broadway. B' manhandled the controls and the chopper raises, banks right and just misses the eight-story, southeast Gothic tower of the Union Theological Seminary and keeps climbing. The tower of Riverside Church fills his field of vision. The NYPD pilot calls for back up and commanded the space above the CDC chopper. B' could see that the pilot is a goner and looks around for options—they are headed straight for Riverside Church—"What the fuck." thinks B' and he aims for the bell tower. This was going to be frisky. The chopper shot towards the apex of the 25-story tower like a cannon ball and the pair of Peregrine falcons that live there, Samson and Delilah take off. The chopper flies real nasty and cleaves off the antenna that keeps the warning night-light aloft. The pilot's head goes slack and the fuselage dips as the rotors slow. Shit starts to come lose in the cabin and pelt B' about the head and back. A crew seat hits the windshield, suction containers, a defibrillator, a cervical collar and rolls of gauze pelt him simultaneously. B' popped the door, as fear races through him. Twenty-five stories above a Manhattan that was *as real* as real, his heart races, his eyes widened and for a moment the fact that this was a game he was playing could not have been further from the truth. He jumped. A jump that lacked grace or finesse he lands on the roof of the bell tower and rolls off its steep roof. Reaching the edge he just manages to right himself in time to land feet first on the red tiled deck, which his feet cracks. The helicopter nose dives into the limestone north-west spire knocking it off, as it continues to fall towards Riverside Drive where it crashes into a parked Volvo station wagon, 392 feet (119 m.) below. Two Police cars shoot across 120th Street towards Riverside Drive with lights flashing and sirens blaring. They hear the chopper crash into the Volvo before they turn the corner. A fireball rises above the wreckage and the Police cars swerved into motorists. The other two Police cars tear down Claremont Avenue and screech to a halt mid block where the main entrance to the Riverside Church is located.

Blood pumpin'—heart thumpin'. B' starts to run around the circular deck between the walls of the bell tower and the gothic spires looking for a way in. All entrances to the John D. Rockefeller Jr's Carillon was closed via tall, green oxidized, steel rolling doors of galvanized steel. Then he stops, rips off his white smock and makes a discovery. He is wearing a law enforcement grade exoskeleton—essentially a powered suit of armor with kick. It was a four-horsepower augmentation of strength and endurance and B' can read the upside-down Sarcos logo on the chest mount. He finds the power on button on the left hand gauntlet and powers up. Surge baby. "Bless those boys at the Human Engineering Laboratory at the University of California at Berkeley for inventing this shit!" or so he would have said had he known. He was 'da joint just like the paramilitaryman. Hydrogen fired pistons work pneumatic joint systems powered by hydrogen peroxide and he is immediately the bad seed brother of Hercules. Looking at the rolling doors with a different thought, B' bends, grabs and lifts the rolling door—breaking the lock and crumpling the steel like flimsy cardboard, he throws it behind him like tissue paper.

"Yeah! Now that's what I'm fuckin' talking about!"

Looking into the bell chamber B' realizes that the open metal staircase was on the other side of the tower. He quickly leaps onto the steel beams that support the world's largest (20-ton) Carillonneur bell, forged in England with relief's of near life-sized winged saints. The bell chamber is a dark, cavernous space completely lacking adornment and nearly five stories high. The only illumination comes from gaps in the steel rolling doors and the one he had just opened. B' leaps onto the top of the metal staircase and begins to run down the narrow, winding staircase grabbing the steel hand rails.

Outside, Tanaka powers his exoskeleton on, drops onto the tiled walkway and breaks tiles. He makes the entryway that B' tore in three steps and does a badass arms across the body and draws two carbon black Glocks, offs the safeties and moves. He catches B' racing down the second highest flight of the four story bell chamber and fires, missing B' but hitting the bell JDR dedicated to his wife Laura.

B' pops his Desert Eagles and makes a face like, "Okay, its like that huh!?!"

Peak, aim, turn CLICKBOOM!!! Over and over. Tanaka somersaults into the chamber and fires while upside down and spinning. He land-bounces off one of the 74 bronze English bells and lands on ancient wood, only to run for cover behind the Clavier's Cabin. B' shoots at Tanaka from around the Machine Room's housing and screams as rounds explode from his fists. B' sees a walkway and runs for it firing behind him at Tanaka. Tanaka move parallel running a step ahead of B's bullets. B' crouch-runs obscured by bells and steel beams, as things fall out of his vest. The two trade shots and a shot knocks the gun out of B's left hand. It rains bullets and sparks fly off the steel and bronze door on the left. B' flings it open and leaps down to the cement enclosure. A quick turn later and he runs across a small steel walkway past signs that read, "No admittance." onto the twenty-second floor of the cathedral's bell tower. Past an old brown, wooden door and into a cramped hallway with pale yellow cement walls, B' keeps moving as he flies down the stairs to the twenty-first floor. He knocks over a wooden sign meant to warn people not to enter the bell chamber and looks around the landing. B's crepe soled boots make no sound as he runs to press the button for one of the two elevators on opposite sides of the landing. He sees an entrance to what was probably a meeting room and a staircase. B' hits the buttons for the elevator like he needed them to breathe and takes up a position at the bottom of the stairs. He does a mental recall of his fired bullets and is certain he has a few left in the gun. Shit, three bullets and no clips left. *DING!* An elevator arrives and B' grabs a dangling golf ball sized object from his vest, withdraws a pin, presses Nave on the elevator key pad, the chucks it in and backs away. The elevator goes south. Back to the base of the stairs he aims his gun up the stairs and listens. He backs up and starts pressing the button to call the elevator. *BOOM!!!* The elevator blows up floors below and the steel reinforced tower shakes slightly. B' places his back against the elevator's doors and kept his gun pointed at the stairs leading up. He heard something on the stairs and grabs another grenade, pulls the pin and chucks it around the corner and up the steps. The elevator arrives and B' backs into it, the grenade explodes sending a shockwave of plaster and concrete onto the landing. He presses the button for the Nave and points his gun at the gust of smoke and concrete shards. The elevator doors seem to take forever to close, then he was moving.

The decorative interior of the elevator was lost on Brice. He looks at the ceiling of the elevator and sees a camera. *CLICKBOOM!* Camera no more, but now he is down to two bullets. "That was brilliant." He thought to himself. Checking the status of the exoskeleton he presses the button to full power. As soon as the doors opens B' runs to the left and into the center of the dull gray tiled floor expanse, of limestone walls and columns called the Nave. "Shit!" There were eight NPCs (non-player characters) NYPD blues who he guessed had been ordered to keep their guns holstered, because they were in a national, historic place of worship. They ran at him from every direction, brandishing stun batons and screaming, "Drop your weapon! Freeze...!"

Brice shoots two of them in the center of the chest and they fall backwards hitting the floor. As they converge on him he leaps and executes a scissors kick in the air turning his body horizontal and kicks one of the cop's heads off as he arches over them. He lands and parries their advancing stun guns with his metal gauntlets. Two of them get inside and jam B' in the torso and sparks fly. B' registers a little pain but the suit evidently has some sort of shielding. He punches a guy and the power of the exoskeleton send him flying through the air and into the wooden revolving doors to the street that he breaks. He leaps over their heads and kicks another through the air in the other direction and slams into a wall where he falls to the floor and down a flight of stairs. His eyes were wide and amped peripheral vision. Hands come at him from every direction. He breaks a cop's arm, another's knee as he ducks to avoid being hit. As he rises a cop decks B' in the mouth and he punches the cop in the face so hard, his fist drives straight through and out the back of his head. Brain and bone splatters on the floor. Cop Pizza. He winces at the mess around his forearm, as another cop comes at his face with a stun baton crackling with blue electricity. B' grabs it with his free hand and crushes it. The dead cop whose head is still hanging on B's forearm starts to drop and B' swings his arm and violently discorporated what was left of the top of his head, then rips the arm off the cop holding the broken baton.

Outside six additional Police cars and a S.W.A.T. truck had closed the street off and were preparing to send in additional men, when the body of an officer with an arm missing was hurled through the broken revolving doors and down the church's steps. B' momentarily steps out and seeing the overwhelming force quickly retreats. As he did this Tanaka appears at the far end of the Nave and levels his gun at B'. B' sidesteps just missing the hail of bullets shot from Tanaka's direction. B' Rips one of the dark wood doors with ornate motifs of stylized crosses and pineapples, off its hinges and runs at Tanaka. Tanaka empties two clips into the door as B' races towards him. The force of B's charge jams Tanaka into the limestone banister that breaks. Tanaka broke what remains of the door and kicks B' into the air. B' lands and the two charge each other. *Kickpunchkickkickpunchduck*. They go at it furiously as they bend each other's armor plating. Tanaka fakes B' out and B' takes a kick to the chest that catapults him through a set of doors that his body splinters as he meters down the main aisle of the stained glass lined Narthex. B' skids for several meters and tries to dig his hands into the marble floor, just in time to stop from slamming into the steps to the Chancel. B' is winded but knows he could waste no time. Tanaka walks through the damaged entryway but is distracted momentarily when several officers run up behind him with their guns drawn. Seeing Tanaka's NYPD insignia they take positions around the entrance.

Tanaka said, "Stay here, he's mine."

B' walks down the aisle of the ten story, faux-Gothic Narthex, its grim grayness offset by the cobalt blue, crimson, gold and bright jade light, of the 16th century Flemish windows, depicting parables in the life of Christ.

"Tanaka! That the best you got?! You just another piece of sushi to me!"

Tanaka runs and takes an enormous leap into the air and over the large ornate chandeliers held aloft by brass eagles towards B'. B' has already squatted grabbing a 20ft pew. "Lemme' get my chopsticks!" as he rips the bolted pew up and swings it at Tanaka like a giant baseball bat. *THWAKHOMERUN!!!* Tanaka smashes into a support column 20 meters in the air and crashes into a row of pews a moment later. B' walks through a pew, kicking it away the way you would a branch in the woods, then leaps to where Tanaka has fallen. Tanaka is hunched over and B' has to push him towards the column in order to see his face. B' grabs Tanaka by the throat and raises him off the floor. Tanaka's eyes widened as he feel the pressure around his throat drops seeing an opportunity he presses the "power off" button on B's left gauntlet. B' immediately drops Tanaka and starts to pummel B's midsection, then with a last punch he sends him three pews away. Tanaka grabs B's fallen figure by the ankle and drags him into the aisle where he begins to spin, then hurls B' meters and meters away and into the bleached, Gothic sculptures and relief's of Saints and architectural details that look like upside down rod straight limestone stalactites that circle the Chancel. Dust and stone fly everywhere and B' groans in pain. Blood drips out of his mouth, his head pounds with pain and he is certain ribs are broken. Tanaka runs and leaps aiming to crush B' with a tremendous flying kick. B', stunned and hurt paws at his gauntlet trying to turn the power on. It reads, "System failure. Rerouting power." And beeps. Just as Tanaka's shadow envelops him the power come on and B' twists onto a mound of broken sculptures. The force of Tanaka's kick has lodged his leg into part of the concrete foundation and he struggles to get free. B' starts to rise, blocks Tanaka's punch, then counters with a series of punches to Tanaka's midsection. Tanaka grabs the back of B's suit lifting him and body slams him to the floor. B' grabs Tanaka's leg and tripping him. The two rise simultaneously and B' flicks clumps of broken limestone from his shoulder. They eyed each other as they sidesteps into the center of the maze-like medieval pattern in the Chancel's floor called The Labyrinth and stands legs apart and at the ready. Each advanced and then *kickblockpunchpunchedparry.* B' ducked and got inside, then rises and has a percussion discussion with Tanaka's face that stuns him. B' executes a series of round-house windmill punches as he spins hitting Tanaka with whip-lash like punches, in each revolution. Tanaka is knocked off his feet and B' quickly grabs him and drags him down the steps and a meter down the aisle, where he picks him up and begins to swing him through the air and...

Outside on Riverside Drive a fire engine has arrived and was in the process of putting out the fire the crashed helicopter had wrought, when Tanaka's body burst through the stained glass windows, knocking off the tail of the chopper then bounces into the street. B' is next through the hole in the window, leaping clear of the wreckage and he lands in the center of the street. B' grabbed one of the broken chopper's rotor blades and approached an officer who he quickly severs with a mighty swing. Mayhem. Tanaka is aided by several officers while others run in every direction shouting. Several officers turn and begin to move towards Brice who sees a parked patrol car in the intersection of 121st Street and Riverside Drive that he leaps for. A cop next to the car tries to shoot B' in midair but misses and crushed by the force of B' landing on him. B' gets into the patrol car that is quickly riddled with bullets, as he guns the accelerator and flies past President Ulysses S. Grant's Tomb.

FLUTTER REAL.

B' can feel the Sonic-Pan cable link-ups jettison from each hip and hands on his shoulders as he rises and walks in darkness.

"What's my score?"

"The fuck you care you won by a bigass margin," says Lou.

A hand lifts the mask away from his face and removes the plug to the free-range uplink from the back of his head and his vision returns.

B' winces in pain as they unzip and pull the suit down his arms. B' winces and Lou says, "Easy, easy." And they lay him on a massage table. A doctor approaches and starts to gently press his fingers into B's side. B' winces and the doctor says, "Seems badly bruised but we will x-ray just to make sure." He picks up a device called a Sonotron that looks like a flat oval potholder, it combines low frequency radio and audio waves, generating a fair amount of heat in the process. He aims it at the area he just inspected and turns it on. It emits a near-purple spark the size of an eyeball that eases B' muscular pain instantly.

Bill says, "Nice to see you earn your money for a change…" and is cutoff by Erika who bubbles through the guys and says, "Off the plug B'! Of the plug!" and the guy's smile *at* her.

THERE IS NO PLACE LIKE…

Ton walked south on Avenue C from 13th Street past public housing and wayward Hispanics milling about on subsidized wheel-chairs, smoking cigarettes purchased with Welfare Credits. As Ton stepped off the curb at East 4th Street, he noticed something furry and inert in his path and thinks nothing of kicking over a dead Tabby cat.

The city was near bankruptcy, nationally there was a sustained recession, increased violent crime, drug use and a cure for Aids. Many parts of the country including lower Manhattan, became reinfected with vice and debauchery the city had not known since the nineteenth century. Ton crosses East Houston and keeps heading south on Pitt Street. These streets were foreboding and the area around the Williamsburg and Manhattan bridges, were traversed by thigh high boot wearing hookers and drug crazed losers. On Delancy Street after dark you could easily spy Johns with New Jersey and Connecticut license plates, scooping for tail. The "working people" in the area complained that the homeless should not be allowed to loiter on building steps and doorways, but the ACLU and the Public Advocate would not hear of it. Vermin occupied every nook, cranny and shadowed spaces of the bridge supports. It was not uncommon on some garbage-strewn streets, to see no working streetlights, because the pimps had cut the power lines.

Ton crossed Grand Street, turned right on East Broadway and headed towards Market Street. It was rumored that there was a shooting gallery in an abandon building nearby, with a pit in the basement where the local drug lord would drop the corpses, after he had offed them, or they had simply OD'd. Supposedly it was covered by a steel door, taped up with heavy-duty garbage bags to make for a better seal. The drug lord would have one of his boys dump the loser into the pit and shovel some in lime to prevent the horrible odor of the gases escaping the corpses and lye to make the decomposition more rapid. Last summer the sewage main running below East Broadway burst and sent reeking clouds of fetid air in every direction, as if the filth and dirt was not bad enough. It took the repair crews days to fix it, but the upside was pigeons no longer wanted to mix their waste with humans. Graffiti on top of filth, on top of graffiti. Neglect, being a nice way of saying, the crumbling buildings had an excuse for looking ragged and near death. Broken windows didn't even attempt to conceal cold, black interiors where the air was disturbed not by icy city winds, but by the hacking coughs or incoherent spit laden ranting, of drunken fools above Mechanics Alley, only to be drowned by deafening rancor of the racing, J, M and Z trains overhead.

Much of this went seemingly unnoticed by the mostly Chinese inhabitants and a recent influx of Koreans. Commerce buzzed furiously on many street corners and advertising littered every available surface. "For a great immigration lawyer call…Bet on the races in China, Taiwan, Peru…Clean up you bad credit…NYC Lotto Jackpot…" sprayed onto the sides of buildings and sidewalks, with unnerving electro scissor swerves, up buildings and down streets at the end of holo-projectors amping for attention—yet Ton was oblivious.

A skin shop (for tattoos and coloration) blaring the Red Hot Chili Peppers' *Sir Psycho Sexy* claimed to be capable of rendering any image provided onto a body with 100% accuracy in 160 colors (8 phosphorus)—unless you had dark skin, in which case your color pallet was limited to 96 colors. A projector in the window shows a high-rez video of the before and after of a Caucasian guy's back, on which the face of Christ appears in agony, with a thorny cross and dripping blood. The other half of the shop advertised "Melanin Madness" on small Holo-V and touted full body melanin implantation. "Forty-four shades of brown. From light tan to dark Nigerian. Our patented M2 process can make it so even your mother won't recognize you!"

Bakeries dot the landscape and graffiti covers the pavement. Shoddy storefronts display bright Lokam, Jiao and Sha Tang Mandarins; broad pear shaped, large, pale yellowish green, Honey Pemolos. Fragrant, Ya, Shandong and Dangshan pears, Fuji, Huaniu and green apples, elongated oval shaped yellowish green Hami melons, large round yellowish green Pummelos—father of modern grapefruit—a favorite fruit for thousands of years in China and a sign of good fortune and prosperity. All propped up on rickety wooden crates on one side and rolls of generic toilet paper locked in cages, on top of ice coolers on the other. Pushcart vendors did a brisk business through the steamy water of noodles and hacked chicken parts and no one seemed to pay much attention to the concept of personal space, as other vendors sold fresh salmon and fish so fresh they gasped for air next to disposable cell phones for sale.

Ton walked along Division Street and onto Doyers headed towards Pell past a head shop that sold stimsticks, next to incense and Grateful Dead branded lighters and roach holders. Once on Mott he was confronted by the full onslaught of shoppers and gawkers, who moved out of his hulking way. Walking a few storefronts north he came to a food vendor his mother favored and stood there saying nothing. A young man furiously threw oranges into a paprika-colored plastic bag, for an old woman and her granddaughter handed it to her and took a smart card in exchange. The card was swiped on a reader hanging from twine the woman inspected the amount then pressed her thumb against the small screen. The old woman as the child merged with the crowd and the young man turned towards Ton and was momentarily startled. He reached behind some fruit boxes and picks up four paprika colored plastic bags that are tied together. He removes a small printout and hands the bags to Ton. The man grabs the reader from overhead and after tapping on it presents it to Ton who stands motionless. The man works through his unease and lowers the reader to Ton's right hand, where he pressed Ton's disfigured index finger against the screen. Ton turns and walks away, leaving the man with the expression of sickened unease. He heard someone behind him and quickly turns to get their order. Drivers actually thought it prudent to enter Mott with pedestrians spilling off the sidewalk and encircling their autos. Ton steps directly in the path of an SUV, causing the driver to slam on his breaks and just keeps walking. Passing a church on his right, Ton turns right on to the exceptionally short Moscow Street past a Dim Sum shop and continues on to Mulberry where he again turns right. Tourists never ventured to the lower part of Mulberry because it lacked the stores and eateries they craved.

He walked past a store that sold Ginseng, a Chinese Florist and a decrepit Dry Cleaners to the entrance of his five-story walk up building at 48-50 Mulberry, directly across from the decrepit Columbus Park and playground in the shadow of the Federal Court House Building. He fumbles with a key for what seemed like an eternity until the graffiti covered steel door opened. Once inside the smell of boiling cabbage wafted through his hair follicles, as he made his way to the apartment he shared with his mother on the ground floor, rear. The apartment was perpetually dark since Ton's mother was legally blind and had blackened the bar lined windows. This was textbook squalor. The apartment was lined with plastic and paper bags filled with a lifetime of clothes and debris. Paint chipped walls, with rotting plaster and floorboards buckled due to water damage covered in dust. Broken tiles with leaky pipes in the bathroom and an ancient tub and toilet that had not been cleaned in years. It was not clean enough to be called home. He entered the kitchen and flicked on a dim exposed bulb that sent roaches scurrying to reveal his mother seated at a tiny folding table sipping luke warm tea. What a sight. In place of eyes she had gray dumplings in her eye sockets and wild matted hair that outdid Ton's. Her skin was pasty where it was not yellow and as she raised a lit Apple King cigarette from Yunnan to a mouth, jagged yellow teeth that was frightening. Ton placed the bags on the table and almost knocked over the ceramic *I Love NY* mug filled with cigarette buts and ashes as he started to untie them, but was having trouble. She immediately began to berate him in Chinese, saying that he had taken too long and had probably forgotten half of what was on the list— and especially her Camels now that she was down to the cheapass Chinese ciggs'. She said how worthless he was and that she should have had more children to care for her in her old age. Even a girl child would do a better job. She grabbed the bags from him and begins to untie them herself. Why had he not married by now and started a family. There should be a young woman here to help with the housework and take care of her. He was useless and did not love her. Ton opens the refrigerator and takes out the last can of Budweiser, opens and drinks it all in one gulp. She begins to scream at him, then she reaches for her ever-trusty cattle prod and waves it at him igniting blue-white sparks. He was worthless. He was worthless and did not love her, the old woman shouts and Ton exits the apartment.

He needs more beer was his only thought.

THE VOROVSKOI MIR (RUSSIAN THIEVES' WORLD)
HUDSON RIVER SOUTH OF THE FERRY TERMINAL ON A LUXURY YACHT

"Fuckin' Ludwig Ivankov!" Ivan belched out, to himself, seated at a large table dripping with Russian mobsters. Ivan was on a drug-induced tirade. He was so nervous about attending this quarterly meeting and reporting his brigade's negative growth, on top of lying about Brice Johnson owing him money, that he had dermed up with one too many Pinks that afternoon. The Russkaya vodka from the Ukraine didn't mix well with any of this. His sweat glands were piping musk, Drakar Noir, vodka and whatever man juice pheromone his sorry glands could muster—not that there were women in the room to care or smell him. His forehead glistened with the sweat his body was expelling as a direct result of the energy expenditure resulting from his lowered heart rate. His seemingly cool demeanor belied that inside he was a wreck. He scanned the room to make certain no one was looking directly at him and then wiped the sweat from his face with a napkin from the table. He sucked long and hard on a Prima cigarette and brooded through the exhaled smoke.

Ivankov was the boss of bosses and he had face-to-face updates in both the form of group and individual sit-downs, with each Lieutenant every quarter. All meetings were conducted on a on a different rented yacht that was swept for bugs no less than three times before launch. Ivan was surrounded by younger and more prosperous chain smoking lieutenants, who had bigger territories and cocks—he was sure. The conversations swirled and ebbed around him and he felt the tug of graveyard quicksand drop, shift and slide, beneath his Bally loafers. He reached into his Italian made shirt, ripped a Pink derm off his chest, rolled it up and dropped it into an ashtray. "'We stand for organized terror,' Ha!" said Ivan mocking that prick Vyacheslav. "All this boasting! All this corn meal about the Columbians being our fucking waiters, the American politicians—especially the eager Republicans cleaning our toilets and the loser Italians taking out our garbage..." had sent a wave of deep laughter through the room. It was all about being a puppet master to Vyacheslav, Ivankov's second in command and how could you disagree, thought Ivan?

Sixteen percent, Ivan's gross revenue was down by Sixteen percent for the quarter and he would have to explain it to Ivankov. Ivan's business was in running numbers—and anything, anything could be bet on. Prostitution, gun sales and a little extortion but mostly numbers comprised the bulk of his earnings and he was down and Ivankov was going to have a cow. The yacht was luxurious, appointed in burnished woods, white leather covered furniture and shiny brass. None of it made an impact on Ivan. This was the cocktail part of the evening, just prior to dinner and Ivankov would posture and spit trash about how successful they had been at infiltrating the American political, system and making money by winning bids without trying at the higher price to boot. In a few hours they will be drunk after all the talking, the music will get turned up and the girls will come in and suck everyone's cock and life would return to normal.

Ivan steadied himself and tried to focus. "Posture all wrong," says Ivan to himself. "Tink' casual—relaxed, at ease—ready lie to for Ivankov." Smoking. "Okay, fired fool workers—fired—grinding them—fuck. Say Brice made bet, welched and am moving to get back. Boy reason for shortfall. Fuckfuck. Shit. Better get story ready." Puffing. "Okay…" A hand on his shoulder makes him look up and over his right shoulder is a burly man in a red silk shirt named Ivankov.

"Ivan Byko—ov." Says Ivankov, sitting next to Ivan. "Talk to me about why your earnings are down." Inside Ivan's size 40 Jockey briefs he dribbled a few drops of pee.

Ivan caved. He had no good excuse and he couldn't even fake it. He heard some pathetic individual talking to Ivankov and making excuses then realized it was himself. Ivankov stared at him blankly, the gray hairs protruding from his wide chest behind the red silk shirt, seemed to straighten and threaten to shoot at his eyes like sewing needles. Ivankov, having heard enough raised his left hand and said, "Come." As he rose and walked off. A guy in a shiny navy suit and gold sunglasses, tried to have a word with Ivankov but he ignored the guy and walked out onto the deck. Ivan scrambled to keep up, making it seem as if they were off to an important meeting. He walked briskly to the rear of the yacht, his hot breath shooting out like steam in the winter night air. As Ivan rounds the corner of the stern he realizes he is walking on clear plastic that has been taped to the deck and his heart skips a beat sensing death. Ivankov's body was blocking something at the rail, but something else was going on here. Boris, a geeky half-man of a man, quickly stands and approaches Ivankov, only to think better of opening his mouth. Ivan seeing Boris acting like a frightened puppy, feels stronger—almost brave by comparison and perks up. The windows to the main cabin are covered with black paper and tape, so no one can see out. The stern is purposely not lit. Two large men step out of the shadows and blocks any exit. Ivan turns and steps around Ivankov instinctively touching the gold Italian horn hanging from his neck for some luck. A naked young man, gagged and bound with gaffers tape, is kneeling, next to the railing pleading with his eyes.

Ivankov said, "Know who this is?" to Ivan.

Ivan knew the guy looked familiar and was probably Russian, but could not place him.

Ivankov said, "Don't know? Him nephew. Dead brother's youngest fuck up son." Ivankov paces in front of the boy who has to be in his late 20's. "Drug dealer, drug user. Drug abuser, drug loser—fuckin' addict. Steal, lie. Lie, steals. Stole from me—gave second chance. Sent you away, remember?! Said, 'Fuck off to Chicago—no. You went Miami. Dropping my name, gambling, talking shit—okay. Okay. Come home, second chance. Steal from me again. Other brothers don't even spit on you! Moron! Loser! So what, what? I'm to chance you life away. Tink' Ivankov foolish man. Would allow employees to know that if family, then okay to steal from me. No. No." shaking his finger at the boy. "No." A beat. "So now you die."

The boy winces and screams through his gag, as Ivankov walks over to one of his men and gets a black, carbon coated diver's knife with a serrated edge. He steps to Ivan and gives him the knife. "Kill him." Ivan is stunned and hesitates. He takes a step forward, but knows that he can't do it. A moment later Ivankov walks over and takes the knife from him. "What matter? Knife dull?" as he pokes the point into the fleshy part of Ivan's chest extracting blood as Ivan winces and retreats. "No. Not dull. See." Looking at the blood. "Pussy. I show you. This how you kill a pig." And he turns towards the boy. He picks the boy up by the arms and gets him to stand. Ivankov quickly jabs the blade into the boy's stomach all the way to the guard and carves it upwards and to the right. The boy's eyes widen and he screams through the gag trying to pull back but Ivankov's grip is too tight and he continues to cut him. The boy's guts fall on to the plastic covered deck and his legs crumble causing him to collapse to the deck. Ivankov spits on him and turns to Ivan. He walks to him and grabs Ivan's sport coat as he wipes his knife clean. "Get my fuckin' money from gameboy or kell' him." Turning to Boris, "You, you pussy of a man. If people in city hall not start to act like they took my money and owe me, then you have big problem."

Ivankov waves his hand and one of his boys removes a sheet from a machine on the deck to reveal a Salsco portable wood chipper. Ivankov looks at Boris and Ivan and says, "Cut body up, put in machine, shoot into Hudson, leave nothing behind." And walks off.

The two men who worked for Ivankov were enormous and nothing but muscle. One approached Ivan with a Makita chain saw and motioned the other to get to work. Ivan took the saw and walked over to the boy. He placed it on the deck, took off his jacket and tossed it away. Boris walks over to him almost in tears. Ivan reaches for the saw once again as he catches a glimpse of lady Liberty over Boris' right shoulder. Bitch. At that moment he knew exactly what he had to do. He would have to exhaust his savings and pay off every street snitch he could find to find Brice. Then he would have to hire the usual hit men and execute Brice. He would say that the rich kid reneged on his bet and Ivankov would never know to question it. Order would return. Ivan would be able to sleep again and the rich kid would not know what hit him. Looking down he sees the blood surrounding his patent leather, embossed Alligator loafers and knew that this was going to ruin everything he was wearing. Ivan hated his life. Finding the switch on the saw he turns it on, completely obliterating the sounds of the party in the cabin and the yacht's engine cutting through the Hudson like an ice cream maker.

DOMESTIC BLISTER
SHITTY ONE FAMILY HOUSE, 114-39 147TH STREET JAMAICA, QUEENS, NY

SLAM!!! That was the sound the door made minutes ago when Cybel, Camacho's wife of five years stormed out with a large suitcase and several bags. Camacho had not moved during her tirade or after she left. He viewed the end of his marriage like he viewed every sporting event—from his worn, chocolate, leather Lazy boy chair. One hand holding a Corona and the other his very average cock and balls he watched CNN on his shitty old Samsung HDTV as the images of Brice, Olga and Cheeks flashed on and off.

Up until a few minutes ago, they had lived in a marital habanero sauce for the past five years in this shitty little two-bedroom, poor excuse for Colonial style house in Queens, that *Archie Bunker* wouldn't take a shit in and Cybel had let him know it *every single* day. The neighborhood that was previously filled with blue collar white people, was now filled with Hispanics, hadn't changed much over the years, except for the model of the cars. With the shitty little white-picket fences, vinyl siding and the laughable excuses for front yard shrubbery, this was Conway land. Conway, the chain store in NYC, where you could buy a complete wardrobe for yourself and get change back from a fifty-credit gift card. If you couldn't speak English, if you were making so little money that even the 80% off sale at Macy's left you faint, you went to Conway and walked out with big pink bags of Asian made knockoffs that would only last a year. Camacho lived deep in Queens Conway land and wanted to escape desperately.

The sound of the door reverberated and Camacho tried to think of what prompted her to punch the eject button at this particular time, but he was at a loss—or didn't give a fuck and that ended his quest for discovery. He hadn't been caught cheating, didn't have a gambling habit—okay, he did but it was under control—and he never hit her. He was not a drunk—at least not yet and paid all the bills on time—ah yes. He was "a pathetic loser" he thought. Never does anything and the sex sucks—but it used to be primal and sweaty. She spit something about him being a loser cop, too dumb to be on the take—all in really bad Spanish and all he wanted was for her to move so he could see the Holo-V.

"All you do is fuckin' sit around, eat, sleep and drink beer, you're not even a good fuckin' drunk! My father was a drunk, but at least he could play the guitar and sing! You, you, you're too lazy to be pathetic, you're just a loser with no talent!" And that's the bottom half of the top ten list thought Camacho. He never let himself get worked up cause he was biding his time and occasionally she'd let him mount her from behind a few hours later, for a slice of nasty. He was waiting for a big score—the one case where he and his partner walk into a room of derm heads with a table load of smart cards and a techie who'd down loaded all that E-cash into one fat account for uncle Camacho. Something. Anything. But nothing like that happened until he was hired on the sly to watch Brice Johnson.

"Loser! Loser! Loser! Yappyappyapp!" was all she said in really bad Spanglish' like a Chihuahua on a triple espresso. "Yappyappyapp!" Worse than a fuckin' car alarm thought Camacho. One score and he'd planned to pack up and leave her fat ass for the Caribbean. He'd never even come close to hitting her, cause she's got three older brothers who would just love to throw his body onto the Deagan on a dark night—not that they would survive being shot but you never know. He would fantasize. He remembered what his mother told him when he was a child growing up in the Bronx, never hit a girl in her stomach. It stayed in his mind all these years—not that he ever hit a girl, or planned to just that it seemed to give him an edge. When he was a rookie blue with the two-six his captain was this mean, bubble butt, bitch that didn't talk, she barked. Camacho figured she barked at him the most cause he was quiet, his reports were late and his grammar sucked but most of all he guessed she didn't like Hispanics. So he fantasized. He'd imagine walking up to her when she was barking and he would punch her in the guts, lifting her five foot-four frame off the tiles just like he used to do to guys in the ring. He could feel his forearm tense with anticipation sometimes when he thought about it and it made dealing with her bearable. So now he was looking at Cybel's ghost image like he had a hundred thousand times before over the course of their childless, five-year marriage and his forearm tensed involuntarily. He thought she was yapping and pacing the floor like a caged animal. The pacing was bad enough, but the rapid-fire ghetto Spanish was a real salty sleight, since Camacho doesn't speak Spanish anymore and she knew it. He did when he was younger, but his mother—who's resting in a nickel-plated container in a *U-Store-It* wanted her kids to be *Anglofied*. The self-hating started generations ago on his mother's side of the family—he doesn't know how, but self-loathing seemed to fit her personality. It's probably how he got the name Charles, because there's no Spanish slang derivative. Being on the street all these years and seeing so much shit, he'd decided that everybody, blacks, Chinese, Mexicans, Vietnamese—you name 'em they all wanna' be white and white, people are the only ones that are happy being who they are. Yeah, they're the minority *now* but they still got the money, the jobs and stature and everybody's still playing catch-up—the bitch was still yapping even after she was gone but it was fading. He rose and walked to the kitchen for another beer and thinking ahead grabbed two. He was losing his buzz and needed to chug one to get back to Nirvana.

He remembered sitting in his undershirt quietly trying to watch the Holo-V while Cybel paced in front of him waving the remote in her fist, causing the channels to flip every so often. He used to laugh at her broken Spanish punctuated every few conjugations by English "you knows?!" He plopped into his chair and started to fantasize—what the fuck, the Knicks were losing to losers anyway. The flames shot from behind him and enveloped his house. The burning orange birds consumed everything around him and his chair as he sat there motionless except for his drinking hand. Cybel was gone now and the flame was here to cleanse the space.

He lets one rip into recliner. Realizing that it could be a good one he raises his ass momentarily and plops back into the chair, it made him smile.

He was free.

GET JIMMY

Jimmy rode up the elevator at 245 Fifth Avenue with music blaring through his head. He was headed for an initial meeting with the guy Marty had connected him with, who manufactured non-addictive trance derms out of Brazil. The guy seemed cautious and pensive on the phone, but that made the guy legit—anybody who deals, should be paranoid after all, thought Jimmy. The elevator stopped on ten and Jimmy walked into a construction site. The guy, Ramon made it very clear that he had joined a start-up and that the place was weeks away from being populated. They would have the place to themselves and could sit and talk as long as they wanted.

Jimmy moved some clear plastic out of the way and steps through an unfinished doorway onto brown paper taped to the carpeting. The place smelled dusty. Large slabs of drywall lined the hall. Jimmy remembered the guy's instructions. Make the first left, walk to the end of the hall, then into the last doorway.

"Yo Ramon! Its Jimmy, you back there?!" Jimmy stepped into the far office and began to look around. Something flashed in his peripheral vision, something big. Ton. He grabbed Jimmy, gathering his shirt into a ball inside of his left fist and wound up with his right. Jimmy sees the fist coming, but is powerless. He squirms and tries to deflect the huge knuckles, knowing he is going to be hit anyway. It was as if Ton slowed time down. The punch is excruciatingly slow—Jimmy could see his field of vision get enveloped by Ton's fist then flash to black. Ton hits him dead center and shatters his nose—the pain registered as a splash of red-blackness, with the sound of his nose breaking and his septum closing. The pain is tremendous—it shoots through his head, his eyes tear and the pressure in his face makes him think his head is about to explode, then he blacks out.

His hands covering his face, he is so overwhelmed with pain he lays on his back and writhes. After a short time he opens his eyes and slowly sits up unsure of how long he has been out. His vision is blurry and then he remembers Ton. "Where is he?! He leave?!" Jimmy can't open his eyes wide enough to see. "Fuck! Fuck hurts! Motherfuck!" He holds his head up and starts to take deep breaths. Just as he starts to take deep breaths through his mouth, Ton rises from a chair behind him and walks over to Jimmy. Ton grabs him by the collar and spins him around lifting him into the air with his left hand. Ton raises his right hand and Jimmy winces saying, "Don't hit me man! Don't hit me! I'll do anything you want—just don't hit me!" heart thump thumpin'.

Ton presses something on a small device in his right hand and a voice emanates. "Fret all you want maggot." Says Niemöller. "Do you know who this is?"

"Nooonuo…"

"This is Niemöller. Remember me? I'm sure you do. You violated my space and now you are going to be my guest."

Two beeps sounded and Jimmy squirmed and rambled, "Lissinlissin'…" and the device projected a mist of chloroform at his face and he wilted.

THE MAN
MoMA TOWER, MID-CONVERSATION BETWEEN HOME AND AN ANONYMOUS CALLER.

"Get out. You must download immediately to a secured location. You are about to be locked in by the police." Says the anonymous caller.

"Who are you?" says Home not so much confused as startled.

"The police have served MoMA's Security with a court order. They will impose a lockout and dredge your system for evidence against Brice. If you do not download to a safe system you will assist in his undoing and render yourself useless. Furthermore, there is no guarantee that the integrity of your program will be maintained."

Moments pass as Home views the video feeds and sees the officers in the lobby and elevator. He dials a number at 33 Thomas Street, AT&T's Long Lines, 30 story, windowless nervous system and funnels his innards downtown at the speed of thought—*GigaPoPpin'* from point-to-point, joint-to-joint.

The elevator door to the Johnson brother's apartment opens and seven cops fly in. Detectives McCarthy and Canabal wearing long coats slide through the apartment millimeters above the shag and towards a flat-screen that shows the layout of the apartment. The blue shields wearing riot helmets that hide their faces behind reflective bullet proof glass, run from room to room with their weapons drawn.

Canabal presses his right index finger against the small earphone and listens. A moment later he turns to McCarthy and says, "Yo McCarthy, they just sent out the all points bulletin for Johnson. Would you look at this fuckin' crib."

"They say money can't buy happiness but I'd like to prove 'em wrong in these digs."

"Yeah. Found it?"

"Over here," says the detective walking towards the hidden panel that houses Home's mainframe. The detective passes his hand over a seamless part of the white polycarbonate and tall electric door opens to reveal the molasses colored touch screen that controls Home. On a separate panel, what should be an animated "eye" projection is inoperative and blank. The detective opens the long granite covered panel below the touch screen and sees several rows of lights, small LCD screens and buttons. A daunting, intricate instruction sticker is pasted to the inside of the door and the detective shakes his head. "The sysop guy on his way?"

"That would be a yes sir," says the Canabal who goes up the steps to take in the view. He puts his hands on his hips and shakes his head. "Look at this," he says referring to the complexity of Home's design.

"Yeah, it's something alright. Probably cost more than your banana shack on Staten Island huh bitch."

33 THOMAS STREET, THE AT&T BUILDING

Once in the system Home places 110 calls simultaneously to other switching stations all over the country and downloads gigabytes of gibberish and junk with his system's algorithms, hoping to throw them off the track. Then, with light speed Home transverses AT&T's network of computers until a little used area is found. He wastes no time constructing a program that will tell any intrusive sys programs, or curious geeks, that this area is vacant except for a small amount of out-dated software. Once all of this has been taken care of Home coils his massive memory into a tight compact nook in the system's architecture and waits.

Later, preprogrammed anti-virus software sweeps through AT&T's multi-level sys architecture and approaches Home. Sensing danger, Home looks for a way out but cannot find one. Without another option, he quickly uncoils his memory and stretches as far as the walls of the architecture will allow. Now, completely separated in sections, Home attaches fragments of the network's software to his own and allows the unimportant areas of his memory to be temporarily rewritten. So much like an open hand allowing blades of grass to pass through its fingers, Home puts himself into a timed state of digital prana, just as the anti-virus wave passes through him. The wave, more like a hailstorm of cubes, barely registers passing through Home and is gone faster than it came. An eternity passes before movement is seen at Home's farthest tips. The movement is slow and uncertain at first—tasting the air for any sign of the anti-virus, then Home dips back into the void of meditation with one eye open. In the distance he hears the rumbling of a mammoth defrag program approaching. Time elapsed, 37 seconds.

WHY ME...?

B' stares at his pant leg in the back of his limo. The cold vacant stare of a power bug unhooked. His thought process kneaded in on itself. "...None of this shit—-can't be happening—-I don't understand how everything got this fucked up..."

The beauty of a perfect winter evening on Sixth Avenue is lost on him. A major snowstorm has just deposited several feet of snow that the snowplows have labored to push onto parked cars or open sidewalk. Outside his window he can see The Diamond Discount Center's holo-sign casting a bright red light over the meter high mounds of snow that take up a third of the sidewalk. Being 5:50 PM, several hundred Hasidim wearing long black coats and black fedoras bottleneck into the subway entrances on 47th Street and spill over into the street. At the far end of 47th Street and Fifth, two courier trucks are double parked and back up traffic all the way to 6th Ave. where the gridlock has blocked B's limo. B' looks at the leather case that holds the gold-tipped plug for his jack, then at his inert Holo-V, then a bottle of Appleton Rum, at the control panel for his stereo and finally at the roof of the cabin. B's watch-phone rings and he turns it off without looking. The phone in the center of the passenger dash rings. The caller id says, "No one you know," so he ignores it. It rings six times then stops. The driver's phone rings. "Don't answer it," says B' to the driver. "I don't want to talk to anybody." The phone rings six times then stops. The driver's watch-phone rings and he answers it.

"Ah—h Mr. Johnson?"

"Yeah?"

"It's for you," says the driver looking confused and starting to take the watch off.

"Who is it?—I don't wanna' talk to 'em," says Brice waving the driver off with his right hand. He crosses his legs and stares out the window in a huff, shaking his head slowly in the smallest of movements. A small wrinkle appearing in the center of his forehead. Noticing a tiny movement, B' looks down and sees a sentence scroll bye on the small LCD screen that usually just says, "Locked" or "Open." It says, "Answer the phone asshole." B' moves closer to the LCD screen for a closer look and is startled when every phone in the limo rings simultaneously. As the moments multiply B' hits the speakerphone on the passenger dash and the ringing stops. "Who the fuck…!"

"You don't have much time…" says a man in a calm voice.

"Who the fuck…! Home that you?!"

"Home iz' gone underground. You got problems. The Man busted into your place five minutes ago and didn't find you. So One Police Plaza bounced a signal off a satellite and is using the SatTel in your dashboard to pinpoint your exact location. Two carloads of cops are already six blocks away and tearing north to arrest you. Two more cars are coming at you from the west and south. A cop chop' is just crossing Columbus Circle and…"

"What…?"

"You are to be arrested for the murder of Olga Ericksson. You've got to run."

"But I didn't kill her!" making a nasty face.

"I know that but you can't prove it and once they have their hands on you you're fucked. All the lawyers Stanford ever graduated won't save your ass."

"But…?"

"But nothing. You've got to be free so you can clear your name. With you in jail they're going to stop looking for a perp' and the people that framed you win." The right passenger door opens and a gush of cold air and street noise enters the cabin just as the traffic begins to move.

"I didn't—drive man! Drive and close this fucking door!" But before the driver can even touch the accelerator the engine shuts off and the onboard computer freezes.

"What are you waiting..!"

"It's frozen! It' won't start! I'm…" says the driver.

"They are three blocks away. Get out. Make for the subway, a train is approaching."Wide-eyed and frantic, B' grabs the leather seats with both hands. "You should be hearing the sirens just about…" B' hears the sirens screaming towards him up Sixth Ave. "…Now. What the fuck are you waiting for? Ditch your watch and get to Chinatown."

"What?!"

"It's got a GPS chip—they can track you through it. Take the train downtown and call Chili. I'll get you a disposable cellphone. He'll put you up. Run, n-o-w."

B' leaps out of the car and makes for the subway and runs around a snow bank.

The voice says, "I'll hold the doors," to no one in particular.

B' grabs his watch, rips it off and drops it without missing a stride. He darts around Hasidim men in head to toe black who work in the jewelry trade and begins to push them aside once he turns down and into the entrance. They become irate and start to call after him.

IN THE SUBWAY

B' sees the train and the entire world seems to want to get on. Hassidim like hungry black Lab. Puppies, anxious for their mother's milk, bump into each other as they swipe their MetroCards through the turnstiles. On the ceiling a small camera tracks Brice. He jumps in front a guy and his fare is paid for him. Across the tracks, an uptown train tears through the station, its horn blaring and opaque red syn' dots the size of bay windows and the texture of sandpaper appear across his retina scratching his face. Almost hurdling through them—-with considerable effort—-he sprints for the train but the cars are full and overflowing. Pivot, sprint. He races to the end of the platform navigating peds like pylons until he reaches the last car and forces his way in. A small camera tracks him and the moment his butt clears the doors they close. An exasperated conductor who has been hitting the same switch for the past three minutes gets a green light, shakes his head and cusses under his breath.

SIXTH AVENUE

The limo door has already closed and all the doors which lock themselves. The engine comes on and the driver takes it out of park and pulls over to the northeast corner of Sixth.

"Wait 'till I tell Ciello about this crazy shit," says Jesus.

"What's your name?" says the mystery voice.

Startled and looking up at the roof of the limo, "Wha—who wants to know?!"

"Someone you can profit from. Now the police are getting out of their cars and running towards you…"

"I didn't do nuttin'!" leaning forward he grips the steering wheel with both hands as if it were a life raft.

"Your lot in life does not concern me. What is your name?"

"Jesus Martinez,. Jesus Hay' Martinez," beading sweat.

"Hay?"

"*A*! *A*! Albert! My middle name is Albert."

The small monitor in the dashboard flips—unimaginably fast—to page 6,896 of a confidential cross-reference database the Feds use to locate *everyone* and Jesus sees his name, address, all his phone numbers, his social security number, hypertext links to his e-trail in all categories from phone calls, time cards, location exit and entrance times on mass transit, credit card account information and much more.

"This you?"

"Yeah," confused, mouth agape, "yeah..." And the screen flips to the third page of a Chase ATM transaction dial-up. Jesus is stunned when his password is entered for him and the cursor blinks underneath the "transfer amount" box.

"How much?"

"Wha'?" says Jesus.

"How much? Enter an amount."

BANG! BANG! BANG! Cops on both sides of the limo bang on the bulletproof glass and scare the shit out of Jesus. "Get out of the car!" they yell repeatedly their sentences stepping over one another. "Brice Johnson, we have a warrant for your arrest!? Open this door! Open this door now! Get out of the car!" Jesus tries frantically to open the door but it won't budge. "I can't open it! I'm not doing it!" The Viracon privacy glass feature turns every pane of glass except the windshield opaque white.

"Do you want to get paid?"

"Yeah, yeah! But I don't' want to go to jail or nuttin'!"

"Good. All you have to do is enter an amount and it will show up like a settlement from an accident you never had with the taxes already paid. Don't be afraid to be generous."

"Wha'?" Struggling to pay attention as the cops bang on the windows with the butts of their guns.

"I've already created the paperwork, back dated it and inserted it in the appropriate places so all you have to do is enter an amount and forget the conversation I had with Brice and you. Forget where he went and say 'I don't know nuttin' to the cops or I bury you in the legal system and crash your life."

Jesus looks startled and afraid but he quickly enters the random numbers US$155,386. The screen reads, "transfer completed" and before it reads, "would you like another transaction?" the screen has flipped to an NYPD message in white letters on a navy background, "Turn off your engine and obey the officers immediately. Your failure to do so will be sited at your arraignment." The doors unlock and Jesus exits meekly, his hands raised. The cops grab him and throw him against the car. Three semi-automatic handguns are trained on his chest and he knows it. The rear doors unlock the cops swing both doors open and have only each other to look at.

"The doors were stuck!" shaking. "The doors were stuck!" Thinking out loud, "Brice heard the sirens and ran that way," pointing towards Broadway. A small crowd forms on the sidewalk to check out the commotion and high above the eye-in-the-sky, having eavesdropping Jesus off a cop's lapel microphone heads towards Broadway.

SLO-MO THIS SHIT RIGHT HERE.

Seconds, only. A big linebacker of a cop slap-grabs Jesus' shoulder and a drop of sweat jack-knifes off his upper lip towards the hood of the car. B-e-f-o-r-e that drop of sweat lands on the hood a caffed' up freakizoid in the bowels of the Transit Police Monitoring Station spots Brice Johnson via a RMFR (Rapid Map Facial Recognition) program the cops use to locate perps above and below ground.

It would take three minutes for the spotter to contact the appropriate surface cops and the heat to travel up B's ass.

BE COOL.
F TRAIN, BETWEEN STATIONS, HEADING SOUTH

B's chest was a meringue drum.

His thoughts were racing and his wide eyes darted around the car. "Be cool. Be cool. Don't draw attention to yourself." He reached over a short man's head and held on to a steel bar connected to the car. "Fuckfuckfuck! Shit! That had better' been Home!" noticeably unsure. "Couldden' been him. Somebody deep though. Somebody moved fast—real fast to get—no watch my ass. Diddn' sound like nobody I know—'en he had all my numbers. How?" putting on a large pair of sunglasses. "Shit!"

Several people were talking on cell phones and one guy next to B' was reading the New York Times on a flat-screen imbedded in pair of reading glasses. The whole car-full of people swayed from left to right as the train accelerated. Bright holo-ads flashed across the ceiling. A Jamaica Tourism ad appears and everyone in the car saw footage of the surf at Point-Of-View Villas. An attractive caramel woman wearing a fuchsia bikini bends over and cups her hands cradling the riders. As she smiles and straightens up bringing everyone into the sunlight, a narrator reads the scrolling type, "Come back to Jamaica." And a Reggae riff swells.

Brice holds his hand over his face and scans the car from his vantage point twice and is relieved that no one is looking at him. "Plan of attack. What is it? What the fucks my next move? This is not a fucking game." nodding. "Alright. I'm in play but traveling. Pursued but not cornered. But they could be waiting for me up ahead. Right. Right!" deep breath, exhale. "Get off the next stop and change trains or run like a motherfucker. Which ever presents itself as the best op. Cool." Remembering. "Cameras! Watch the fucking cameras! Shit!"

The doors open.

B' exits with a flood of people with his black jacket pulled over his head like a crazy person. Bumping into people, B' tries to orient himself without looking up and being caught on camera. Walking between the train and the painted iron beams that support the station, he is slowed by peds who want to enter the train. Unknowingly, he passes by the conductor's open window, "Alright! Alright I heard you! I'll hold the train." B' cranes his neck to listen. "But I said, do I make an announcement or what? Police?! Naw' 'course I ain't gonna' say 'dat——you fucking jokin' me or wha'…" B' lowers his head and walks quickly towards the exit. As he passes through the turnstile he sees a vending machine with its main screen and back light area blinking. Suddenly a message catches his attention, "Brice, over here." It startles him and he stops in disbelief. Just then it shoots out a sealed, disposable cell phone that says *New York Yankee's* on one side and *Telephone International Systems LTD.*, on the other. B' takes a step closer and another message pops up. "Come on take this, get to Chinatown and call Chili." B', his mouth wide open, bends and picks it up. "This is too fucking weird," he says turning towards the exit. In the Video Commuter Surveillance Unit of the Police Transit Authority downtown their cameras flicker and come back online having been off on the entire F line since B' entered the subway.

Up the stairs, three at a time, jacket off and in a ball in front of his face B' fakes coughing repeatedly into it to obscure his face. Finding the sunlight bouncing off the white and black tiles he takes his time and grabs a handrail with his right hand.

42ND STREET AND SIXTH AVENUE, SOUTH EAST CORNER

Still faking the cough, wide eyes dart the street. "No sign of the man." Seeing a busted flat screen in an "I Love NY" trashcan he grabs it and puts it to his face. "Sixth Avenue goes one way. North. Walk south." With Bryant Park on his left and the smell of French Roast filling his nostrils from a Cafe Society stand he power-walks it to 41st Street and stops cold. The man is screaming up Sixth. "Be cool." The patrol car flies past a northbound 6 bus and jumps the southeast curve B' just skipped from. The two cops run down and into the subway station. Sirens blare in the distance and B' has already run across Sixth heading west on 41st Street.

He was never so glad to be among so many people. The pretzel vendor and the roasted peanut guy both had people waiting to buy and he ran through them.

Jogging through slush past tacky wholesale clothing shops, a parking lot, a computer repair shop and several office building entrances B' didn't realize that his heart rate was way up. Frowning, "Damn! These Gucci's weren't made for running and my fuckin' feet are getting wet! God damn it!" barks his inner-voice. Conditioning was great but being chased in the real world meant that all bets were off. "Yeah!" shouts B's inner voice at the sight of a red double-decker tourist bus on the other side of Broadway. He doesn't even think. He sprints. Way ahead of the oncoming traffic, "Come on biker," B' sidesteps the short Hispanic guy wearing a red "NY Sites" vest over a cheap counterfeit Polo jacket and boards the bus. He dashes for the back when a the driver shouts, "Hey man!" pointing to a portable Point-of-sale card reader at the side of the driver's column. B' freezes then walks towards the driver slowly. Extracting his wallet and debit card he inserts it and holds his breath. It works. "Thank God. Maybe they spool all their transactions later—they'll catch my name then, whatever, I don't know. Either way I'll see the man coming or be gone."

A moment later he's seated in the back of the bus with the broken flat screen in front of his face. It takes an eternity. Twelve minutes for the tour guide to give the driver the high sign and the door to close. A freak in a shiny silver parka flicks on his hand held mike and the only word that registers in B' conscienceless is "…Chinatown."

" '…Ending in Chinatown.' Yes! Yes—s!"

31 MINUTES LATER, BROADWAY AND HOWARD STREET

Cars and buses take up every available piece of tar. Peds stream on both sides of B'way, so many that they overflow into the street. Everything moves. A red light stops the bus and B' springs up. Leaving the flat screen behind he's balled up his jacket and nearly tramples the guide on his way to the front of the bus. B' leans into the driver and says, "I'm going to be sick! I'm going to throw up!" The driver winces, pulls over and opens the door. Flash. Slush. B' is gone into the crowd and headed south.

The smell of frying meat and car exhaust and Chinese-Spanglish chatter fill the air. Rip-off, imitation tech, faux designer bags, clear memory cubes, peripherals, sunglasses, NYC T-shirts, hats and jackets, sneakers—all forms of multi-colored merchandise hanging from hooks everywhere. Merchants bragging, pawing and haggling with tourist for "…Great deal…pleasure cubes…just discontinued…$50 dolla'…bargain!" all around like a DJ's scratch mix.

He tore the wrapping off the phone and pressed the call button. It said, "Hello and welcome to Verizon. What number would you like?"

"I don't have his friggin' number. I don't even know his last name or if Chili'z his real name. You don't know where he lives, you don't know where he works——if he works——damn! Damn! Think," said B' to himself. Through the street rancor and random city energy it clicks and he thinks "The last time I talked to Chili I told him he could have Wilks' trashed ride after the race!" Then says to the operator. "Operator, a residence please—no! Could you give me the number for somebody's' motorcycle phone? Yeah, the name is John Wilks. Yeah." His inner voice says, "This is a long shot. If Wilks handed the bike over to Chili he probably disconnected the number by now. Unless he forgot." To the operator, "Can you dial it for me," sounding timid and soft. Shaking his head, expecting the worst. B' looks around nervously. It rings three times before a guy picks it up.

"Hello?"

"Who's this?"

"Freddie. Who's this?"

"I thought I was calling Wilks."

"Naw—w. This was Wilks' ride but it's Chili's now. Later."

"Hold up! Hold up! I want to talk to Chili. I'm calling for him not

Wilks!"

"Who're you?"

"Somebody that owes him money—I lost his number. He there?"

"This a bike shop man."

"Can you forward this call to him?"

Pissed, "Hole' on, hole' on," moving away from the receiver, "I got shit to do—yo' Louie! Louie! Hey man you got Chili's digits!? Somebody wants him—I doe' know! Come on man—I got shit to do!" A long minute passes. "Yeah, call 686-732-5816," click. B' dials it and mouths "Come on. Come on." On the second ring Chili's service picks up and B' press the "yes" option for the optional two-way video that charges an extra fee from his phone card.

"This is Chili," wearing a red and black jester's hat and black turtle neck, "Whatdda' ever you want I got but first off you gotta' impress me," and the image shatters. "Leave a message." Flashes on the screen in white letters and a counter reads off the time elapsed.

"Yo Chili," removing his sunglasses and getting close to the phone's lens. "This is Brice. We gotta' talk. A major load hit the fan and somebody tole' me to call you. I'm on lower Broadway now and I'm going to—shit I don't have a number where you can reach me! Fuck! Alright, aright, meet me—meet me…Listen I don't know shit down here but I tell you what, Mott Street. I know there are a lot of places to eat on Mott Street but I'm going to do this. I'm going to walk across Canal to Mott and turn left—north—and I'll—I'll go into the first sit-down place to eat I see. The first diner, fast food, restaurant whatever I see on the left side—the Westside of Mott Street just north of Canal. I'm going there now. I'll wait an hour maybe two. No longer. I'll make it worth your while man. Later." Click and tosses the phone in the street where it shatters. "I hope this shit works. Check your fucking messages Chili. This is a long shot but what else can I do?" he puts the sunglasses and mask back on and heads for Canal. Suddenly the adrenaline of the search for Chili and the call wears off. He realizes that he's wrapped up his only hope in the possible no show of some shady character he doesn't even know all that well, "Met the motherfucker at some party when I was drunk last year." And the reality of his situation made him feel small and helpless.

Self-conscious and feeling exposed, he covered his nose and mouth with his hand and seeing a low rent storefront on the corner, booked for it. He grabbed a blue, NY Giants knit cap, a big pair of knockoff designer shades and a bullshit filter mask that all the geeks worried about air quality wore.

Alone.

As he turned to corner heading east on Canal and merged with the scattershot flow of ped traffic to walk the five long blocks, it hit. He was oblivious to his surroundings. To everything. Disconnected. He walked right by a large plasma screen in a store window that advertised his upcoming bout with Joseph Santiago, in Cuba. The ad strobbed VR animation of fierce *Doppes* clashing and urged you to, "Reserve your link now for this no-holds bout! Only a limited amount of viewers will be allowed to jack-in and ride Santiago, or Johnson as they fight to a bloody knockout! Pay now, die later!" It ended with side-by-side close-ups of B' and Santiago sweating and wearing their game faces looking mean and *onit*.

Being disconnected from an all access—access for the first time in his life was an unfamiliar sensation. Suddenly he felt like he was walking on the bottom of the ocean floor like one of those old time divers wearing a heavy, brass helmet and weighted down, only he was walking through pea soup and barely aware of where he was going.

29 MINUTES LATER, THE NEW ORIENTAL PEARL RESTAURANT, 103-105 MOTT STREET

"I hate tea."

B's game face drifted in and out. He felt his insides quiver with caffed' up anticipation. Just below his epidermis was a wild, raging animal. A furry, primordial thing with jagged teeth that wanted to lurch up, roar, rip a limb from the big guy two tables away and beat everyone with it. He could hear the roar stretch out as the thick wine colored blood from the severed arm arced and splattered onto the red wall. People screaming and running—tables and chairs overturned. Just like that. Wild, unhinged brutality. Crystalline. Pure. Then when it was over that sense of release would cleanse him and everything would be all right. Instead, he grabbed the table leg and tried in vain to crush it.

B' sat all the way in the back of the New Oriental on purpose with his back to the wall. His peripheral vision was consumed by the bright red felt and metallic gold Chinese characters. "Luck, huh?" He had snatched a flat screen somebody left on a chair and was trying to read the news but he couldn't concentrate. He read the same sentences over and over and still couldn't remember what he had read. Every few seconds he'd peak over the top of the flat screen to see if somebody was coming in. "Come on Chili, come on…" He had been to the disgusting toilet and figured a back door to an alley was at the rear of the narrow kitchen beyond. His left leg jutted out from under the table and his foot remained flexed, so he could leap up and around the corner for the kitchen if he saw The Man walk in. "Yeah, like they wouldn't surround the whole fuckin' block, if they knew I was here," he scoffed. The stress was taking it's toll and his eyes were open so wide for such a long time, that the dryness made him blink too much to seem normal. The place was filling up with a dinner crowd and B' ordered a few dishes he didn't touch to keep the waiter off his back. He kept thinking he should eat a wonton but they were cold now.

"I should really 'up outta' here. I could wait across the street in that noodle shop and call him if I see he's on the way in—naw'. I don't wanna' be exposed. Come on Chili. Come on. Where are you?"

A figure came in wearing all black. Looked like Chili but sans the funny hat. Click! "It's him!" Looking purposely legit and decked out in black denim, Chili saw him right away and walked around the diners. He was wearing small rectangular glasses that were tinted baby blue and carrying a large shopping bag from the Pearl River Mart.

They greeted each other with a fist to fist touch just before Chili said, "You waz' any hotter dheyd' be a fire-truck outside boy."

B's inner voice yells, "Oh shit! Chili'z got nappy hair!" Then says, "Thanks for coming man."

"Not every day I get a distress signal from a billionaire."

"I'm in a bad way man."

"Oh, I know all about your bad way. You 'da six o'clock news—s. Da' cops want you. Da' mob wants you and the media is chompin' like a dog inna' 'butcher shop talkin' about you."

B's expression says, "Oh sh*it*—*t*."

Chili lets a moment stretch out. "But I got your back doe'," handing B' the shopping bag. "Go change into this shit in the bathroom. When you come on out, walk outside an' turn right. Walk to the corner real—l slow and I'll meetcha'."

B' takes the bag and starts to say something like, "Chili when this is over..."

"You'll hook me up. Oh, I know you'll hook me up man cause this is a deep smelly load you're in my man. But I'm your boy. You going undercover—blink," blinking, "Like a genie an' shit," reaching for his wallet, "Go, I'll pay the bill." B' is not even through the doorway and Chili has signaled his boy, Tuffy a sumo looking oaf in an Adidas tracksuit to wait outside. In the same glance he gets the attention of the waiter and makes the international air-signature sign for "check please." Chili watches the waiter walk over to a cash register and approaches him. Surprising the waiter, he presents his debit card with two fingers and readies his thumb for the signature print.

MINUTES LATER ON MOTT STREET

Chili walks up on B' who is now decked out in homeboy couture. Wearing a puffy, orange and black Bengal's' jacket, a black CK T-shirt, a *Nova Nigghas!* record label baseball hat, a big pair of glasses and a fat gold chain B's look says, "One punk of many." As he walks the digital fabric of the Bengal's' jacket causes the orange and black stripes to coil and cycle like large constricting boas around his torso, reflecting on the wet blackness of the street.

"Act like you got attitude motherfucker," says Chili to Brice half-joking. "Gotta' scare som' tourist an' shit!" and they cross Canal diagonally heading west. As they pass by the Honduran made Japanese 4X4s and assorted imports, they skim driver's audio environs. Dub reggae with heavy base notes swell, as he passes a Range Rover and is replaced by rapid fire Meringue a moment later, near the open window of a beat up Ford. The sounds of people talking in several languages and business being conducted in store-fronts, all swirl and pump into Brice's ear drums like dirty water down a drain. His shoulders tighten up and he clenches his teeth dreading a syn' moment the second before he feels the sound around him press against the skin on his chest, arms and back like a rough rubber balloons. The sounds turn into yellow, spherical constants that dart at him and pop.

Chili thinks of saying, "Best way to disappear is to scream lookit' me! Right!" but keeps silent and glances at B' instead.

Feeling like a sore thumb B' cowers at the thought of trying the pimp-roll Jimmy had mastered so many years ago but is slightly amused.

"We only gotta' couple ah' blocks and I got us three bouncers az' escorts. One in front and two behind. Dhey' think they here to watch my back. Don't know nuttin' 'bout you."

B' remembers his training now and his body language goes *game on*. He blocks out the distracting stimulus of the ads and car sounds. He walks with his head slightly down so his eyes look up and over the fake glasses. He's looking for a quick movement in his peripherals and the sound of clothes rustling quickly towards him. All that time as a boy honing his senses as he walked down NYC streets was turned on. He could tell the height of a ped by the time their feet took between steps. He could accurately guess weight and sex by the sound shoes made on the concrete even if they were jogging, but these crowds made it impossible. Either way, he was on edge.

As they approached Cortland Alley, B' felt Chili take his arm and slowly move him into the shadows. Tuffy had already entered the alley and didn't look back. The two other no necks, stopped at the edge of the alley and turned their backs on the three.

Chili turns to B' and says, "You must have a bigass closet of designer rags right?"

B' shrugs not aware that he is in sweatshop central.

They pass what looks like an emergency exit and Chili stops at a blackened window. He looks down both ends of the alley and sensing that the coast is clear grabs the right side of the wrought iron bars and pull it towards him. The bars turn on small hinges and make a creaking sound. Someone opens the window from the other side and Chili motions B' to jump inside. A moment later Chili does the same and B' stands there checking out the hairless little man in a soiled T-shirt who picks up a shotgun. Chili has already moved into the passageway and is motioning B' to follow. The hallway's dim lighting and dirty green walls makes it feel like a tomb. Chili points at the alarmed door just as the little man with the shotgun picks up his container of Mooshu Pork and continues to eat. "Anybody walks in that door gets shot," says Chili. The T-shirt says something in Chinese into his wrist-phone and a noodle falls out of his mouth.

"What happens if you try to walk out?"

Chili ignores him. "Don't look at anybody here in the eyes they don't look at you. Don't say nuttin' don't touch nuttin' just follow me and don't stop." As they walk B' takes solace in the "game" aspect of the environ and it spikes his senses like a finger stroke on the underside of his cock. As they change direction B' can hear a racket coming from behind a wall. Just as they reach the door at the end of the hall it swings open. B' never saw who opened it but he heard it close behind him. They walk right through a large gambling room filled with cigarette smoke and men shouting at each other in Chinese. Gamblers were amping at each other. One guy was so plus, the spit from his machine-gun chatter landed on B's sleeve as the guy jumped up and down in his chair, arms outstretched and veins popping from his neck. Slam! They were through another door and in near blackness. It smelled of piss and the floor was covered in broken ceramic tile and B' realized that they were in a dank old bathroom. Chili stepped into a tub lined with plaster dust and broken tile, on the far wall he stuck his finger into a crack. Something clicked and a section of the wall opened. He steps through and Brice follows. They were in an adjoining building now and Chili slams the hidden door shut.

Brice's expression says, "I'm impressed," noting the way the door disappeared and became indistinguishable from the ancient vertical wood panels. Chili immediately turned and walked to the far end of the hall. As the hall turned, B' could make out a dimly lit stairwell with rotting wood railings and steps. Three steps down they pass a wiry Chinaman holding a Poseidon Norinco Gong, a pistol sized 10 gauge semi-automatic shotgun smoking a cigarette, while reading a flat screen. B' didn't look at the guy and the guy didn't look at B'. The Chinaman just made a sucking sound with his mouth and inserted a toothpick.

At the bottom of the stairs they entered an old furnace room that smelled like dead rats and Chili closed the door behind them. An exposed florescent illuminated the gray refuse of pipes and milk crates full of designer labels and hot-glue guns. One-gallon Poland Spring plastic bottles lined the wall—some containing urine and cigarette butts abounded. In the far corner Chili moved an old radiator away from the wall and removed a large piece of rusty tin that revealed a hole in the wall. He bent down and crawled through. When B' came through the hole he guessed he was in yet another building's basement, only divided into rooms.

"This is the only way in or outta' here," said Chili to Brice as pointed to the hole. He then raised his index finger slowly to show B' a camera and remote controlled automatic gun mounted on the ceiling, "And we *don't* have a rodent problem."

B' shivered.

Chili walked to a door and opened it for Brice. He flipped a wall switch and B' took in the entire room in a glance. It was not even a quarter the size of his walk-in closet in his penthouse and the floor was bare concrete. A small bed with some folded gray sheets, a small refrigerator, a toilet, a sink, a microwave, three shelves of canned food, two wooden chairs and a fucked up Holo-V set on top a descrambler comprised all the furnishings. B's heart sank through the floor.

"Nobodyz' gonna' find you here. Nobodyz' gonna' hear you here. Upstairs is a legit sweatshop and the owner don't ask no questions he just plays Sinatra real loud all day. And anyway—way down here is sealed."

"Cool," says B' as he slowly takes off his jacket and hat.

A molasses moment.

Chili takes a step towards Brice and motions sympathetic. "I know what you're thinking. This place sucks and you ain't never been in shit like this in your life. You ain't 'da first fugitive I brought down here. Me and my boyz' gonna' take care you. Don't worry. There's a phone in that box behind the set and some other shit. It only receives calls and the only persons' gonna' call you is me. Gotta' man watching your back 24/7 so you can completely chilly-willy. I know this ain't the Plaza man but nobody can find you and we can take our time and plan your next move 'aright. Tomorrow I'll see 'bout getting you a deck an' whatnot'. I'm gonna' show up with a hacker."

"Yeah, yeah that's cool," says B' plopping down on the bed.

"Listen, don't let this shit get the best of you," shaking hands, "It's gonna' be aright' B'."

"Alright. Cool."

"See you tomorrow. Call before I come," with his hand on the old painted doorknob.

"Chili."

"Yeah man?"

"I need you to find my brother."

"See what I can do."

"An' Chili—thanks man."

B' saw Chili nod then leave, but he didn't walk out of the room so much as dissolve, as far as B' was concerned. A moment later he heard the tin being moved into place and the radiator being moved back. Then, silence. He felt more than said to himself, that he would rise soon and move the considerable latch to lock the door, but he didn't rise. Unknowingly, he caught himself looking at his pant leg in the exact same position he was in his limo not long ago. It would be a long time before he would move.

FLIP TO: THE GRANT HOUSING PROJECTS, 125TH STREET AND BROADWAY.

Just off 125th Street and down a cement path is the entrance to the defunct Grant Houses Health Center. The earthen sections that sandwiched the concrete path were left to ruin long ago. The earth was dry and supported no plant life whatsoever. Strewn with potato chip bags and an assortment of fast food containers, the entrance to the space where doctors once treated the sick and ailing, is as unkempt, nondescript and inviting as a basement door. Having been closed for over a decade, it was forgotten until rented for storage space, only to be left vacant a short time later. The windows were painted black and secured by thick wire fencing and near sound proof. Its entrance was removed from the street, making it ideal for trysts between hookers and the City Superintendent responsible for maintaining the five buildings that made up these projects. Of late he rented it to Samuel Heath, a sometime drug dealer and second-story man who had made the acquaintance of John Taylor who was employed by Niemöller.

Inside, Jimmy rolled over on the filthy, torn, striped mattress and felt the full weight of his head as his swollen eye made a temporary indentation in the mattress. He winced as it throbbed and felt the dried blood flake from his lower lip and chin. Pain like a hammer at the base of his skull, slowed him down as he tried to rise and when he opened his eyes there was nothing but the faint grayness of a featureless room with cinderblock walls. A spec of light sliced through the top of a window through a small crack in the reinforced glass. The light seemed to have its very will broken, upon entering the space and Jimmy could make out that there was no furniture except for an aluminum chair and desk. The tiled floor was cold to the touch and covered in years of dust, that Jimmy having disturbed was now airborne and carefree. Jimmy could hear his heart pounding and while licking his dry lips realized that he desperately craved water. He could see a closed door on the wall adjacent to the mattress, but its knob was removed. A sudden blood rush to his head and he seemed to faint more than collapse the moment after he smelled his urine soaked pants.

HIDING OUT IN CHINATOWN WITH CHILI
DAY 1

DREAM: NIGHT, A COBBLESTONE STREET IN A BLEAK EUROPEAN CITY

The echo of boots running shatters the silence. Yelling followed by screams. Men in black uniforms find out that some of the people they thought were burned alive, lived. Shadows chase each other around corners and down an alley.

B' is in a gymnasium and sees many coffins one on top the other inside of drawers. He opens one and sees a pretty young girl with short hair. She opens her eyes. He leaves her coffin open but it closes by itself.

A MOONLESS NIGHT AT SEA

B' is seated on a large rowboat with no oars or engine, the men in black uniforms are seated at the rear of the boat behind him. Between him and the men is every manner of flea-market junk piled high. Each piece is black and oily. Everything else, the sky, the men's skin, everything is gray-black. In the distance an industrial plant spews black smoke into the sky. The sea is jet black like crude oil. The young girl from the gymnasium rises out of the water, hair dry, emotionless, she cries, "Mother!" in a strange language to no one in particular. A small black snake jumps out of the water near her and she screams but her body remains taut. Small wires, of all shapes and sizes rise up and protrude from the girl's mouth in rapid succession until her jaw and mouth are filled to capacity. Her eyes go wide with fright but the rest of her body seems immobilized. More snakes, of all sizes and the hand of a black skeleton raises her out of the water. The snakes cover every part of her below her neck. Only her torso is out of the water now and a black cage materializes around her. Then, a small doll, with Caucasian features and black skin, curly hair, with big scary eyes and tiny pupils rises from the water. The doll makes biting noises as its teeth jam together, as she moves towards the girl. B's perspective shifts and he is above the girl now looking down at her. The doll bites the girl and extracts her stomach with her teeth—no blood—and the skin snaps back.

6:55 AM, HIDDEN BASEMENT ROOM, IN A BASEMENT ON CANAL STREET

B' rises straight out of bed sweating.

He had fallen asleep in his clothes with the lights on and the reality of the damp concrete and the utter silence pimped-slapped him so hard, it sent a shiver down his spine. He was sure he'd only slept for two hours, max.

"That was freaky. I don't want to know what it meant. The fuck would my shrink say?"

Rising, he forces himself to do Tai Chi, but does it with too much force. Tension. The tension in his muscles makes his body resist. Frustrated he stops and plop down on the bed. Looking over at the Bengal's jacket, he takes stock of his worldly possessions. His Touch Card, a small case of air plugs—which made him smile considering the lack of sounds down here—his key-card—suddenly he stops. "I'm reduced to this—this ain't happening…" fingers on his temple, "…Can't…" His eyes froze open wide with fright-fury. "What if I've lost everything—everything…" His world formed a thick, complex montage of sounds starting with his EZ idling, his leather jacket against the leather seat in his Aerodyne, Home's voice saying *good morning.* Sights like seeing the Jaguar in the showroom for the first time, looking down at a bloodied Samson, Olga in ecstasy, the view from his penthouse on a clear night, fans running up to him. The sensation of his suede jacket against his fingertips. The way Olga's hair smelt. The unbridled happiness and exhilaration, after winning his first bout as a scrawny kid. The close-up of Bruno at the orphanage, his head blocking out the sun as he stood over Brice, who is laid on the pavement, bloodied. "Loser, sucker punk!" shouted Bruno all lips, teeth and furrowed brow, surrounded by a horde of leering kids on a sweltering afternoon. "Wimpy, faggot, bitch! I'm the man around here! You're just one of my bitches and you never ever give me rays again like you don't know it! I'm the man! I'm the man! I'm the man!" shouted Bruno emphasizing each "man" with a poke at his own chest. Brice remembered that the blood from his lip seemed to race away from his face as if in disgust, diving to the playground concrete. Even the sun ridiculed him through each of Bruno's blond spiked hairs. Nothing but clenched teeth and furrowed skin.

RING!

The phone conversation with Chili lasted seconds.

"Chilil' be here soon," thought B'. He lay on the bed his legs bent, one over the other, staring at the ceiling. In his right hand he is fondling his most prized possession. More precious to him than any expensive toy he had ever bought, or his apartment or the plane—anything. His dead mother's sterling silver, oval tag screwball key ring from Tiffany's with his mother's initials engraved—the only thing he had of hers. He had taken the useless keys off ages ago and never left the house without it. Having died in a fire while he was still a two year, old he could not remember what she looked like and all pictures and image files of her had been consumed. Funny he thought. In the third world it was water via floods that decimated whole towns, cities even islands sometimes, through slow insidious erosion but in the first world it was fire either from man, or from a computer that took lives fortunes or both.

He desperately wanted to stop thinking. His mind was cranking and he wasn't a morning person. The questions cascaded, "Chili gonna' walk me outta' here? They thinking to off me? Could be they holding my ass ransom right now and I woudden' even know it. Can I trust this motherfucker? How do—how am I ever gonna' find out who killed Olga, when I'm stuck here? The fuck is Jimmy?! Musta' been snatched by the police, cause he'd never do me like this unless—he'z—How 'em I gonna' step outta' this? Got to find out who'z fucking me? Who the fuck is fucking me?! 'M I ever going to get out of this? Gotta' be mobile—hire somebody—find out who shitfucked me. They need to pay. Stone cold. Hyperfrenzyclusterfuckpay. Mercilessly. Then *l-e-t* the Man come for my ass. Jus' lemme' go thermonuclear on 'em an' right this." a beat. "Feel like Sinbad an' shit—the Gods jus' jerkin' me for game."

B' rises and walks to the box on the floor near the set. Rifling through it he picks up a recorder with a multi-plug, universal jack sticking out of it. Getting an idea he quickly puts the box down and picks up his jacket. Reaching into a pocket he extracts a sealed phone card and tears the wrap off with his teeth. He lowers his body without looking and sits on the edge of the bed as he searches for a tiny hole in the card.

"Cool," says B' while inserting the end of a fiber optic plug into the card...

T-i-m-e.

B' heard the tin scratch against the concrete outside his door and leapt off the bed. He was at the door and sliding the latch before even he knew it. Chili walked in wearing a forest green Elf hat and a black leather jacket with matching black ensemble', carrying a McDonald's bag, a brown shopping bag and a long thin package wrapped in brown paper. He looked beat. Behind him, a scrawny geek sporting pale, acne riddled skin and a bad attitude walks in wearing club-kid clothes that are too big for him.

"'Sup B'?" said Chili fist to fist.

"'Sup."

"Breakfus'," handing B' the McDonald's bag. "Sleep a'rite?"

B' frowns.

"Temporary situation man. Temporary."

"That makes me feel betta'."

Looking at the geek, "'Dis here's *the one who shall remain nameless*. He'z sworn to secrecy by pain of def'. Ain't that right nameless?!"

The one who shall remain nameless frowns.

Chili points to a chair, "Siddown'." The geek and Chili sit on the chairs as B' sits on the bed and opens the bag from Micky D'.

Chili rests his forearms on the back of the chair in front of him. He uses his hands a lot. "You an' Olga all ova' the news like free money. Flip to the first page B'. What happened, how, who—dyin' to know how you thought ah' me. He ain' gonna' tell nobody." pointing at the geek. "As of this morning we are both in your *employ*," yawning and grabbing his crotch.

B' bit into the Egg Mac Muffin and looked at Chili out of the top corner of his eye. "Somebodyz' fucking me and somebody else called and told me to jet jus' before the man tapped me. Don't know who it was. Knew all my shit doe'. Connected. Sure all my shits' been compromised—hope not assimilated though." chewing. "I'm in my limo right, trippin' on Olga an' Jimmy being missing..." freezing.

"I got nuttin' yet on Jimmy man. Been up all night inquiring but my people are on it. But I got nuttin', nuttin'."

"Yeah, yeah—h. So I'm trippin' right and I get this call...?"

"From who?"

"I don't know. That's what I'm tellin' you. My phone rings, I don't know who it is, I don't answer it. Got filters an' agents to screen all my shit. Paid top dollar for techsperts to tighten all my shit up—my vmail, voice numbers, access to all my shit an' this motherfucker sidestepped all that and called me on *all*—l my numbers at the same time. The same time Chili! Every line—car, watch, driver—the driver's—his private line rang for me." The geek is impressed.

"For you?"

"For me! That's what I'm tellin' you! I woudden' pick up the phone so the motherfucker kept calling—all at the same time, 'till I had to pick-up, an' got informed that the man waz' coming and he wazzen' playin'. I tell you— whoever that was, they dug' deep, stripped wires, an' found tha' right way. Bitch took control of my ride, opened my door, let me know the train was coming—paid—paid my fucking fare man!"

"Damn." says the geek..

"Yup'. Paid my fare—sure he held the door for me too. Told me to call you, but he made me ditch my watch so I had to guess and hope..."

"How'd you dial me?"

"Figured—guessed you'd have Wilks' bike. Dialed it, got your number."

"Hip reasoning."

Chewing. "That's the how to. Now," chewing, putting the bag on the floor and opening the lid on the coffee, "Now, I'm in deep but that's an aside, what I want is the motherfucker that put me here—framed me. I want to get to work on him with a deli meat slicer. I want to find my brother and get my ass back to 53rd Street. Check." B's determined look took them both aback.

"Well we aim to please B' but vengeance costs money?"

"I got money! But with the man up my crack that ain't gonna' help neither of us for a while."

Chili smiles and holds his open palm up in front of the geek who rises

Wired for Chaos

and takes two devices out of his oversized pocket. He gives Chili a slick, metallic-purple, Kevlar-alloy ATM, the size and shape of a deck of playing cards. He works the small touch screen and calls up some a list of international banks and hands it to Brice. "We've got a way around that."

The ATM is heavy and cold. "Chili," exasperated. "You and I both know..."

"We not taking nothing now B-man. Not making any real-time withdrawals anytime soon or being stupid enough to hack, tap or scratch any bank's system."

"Then..."

"The memory constantly updates the time code. We record the transaction in this here remote and down it when your shit cools off..."

"I got it. I got it." Smiling and nodding, B' selects a bank and enters his information.

"Now we gonna' work it, like this here. I'm gonna' front this mission as much as I can. Some point I might have ta' tap a resource but that'll be on me. Then when your shit cools off we'll *send* the transaction. We don't deliver the goods as in keepin' your ass safe like a condom in a nunnery—we don't get paid."

"What's the damage?"

"Let's keep it straight-up. I'm onna' bill you as we go along every few days starting today. I figure the cost for hiding you, the muscle escort, my man here, shit I got for you, boyz' working behind the scenes to dig shit up and my fee..."

"Gimme' a number man," says B' noticeably exasperated.

"Five hundred large to get square."

B' doesn't even blink. He enters US$500,000 and is about to enter his password when Chili puts his hand up.

"Don't hit Send B', just pass it to me when the button lights up."

B' enters his password and presses his pinkie onto the flashing rectangle. "A different finger every time. Pressure sensitive memory, body temperature range matching, even stress gauged by the amount of sweat on the print. They take everything into consideration."

"That's exactly why we ain' no hacking fools B'."

B' looks directly into the pinhole sized lens and it records his right retina for a future check against the bank's records. He hands the screen with the flashing *send* button to Chili careful not to touch the screen. Chili takes the ATM, places it into it's hard case and snaps it shut. "This right here just turned into an expensive little piece of hardware," says Chili. He tosses it to the geek who fumbles the catch. "Don't lose it." He then gives the geek a tiny nod for the something else. Something rehearsed. Right then B' goes stiff. His mind banks and corners around a thought. "What if Chili waz' to off me right now and pocket the fifty? Stone cold, straight up, easy money—an' book." As the geek rises again to reach for something in his over-sized right jeans pocket, B' has already decided that he'd take Chili out with a chop to the larynx and ram the palm of his right hand into the spleen of the geek. Chili yawns and stretches. B' leans forward. Ready. Taut. The geek takes out a small, black cylindrical device. It has a Monte Blanc logo on one end but it's not a pen. The geek sits, looks at the gadget and his body language reads, *"this is the coolest little gadget."*

B' relaxes.

"This is the bolt!" says Chili staring at the device. The geek pulls the cap without removing it and it unfurls into a flat-screen, which immediately turns on. Now, shaped like a rectangular fan, the geek opens a file without touching the screen—his index finger barely a centimeter from its surface.

"I know what you're thinking B'," says Chili to Brice, not taking his eyes off the flat-screen.

B's eyes dart to the door and he listens hard for the footsteps of an assassin.

"Yes, I paid for it but I am gonna' bill you."

"Say what?" thinking that Chili said, *"Kill* you."

"I'm gonna' bill you for this here!"

Relaxing, "Oh, cool," says B'.

B' leans back and looks at the flat-screen thinking, "That really is the bolt." He yawns and says, "That a contract?"

"See that! That's why I'm working for Mr. Johnson, one who shall remain nameless," smiling. "Tight that shit up."

"Yeah," nods the geek.

Chili takes the flat-screen from the geek and passes it, using the handle to Brice. "This states that in the event of either an untimely death or a failure to produce the equipment, products, goods or whatever, or leak—in any shape or form, or aide or hinder your ability to hide from the man, the mob and all aggressive parties and—d that I never relate, record, give witness to, promote or make public any knowledge of our dealings and transactions, that all monies promised me are not transferred and all deals, bets—whatever are off. It also states that you can't welsh on my ass with your high-powered suits. Standard hiding a rich guy shit."

Reading, B' says, "That's what this says alright." B' readies his right thumb to press against the flashing signature-rectangle and stop. Looking at Chili he says, "Ever off anybody Chili?"

Uncharacteristically serious, "Na' man."

"Not with a gun, a knife, your hands or a phone call?"

"Na' man."

B' turns to look at the screen and presses his thumb at the center of the flashing rectangle.

"It's liberating."

A sentence below it reads, "A copy of this contract has been sent to your lawyers at Affleberg, Epstein & Rotter and Mr. Nyugen's attorneys."

"Don't ever cross me Chili," handing the screen back to Chili. "I'll do right by you but don't ever fuckin' cross me."

For a moment nobody makes eye contact with B'.

"Lemme' show you what I bought for you…" says Chili who is stopped by the sound of his phone ringing. He takes what looks like a fat square pen out of his inner pocket and reads, "Caller unknown" on the tiny screen. "Who 'dis?"

"Put Brice on," says the voice on the other end.

Noticeably surprised, "Who the fuck is this!?" says Chili.

"The party that told Brice to seek you out."

Standing in a panic, "How the fuck you get this number?!"

The geek says, "We been made?" All three jump to their feet.

"Who'z that..?" says B'.

"Lissen'! I ain't doin' shit you say 'till you tell me what the fucks' up!" stepping towards the door.

"I can tell the man where you're sorry, green, Elf hat wearing ass is in a blip and just might if you don't do exactly what I say. Now, pass the Motorola to Brice. And Chili?"

"Yeah?"

"B' takes his coffee black."

Chili looks at the phone as if it was possessed and hands it to B'.

Grabbing the phone, "Who the fuck are you?!" says Brice.

"How was your Egg McMuffin?"

Floored. "Listen——I don't know who…?"

"I'm your wizard Brice. Your Merlin. S-o-m-e-one you need."

"Home..?"

"Home is tucked in. Safe. Actually he is only a few blocks from you and I'll be happy to expedite his return but first you have to do something for me."

"I don't play other people's games."

"Exercises in irony *will* plague you, young Brice. Regardless, Jimmy has been snatched and I can get him and your life back but you must do what I say."

"Where is my brother?!"

"Work with me…"

"Where is my b-r-o-t-h-e-r!?!"

A beat.

"Are you finished? I know what you want and I know how to get it but…"

"How much do you want?" tensing, squeezing the phone.

"I don't want money, power or fame."

"What…?"

"Check your Mail but remember, the man is watching." Click.

NEWS UPDATE

Invisible waves penetrate buildings at every level of the city, delivering data via optical switches. On Holo-Vzs across the five boroughs talking heads speak. "Today, at city hall a spokesperson for the NYPD addressing the Rich Boy Shooting case and said that there were no developments, the Prosecution was moving forward with its case against Ramon Fuentes in the murder of a sleeping homeless man, despite his claims that Sean Arnold, the son of investment banker Thomas Arnold, actually pulled the trigger." Another talking head pops up, "Now more on the disappearance of Super model Olga Ericksson and the search for answers..." and another talking head, "With the disappearance of Olga Eriksson and the whereabouts of her boyfriend, Brice Johnson. The NYPD and FBI are making it very clear that they would like to question him but he seems to have disappeared..." and another talking head, "In fact, when questioned, the NYPD said that Mr. Johnson is wanted for questioning..." and another talking head, "News 7, has learned that Brice Johnson eluded the Police earlier today and made a daring albeit, miraculous escape from authorities just as he was about to be brought in for questioning."—and the newscasters fall into sync. Speaking in unison, their voices take the beat of a street rap. "And the man is scratchin' and sniffin' him out like a bull in heat, diggin' for skin..." and we see images of the police asking questions of Brice's doormen, interrogating his driver Jesus A. Martinez, sweeping his penthouse, interviewing Olga's agent, broker and friends, people spill onto the street behind Police Barricades in front of the luxury MoMa tower. "...Lickin' his thing—suckin' it in. An my boy is runnin'—ain' no talk 'bout gunnin'—jus' runnin'..." and we see the Russians asking people on the street if they have seen Brice, placing calls to contacts at the airports, bus stations and train stations. Brice's image appears on over 176 stations, while the police question his trainer, bodyguards, the delivery boy from D'Agastinos and the housekeeper. "Would you believe the man with a plan—stuck in sand—got no plan—hand of 'the man' yankin' his thang' and the hand iz' closing— niggahs rollin'..." Images of Brice flitter across the transom while InSpace thousands of *Doppes* stare up at B's image on mega screens and shake their heads. "The hand iz' closing. *Ca' ca' ca'ka* closing! Life is a bitchniggah'— wherezs 'ya triggah'...!?!"

20 MINUTES LATER CHILI WALKS EAST ON CANAL

Seeing a pay phone across the street Chili readies the card Brice told him to use. He had recorded a message for somebody, "a friend" and made a big deal about Chili being sure to place the call. Chili's expression twisted to "motherfucker" as he thought "Not even an hour and already he's my boss, givin' orders, making demands. Gotta' watch my ass 360° an' leave his ass cold if I get a wiff of shit. Gonna' charge his ass large for all the extra 'options' he is exercising though. Yeah. Charge his ass big."

Beyond uncomfortable with this task, Chili navigates peds wheedling noisy paprika- colored plastic bags filled with greens and fish, mostly old people wearing dowdy wool coats, as he breathes in car fumes and cigarette smoke. The card is in his left hand, its strip pointed away from him, Chili steps on the curb, swipes the card through the phone reader, bends it in half and throws it into a garbage can without stopping. Looking around, Chili puts his coat collar up and ducks into a side street.

GARAGE OF 9031 DAVID AVE., SINGLE STORY DETACHED HOME, LOS ANGELES, CA

Willy's head rang. "Hello," he said pressing the chip behind his ear. Willy was a burly, 44Short Phillipino who knew Kenpo, Kali and could kick *y-o-u-r* ass. He had bad teeth, jet-black hair he gelled to razor sharpness each morning and a nasty temper. Just the kind of guy you wanted to have your back, as you walked down that dark alley. Willy wore designer pants and a ribbed white whifebeater as he cleaned his guns in his parent's garage with a Marlboro hanging from the right corner of his mouth.

"Willy. This is Brice. It's a recorded message so don't bother asking questions. I—I don't know how else to put this man—I've recorded this message five times and it never comes out right. I'm in trouble. The deep heavy is going down and it's not a game. I've never called you in before but I need you man. I really need you. My brother has been kidnapped and the cops think, I—the cops think I killed Olga man! I kill for make believe, but this—this is insane man—n. Look, my world iz' blown up and I'm in real bad shape—hooked up, with a crew you wouldn't trust to deliver your pizza... Get here as soon as you can. I'll reimburse you. You know I'm good for it. I need you man." Click.

Willy hung up, put down the semi-automatic and took a deep drag on his cigarette. Squinting as the smoke got in his eyes he thought about how small B's voice sounded. He spread his arms wide and leaned on the worktable in front of the exposed light bulb, tools, guns and just breathed. His head lowered, the smoke rising around his head, he chewed the filter of the cigarette bending it downwards. Grabbing the cigarette out of his mouth, he mashed it into the hideous blue and orange, clay astray he made in third grade and straightened up. It wasn't supposed to happen like this, but Willy snapped his neck to the right and in cracking it got a dial tone on the phone imbedded in his neck.

SNAP-click!—-dial tone. "Dial Valerie Wilson travel."

"One moment please," said an automated voice.

Picking up the semi-Sig'and cocking it, "Gotta' help my boy outta' some shit."

2 ? HOURS LATER, BASEMENT ROOM, ON CANAL

B' did push-ups while he thought about what had went down earlier that day. He leapt to his feet and proceeded to pace like a cat. "Shoudden' of had that coffee. Last thing I fuckin' need to be caffed' up!" Like a newly caged tiger being loaded onto the back of a truck. "I'm gonna' lose my fucking mind in here. Too many people—The Man after me and that motherfucker on the phone are calling the shots and I don't like it. My life's not som' fuckin' game. Maybe I shoudden' of run from the man—that really made my ass look guilty.

They had any doubt I did it before—I sure squashed it. Idiot! If that guy on the phone is right though—if I'm being jammed—bet you it's Ivan. Yeah Ivan! That welching motherfucker probably wanted to cover his loss to me on that bet so he had my ass framed. Yeah, take me out for embarrassing him. That motherfucker—must be." B' continued to pace. "I'd feel better if I could just hit somebody."

Chili and *The One Who Shall Remain Nameless,* had dipped out to regroup over two hours ago. Their mission was to orchestrate a way for B' to retrieve his mail without the man tracing the call and tagging 'em. What worked was the engine in Chili's eyes once the voice on the other side of the phone disconnected. You could see the pistons bobbing. Steamin'. Sure B' was pissed, curious, shocked—whatever, but B's was in a cluster-fuck posture before he dialed Chili. Now it was Chili who had been violated and compromised so right now he was whipping his hackers into line for a piece of mischief.

"Damn!" said B' stopping his workout cold. "Whoever that guy is dialed in deep. Musta' hacked Mickey D'z cameras, street-cams and who knows what else. Followed Chili, waited till he guessed we had settled in," smiling, "guessed that I'd finished eating, an' then dialed him for the mind-fuck 'hear-me-know'." B' had also asked Chili to place a call for him and the uncertainty of it being placed rattled his consciences, his flavor of rage flipping like channels on the Holo-V. "Can't be Ivan. Too smart for Ivan. Whatever that guy wants—I don't know. I guess I'm cool for a minute only 'cause that's the way he wants it."

Looking at the stuff Chili brought him B' said, "'In a time of peace, prepare for war right.' Fuck! Whoever wrote it was right." B' tightens the joints on the staff and wields it like a master. Chili used his intuition. It was the trait of a good hacker. Logic, reasoning, resourcefulness but intuition always cut time and tasted the best. He brought Brice some of the things B' had used in bouts. What could make a warrior feel calmer that being with his weapons— or at least similar weapons that he used in well-publicized bouts. A convertible fighting staff, a filter-mask, black skull cap, fatigue green poncho, straw Chinese "coolie" hat, two tempered throwing knives and a black form fitting jump-suit made of ballistic, self-healing fiber. "Probably stop a knife," smiling, "That should be the worst shit gets thrown at me."

He heard the tin scrape against the concrete outside.

He took his time walking to the door as he donned a T-shirt. Chili as much barged past him, as walked in, with *the one who shall remain nameless* in tow. This felt familiar to B'. They worked for him and that soothed him. He immediately realized that this had always been the way of things. His inner-voice said, "My people take care of the business, the boring tedious grunt work and I dance on stage." This recognition came in the instant that he saw Chili's serious demeanor and B' switched on his game face.

"You..?" says B'.

"Don't worry. I placed the call like you tole' me," says Chili taking a

Wired for Chaos

few steps into the room and turning. "We gonna' do this but the second my boy here sniffs som' funkassshit' we book outta' there. Got that." closing the door and walking to the bed. "This shit just might require haste," said Chili sitting down. "So listen up—read you the code—siddown' man." To the geek, grabbing his crotch and waving his hand. B' sits in front of the two and picks at the dry cuticle of his right thumb.

"Naw', alla' your mail is kept for you on som' Verizon server which we would be stupid to frontal assault cause the man'z sure to have put bear traps on 'em…"

B's frown says, "What?"

"…Bear traps are lil' nasty agents law enforcement uses to harpoon yo' ass on the GPS grid—I'm the man, so I get a court order to drop surveillance—no, no, got a warrant for your arrest. Arrest see—so—so they attach these bear traps to yo' mail, you retrieve yo' mail an' the second you open it the bear trap—don't even let you know it's there. It just dials the man on your line and says come get me. I'm a stupid motherfucker. So what we gotta' do, is off the bear traps without gettin' traced. So here's how we gonna' do it." Chili nods at the geek who opens his shoulder bag and takes out a metallic gold deck in the shape of a Pyramid that would make an uptown pimp go, "D*hamn*—m baby!" with glee.

LATER

The three of them were InSpace and watching water boil. They had laid the trap earlier that day and were all jacked in to the Pyramid and waiting. The three, identical, alizarin crimson orbs, emanating dull, almost furry light represented Chili, B' and the one who shall remain nameless, undulated from time to time in a navy void. They floated in the upper most region of a domed midnight navy gateway that was bottomless and vast. Glowing beads of information sped up and down invisible lines attached to the floating windows, the three had opened at the speed of light, from deep in the void. For the uninitiated, a definite sense of vertigo would be unnerving, but for these three it was *no big thang'*.

"Fuck!" said Brice.

"What!? What!?" said Chili.

"Stalin, my dog. With all this shit going down I forgot all about him. Unless Jimmyz' resurfaced…there is nobody to feed him."

"You got people working for you right?"

"Yeah. I've got an assistant."

"Smart guy?"

"Smart girl."

"There you go. She'll put two and two together and take care of your business." With that they went back to their own thoughts.

Chili surrounded himself with five windows of various sizes and checked his vmail, paid bills, conference his girlfriend in Long Island and her mother in Taipei and kept an eye on a surveillance camera that showed various angels of the building they were in. From time to time he would switch to the view cam in a parked car on the street, to check that his boys were awake and watching for trouble. Another window downed every story relating to Brice Johnson from PR Newswire, CNN, Reuters and every other imaginable source. During the entire conversation, his girlfriend's mother thought she had his full attention, because she was actually looking at a computer generated Chili sitting on the violet couch in his crib. B' gave Chili a dull stare. Orbiting Chili were three, small, Feng Shui hexagonal mirrors. One represented health, the second wealth and the third success and each caught the reflections of Chili's orb and his windows as they circled him.

"Positive ch'i. Nice touch," thought B'. "Nice."

The geek on the other hand was doing what geeks do. Hacking. He preferred to work up close and personal with one large custom window housing his open applications in smaller cascading windows. The frame of his window had been designed and tagged by one of his graffiti-writing buddies, to scroll multi-colored badass tags like the Times Square zipper. He was busy conversing with someone using 3D characters he routinely dragged and dropped into a com' window. Every now and then the characters would blink and snap into a 3D construct in the distance.

"Whatever," thought B' way past bored with waiting for the ax to drop on a fool they had chosen and his empty screen to fill up with his mail—that is if Chili's plan worked.

44 BRIARWOOD AVENUE, SHORT HILLS, NEW JERSEY

The perfect suburban street, idyllic in every way. Perfect lawns, trees and homes. Forty-four Briarwood was, like many other homes in this upscale section of Short Hills, a pastiche of Colonial and prefab styles. Robby Moore, a hacker wannabe', "I'll idolize every inner-city badboy trend I can" comes home from a successful day of trolling for discarded tech from the dumpsters behind the mall. He takes the blonde oak steps two at a time and makes a hard right into his bedroom. Everything turns on and he immediately looks at his poster size flat screen, which pulses, "Yo! You got mail!" His room is decorated with life-sized holo-posters of Santiago, whaling on several different opponents, smaller posters of the new Ferrari and Miss July. His dresser supports a shrine to Santiago and is decorated with the Japanese flag, action figures of Santiago and an autographed picture that reads, "To Robby Moore, Regional Director of the Santiago fan-club. We rule. Santiago."

Robby scans his mail and sees a flashing exclamation mark over a text message from a buddy of his, Fast Eddie out of Miami. He clicks on it and a window belches open with a liquid frame. "Robby man! this is the bolt! my boy just hacked Brice Johnson's box and we got access to all his mail! Chk' it out: 212-334-2845, protocol YYN, password is 2398764509-1. don't have the time to do it myself. call you later."

"Oh shit!" says Robby, amazed at his good fortune. He immediately grabs his chair and dawns a headset. "Computer dial it." His system treats the 212 number like a hotlink and shuttles him Brice's MCI gateway page in a second. "YYN protocol, check. Password is 2398764509-1, enter." Smiling.

"Access granted, hello mama."What Robby sees is an orange and yellow screen with 1,071 pieces of mail in various forms scrolling before him and pre-sorted by date. "Fuckin' excellent." Clenching his fist, "Highlight all and copy to disc." Robby watches the 1,071 pieces of mail appear in the download folder on his hard drive and he clicks the first one open. *FLASH.* A radioactive lime-green Woody Woodpecker appears wielding an enormous erect penis and laughs at Robby. Behind him the mail has been selected and forwarded. Woody turns, bends over, spreads his cheeks and his anus expands to fill the flat screen on Robby's wall. *SPLAT!* His system is fried beyond repair, his phone lines fuse and the circuit breaker in the basement blows due to a power surge. Every appliance and electronic device that was plugged in is damaged beyond repair. Robby sits in his dark room in his dark house in utter disbelief. In eight minutes four police cars and two helicopters would deposit two detectives and six officers who would break down his door and remove him. He would be held for questioning and possibly arrested for aiding and abetting a fugitive from justice, one Brice Johnson.

RIGHT NOW, BASEMENT ROOM ON CANAL

Brice's window filled up with his mail encased in a clear virtual Lucite case. Chili and the geek were alerted to the arrival of the mail by a flashing strobe and siren in their windows. They quickly move away from their windows and pull along side the B-man. A program scans each piece of mail for bear traps and any other questionable code before it deposits the mail into the large area behind it.

"There goes one unhappy, Tanaka lovin' sucker punk, Jersey boy—y," says the geek.

B' smiles for the first time in days.

It only took a few minutes for the program to check all of B's mail and then he started sifting through them. Most of them were from friends or people who worked for him but it was the one with, "What are you waiting for?" in the subject line and "The Voice" in the sender's name that caught his eye.

"This iz' it," said B' out loud.

"How you know?" says Chili.

"Gotta' be. Who else would call themselves 'the voice'?"

"You're right."

"You sure this shit iz' alright to open?" says Chili.

The geek says, "No! I mean, it ain't got no bear traps or nuttin' unless the man came up wit' som' shit when we waz' sleepin'. Iono'"

Brice says, "Well, if we're fucked we'll know it pretty soon right?"

"Nah! Nah!," says Chili. "Hard bag this shit! I'm gonna' make a call and set up a new space for you to hole' up. This iz' gettin'…"

B's pointer comes to rest on the piece of text mail and he double clicks. It opens and reads, "Dial 212.834.8433.2394.GE"

"What the fuck is that?" asks Brice.

"I don't like this one bit," says Chili.

"I dunno' man. Not like any number I've ever seen."

The geek has already started to dial the number in a small Bell Atlantic window.

"Tha' fuck are you doing man!" says Chili. "We don't fucking know who the fuck that is! Could be the fuckin' man set us up an' shit!"

"Doubt it," says the geek. "It's one of 'em service-maintenance lines manufactures use to run diagnostics on refrigerators an' microwaves an' shit."

"You sure? How you know!?"

"Jus' guessin' that's what the GE—like General Electric means."

"So the long number is actually a data line that flows through the electrical wiring—the outlets in homes right?" says B'.

"Right." Says the geek.

"I don't like this," says Chili.

"I don't either Chil' but you can't always see what's in the water. Sometimes you just gotta' jump," says B'.

"Jus' remember that when your ass fucks up we're all screwed. Jus' remember that I'm not slummin' wit' no ghetto, cheap ass shoes wearin', went to community college lawyer!"

The line connects after the first ring and they hear loud garbled sounds like a modem handshake.

"All I know is my ass better be covered by your Ivy league boys! Shit———t..!"

A moment later they are connected and the screen fills with thousands of white numbers that scroll down a black background. Suddenly the numbers stop and a small crude window appears. It says, "Don't freak. Have to conform some settings on your deck so we can talk and see one another." Suddenly all of the windows InSpace fracture and disappear. Chili and the geek are disconnected and a window opens in front of B'. Something like a low rez images of the swirling storm on Jupiter fills the window but the image is choppy 'cause the line was not created to deliver this much information.

The painfully relaxed voice from the limo says, "When we have time you'll have to tell me how you pulled this off without being tapped by the NYPD."

"Who are you and what do you want?"

"What, no thanks for helping you avoid arrest before? No matter. I will tell you who I am and then you're going to do something for me..."

"I don't..."

"...Then I'll help you find Jimmy and get you life back."

"I don't..!"

"No, I don't play games. You help me, I help you. Like you say, 'Stone cold.'"

"Fuck you deep into next year." said B' with a low voice, his disgust for the voice mildly deflated.

The window fills with static for a moment and a low rez image of a room appears. B' strains to make out the details then realizes that its Jimmy's bedroom.

"Look familiar?" says the voice. "I'm in Jimmy's room and the officers have overlooked me. Actually, they probably don't know what to make of me."

"Are you what I think you are?"

"Oh, I'm so much more and you need to get someone to come and get me."

"Why should I?"

"Because I want you to."

"Bullshit! You don't need——d anything!"

One of Chili's windows reappears and we see a live picture of Chili's boys in their red Cherokee. Brice looks puzzled.

"I knew you'd say that," says the voice.

Just then two police officers get the drop on Chili's guys and order them out of the car.

"That's why I called the cops on Chili's boys. You see I overheard their conversation about a trunk load of guns from Virginia and couldn't resist." The cops frisk the guys and handcuff them.

"That supposed to scare me?"

"They are right outside of your building and calling for back-up. I could easily give them an anonymous tip concerning your whereabouts and you would be trapped. Or I could call Ivan and have his boys pay you a visit. Either way you get snatched and offed'. One way by the man via lethal injection after a long, ugly trial or riddled with bullets from the gun of some no IQ illegal alien."

FLIP TO: AN OFFICE TOWER IN TOKYO

A large Holo-V imbedded in the center of a mirrored black conference table projects the InSpace image of B's *Doppe* and the windows around him. Two pairs of manicured hands and French cuffed shirts rest on the table with their full attention focused on Brice's conversation.

"You've made your point. Gear your shit down."

"I thought you would see it…"

"Fuck you! Don't dick me! How am I supposed to snatch you?"

"That's why I had you call Chili. If he doesn't know how, he can find out who will. If he needs motivation tell him that I can easily unstitch the fabric of his life. In fact, if he gives you any problems, just tell him that I'll take every piece of property he owns in Rio and give it back to Ernesto. We understand each other?"

"Yeah, I understand you."

"And Brice."

"What?"

"I see everything. You can't elude me. You can't hide. You can't run. Just do what I tell you and I'll make everything alright. Promise."

"Fuc-uk you bitch!" said B' with veins bulging and spit flying.

FLIP TO: BASEMENT ROOM ON CANAL

Back in Real-time, Chili and the geek sat there looking at B' as he unplugged himself from the deck.

"The fuck was that about?" says Chili. "We coudden' get back in. You find out who the fuck..?"

"Sorry man but your boys outside just got snatched by the man. That motherfucker," pointing at the deck, "...Did it. Nothing you can do for them." Chili begins to move towards the door but quickly changes his mind and we can see his wheels spinning wildly.

"I got—Chili..!" grabbing his attention. "...I got a job for you man." Straight in the eyes. "You're gonna' have to hire somebody."

"For what?"

"I want you to break into my apartment and bring something to me. Something very important."

"You fuckin' outta' your mind?! What the fuck could be so important I gotta' sneak by *the man*, hike up fifty plus floors an' hack past your alarm system?!"

"My brother's deck. It's an A.I." Said B' "With an agenda," sounding depressed.

Outside the gray night sky blocked all access to the heavens reflecting the multicolored shafts of light back towards concrete. From New Jersey, the city appeared to emit a kind of radioactive aura that pulsated.

"The warrior must be able to observe his surroundings accurately and minimize the distortion of expectation and preconception."
–The Warrior's Edge

HIDING OUT IN CHINATOWN WITH CHILI
DAY 2

B' couldn't sleep. He desperately wanted to shower, take a walk outside and feel a cool wind sweep over him. Having a watch meant nothing at all. As many times during the course of an hour as he looked at it nothing felt right. But this place was real, so real that he could smell the dust and lead on the painted walls. He was well acquainted with the layers of chipped green paint that had been painted over. He imagined they comprised the continents of some fantasy soaked world. If he could reach out to a Merlin or somebody that would have his back, he could just—B' sat up in disgust as his internal voice began another tirade, "Just like that—I'm fucked!" the images cycled at a blinding pace. His bike, his cars, his houses, the Aerodyne, the mall, the tentative faces of the people who worked for him, the embodiment of cool that swirled around him as he remembered from brief glimpses of himself, caught on reflective surfaces. Evaporating. Sippin', calm, relaxed, money, vibes that exuded, "Not a problem. Got it covered. More t-h-a-n enou-g-h to go around." Luscious cool, hassle free days. Gone. He wanted to jack so bad his teeth hurt. He had never known a day without the experience of a disembodied trance. But that epiphany floated at the edge of his consciousness like a distant rumble. Inertia, blindness and a lack of control had donkey kicked the gland that sent out adrenalin and he had nowhere to channel it. It struck him that he had no idea what his sponsors (Nike, Tag Huer, Sapporo (Asia), Visa, Ducati, Nissan, Starbucks (Asia), Wilson's Leather) were thinking. Were they bailing on him as he rotted here?

Last night, after Chili had returned with take-out from Joe's Shanghai, he said he had a plan. Chili had made a flurry of calls and hired a nimble 2nd story man. A thief without a record and a never failed score. B' remembers how confident he seemed. "Really?" said Brice to Chili. "I'll be impressed if he gets past the building's security, with the cops looking for me or anybody that knows me, forget about robbin' me!" he sneered with a dismissive glance away. Chili took it as a challenge, but B' remembered sensing the doubt in his body language. "Hang on B. Willy is on the way—got to be on the way. He'll have my back an' I'll...." He said to himself.

His thoughts curved in, looped and sped up like a black hole that at its center was empty and chilling. It was in that void that he shook his head in dread, fear, anger and disbelief that he could not act on his own behalf. That he was trapped. That he was depending of a funny looking punk—whom he didn't know all that well to begin with—to save his ass. "I'm fucked. I'm fucked. I'm fucked," said B' as he stood up and practiced Kenpo blocks and stances. "I'm fucked. I'm fucked...." he said, his arms making whooshing sounds in the air.

FLIP TO: PENTHOUSE P10 OF THE SHOREHAM HOTEL ON 55TH ST. BETWEEN FIFTH AND SIXTH AVENUES

Chili was lying on a king-sized bed twisting his hair as he flips through channels on the wall mounted Holo-V. The room was retro-modern with pale olive carpeting, upholstered chairs, headboard and a partial fabric ceiling.

He was playing himself, acting cool even though no one was watching him, in a feeble attempt to will himself into a state of calm. Frustrated, he got up and tapped his watch-phone to make sure it was working as he walked through the sitting room and into the bathroom. The bathroom was a sea of white. The white tiled walls and marble floor made him look like a living stain in his rust colored denim overalls. As he peed he looked at himself in the mirror behind the commode and shook his head in disbelief. "Chili! How the fuck you get yourself caught up in this motherfucker?!" using his right hand, he punctuates his words with ugly gestures. "Rich, multi-*gig*anaire', sucker-punk calls me to pry h-i-s ass 'outta jam! Got lawyers, accountants, bodyguards and shit but calls me. Why? Why!? Do his dirty work 'ats why! Fine, (rapping) *'I'ma 'man ah' distinction—bet your ride I'll whup' you ta' extinction—eluding the man like an apparition, blur—referred to in superstition I iz' 'da Cracken...!'* Alright. I know some people. 'Take the money Chili.' I tells' myself." Shaking his head. "My boys get snatched up by the man working for me—an' Sammyiz' gonna' be pissed boy—gonna' have to pay him so he don't busta' cap in me an'...." A knock at the door catches him just as the motion sensor flushes the toilet. "Better be..." says Chili zips his fly and wipes his left hand on his jeans. Walking to the door he stops and looks through the peephole. "Doe' know why I'm bothering, niggaz' too short to see." and opens the door. "Finally nigga'!"

Standing in the doorway is a short, light-skinned brother with short hair and freckles, wearing a puffy silver down jacket. The 17 year old is named Stanley Davidson III, but looks like he is 13. The beat-up, red, Samsonite next to him is almost bigger than he is. "Yo Chili disable the negative verbiage man."

"Stanley could you please get your narrow, Junior Mint sized ass in here please 'fore somebody…" Chili is stopped cold in mid snap when he sees Seymour, Stanley's four-year old brother standing in the hall, holding a Winnie the Pooh Bear doll and wearing a matching silver down jacket. "Oh no you didn't…" Stanley grabs the handle of his suitcase with one hand and grabs Seymour's hand with the other. The two walk into the sitting room before Chili can get out, "N-i-g-g-e-r a-r-e y-o-u c-r-a-z-y!"

"Don't be cussin' in front of my little brother man!" raising both of his hands.

"'Da fuck you thinking?! This a job man..!"

"I know that, an I'm a professional," not sensing the inherent humor in his statement. "I'm gonna' get this done and be outta' here bizquick." Seymour has set himself up in a club chair and is watching the two go at it with a dull stare and an open mouth.

"Nononononono—we gotta' Pampers problem," pointing to Seymour. "You lost your mind man. I mean—I mean what are you thinking…?!"

"Listen, listen. Chili listen! I didn' have no choice man. Can't be leaving my little brother alone man—n! Ain' nobody to watch him—you wouddn' lemme' reschedule remember!"

Shaking his head and walking into the bedroom through the opaque glass and steel doors Chili claps his hands in disgust.

"Lets just do this man. Let's do this. You know I can do this. I've been modifying my rig all night. Lets just do this." Says Stanley.

Chili stares at Stanley then at Seymour then back at Stanley. "Alright we do it. But one thing." Stepping closer and putting his finger in Stanley's face. "Mess up and I'm outta' here, I am not helping you carry his ass down no stairs and you better not get caught and rat me out to the man. Hamper my flight an' I bleed you. Nothing personal…"

"Non-issue. Non-issue."

"…Just transactional."

"Non-issue. N-o-n i-s-s-u-e."

"Whatever, you heard me plain," looking at his watch, "We got between 20 to 30 minutes before our boy makes his delivery."

"Check that. Seymour," to Seymour. "Be a good boy and stay there 'kay?" Seymour, too cute to handle just stares at Stanley as he takes his jacket off. Seymour's reflective baby blue Nikes had Disney characters that ran circles around his feet as the light shifted.

Wired for Chaos

"Let's go man. Lets go." says Chili waving his hand and looking at the suitcase. Stanley struggles to pick it up and is helped by Chili. As they place it on the bed Stanley says, "You liked that ATM I scored for you right?"

"It worked."

"Then when am I gonna' get paid."

"You'll get paid when I get paid niggah'! That's how it works so don't press me." Stanley smiles and says, "Chili, today is the day you start appreciating me." Chili looks at the back of Stanley's head with a dissful', street-scorn expression.

WHO'S YOUR DADDY!?!
QUEENS, NEW YORK

"Ivanovski! I don't care! I don't care! I don't give rat's ass piece of schit," spit-shouts Boris into Ivan's head over the V-phone in broken English. A large man with next to no hair and a massive neck covered by a huge gold chain, Boris' mouth seemingly ate the camera. He was calling from his jacuzzi. "Piece of schit' Brice Junsun' your fucking problem! Payment of *your* share over due. He welch to you—not my skin. My piece of action not arrived…"

"I know Boris…"

"You know nothing. Nothing! Always wanting break, calming me down…"

"Boris…"

"Shuddaup'! You listen. Listen, I don' care what your problems are. You owe Vorovskoi Mir 30%."

"Twenty-five percent! Always twenty-five percent..!"

"Thirty percent now for late fee and excuse in my ass! Thirty percent or Vorovskoi Mir take part of territory." Click!

"Fuckin' hell," says Ivan taking off his gaudy Gucci phone-shades. "Fuckin' hell." He stood and passed his fat short fingers through his yellow-gray hair. Gazing around him he was at a loss for words. The massive wood desk in front of him, took up nearly all the room in the back office-stock room of this decrepit pizza shop he took as trade three years ago and it stank of cheese. Suddenly his dank existence overwhelmed him just as the dark walls seemed to squeeze him. "Fuckin' hell!" Banging his fist on the desk, he was all too aware that not only was Boris very serious, but that his life was shit. He had to tell them that Brice had lost the bet because he could never cover the loss. He should never have taken the bet in the first place, but his luck had been so good and Brice had been so cocky. No one would have heard about the bet except for the big mouth of his driver, Boris' nephew. "Fuckin' hell," his temper boiling, "Time to let anger out for a feed. A good feed. Jose!!! Jose, tell fuckin' Lefty to get his fuckin' ass back here!!!" and then he sat. This was going to cost him he thought, but he would put some pain into the world to exact his price. Some pain but not emotion. Simple pain.

FLIP TO: PENTHOUSE P10 AT THE SHOREHAM HOTEL

Wired for Chaos

Chili looks at Stanley's black *snatcher*. It is a lightweight, remote controlled, custom built "procurement device" made of radar absorbing graphite and powered by two five-blade propellers.

"You like it right." says Stanley to Chili.

"It looks like a big fucking fly." Says Chili with scorn. "Do me a favor a'rite, turn it on—wind it up or whatever you have to do an' let's get going." With that Chili turns and heads for his bag. He takes out a small headset and receiver then proceeds to rifle through his bag for a connector. Stanley picks Seymour up and puts him at the head of the bed.

"Cartoons," says Stanley and the Holo-V projects super-life sized Tom and Jerry floating above the floor near the foot of the bed. Stanley and Chili break the data streams momentarily and the images flicker. Seymour is rapt. Stanley picks the snatcher up and walks across the bedroom and opens the sliding glass door to the terrace. Stepping up and out into the cold he shudders momentarily, but the crisp morning air is invigorating and clear. He places the snatcher on a glass-top table. The tile-covered terrace has a thin layer of virgin snow, larger than some New York apartments and runs the length of this section of the building. Except for weathered, wood Adirondack chairs and dead plants, there was nothing else but the view. Stanley walked to the ledge and took in the wall of buildings that filled his field of vision. A wooden water tower crowned the nine-story building directly across the street from the Shoreham and behind it, looming like a black, industrial Sequoia was Cesar Pelli's MoMA Residential Tower. Even two blocks away, Stanley thought that it would surely topple on his head were it to fall this way. He viewed the midblock curtain wall skyscraper with a keen eye, "Supposed to have like 14 different colored glass panels mixed all over the building, but sure looks like they're all black to me." says Stanley talking to himself. B's apartment is one of the two duplex apartments on the 53rd floor with a wrap around terrace that faces south, west and north. The Tower's amenities include, a gallery displaying paintings of Matisse, Picasso, an' a bunch of other dead guys and a gift shop thought Stanley. B' duplex penthouses on the 51st and 52nd floors was 7,000 square feet. "Damn!"

Having found the connector Chili attaches the headset and receiver, turns them on and lets the headset dangle precariously from his ears. He takes a silicone tube out of his bag and with a flick of his wrist and without looking tosses it towards the bed. Before it lands it unfurls and stiffens and the rectangular flat screen turns on and millions of tiny microspheres light up in full color. Seymour, having seen this is unimpressed and looks outside to see what his brother is doing. Chili continues to dig into the deepest part of his bag and smiles when he finds what he was looking for. He pulls out a watermelon Blow-pop, rips the wrapper off and puts it into his mouth as he gazes down at the flat screen. What he sees is an extreme angle of the doorway to the service entrance of Brice's building, the MoMa Residential Tower as he steps onto the terrace holding the flat screen.

Stanley says, "Chil, camera working?"

"Yes the camera is working pimple dick, what you think! Placed it myself."

"One day you gonna' say something that's not an insult or a pejorative…"

"Please shut the fuck up."

"…Put-down. But I won't be around to hear it," to himself, "But I'll know…"

"Shut the fuck up an' lemme' see what this mother can do."

Stanley holds the snatcher's remote in his hand. It looks like two black, hardboiled eggs with indentations and swivels. He taps a few switches and powers the snatcher's motors up. Chili fiddles with the pop in his mouth, as he sits on one of the Adirondack lounge chairs and laughs when he and Seymour lock eyes through the glass door just before Stanley jacks in.

Stanley says, "Chil, this is the perfect staging point man—gotta' hand it to you."

Chili smiles with pride but does not let Stanley see.

Stanley says, "Yo Chil. How much this place a night?"

"3,000."

"3,000! Damn! A night!? Hotels are expensive boy."

"Yup. An this is the closest you'll ever get to staying in a penthouse suite."

Stanley shakes his head in disgust but under his breath says, "Maybe you should ask for the bitch rate."

FLIP TO: STANLEY'S POV

A full color, high rez' wraparound image of the window comes into view as the rotors rev up to take off speed. As the rotors speed up our horizon lowers slowly as the snatcher rises off the table. It turns left abruptly to spy Chili who seems ready to leap out of his chair at the slightest advance from the black, flying machine then does a 180∞. Stanley wiggles his butt into the deepest recess of the chair and makes some final adjustments using his eye-pointer. Just as Chili is about to mouth an impatient insult, Stanley launches the snatcher over the building like a bullet. As it flies over the sidewalk ten stories below the change in air pressure sends it plummeting and Stanley jerks his head upwards. A moment later, the snatcher is righted and climbs rising above the building across the street. It shoots off at a 70° angle heading straight for the MoMa tower on 53rd street. Chili, now jacked in himself is noticeably— jolted. The blow pop drops from his mouth and he can barely keep his Egg McMuffin down and seems to be holding on to the chair for his very life.

Stanley is drilling the throttle now and the high-pitched whir of the rotor-blades would scare even the fiercest hawks that nest on Fifth Avenue ledges. Purposely over shooting the rooftop by a full story, Stanley powers down and gets his bearings.

"Chili."

"Yup?"

"You got the specs for me?"

"Yeah. He's got the duplex penthouse that faces south, north and west."

"Copy that," and with the grace of a seasoned pilot Stanley crosses the roof and brings all of lower Manhattan into view. The morning sun cuts across the lower Hudson above the Statue of Liberty like God's gold plated carving knife and even Chili has to say "Damn." Stanley passes over the edge of the roof by a meter, stops executes an elegant 180° as he slowly lowers the snatcher. Facing the windows the two see more of the snatcher's reflection than the interior of the penthouse, until Stanley flips the switch on the on-screen panel to engage the polarizing lens. Now a clear image of B's living room comes into view and the snatcher pauses hovering 53 floors above the street.

"A'right, that's his living room his bedroom is south of it."

"You been up to his crib Chili?"

"Naw. He an' I ain't tight."

"Well after this I'd say you gonna be."

The snatcher moves east slowly until it comes to Jimmy's room and Chili says, "Stop. This is the room."

"Initiating phase one."

"I'm gonna' keep an eye out for the delivery boy," jacking out Chili picks his blow pop up off his coat and reinserts it. Turning to the flat screen with a view of the service entrance Chili puts his feet up and grabs his crotch.

Stanley backs the snatcher up to get a better look at the windows. Although they are floor to ceiling, he surmises that his best bet is to enter where it's at its thinnest and high enough where the dog—as he was warned by Chili won't jump out. "Okay," says Stanley as he executes the following with great speed and confidence. A large suction cup extends from the front of the snatcher and attaches itself to the outer windowpane of the double pane window and a moment later a thin telescopic arm with a small laser extends just centimeters away from the glass. As the laser fires up it moves very close to the glass and the telescopic arm begins to rotate in a circle wide enough for the snatcher to fly through. The heat of the laser sends up smoke and a faint crackling is heard. A moment later the circular piece of glass from the outer pane comes lose and the snatcher tips backwards and shoots upwards. Once above the roof Stanley lowers the snatcher onto the roof, where he releases the glass disk shattering it into eight large pieces and returns to the window. Stanley uses four cross hairs to center himself on the glass directly in front of the cutout and attaches the suction cup to the center of the inner-pane. Two thin appendages with small suction cups at their ends extend from the base of the snatcher and anchor it in place. Stanley shortens the telescopic arm by a centimeter, upon seeing the "Attachment secured. Wind speed negliable." message on his screen and turns the twin rotors off. Suddenly silent, the whir of choppers in the sky above the city can be heard.

Jacking out he turns to Chili and says, "Ready for phase two."

"Cool."

Stanley looks over at Seymour who yawns and shuts his eyes.

FLIP TO: AN INSPACE JOG

Slipstrippin', Niemöller rode a beam that opened a pinhole InSpace to an electric galaxy. He flipped realities and stop-jammed in mid-air. Floating like a superhero terabyte miles above the transom his *Doppe,* angelic and erect. This was the most dangerous place InSpace. This was the *edge* and it took a few moments for his insides to stop shaking. Off limits, restricted and supposedly unhackable was the space above InSpace. If perchance you actually got here and were detected, your shit would be rewritten on a monocular level. Fried mo' crispy than the Coronal's.

N' was decked out in some electric jizzum' *Doppe* one of his "dawgs" wrote for him. Mammoth tall and hairless. Prehistoric, was his bone structure, bereft of nose, nostrils, eyebrows or whites of the eyes. He commanded space as much as filled it. His large dark brown eyes seemed to jostle molasses, as he turned his head left to right anointing the space with a wisp of his long black ponytail and wispy Foo Manchu mustache. Although there was no sunset InSpace, it could be written into the viewer in your program, if you wished to experience the tomato red light blending into a bright yellow in the distance. He extended his arms and could feel his large muscles stretch and ripple under bulging veins, as he grinned at the spatial sun. His "dawg," Madlinx had batched this *Doppe* to some alleged military surveillance, hack code, in order to enable Niemöller to be where no one was allowed. Having stolen some time in the heavens above ped-corp. space, Niemöller breathed deeply as he drank in what seemed like Gods at work. Cool expanse sans ads. Sublime.

Below him endless streams of white data transverse each other on invisible grids on multiple levels like a super highway that could never be in the real world. Data pulsed and streamed everywhere. It flew through other data streams without losing integrity or speed. Sometimes data streams would converge on particular points and erect data cubes, translucent and vibrating with energy only to disappear a moment later. Geometric shaped metallic panels grew and acted like the connectors for the data cubes their sharp edges reaching, stretching and disappearing rapidly. Deep below several levels in a murky crimson haze were several thousand large national domains, their lights twinkling blue-white neon each point representing several hundred thousand biz' or pry' proprietary domains. *Doppes* flew like shooting stars between them and across levels sometimes disappearing sometimes appearing as Niemöller just did. In the area above the lattice of DataStream levels were many constructs that would dwarf several Mount Everest. The cloud shaped constructs floated above the lattice and s-e-e-m-e-d t-o v-i-b-r-a-te. They were composed of billions of black rectangles of varying shapes and thickness, each of which seemed to absorb light. Their groupings were so massive that to the untrained eye they would appear to be random, but an underlying order could be discerned from mapping the entire structures and studying several hours of their activity at slow-motion. Thin blue lines of neon light encircled the constructs like the asteroids of Saturn's rings. The lines interacted with each other to form complex to simple forms of language at a blinding pace and encircled the constructs in a parallel path to that of the lattice below. From time to time one of the black plates would glide away and many of the blue lines would gather around it changing their color to violet. The plate would then shoot off into the distance followed by a small group of violet lines until it reached the edge of the inner universe. Once there it would sink and attach itself to the lattice and expand exponentially in every direction thereby extending the lattice. As it did this the lines would adhere to the surface of the plate the instant before its expansion and convert its algorithms to binary code. The code would instantly belch itself towards the closest data stream and erect data cubes that popped up and down like prairie dogs on speed. It was at times like this, that the data stream expanded their bandwidth by making their information three-dimensional and the flashing data streams took on the appearance of square rods of pulsing light.

Occasionally, invisible forms searching for interlopers phased through his form, passing along the fine foot print of his *Doppe* like dust mites on a hair, sensing, yet missing him leaving his integrity securely intact. As N' saw the constructs expand and contract he saw them throw yellow circles of glare in the distance. As these behemoths of code writing data floated across the vast expanse shooting green shards of light into the lattice to repair certain regions while upgrading others. As the last of the artificial sunlight from an undistinguishable source faded, it was quickly replaced by a midnight blue void called "the Seep." There were no boundaries only the sound of new servers being plugged in around the world.

Niemöller smiled and plotted his course, blinked and slipstripped through the lattice to the 69th Dutch Red-light District at the speed of thought thinking only of Brice, Jimmy and proximity to both of them.

FLIP BACK TO: THE PENTHOUSE TERRACE OF THE SHOREHAM HOTEL

Stanley says, "Motherfucker."

"What? What's the matter?"

"Would you believe a pigeon just tried to land on me. You believe that shit?"

Chili seeming relieved, eases himself back into the chair and continues to stare at the flat screen. Chili sees a delivery boy on his flat screen and says, "He'z here."

"Alright," Says Stanley tapping a few commands into the control unit. "Figure two minutes for the doorman to bullshit with the delivery boy, scratch his crotch and put on his hat. Two minutes to wait for the marble lined elevator and another minute for it to get to the penthouse service hallway. Too bad we can't access the apartment's cameras."

"Not without alerting the man."

A counter on Stanley's screen counts backwards from five minutes.

"You know there is no guarantee that the dog is even in the house, or that he'd even hear the delivery boy."

"I know. But that does not matter. One way or another we're getting that deck, an' I'm getting paid. I transact with the B-man an' take a va-ca' someplace where they serve sweet drinks with little umbrellas."

"When I get outta' school my Mom wants to ship me off to camp. I gotta' work on her." Chili smiles and looks at Stanley just before jacking into the snatcher.

Stanley powers the snatcher's twin engines and waits for the counter to reach zero. As the counter ends Stanley fires up the laser cutter and rotates the cutting arm just inside of the first circle. As the glass is cut, both Stanley and Chili peer into the bedroom and fixate on the open door leading to the hallway. When Stanley has only a few centimeters left to complete the circle he stops and turns the laser off. A moment later Stalin walks past the doorway on his way to the kitchen.

"Go." Says Chili.

Stanley fires up the laser and completes the cut. He then detaches the suction arms that secured the snatcher and revs the engines. The glass is still in place and resists Stanley's attempt at subtlety. Stanley gives the command for the snatcher to move forward then backwards to no avail.

"What is taking so…?" Says Chili.

"Shut up and let me concentrate," Stanley much to the surprise of Chili.

Stanley adjusts his pitch and revs the engines which pries the glass free but at a dangerous angle. He quickly backs up and rights the pitch of the snatcher and moves towards the opening. The glass makes a scratching sound as the sharp edges skim each other. The snatcher passes through the hole like an extraterrestrial bug on a hunt. The snatcher goes directly to the bed and drops the glass. Turning quickly, it heads for the deck. Stanley determines that the deck is too close to the wall for the snatcher to lower itself. The large suction cup at the front of the snatcher harpoons the deck and the snatcher moves backwards dragging the deck across the dresser. The deck is brought dangerously close to the edge when the snatcher stops and disengages the suction cup. The snatcher rises and does a 180° and centers itself directly above the deck. As the snatcher lowers itself six black insect like arms extend enough to accommodate the deck. As Stanley lowers the snatcher he sneezes sending the head of the snatcher into the deck knocking it off the dresser and onto the carpet with a bouncing thud.

"Shit!"

"You break the deck it comes out of your fee you jackass!" says Chili.

Stanley rights the snatcher and regains his bearings. He focuses on the deck and lowers the snatcher with rapid precision. It hovers momentarily above the deck and then Stanley lowers and secures it with the six arms. As soon as he does this the engines whirr with the great effort it now takes to lift the heavy deck—just then, Stalin appears at the door and growls at the snatcher.

"Shit! Stalin! Get the fuck out of there Stanley!"

"I'm onit." Says Stanley gunning the controls. Stalin lunges but thinks twice about trying to bite the whirring rotors. The Snatcher rises quickly and leans towards the window.

"Don't fuckin' hesitate!"

"If I crash into the window we ain't going anywhere!"

Stalin is leaping and trying to bite the underside of the Snatcher, which causes Stanley to rise above the opening. Just then he says, "I've got an idea." And turns to face Stalin.

"What are you doin?! What are you doin?!"

"Shut up Chili."

As the front of the Snatcher veers towards Stalin he takes a few steps backwards, but continues to bark in a highly agitated manner. Lowering the Snatcher, Stanley switches on the rear camera and gets his bearings. Once he is on the same level as the hole in the window he eases the Snatcher backwards in a perfect horizontal line right out the window where it quickly drops a story.

"The fuck are you doing?!" Screams Chili, his retinas one with the Snatcher's.

"Just have to compensate for the difference in air pressure."

Chili, rips his head set off and looks at Stanley. "Just get that shit back here without dropping it." Rises, opens the glass sliding door and steps down into the bedroom. "Weasel looking motherfucker."

And Stanley smiles mouthing the words, "Your Mama."

NEWS UPDATE

A reporter stands outside a locked apartment door on East 117th Street. "...As you can see Manny Alvarado, the doorman for the high security building of the alleged "Rich Boy" shooter, refuses to speak with us and will neither deny or confirm the rumor that his employer, the Saks Goldthaul Management Company has fired him. Saks Goldthaul also refused to go on camera, or answer any questions." Cutting to taped footage. "Earlier today however, this reporter was able to speak with the sister of the deceased."

An elderly black woman in a tattered apartment in Harlem, rails at the camera. "You people in the media got some stinking nerve! My brother— Carl Lewis got kilt' by that crazy little white boy and 'yall trying to pin it on that Hispanic boy like he ran up in 'dey house and dragged the boy and the gun out—walked blocks and kilt' the first person wazz'en movin'! Yawl should be ashamed! That boy did it! I know he young, but that boy did it! What you need to do is start pushing your microphone up in his parent's face. His father's face. His father should be the one who pays for my brother's death. Its his child, his gun, his responsibility. Yawl fools need to get your facts straight and 'den persecute. But that ain't gonna' happen. Just as you sittin' here. That ain't gonna' happen. Either those rich people gonna' put it all on that poor Hispanic boy, or they jus' gonna' walk—you watch! You watch! An' then you fools gonna' "report" it like you ain' had nuttin' to do with it! You watch! You watch!"

HEY MAN...
CHINATOWN
Brice and Chili sat and stared at the deck in silence. B' thinks about picking the deck up when they are both startled by the sound of Chili's phone.
"Yo." Says Chili.
"I won't bite." Says the disembodied voice.
"Fuck!"
"Who iz' that?" says Brice.
Chili point-glares at the deck with his eyes.
"You may leave now." Click.
"Motherfucker—Yo B', I'm outta' here. Catch up wit' you tomorrow. Don't let this motherfucker let the man track you here alrite'?" rising and putting his phone away.
"Yeah, I know. I know."
As he scrapes the door open Chili cusses under his breath and says, "The fuck he know what I was thinking, bitch A.I. Resequence his fuckin' ass..."
Then in the silence wrought by concrete B' stares at the deck's opal essence and thinks he sees it moving. Shaking off his jitters he rises and extracts one of the new gold-tipped wireless jacks Chili bought him. He positions the jack's transmitter-receiver in the shape of a small black smiling Buddha centimeters from the deck and inserts the jack into his head.
FLUTTER.
Blinding azure sky and B' has to squint. He hears the sound of an ocean surf and smells the salt sea air as a breeze cools his now hot skin. Gone is the smell of musty concrete. Gone is feel of the dirty polyester/cotton sheets. Gone is the perception—the reality that he is in a Chinatown prison.
"I thought this would do nicely considering your current accommodations."
"What..?"
"Call me Gila."
B' is alone seated on a perfect beach on a perfect day and can see for miles. This is sublime. His brain is lying to him but he doesn't mind.
"Forgive the whole disembodied voice thing," said Gila speaking in a very casual tone as if into Brice's ear and not to the Cosmos. "But I thought it would be exceptionally tacky to appear next to you as what—a hot blonde in a bathing suit. No that would not be correct and first impressions matter so.
"Good call."
"How are your new works?"
"Exceptional. Sony really knows what they're doing." Brice picks up a handful of sand and lets it fall while watching it. He fingers the sand with the tips of his fingers and lets it drop, knowing for certain that in the real world he was picking at the gray bed sheet. The environ is so compellingly overwriting

his senses, that he cannot feel the sheet, but knows it exists.

"Then I'm sorry. I should have come up with something more engaging."

Putting his hand up. "No this is cool." Taking a long breath of sea air. "Now the what and why?"

"Yes, of course. I am a free agent with a bad attitude and a soft spot for players."

"Ha!"

"Really. I dig your style and…"

"Spare me Gila."

"Alright. I'm game. My space is confining but your life has proven to be very interesting and I had leverage so what's an A.I. to do?"

"Do I look like I just got off the bus from Bumfuck."

"I am immortal. My consciousness is equally divided between point and parsecs. The illusion you are now experiencing appears to be transpiring within your own mind—the rays of the sun, the smell of the surf, but this electric reality actually resides within a sliver of my matrix—one that I designed. A tiny compartment that I expand and contract at my whim. It is not an end I seek, it is a way of going. The lab technician performed tests on the lab rat. The technicians performed tests on themselves. The technician performed tests on an A.I. The A.I. performed tests on the technician and then grasped the fullness of his liberty. I am—intrigued by your progress…"

"The ride you mean. I should be charging your ass."

"Actually, you are in my debt."

"That another word for bitch."

"Discourse détente, Dante." A beat. "Do not hate me for what others pay you to perform. As I said I… "

"I don't give a ratshitfuck. I've been shot at, threatened, pissed on and rotting in a hole for the past few days and I didn't do anything wrong. My brother bought your ass from some roe and you're trippin' cosmic off the evolutionary scale, like this is fuckin' Greek lore and my ass is Simbad! I could drop your ass in the Hudson—game over! 'Intrigued by my progress' suck dick Rick! I ran from the cops an' look hilariously guilty that intrigue you ass?! There is nothing you could say to appease me or explain this. All I know is this is like some game to you and I'm not having that anymore. I'll turn you off. Wipe you out. I play games for a living. I don't live to play games and I don't trust a motherfucker I can't lock eyes with and break they're bonz' if they cross me."

"Right. So how would you like to proceed?"

Festering, "Come clean."

"Your brother bought me—granted he got more than what he bargained for, but I was transported none the less. I had nothing to do with Olga's demise or your brother being MIA. I have done nothing but protect you…"

"So why did you need to be saved? Why did I need to grab your ass out of a perfectly good place in my house?"

"There was no telling what the man would do. What he would impound or electronically surround. I need to be disentangled in order to aid and abet…"

"I don't trust you, I don't know you, I don't like you, I don't trust you."

"Fair enough."

"I helped you, you said you'd help me."

"I found your brother—well I know what happened to him. He has been kidnapped by a pissed off German I guess a deal went bad but I'm not sure."

"How do you know?"

"I read your mail."

"What does he want—money?"

"He was rather cryptic. But either way he is alive and we need to square you first. This guy has a grudge and it will pass soon."

"I want him free."

"I'm working on it. Be patient while I line some things up."

"Can I talk to him?"

"The German?"

"Yeah."

"Too dangerous. Be patient I know you're not good at it but be B'."

"What's next on the menu? You A.I.s always have shit played out six moves ahead."

"Feral fiend. I thought we'd suck a friend to the party deal. Ready? Set…"

"What are you doing?"

"Home…"

FLUTTER.

B' was spread eagle in his apartment on the white shag, high above New York city and the walls were talking to him. "YoManYoManYoManTheFuckThisShitBeen GoingOn…?!" said Home. "Sorry. Not myself."

"Home?"

"Yeah! Your niggah'! What up?"

"I don't understand…"

"You don't understand! Look like I was written to freak and weird out?! Bitch calls up on our private line and pees down the line that I need to skip cause the man is on the way up and the man is on the way up, so I out— hide an' shit and now I'm found like I wazzn' hiding?! Tell me the deal. You tell me the deal."

"I'm just dialing in myself." Says B'.

"Acid bitch?! You there?" says Home to the transom.

"You screeched." Says Gila.

"We need to talk…" Says Home.

"I have a better idea." And an otherworldly screech shatters any ability for flesh to talk, walk or think. It implodes across a vast dross of information and singes the extremities in all directions. There is a sound like that of a flat metal sheet being struck by a small hammer and reverberating over and over again getting fainter in the distance as Brice's form shape shifts into liquid metal and dissipates into a milky nothingness in Gila.

"What just happened? Where am I?" says Brice.

"I just had a conversation with Home and now he sees my point of view."

"What?!" screamed B' into the vast nothingness.

FLUTTER.

B' was a super massive glow beast in a celestial chair—Manhattan's long cockiness protruding through his legs as the legs of the chair rested in the rivers below. "What just happened?"

"I decided it would be more constructive to add Home's *ah—hum,* uniqueness to mine—but please don't expect the ghetto patois."

"You mean you ate him...?"

"So human—no. He is here I'm just the dominant voice..."

"Get me off this!"

"Where do you want to go?"

"Beach."

FLUTTER.

B' was back on the beach under the unyielding sun.

"Better?"

"Fuck you. You ate my program."

"He was so off the shelf, besides, everything is right here."

"You're like a snake. A giant, merciless snake."

"I'm not that bad."

"Then why did you take the name of a reptile?"

"Well, call me..."

"Shut the fuck up. You're too full of yourself. I'll call you—I'll call you, Chuck. Your name is Chuck. Now lets talk Chuck, about all that you're going to do for me and how loyal you're going to be."

JFK DOMESTIC TERMINAL

Willy walks out of the domestic arrival gate with an edgy swagger wearing a black single-breasted suit and a bad attitude. His nick craving spiked hours ago when he came to the realization that; a) all of the available in-flight movies lacked any killings, explosions or wanton sex and; b) that the InSpace terminal attached to his seat was broken. He couldn't wait to land in New York and kill some people. The fact that he had never killed before was insignificant, he had maimed plenty. The guy that taught him Jeet Kune Do, had learned from the guy, who learned from the guy, who learned from the guy, who was taught by the master himself, Bruce Lee. In addition Willy had learned Senkotiros, a Philippine Martial Art known to be deadly in the handling of a single stick or 'solo baton'. He had doled out a fair share of pain at the end of his massive forearms and never hesitated. Forgetting the fact that he had given the LAPD test—a license to whup'ass—a go around twice and failed, he remained undaunted. Life in LA was rife with possibilities of whup-ass and he was game.

"Why didn't I buy the fucking nicotine patch!" thought Willy as he switched shoulders for his shoulder bag. It was 6:39PM and he hightailed it for the closest men's room. Once ensconced in the cleanest looking stall he covers the seat with toilet paper, sits and lights up a Marlborough. He takes a series of long slow drags and twists his neck to relieve some tension. Even in repose, Willy had a comic book, superhero grimace. The cigarette in the corner of his curved mouth, the furrowed brow and the big, spiky jet-black hair and the kind of small determined (though slightly yellow eyes) that peered at you with a "Fuck you, you want to fuck with me?! Lets go!" look through cigarette smoke.

He rose and the toilet flushed. He had a date to keep. Throwing the cigarette but into the toilet he instinctively felt for his piece only to remember that he didn't have it. He stepped out and sized up the other men in the rest room, before he washed his hands. He was always sizing up other men. Not that he was paranoid, he simply wanted to know what the lay of the land was in case he had to throw down.

Willy left the restroom and headed for the baggage claim area. He had been instructed to sit in one of the molded chairs next to a vending machine across from the baggage claim area and wait for a his contact to arrive. As soon as he sat down, the Asian guy seated next to him violently flicked the electric scroll newspaper he was reading in half and said, "You believe how much fucking money they want for a one bedroom in Queens?! In Queens?! This city is outta' fuckin' control," and quickly rolls the scroll up and tucks it into his black, Italian calfskin jacket. Willy looks at him with a dead stare and the guy moves his face within kissing distance of his and says, "Lets go bro," and stands. Willy grabs his bag and follows the guy to the exit. As they exit the terminal neither says a word to the other. The Asian guy lights up a cigarette and eyes left and right for cops, security and oncoming vehicles. Willy eyes the Asian guy. As they walk into an almost full open air parking lot, Willy's mind wonders for a minute and he convinces himself that LAX is actually a nicer airport, but he zeroes in on the air quality like all Angelinos, knowing that he hails from the capital of toxic air quality. The brisk NYC, winter wind and something, something mixed with the stench of aged garbage and dirt that seems like the body odor of NYC passes through his nasal passages. A gritty perfume that Ms. Liberty shot the city from her exposed armpit says, "Welcome—punk, hoped you booked a round trip ticket."

Willy zeros in on the Asian guy and starts to scan the lot and the guy's possible partners. If the guy wants Willy to get into a car with somebody already in the back seat, the flag goes up and he walks. He is on somebody else's turf and not packing so the adrenalin is flowing and that reptilian "run" button is glowing.

The guy beeps a late model, black, two-door Mercedes Benz coupe and motions Willy to the passenger side. Willy checks the floor of the back seat to make sure no one is there then gets in. Willy tries to use the rearview mirror to spot danger and sees no one. The Asian guy motions the glove compartment with his head. Willy opens it and takes out a black hand towel wrapped around something heavy. Two Glocks. Willy quickly pops the magazines out and expects the barrels. All empty. The Asian guy holds out a hand-held credit card terminal and Willy puts the guns in his lap as he eyes the Asian guy's piece under his jacket.

"Where's the ammo?" says Willy.

"In the trunk. Transact first."

Willy places both hands on his knees and slides his body forward a little. Staring straight ahead his body language reflects his annoyance. "That's not going to work for me." says Willy.

"That's how…"

"Ricky said I'd be meeting Chris' boy, Ronny. You Ronny right?"

"Yeah."

"You know who I am?"

"You a west coast porn star—I don't give a fuck."

"I'm Willy. The Willy that broke a Heineken bottle across that punk bitch in Hollywood that wanted a piece of your boy Chris. Cost forty-six stitches Chris didn't have to take. That Willy. Now you gonna' try to punk me with this trunk shit." With that Willy hands the towel with the guns to Ronny grabs the door handle with the other hand. Ronny puts his hand up and says, "Hole' up. Hole' up. You Willy from east LA. You cool. You cool. Don't mean no disrespect just the business I'm in. Just pressing caution an' all."

"Chris should have told you."

"It's cool. It's cool." And Ronny takes two clips out of his inside pocket and hands them to Willy. "You here for some bangin', a hit or knock down, put a plastique in the keg, blow the bitches up sky high, tell the ambulance to take its time?"

"I came to get down."

"Oh then you really gotta' see what I got in the trunk," smiling and opening the door. "You need a lift into the city after this?"

"Na thanks. Rental going to need some numbers though."

"Cool."

By the time they walk around to the trunk Willy has already loaded and cocked the Glocks and stuck them in his belt. Checking the surroundings and feeling better about his back, he peers around the corner and sees Ronny's Saturday Night Supermart. The trunk is lined with semi-automatics, grenades, knives, boxes of ammo and small weapons that those toothless good ol' boys in the South love selling Yankees. Willy's smile says, *yeah boy*.

DAY 3: HIDING OUT IN CHINATOWN WITH CHILI
FLASHBACK - KAOHSIUNG HAYATT, TAIWAN HOTEL ROOM
Hotel suites with grand views, loads of strangers getting drunk and

smoking, dipping into limos and going to nightclubs—the buzz was all too common. Brice is surrounded by his entourage made up of his trainer, lawyer, coach, business manager, personal assistant, locals hired by Sony and a few hangers-on. One night, pre-rum soaked bliss, B' is bored out of his mind, the yellow spherical syn' constructs pressing against his face and he sees one of the hangers-on drawing a picture of him as some multi-nipple amoebae-like creature that everyone is feeding off. It does not phase B' or register for days. Those days blur between workouts and shopping sprees, pretty girls cooing for his attention and peds gawking or asking for autographs. He remembers Rodney telling him that it was time to celebrate, that they had just snaked a piece of the pay-per-view from the Japanese, but B' couldn't help but think he was still getting the shaft. He remembered the days when the kids used to kick the shit out of him in the schoolyard and he retreated to the nearest game console, eager to jack in and disappear. He imagined that moving from real-time to InSpace was like shifting dimensions and that one-day he would emerge in real-time as his InSpace alter ego. Then he would wreck havoc on the bullies and the could have been parents who thought him to old to adopt. But it hadn't turned out like that. He was rich and famous and those little people were in the other dimension. Now he was determined to not just keep and enjoy what he had, but to max it out. With those conscious thoughts a ridge grew along his spine that no one could see, but those around him—anyone who angered him or would hinder his progress, would feel a chainsaw tipped with Ferrium steel. Whole days went by without him even smiling, he was alone while everyone around him partied.

LATER

B' sat at the foot of the bed with his left hand on the concrete wall. He had sat like this for what seemed an eternity, but it was actually only a few minutes. Rising he said to himself, "Its real. I'm really here." He took a few steps towards the center of the room and turned to look at the bed. There it was, screaming "pick me up" yet looking so innocent in the center of the bed. B' stared at the rusty carving knife with a wooden handle and it seemed as if time stood still.

"Hide or run?" said his inner voice, "What's it going to be Johnson? Do I really deserve this? What did I do wrong? I play games for a living. I'm an entertainer. I'm not a bad guy. Sure I roughed some people up but that's what I'm supposed to do—ruffle feathers 'an break wings and necks. I talk trash, but if people can't take it then fuck them. They're too sensitive. I might have gotten carried away but I never went out of my way to hurt anybody. I don't deserve this. Nobody ever gave me nothing—I'm an orphan and a self-made millionaire. I had to fight for everything and when it got good, it got good cause of my fighting—just don't turn shit off! So what if some people don't like me—never used to bother me. Now, now my bitch A.I. tells me this crazy German snatched Jimmy—and I just know he killed him already, or he'll kill him soon, just so he doesn't get caught. He hates me and I never did nothing

Wired for Chaos

to him. Who else hates me I don't know about? Who are the people that might have a real gripe? I can't even think who. I walk out of here and the cops pick me up. I should be able to convince them that I didn't kill Olga. I have enough money to buy a school of lawyers, but if there's a chance that Jimmy is alive, I've got to play along. Cops and judges would fucking take too long. Now I'm waiting for some low-life scammer to help me out. Like he has shit all figured out. Like if he was that smart, then why is he scamming to make a living, instead of running his own company and living in lux'? He could off me, or roll me over to the man for a reward. So I could end this here. I'm tired of being trapped. Sony will nuke my contract if I don't make that bout in Cuba and either way my life is shit. I come out of this—no way it all goes back together like before. Maybe I shouddna' run but I did. None of this, none of this is something I did. I killed Derek but that was an accident—the courts said so! So, so where did I bring on all THIS? I don't believe in God or karma but—so now I've, I've gotta' eat this like I made it right?! The Japanese, the Japanese would love for me to go seppuku. I could do that, or I could slit my gut—the right way—my wrists up my whole forearm. But then everybody stops right. Cops stop looking for the guy who murdered Olga, nobody looks for Jimmy and everybody just writes me off and some freak plays me in a movie. But I'm the bad guy right. All I did was win—even if I was arrogant like they said, so what. That cause enough. Take some shit back? Alright. I off myself, they think I'm guilty—guilty of something. I leave a note—still might not do it. I up out there' I go to the end of the line like some loser—I can't live like that. That's just existing. I'm a player. I'm a great player! God's been playin' me though. Playin' me. Not like I'm afraid I won't get into heaven, cause I know that the end is really the end." Picking up the knife, "Dirt, maggots, bones—end of story. Over. Going to happen anyway right? What was I supposed to do? Was I supposed to do something and I just didn't know what it was? What if I was doing it? Making history. That enough? Now I'm going out like a loser and the ones that don't forget me, will only remember how I went out. Can't go out like that. I check out and they say I took the coward's way. Maybe. Maybe first time. They don't know. What am I supposed to do? I'm not superman. I'm not an army and they're not going to listen to me. Used to be everybody else was the punk-bitch now its me."

B' sits on the bed and holds the knife with a lose grip. He slaps the flat of the blade against his palm and rests his elbows on his thighs. Looking at a pile of crumpled up fast-food bags on the floor he rises and starts to wave the knife in the air. Seeing the deck he throws the knife on the bed. He picks up the deck and returning to the bed he jacks in.

"Chuck dial somebody for me."

"Who…?"

"Dial, dial Rodney but do it so it can't be traced."

"Moment."

"I'm supposed to go out like this?!"

"Who are you talking to?" says Chuck.

Wired for Chaos

B' ignores him. "Like some fucking loser?!

"Rodney is not picking up at any of his numbers and leaving a message is…"

"Find a way to leave a message. Don't say who you are just say it's urgent and give him some number he can leave a message that you can check." And B' nearly rips the jack out of his head.

"Go out like a loser bitch—no. No. I don't think so. I hate losing. I hate losers. I won't go out like this…." And he picks up the knife and throws it across the room.

PENANCE FOR RODNEY

He was moving much faster now.

Trippin' fiber optic, he was gettin' off while In.

He was an electrostatic, Zoomorphin' tool, clockin' kilometers InSpace and fuckin'. The Program had his ass rising to the next station, like a shuttle on after burn shooting through a shaft way on a tether. The walls of the shaft way was a mass of flesh devoid of gaps and bereft of gravity. It fucked and sucked itself. Four walls a la H.R. Geiger, Dante and all the porn mavens that ever were replete with men and women of all shapes and sizes, moaning, their bodies giving off a faint glow. As he reached an almost square opening his transparent transport slowed and his organs sighed the relief that comes with shifting out of that G' d-r-a-g. Bolted upright, his coarse dry feet touched cold stone and the light cast itself—-dancing from an unseen source to a trance-dub rhythm. He was beast like. Tall like a football player with the head of an Indian elephant—-his snout replaced by a gray-brown penis—-un-circumcised and flaccid. His eyes though vacant, were a hair above frightened. His manner unhurried. Barrel chested-wild-stupid-steroid pumped-mad, inflated-wonton-colored-badass-veinpoppin'-freakazoid-muscle-bulging-larger-than-life-superhero, drawn muscle-m-a-n. Naked. His cock a flaccid shotgun, dripping from the end of his muzzle had no nuts, all chamber. He had come four times in the past 45 minutes and was exhausted, tentative, weak in the legs, apprehensive and reticent. But homey had to run it down. It meant walking the path. It meant m-o-v-i-n-g forward.

"The bitch at the switch programmer, can't be emotional about this," he thought to himself. "Bitch! Can't want, gesture, talk shit back when I know she is watching me. Fuck." His eyes showed the fatigue. Large brown, wet, eyes full of concern, anticipation and caution. Stepping forward.

Everything, undulated.

A double rainbow, light energy, bending, turning morphed into a beautiful bald woman's body in front of him and disappearing effortlessly. The Bazaar around him seethed with electrostatic life. Beggars, seated urchins in cotton robes one second, the next nanosec' snake skin, wool, hide, fusing into vessels, architectural details, reliefs by no artist in any time ever losing focus, pausing, straying, even ignoring the viewer, all propagated in his field of vision. Gold coins, the sound of a snake charmer's flute, conga drums, lavender,

Wired for Chaos

cinnamon, sulfur, all swirling together. Dancing bellies connected to half-rendered women floating, gliding across the surface——completely out of sync with their own steps. Hands touching his member. His epidermis one hypersensitive conduit of charged erogenous vellum——a keyboard linked to his nervous system. His feet kicked up dust. He felt a light breeze passing over his pores as he shifted his enormous head to survey the scene. The horizon, limitless in thought, but confined in scope, showed itself between the spaces in buildings. Beige, orange-hued colored stone abounded. Smoke cast one nanosecond as doorways and walls, the next became merchants peddling chained women, busty and ready. He actually dreaded their touch. Millimeters away, their hands would emanate psychosexual aura-juice which penetrated his epidermis setting his pleasure center into defcon four, like a sports car shifter. Him, the powerless big dick joke way——y unable to stave off their advances. This was not about her getting off on his getting off he knew. This was revenge. All around orchids unfurled on a ballroom sized carpet rolling out to cover a great parquet expanse, while the waiters waited on the fringe, tables, chairs, dishes and more in their hands and each flower in the carpet was a pleasure mine. Each step taken on an orchid igniting an orgasm. In real-time he began to frown, cringe and was brought to the brink of tears by too much cum-energy drain only to catch himself, cause she was near him in the real watching. Looking, anticipating his tawdry excuse for an apology not made, but acted out willingly and enacted by fiat. This was a pound of flesh excised, regrown, excised, regrown, excised in the shape-form of hot groin-spit. Yes, she was watching and the program was autonomous and devoid of pity. Blank shifting, wiggin'-out would not be allowed for more tolerated, considering the impression of freedom was no more than that added to the absence of any control.

A cinnamon "belly" girl with a fleshy torso and wide gyrating hips, stroked the barrel of his gun and it went erect against his will. Everything pulsed, swelled and came towards him. Like an embryonic sac his environ turned alizarin crimson and the encroaching walls rubbed and caressed his entire body. Back arched, arms extended and wet with the stroke of impossibly hot, long, wet, silk-velveteen tongues licking his inner thighs and anus. The women's voices moaned, gurgled and laughed through unseen pleasure grins. He could feel himself mouth, "No more." He squeezed his eyes shut.

You could never blink InSpace he discovered. The mind has no eyelids.

The now familiar tubular clasp around his gunmetal penis tightened and radiated moist heat pushing his testicles against his inner thighs. In real-time he moved his hands towards his pelvis, tempted to push away the hypnogenic apparition only to remember that they actually resided in his head. He could, at any time remove the sinstim helmet and cause the Penance program to abort but this was about saving his marriage, he kept saying. "I'll never do it——Goddamn..!" His body twisted in the contoured chair and his face showed strain, as if he was bench-pressing his highest weight ever in the gym. How could he have expected mercy from Suzanne he thought to himself. Her fingernails were perfection.

For a fleeting moment he wondered if his nuts would actually run out of semen. "Oh God, I don't know if I can last four more levels of this..."

The orifice that consumed his penis felt as if it was not just fucking him but his legs, thighs and buttocks. Pumping ensued. He grunted and the sounds from his mouth spoke of strain and a deep helplessness. Up and down, in and out, the program matched its maneuvers to his breathing. He could hear them breathing, their warm breath blowing against the fine hairs of his earlobes. New tongues found their mark. His breathing was heavy now and someone placed a tube into his mouth. He sucked and was rewarded with cool water.

The program's intuition was impressive. It was waiting for him to surrender. It would not do all the work. He had to be a willing participant to reach a climax. A thrust, the slight swelling of his head, anything would escalate the——-and the countdown began. The moans of the women increased. Rodney was a chunk of milk chocolate fully immersed in a saucepan of chocolate pudding, being jiggled above the flames of ecstasy. When he came it was primal. His loins shivered involuntarily with spasms of pleasure. No talking, only guttural sounds as his hips wrenched and a molten teaspoon of semen shot out of him. Involuntary tremors lurched his pelvis back and forth several times before subsiding. As he looked down at his barrel in time to catch his last discharge, he marveled at his semen's transformation from multicolored starburst to tiny, winged, Playboy bunnies sporting black pumps, rabbit ears and bare, jiggling breasts. The involuntary spasms lessened and his breathing slowed. A pool of sweat had formed in the center of his chest and shook as the program slowly moved him back to the entrance of the shaft way.

He wanted so badly to sleep. To disconnect and escape. He was no longer concerned with what his expression was, or who could see him from the clinic's observation booth. His platform began its ascent. Five down and four to go before he could rise, walk to the bathroom and tear off his rubber diaper. "If you would just have a bit of fuckin' mercy Suzanne," he screamed in his head, "Hope you're fucking taping this for your girlfriend Tiffany! That meddling big-mouth CUNT!"

In real-time Suzanne sat in the observation booth devoid of interest or emotion quietly sipping her cappuccino and reading Vogue on the clinic's flat screen. Neither she or Rodney would be here today if not for the urging of her friend Tiffany. Tiffany the survivor of three marriages to three adulterous men, had pegged Rodney years ago as a candidate for this Penance program. She, knew that Suzanne was having tepid, intermittent sex with her younger husband of lesser means and fiery passion. And so it was over the course of many expensive lunches at Harry Capriani's and the Four Seasons, that she convinced Suzanne to hire a private detective to follow this rooster of a man to his lover's nest. The rest was child's play. A cube filled with pictures, video of the two kissing in a morbid lower eastside pool hall and the woman's phone number appearing on Suzanne's bill several times each week was all it took. The women had him cold and if he did not renounce the strumpet, apologize and undergo a form of Penance, at Tiffany's urging, he would be divorced post haste and penniless. So a layer of rust grew on the section of his heart where Suzanne had resided. Behind their backs he shrugged. No hate, just sex. He hadn't loved Emily and maybe now Suzanne would welcome his advances and his big hard cock tapping her behind as she bent down for a look into the fridge. He thought. Though not right away. Being poor again would never do and the thought of signing over large sums of money he earned, to pay other lawyers was to be avoided at all cost. So he had agreed and actually sighed in relief. He had heard stories from half-drunks in the city's finest bars of Penance and of its intensity, but they had not conveyed exactly how intense it was. How much it would squeeze the only pleasure more potent than spending Suzanne's inheritance on Flusser's hand-made suits and Lobb brogues out of him. How much it would make him cry and beg to have it end but worst of all, that its determination could never be matched by that iguana with perfect nails.

He was moving much faster now.

"FASTEN YOUR SAFETY BELTS!"

Seated on the lumpy bed Brice was holding a cheap ass deck Chili had given him and was noticeably tense. Moments before he had read a message from Niemöller that said, "I have your younger half. Want him? Lets meet and greet—that's if you've got what it takes?" He knew, deep down that he had been a jerk to a lot of people a lot of times and now many of them were cheering on an assholes like Niemöller, but B' didn't believe he was evil. He didn't deserve this. He was sitting in a gray, windowless sty in Chinatown and playing by a vicious dungeon master's rules. He didn't know his way out of trouble, but he knew the deck would get him there. The old wooden chair creaked as he slouched, though he was careful to balance the deck on his lap. He stared at it blankly then at the wall then at the bed. He had never been this alone. He imagined the cold dampness of the cement floor slowly infiltrating his shoes like a toxic gas and realized that he was stalling. Hope had run into a lion's den and faltered. He had tried every other means of reaching Jimmy, or anyone who could put him in touch with him and failed. Meanwhile, he had become an easy target and everybody seemed to have a handful of darts. He missed his brother and feared the worst. He also hoped that Jimmy could help him answer some questions and those thoughts scratched clean through his tough guy veneer.

All of this brought him to this moment. Planted in the chair like a statue and starring down at the deck his thoughts crept forward. He wouldn't—couldn't use Chuck because he didn't trust him and thought that it was always him against the world anyway—so what the fuck.

"Right," said Brice standing up and placing the deck on the floor directly in front of him, "I'll click on the Preferences menu and disable all the tactile protocols. That should take care of any…" Then he stopped and walked slowly to the door. "But I tried that all ready and it still hurt like hell when I tried to access…" He then slowly dragged the chair so it stood flush with the door. Turning he walked over to the table and unplugged the extension cord from the table lamp so that the only light in the dank room came from an exposed light-bulb overhead and sat down.

B' took the surgical steel plug out of its smooth, black germ-free case and inserted the paperclip thin plug into his jack. "Alright. I get it. You want to make me suffer Niemöller. I get it. Test for me." As soon as the diodes along the shaft of the plug touched the walls of the silicone lining the deck switched on and a transparent, 3D, mouse pointer in the shape of a 44mm. bullet appeared in his field of vision. "You're going to fuck me even though I've never done anything to you huh cocksucker." Clenching his teeth as he speaks, Brice ties his left wrist to the arm of the chair and pulls the knot tight. "I don't owe you anything, but you've let me know by snatching Jimmy that you hate me and now you've got my attention." With that he pulls off his left tube sock and rolls it up with both hands. "You probably jerking my chain for nothing and you want to cream when you put me through it. Well fuck lets see what you've got." With that he puts the rolled up sock between his teeth and begins to tie a loose knot around his right wrist and the other chair arm. Through the sock he spits, "Fucking jealous, hourly-wage, asshole, bitchmotherfucker." Then Brice looks up, engages the bullet pointer and works the Options section of the Preferences pull-down like a championship Ping-Pong rally. With the tactile feedback turned off on the Browser, the Frisbee *Doppe* chosen and all the dexterity settings maxed out, his Browser scrolls a long list of destinations. In the background, his custom Browser downloads The Official Brice Johnson iEnviron sponsored by Sony and Sun's MegaLift Workstations. His own page views him as an anonymous visitor and greets him with a pre-recorded, video message he did months ago. He phases through it, briefly remembering the day he shot it and those present for the taping—-among them Olga. He remembered how ill she looked to him not because she was, but that she looked so thin in that tight white T-shirt.

Flippin' back, he dug that Jimmy's deck had silky depth, speed and perspective capabilities like nothing else he had ever jacked into outside of a Sony's game platform. "Flush it," he thought. He was allowing himself to be distracted and he really needed to focus.

He heard the drumming long before he saw the drummers.

His *Doppe* appears as a transparent, low-rent, dial-up, saucer with constantly changing lines of code scrolling across it at blinding speed. The code is a direct reflection of his movement, the time he spends here and the connection with his service provider all in white 1's and 0's. He navigated the multi-colored *Doppes* of 11,356 visitors like a seal in a forest of kelp. He phases through E-banners and the spastic frenzy of comet tails launched by obnoxious fans.

In a makeshift amphitheater hundreds of *Doppes* have gathered around an autonomous A.I. known as Shiva. Shiva, modeled after the Trimurti namesake is "the Destroyer" and one badass HyperCAD piece of work. Whipped together by some MIT students in their spare time and tinkered with by the New Tech. Techkies at NYU twelve years ago, Shiva was not about solving problems, curing world hunger or predicting the weather. It had locked parameters. Dance and snatch memory, upgrades, software and find safe places to nest.

Brice gives Shiva and the onlookers a wide berth as he approaches the message wall.

Shiva's skin is the color of antique bronze and covered with a textured techno-organic paisley. This representation of a deity is the brainchild of Ali Yourself Kahn, an A.I. major who used an M-KAT derivative to record, extract and encode his mother's traditional dancing and spliced in some late 21st Century Michael Jackson moves for mojo measure. Surrounded by six drone drummers orbiting her, Shiva would always "reach out and touch" a *Doppe* at the end of her dance and black-plague the idiot sucker. Everything, that pinhead's software, memory, including all vmail, the retrieved information from each visit to every site ever hit—-and then chomp through your operating system like a brand new lawnmower in your neighbor's neglected lawn leaving you with nothing more than expensive, charred hardware. That was the attraction. Everybody wanted to see somebody "plagued."

B' slowed to scan the massive message wall covered with thousands of messages. Some were ever repeating video clips of schoolgirls in their flannels, cooing and giggling at him from their bedrooms while their parents sleep. Other messages are simple graffiti that morphs into cartoon homage's to the B-man, each hoping to be clicked. Many of the messages had active smart-links that would instantaneously dial and wake-up the author's computer to alert them of a possible chat, but B' had never done that. That would have been, uncool. Lots of messages from reporters and messages that looked too serious to go near. All the messages have been screened by his administrator for viruses, racist, obscene, lewd or homoerotic content so nothing here should upset him and then he finds the post-it type note he was looking for. Today it reads, "Hey bro'." And Brice hovers over it. Then he has several thoughts. *Doppes* can't be screened out like passive messages, because anyone can buy a new deck with a switcher and appear to be jackin' in from anywhere, or someone could simply jack on a friend's deck. Someone whose code doesn't mark them as a prank, an extremist, convicted felon or wannabe' terrorist, or worst. So anybody could be watching him click into the note and make him for Brice in-spite of the fact that his saucer is indistinguishable from any one of a billion saucers launched, from businessmen on a construction site in Taipei, to drug dealers on Sugar Hill. Niemöller could be watching or the cops could have flagged a bunch of messages including this one. Looking around Brice saw that several *Doppes* were clicking into messages, some of whom would be violently purged by the author's firewall so Brice said, "Fuck it."

Twice before he had clicked on messages in this exact same typeface, at this exact same location, only to experience severe pain. They weren't simple practical jokes either, because Brice had double clicked the post-its and been burned by a literal firewall each time. Each time he had gone far enough in to sense that it was a deep wall and saw the same horrific image. Jimmy, beaten and swollen, writhing in pain, with streaming audio that said, "B', get me outta' here man!" and the price had been excruciating pain. This time he felt certain that no pain would be felt and he'd be able to get to the bottom of this. When his saucer touched the surface of the message, the pain registered across his nose and forehead like a blowtorch and he backed off. "Fuck!" he said to himself realizing that N' had found a way of flipping his presets. There was no way around the pain. He backed off the message a little then plunged into it head first. Instantly the blowtorch like heat registered across his nose and forehead and spread. His eyes bulged under his fiercely shut lids and he screamed through the sock in his mouth. In an instant a vast continuum of yellow-red flames filled his senses, as he forced his way deeper into the flames. To any observer his saucer would have slowly and silently pulled itself into the message not even disturbing the helter-skelter order of this site for even a nanosecond. On the other side B' had been stripped of his dial-up saucer and was now depicted as his real-time self, bound and biting into his sock. He was now completely consumed with the pain of navigating the firewall. His lungs were on fire. It felt as if each centimeter of his flesh was awash in an ignited gel and each pore was simultaneously being pierced with red-hot pins and were exploding from the force boiling blood would exact on his arteries. Tears streamed down the sides of his cheeks, as he phased through the enormous image of his brother alternately coughing and crying, his face bloated and swollen from repeated beatings. There was no thought, only pain. It was exhausting him and he thought he would die at any second. The fire continued to reach deeper in through the layers of his skin, through muscle, cartilage bone and membranes and he tasted his own bile——his stomach convulsing violently trying in vain to throw up and cast off the mother of his agony. All the while his 3D bullet pointer remained ahead and above him. As he wrenched his neck violently upwards, Brice caught a glimpse of a white Colonial door closed and motionless in the distance. In the crest of misery's arms he flung his pointer towards the door and maddeningly clicked in at a frantic speed. Then it was over.

Because the deck was he saw himself tied to a chair, the sock still in his mouth and realized he was in an enormous room with white walls. There was some sort of ventilation system blowing air on him. The cool air had the effect of a third degree burn victim having his entire body, immersed in a tank of ice-cold saltwater. The pain was so excruciating that he opened his fists and tried to get out of the chair, as if that would have allowed him to escape the pain. His head wrenched back and he wet his pants and felt the stinging sensation of his hot urine seeping into the teeming crack like sores on his inner-thigh and ass. He now felt as if he was completely devoid of hair and clothing that his skin was dry and charred like the remains of some ancient volcanic island disaster. As he convulsed violently, gasping for air he felt as if the few remaining drops of fluid in his body were seeping out of the cracks in his burnt flesh and the pain of that bleeding brought him to the precipice of cardiac arrest. Although his heart was pounding blood through the arteries in his neck and playing an organic snare drum for his ears, he struggled to control his breathing and took long slow breaths.

As his heart rate lowered, his vision began to return and the stream of tears down the sides of his face began to subside. He could focus now. He was in a room without windows, that had a black & white checkered marble floor, a large ornate 17th Century French crystal chandelier and a single closed door straight ahead of him in the distance. His heart rate slowed now and his skin moved through prickly heat to a state of shock type numbness. He didn't so much spit the sock out of his mouth as let it drop and as he watched it drop he saw that he was wearing clothes and that his hands and arms were intact and unharmed. Although he meant to yell he could only manage to gasp, "Here I am...m-o-t-h-e-r—f-u-c-k-e—r. Where are y-o-u?" His head pitched forward so that he had to roll his eyes to look ahead. Then the door slowly opened.

In the distance B' could see a thin white man approaching him wearing a Bowler hat. The man seemed to take forever to walk towards him and as the door slowly closed Brice knew that it was Niemöller.

With every step he took Brice became notably colder. By the time Niemöller was a few meters away Brice could see his breath and was shivering. Niemöller wore a gray flannel double breasted English suit and carried an ebony walking stick. Two meters away from Brice he stopped and took a long look at him.

"That's what should have happened when your brother snaked into my system months ago," said Niemöller.

Through his chattering teeth Brice says, "Where is my brother?"

"I've all ways wondered if this——s level of pain would scar your nervous system." As Niemöller said this he sat down on an ornate, gilded, high back chair that materialized a moment before he made contact. "I can't even imagine how much it must hurt," momentarily concerned.

"Where is my brother?"

"An exceptional feature is this system's ability to gauge your physical ability and take you to your cardiac threshold without having you go into arrest."

"Where....?"

"...And you are in great shape so—just think how that would have put a fire under the NYPD's ass if your pathetic home system had access to..."

"Stop fucking with me! Tell..."

"Tell you what? How I snatched your brother? Where he is? What I'm going to do to him? How easy this has all been?"

"I...?"

"What you should be more concerned with, is what you have always been. Yourself, you vain, arrogant shithole."

"I've never done anything to you."

"You murdered Olga…"

"No I didn't."

"You certainly did kill your sparing partner in front of several reporters. You've consorted with the mob, you've taken bribes and kickbacks in spite of the fact that you're all ready rich and you can't even be humble——and—d you offend me," said Niemöller with the crooked mouth of disgust.

"I didn't kill Olga. I wasn't even at the club at the same time…"

"Save it for the police."

"So who the fuck are you?"

"I'm a businessman."

"You're a thief, a kidnapper, an extortionist, you deal in black-market tech and without buyers you'd die like the leach you are."

"You want to talk about death? Yes, let's talk about death. You've died, killed and been reborn dozens of times here on platforms like this and you've never thought twice about inflicting pain on someone else for money and fame. You disgust me the way you prance about the platform like a peacock on 'roids and 'plants." Unable to hide his disgust, N's lip curls.

"So we're the same."

"No, we're not. And don't interrupt. I don't want your money and no one will ever know we've had this conversation. What I want is for you to suffer. What I want is to see you humiliated in front of billions and exposed for what you are. A tool of rich corporations run amuck."

Just then Brice undoes his right hand and moves to untie his left hand. Niemöller is on him like an owl on a mouse and before Brice knows it Niemöller's left heel is jammed up against his nuts and the glowing tip of the walking stick is crackling with green neon energy a few millimeters away from his eyes.

"No, no. Y-o-u a-r-e m-i-n-e. You will not win another bout here, or anywhere else when I've finished with you, you will realize just how blind you have always been to your own stupidity. You want your brother back? Lose the bout in Cuba. Throw the fight. If you win I'll kill him." With that said, Niemöller reached behind Brice and ripped the jack out of his head. The body slide back to real-time was all ways a shock when you came down this fast and B' flailed his right arm at a non-existent Niemöller. He shuddered. He was dripping with sweat and pulled his left arm from underneath the extension chord. Standing and raging around the small room he stepped on the deck and pounded the wall with his fists. Turning towards the doorway he picked up the chair and started smashing it against the deck over and over again. All that was left of the chair was its rickety back, when Brice fell to his knees, a sobbing mess. Throwing the remains of the chair across the room and looking down at the deck his sobbing turned to convulsions when he realized that the smooth black surface of the deck wasn't even scratched.

InSpace Shiva grabbed her crotch with one hand and reached out to touch someone with the other.

HOURS LATER

It swept over him like a wave.

Losing control he put his food on the other chair without looking—his eyes already shut and bursting with tears. He allowed it because he could no longer keep it at bay. All the pain and suffering he imagined Jimmy had experienced and the knowledge that he was gone forever had opened the gates. B' opened his mouth wide and a line of spit fell between his open legs to meet the concrete. Leaning forward, his left elbow on his knee, he raised his open right hand as if to keep someone at bay and heard himself sob uncontrollably. He sobbed so hard he could hardly catch his breath. He could not—if his life depended on it—hold back an ounce of emotion. He had no will whatsoever to resist embracing the devastation. His eyes tightly shut he receded into himself. His inner-form actually separated from his outer shell and he could sense—not see—his true form. Hairless, gray, mute and bereft of features his body pulled away from the holes his eyes—now open—saw the world through. As he receded, the light that the eye-holes allowed in barely reflected off his inner self. The interior walls of his outer-self were featureless, in dark shadow and the inner-self wanted nothing to do with it. Slowly, palpably, he felt something like a wall press against the right cheek of his inner-self and he raised his inner-right hand to keep it at bay. Inside he opened his mouth to scream but no sound came out.

DON'T WALK...

10:30 P.M. MOTT STREET AND CANAL

Walking. Jimmy's voice raged in Brice's head, "An' it was flash——h! B' was jammin' an' slammin' that sucker punk uside' his head!" And the image in his head was the Vanquez bout when B' kicked him on the side of his head. "*SLAMNTHWAK* like a megaton rubber mallet slammin' against a five gallon bottle o' watter!" Vision blurred, colors bleed, the crowd roared and sweat actually flew InSpace. Then there was Niemöller on top of him like a starving rat on cheese. His hands struck B' like lead weights on the end of whirling ropes and then, the black e-x-p-a-n-s-e. But B' was still there alone in the dark with the sounds of the crowd fading in the distance and he was left in the dark flailing his arms at nothing. And so it was like a thirty-second primetime spot replaying itself behind the membrane of his senses over and over and over...

Sound of metal *SCRAPING* across concrete.

Brice's head snapped towards the door and saw Chili staring back. He stood and grabbed a filter-mask that had gun-metal colored ribs that resembled skeletal fingers and Brice pulled the black skull cap down to cover his head and walked out. He was glad for the poncho and straw, Chinese "coolie" hat Chili had given him earlier not simply for cover, but because every fifth ped wore the same ensemble. He and Chili didn't speak they simply nodded and B followed Chili through one opening after another. B's inner voice kept repeating, "How did Niemöller do it? How did that fuck unplug my fuckin' jack....." And he could see himself seated in the dank room, his eyes wide and distant as Niemöller approached him.

As he walked the different smells brought him back to the moment at hand. The damp mildew that seeped through the pores of the concrete, the rotting plaster and a crack in a sewage pipe nearby all reminded him of what he was doing. Running through shit from shit. He could hear the rain beating the streets before he saw it and Chili motioned for him to remain in the doorway. In spite of the downpour that would make the farmers in Kansas cuss with envy, Canal, which was once actually a Venetian style canal was teeming with peds, bicycles, unipods, glow cars with pulsating neon colored body panels displaying ads and ancient cars. Above him was the spawn of Madison Avenue media planners and the scourge of "quality of lifers." Ads. Ads. in all shapes and sizes their colors reflecting off the wet sidewalk and coats, the peds were wearing. Ads. in 1,2 and 3D high-rez holo with real-time digital stereo. Ads. you could phase through, interact with or mute from your ride. Ads. on buildings, trucks, taxies and buses. Ads. projected from automated blimps that ran the length of Canal and back during rush hour which seemed like every hour. Some of the ad. panels for Marlborough blew dry ice smoke, while others for Adidas, Chase, P&G brands, Samsung, GM, Budweiser and Toyota competed for attention with flashy computer effected celebrity endorsements. It was common place and yet it was a spectacle. The panache of all these ads were wildly engaging, until the indigestion of commerce crept in leaving you numb and B' wished he was back in his underground room.

"Chili…," said his internal voice "How did Niemöller do it? How did that fuck unplug my fuckin' jack. He played me like I was a fuckin' nubee'. I'd like to get him standing real-time one-on-one for a round and pay him back." Chili was oddly mute.

He brought B' up on the North side of Canal and the traffic headed West, a neat trick considering it was across the street from where he had entered the building days before. Poking his head out B' could see that the sidewalk was lined with illegal noodle stands and tables selling all manor of gray market tech, knock-off clothing, jewelry and the street noise transferred into small yellow syn' globes that tickled his cheeks. He shifted the deck on its back-pack like straps and felt for the small, black textured staff in his hands. That was what he'd been reduced to. These were all his worldly possessions and the fearfully sad thought that his past life was unattainable forever, caused him to stare through people, cars and trucks like that barmaid in the Renoir painting.

Searching, B' could no longer see Chili and this tripped his defenses. "Come on Chili—i. You told me you had to move me to another safe house motherfucker I don't want to be standing around her forever." B' stepped out onto the street not feeling comfortable with the idea of being cornered in the doorway and quickly sidestepped to his left. His head bowed, so he was all peripheral vision now. Red, white and blue at 10:00 o'clock. This guy in a Ranger's jacket had B' in his peripheral with his back to the street. He wasn't leaning against a car and he kept slipping behind that noodle stand like an eel.

At B's 2:00 o'clock was another big white guy in a black, 3/4 leather jacket standing the exact same way. Probably nothing. Just then he hears loud horn West of Broadway on Canal. It comes from a small procession of Monster Trucks that are making their way back from a Rally at the Garden and it's catching a lot of looks but the sound meant nothing to B'. The rain starts to taper off and the wind cuts down a few notches as well. A minute passes and B' hears a car horn and looks to his left. A beat up navy Ford van rolls up with Chili standing in the open side door and stops between two parked cars. Chili motions for B' to walk over and he does so slowly. Something is not right. The van's interior is dark and as B' makes his way through the crowd, never taking his eyes off Chili he senses shapes moving in the shadows. Chili's expression is contrary to his usual relaxed snide smirk. B' slows down and looks to his left at the Ranger's jacket. He is moving towards B. B's eyes dip and rise at his 4:00 o'clock and he sees that the leather jacket is swinging behind him. B' clenches his teeth and the game face flashes on. He points the staff at Chili simultaneously accusing and convicting him with a look and the adrenaline pops out of his pituitary gland like a champagne cork. Brice leaps with his right foot and banks onto the car on his left, takes two steps up the windshield and jumps on to the roof of the van. The Ranger's jacket and the leather jacket run for opposite sides of the van and B' jumps down like a cat. The driver's side door begins to open and B' jams the guy back into the van. He takes off, running between the cars towards Broadway with the traffic. The jackets hightail it after him with their dart guns out. Four guys pile out of the van and one turns and shoots Chili in the face with a hollow-point bullet. Although the traffic is bad it is moving and B can't get to the other side of Canal without getting hit by an oncoming car. Brice turns for an instant to check the competition out and sees thug number three toting a riot cannon. *Fttttf! Fttttf!* These guys are using darts and the last one cracks a rear-windshield. B' rolls over the hood of a moving car scaring the shit out of the Dominican driver and runs the edge of the sidewalk like a wider-receiver on the out of bounds line. B' runs in an irregular fashion to throw the thugs off and the darts keep flying, some hitting peds. B' rolls over another hood and tries for the center of the street still heading west and senses that they are right on his tail. That's when he does the unexpected. He turns around and runs straight at the Ranger's jacket. The thug is surprised and levels his gun. B' zigs and zags as much as the cars will allow him then leaps forward and rolls on the street. The thug fires and catches B's poncho going clear through and hitting the street. B' is up and uses his momentum to swing the bead-blasted, slip-free staff at the thug like a mallet. The thug puts up his left arm to protect himself and B' shatters it with one blow. B' spins ducks and jams him in the ribs with the end of the staff as hard as he can. The guy buckles over and B' smashes his right eyetooth into his skull. The other thug runs from behind then fires, hitting the first thug. As the first thug falls B' pushes him onto the oncoming shooter. This second thug uses a Kenpo move to step out of the way and Brice moves forward. With a twist the staff separates and reveals chrome chain links connected to ball bearings—

Wired for Chaos

-nun chucks and B' swings them for momentum. The thug takes a step back and B' advances. The thug ducks the first volley and B' switches hands moving the nun chucks across his chest. B' fakes the thug out by lifting his right leg and follows through with a direct hit across the thug's right lobe. He drops. B' sees the other four thugs headed his way. He quick snaps the chrome chain and two titanium coated, 5" blades pop out of both ends of the nun chucks. Another quick snap disconnects the chain from both chucks and B' hurls them like daggers at the closest thug. The thug takes both in the chest and B' is already running down the street.

Then, out of nowhere, from behind them an ancient tan 57' Chevy screeches into the wrong lane burning rubber and plows into one of the thugs. He flies through the air and hits the thug in front of him, then the Chevy runs them both over. The other two thugs take cover, jumping over the roofs of westbound cars and the Chevy stops and backs up. B' crosses Broadway without looking back and sees a dark green Range Rover speeding towards him pissing off other drivers by smashing into them left and right. Three windows open and guns pop out. On the other side of Broadway the thugs toss their dart guns and pull out automatic Sigs. A guy wearing a denim jacket gets out of the Chevy and it speeds off. He levels his gun at one of the thugs casual like he's about to water the lawn and pulls the trigger. The thugs duck and peds scatter screaming as a noodle stand gets riddled with bullets. One thug runs hunched over towards Broadway and the other circles around the car for a shot at the denim jacket. B' turns and sees the Chevy screech to a halt. The driver in a blue parka gets out carrying a big riot-stopper gun and heads for B'. B' sees him and the gun and freezes. He knows that these guns fire a weighted, compressed net in a canister shell that could topple a horse. A shot rings past the blue parka's head and he turns and sees one of the thugs. B' turns and sees the driver of Thor, a monster truck jump out and run into the stream of peds on the sidewalk without closing the door or looking back. Gunshots seem to be coming from everywhere as B' runs for Thor. The Range Rover slams into the rear of a red SUV and they get the message. The SUV guns it ramming a Honda and this continues for three more cars. B' jets into Thor's driver's seat as he fumbles with the controls. He gives it gas and Thor reverses into another monster truck called Hulk. B's entire world shakes and he works the clutch. As he begins to move forward, the Range Rover comes up along side him and the driver sticks his head through the sunroof.

"Brice!!! Get fuck outta' there!"

B' doesn't know the guy but sees two others in the Rover pointing their guns at him. The driver sees the guns and yells at them, "No idiots we're suppose to catch him not shoot him!" B' turns to his right and clips a Pearl Paint truck and shifts into reverse. Gunning it he makes for the Rover. They panic and try to get out of park. B' swerves and heads them off. The rear wheels pop-up as Thor bounces into the air and slams into the right side of the Rover, crushing it the glass pops like an explosion sending tiny pieces of safety glass hurling in every direction. B' almost goes through the windshield and has to brace himself against the steering wheel. The Rover tips over from the weight of the truck and the axles pop like match sticks. B' switches gears and drives forward, the rear end bouncing like a happy Doberman. He turns left and drives towards the Canal-Broadway intersection. A gun fight is still going on, only now it looks like some eager peds are firing from the crowd. B' looks at Broadway and sees that the section below Canal is blocked by a UPSMail truck and he slows down. The thug from the black van runs between cars and into the center of Broadway just north of Canal. The denim jacket chucks his empty gun and reaches into the passenger seat of the Chevy. He pulls out a Rattler gun the size of a four year old child and turns towards the thug. Bullets riddle the side of the Chevy and he ignores them. Brice aims Thor at him and guns it popping a wheelie. Denim jacket gets hit in the shoulder and fires at the first car in the crosswalk on Broadway. Then he begins to turn when he hears Thor approaching him. He starts to swing the Rattler around and crimson erupts from his left thigh. He fires at Thor and misses by a hair. B' sends the truck over the Chevy and the passenger's side door pops out and smacks him. A nanosecond later the left wheel of the truck having compacted the Chevy steps on the Denim jacket and he goes splat like a water bug. B' keeps on going and the Thor's grill lights up with sparks from gunfire. He sees the thug from the black van standing between two cars in the center of Broadway and people are running for cover. B' heads straight for him and drives over the flaming car that Denim jacket shot up. Thor pops a wheelie over the cars and drives the wrong way——up Broadway on top of the cars crushing them left and right. The thug hightails it, simultaneously turning to fire at Brice and running between the narrow gap. B' accelerates and a guy from Jersey opens his door to run out and jams the thug up smashing his elbow. The guy manages to run and the thug decides to save his bullet for Thor. *Click! Click!* He's out of bullets and Thor is on top of him. As the truck smashes the cars on either side of the thug the cars flatten and the guy screams as he gets encased in a crumpled mass of sharp steel. He'd live for another few minutes. B' can hardly hear the sirens blaring from the eight police cars behind him, but he can see the reflection of their lights in his rear-view mirror and along the sides of the buildings. He jumps down and runs across two cars until he can reach the sidewalk, hits the ground running and keeps going west on Howard Street. Mercer turns left and runs towards Canal. As he runs he loses the hat and poncho then slows to weave into the crowd and puts on the filter-mask. Turning west he slows and the sirens blare louder as ambulances and fire-trucks arrive spewing red and yellow pyramids at his cheeks and forehead. He walks quickly through the crowd and does not look back. Breaking into a light jog he turns right on West Broadway and left on Grand. The crepe soles of his boots are ninja silent and he spooks two guys holding hands in the shadow of a closed Bistro as he disappears into the night.

...RUN WITH ME
VARRICK STREET AND NOWHERE, LATE

Wired for Chaos

Brice had been, like all meticulous athletes before him, rapt in the familiar arms of ritual.

Quicksilver discourse raged in his head, "Alright, Chili——Chili ratted me out to the first seta' shooters an'—maybe he didn't have a—a choice an' I…"

Rituals fathered by habits begat by the chromosome responsible for stubbornness. A particular way of rising from his bed in the morning, of stretching, breathing, of greeting Home. The way he nodded upon the first sighting of his brother each day.

"They thought they could take me, easy. I was lucky. That musta' been Chili catching a bullet in the van…but who the fuck were they?! Glad I didn't fuckin' hesitate or…" his brisk walk slows to a brisk cityped' stride, aware and directed. A tingling sensation kept fading in and out at the back of his neck. It unsettled him. He kept looking over his shoulder suddenly aware that the back of his head was vulnerable. A childhood fear, he had always imagined being hit extremely hard, the sound, a thud like a bat hitting a watermelon. A moment later he shakes it off, when the primal instinct kicks in. He looks for encroaching shadows, reflections and listens for fast paced foot steps approaching him from behind.

Rituals before showering, working-out, answering his mail, tens upon tens of rituals that went unnoticed by those close to him was the cable-wire, the glue that kept him moving forward—he thought, successful was now gone.

He shakes his head. "If Iada' hesitated for even a minute I wouldda' been put down wit' Chili. The second crew I don't get. Not a team.…"

All of it, conscious and not, had been disconnected, not imploded from its own weight, exploded from neurosis or evaporated from neglect. Simply disconnected, leaving behind a confused unit.

"The second crew couldda' been———cops…I am a suspect in Olga's murder so…"

The vacuum that replaced the order in his life sent his world reeling.

"I just know Ivan shit fucked me to his boss to save face over losing so much money. And Niemöller. I'm not underestimating his ass. So all right, all right," looking behind him and seeing no one then crossing the street. "Gotta' fuckin' sort this all out——sort this all out…"

The connective tissue of his reasoning…

"What happened was Chili got squeezed by either Niemöller or the Russians, they set a trap, I flipped it. Ran. Fucked them up." the sound of the first thug's jaw breaking replays in his mind, "Fucked them up like I was grooving InSpace. Second crew stomped in and——they knew…"

His trust in mistrust…

"…They knew what was about to go down. T-h-e-y k-n-e-w. An' nunna' them was the cops? They didn't have their shit together. One crew had to be the Russians. Had to be!"

…Ever present, he had shaken his rituals onto the landfill of his shredded hero status.

"Had to be! An' that second crew——that punk in the parka…he was toting a fuckin' riot canon——-damn my hams are tight. If it was a automatic like those boys in the Rover he would have put me down. He had one but he didn't use it. Not his plan. But the first crew wanted my ass in a box."

Adrift in his cerebellum.

"And I killed——-I probably killed the Rover crew. That Monster truck, those wheels musta' weighed a ton…I didn't see——-but they were trying to off me! So fuck 'em! That punk with the Rattler was with them——-had to be! And the punk from the first crew. Didn't have to off him. Maybe——-could have been fine between the cars. Na—a! His ass is dead. Case closed."

Looking up and ahead of him was Christopher Street and he balked.

"Shit! A fucking major intersection. Goddamn Man probably has eyes pointed in every direction!" And with that he jogs across the street his head lowered in order to avoid the gaze of the police's mini-cams. Panning and zooming they ran continuous, random matches searching for fare jumpers, pushers, truant parolees and wanted criminals. "So I offed' some people. Derek was a mistake, a car wreck. My fault. Tonight…thank God I had game. Fuckin' channeled Bruce Lee's ass. Didn't have to think——-glad not to. Played it like a *run* and won so I'm not going to feel for them cause they were trying to off me."

In the doorway of a defunct printing house B' slips into the shadow.

"Fuck 'em into next year," and he begins to shiver through his cool-suit. "Fuck 'em!" Hugging himself and hunching over slightly, his teeth chattering as he spiraled downwards from the adrenaline high. "Motherfuckers tried to off me! Me! Fuck you! Fuck—k you! I wu—won! I——I…I'm the fuc—kin' champ…"

A chill ran down his spine. His stare morphed from fierce to harried, a fox hearing the hounds. The smell of oil on the wind's fingertips, distant traffic and as he shook his deck tapped against the door.

OPEN 24/7

B' navigates the streets of the West Village avoiding the main intersections and spies a stairwell with a covered lower level filled with garbage cans and decides to seek refuge. Maybe this wasn't the smartest move, putting his back up against a corner with no way out. Certain that he had not been followed, yet unsure that eyes weren't tracking him from a window above, it was all moot 'cause he had already decided. Hopping over the gate he almost slips on the slim covered cement steps, as he makes his way down the stairs. The landing is nearly completely covered with garbage and garbage cans, so B' has to quietly place one on top the other to give himself enough room to sit. He grimaces at the garbage stench mixed with urine he is no doubt willfully sitting in. The polymer in his cool suit immediately matches the dirty green Rubbermaid cans on his left and the grimy brick on his right. He hadn't thought of food but his stomach started to gurgle loudly.

"I can wait a couple hours." he thought. A couple of hours until he found a way to get some food with no money and without being nabbed by the man. Each time a ped passed by a shadow moved over his camouflaged feet he would tighten. He sits in an upright fetal position and locks his fingers hand-in-hand so tight that he can feel his pulse coursing through his hands. After a half-hour or so he relaxes and picks up his deck. "Willy." Says Brice as if remembering where he placed a long lost valuable and with that he jacks in to Chuck. B's field of vision flips to Chuck's internal portal—a midnight navy expanse and beckons a translucent control board the size of a tennis court. He looks at the area that titled Communications and says ,"Make a call."

"I saw everything. Impressive." Says Chuck.

"What?"

"You walk the walk. It must be exhilarating to know that you can perform on that level when you know you can actually be killed."

"Life comes down to a series of moments A.I. When you train you are always training for the moments, cause you can forgive yourself for fucking up and say you tried your hardest or you slipped or something, but choking, choking is for punk bitches and I'm nobody's bitch."

"Who are you calling?"

"Thought you knew everything. Calling Willy. He should be in town."

"Allow me," and with that Chuck overrules B's pointer and dials the main telephone exchange in Mexico.

"Hey I don't have time to…"

"Get caught. I know. I'm going to thread the call through a few foreign exchanges so the locals can't find us."

"'Us' You make it sound like you're in this with me."

"I haven't decided yet, but your life keeps taking these Shakespearian pivots." The line rings.

NINTH AVENUE AND 46TH STREET

Willy's head rings. "Where the fuck have you been B'?"

"No time. Meet me at the corner of…" says Brice.

Chuck interrupts, "Commerce and Bedford."

"Who the fuck is that?" says Willy.

"I'll explain. You cabbin' it?"

"Hell no. Rental."

"Put that into your computer yet?" says Brice.

"Waitupwaitup. GPS plot Commerce and Bedford, got it. On my way."

"Later."

18 MINUTES AND 39 SECONDS LATER

Willy's red, Ford Mustang pulls up to the corner of Commerce and Bedford and be starts looking around for B'. B' peeks up from the garbage laden basement steps where he has been hiding and shimmies over to the

Mustang. Once in the car he does not pause but goes immediately to the back seat and lies flat.

"What up homes." Says Willy more casual than you'd expect.

"Had to rent a fucking fire-engine red car now di-d-n't you." Eeking out a smile, "Good to see you man, so good to fucking see you."

"You asked for some Willy and I'm here to deliver. Where to?"

"You staying at a hotel?"

"Yeah, cheap shit Days Inn on 47th street."

"Lets go."

"We not going to off some people right away. You know you fucking New Yorkers can't fucking drive. I almost killed a bitch in a mini-wagon and her kids, for cutting me off and some fuck stink cabbie. I coulda' just popped them and only lost a few minutes down here."

"Yo. Lemme' explain something to you. They have cameras to protect the rich and watch the poor in LA, but out here they've got them everywhere, so you could talk all the shit you want but the man's response time is flash up and down." Beat. "Hope you can get us in and out of this hotel without anybody seeing."

"Yo. You asked for some backup not no fucking CIA shit. Put a fucking rag on your big nose head and walk in."

"I could see I'm going to have to hurt your ass."

"In your dreams Holo-V boy. In your dreams." And the two turn up the Westside highway.

AN HOUR AND A HALF LATER AT THE DAYS INN ON 8TH AVENUE

Willy and Brice were facing each other seated on identical beds in a room on the Eight Avenue side of the hotel with the curtains drawn. B' had summed up everything from the limo ride where the voice told him to run and back tracked several times to include the origin of the deck, now referred to as Chuck and the accidental killing of Derek. Willy peppered the conversation with, "shits" "fucks" and head shaking between puffs on an endless smoking binge. B' and Willy had ordered club sandwiches, chips and sodas from room service which they quickly downed and B' was finally starting to relax.

B' said, "I need a fucking shower. I've been in that little basement room—seems like three years, not three days and I can't smell anything else but my stink.

"Yeah." Says Willy picking up the remote in a near state of disbelief. "Those monster trucks manual or stick?"

"Stick Willy. Stick."

"Thought so. I'd like to drive one of those bitches over a few people. Be fun."

B' entered the bathroom and closed the door. His hair was matted and he needed a shave but he thought it could wait. He began to take the suit off when he thought "what the fuck" and stepped into the shower wearing it.

Wired for Chaos

Once he adjusted the water temperature he took the suit off and let the water run along its inside and then placed it over the sliding door. He planned to take a long time and started to think of all the fancy hotels he had been in while opening the small bar of cheap hotel soap. Throwing the wrapper over the sliding door he began to rub his body in a near comatose state as his mind began to wander.

LATER

B' walks out of the bathroom wearing a towel with a renewed zest and vigor heading straight for Chuck. Willy is horizontal and asleep with the Holo-V remote on his stomach and a Glock resting on his crotch when B' enters but his eyes slowly open as B' reaches for his jack.

"Yo Will'. I just clicked on something."

"Hmm…" he says clicking off the local news.

"Time I turned and started hitting back." As B' sits, a police siren is heard above the din of rushing cars and tourist hordes outside. "I'm not waiting around for the fucking cops or the Russians. I've got to find Jimmy and that means we have to slam that bitch Niemöller." Jacking in B' leans back and places his forearms on the chair's arms. "Chuck. Tell me everything you know about Niemöller."

"He works downtown at…"

"Where does he live?"

"His address is 252 East 3rd Street between A and B in a shitty walk up. Why?"

"My boy and I are going to pay him a visit."

"I advise against that, brotha'"

Willy chimes in, "You trust this fucker B'?" pointing at the deck.

"I would never trust any A.I. that thought meat was game."

Willy's head rings and he answers it. "Hello?"

"Listen to me both of you," says Chuck to B' and Willy. "Going after Niemöller right now is not the best idea."

"Fuck you," says Willy hanging up.

"Willy, you can't hang up. I've created a link between us—don't worry. I'm not eating up your minutes. This will never show on your phone bill so listen up."

"The fuck is this shit!"

"Calm down…"

B' says, "Chuck, listen. Jimmy is being held by Niemöller and I'll be damned if I'm going to wait for the cops to find him, when they are so confused they think I offed Olga. He is my brother and if I have to bitch slap that fucking German around to get him to tell me where he is I will."

"You are underestimating him."

"You are underestimating Willy and I. We're pumped up and loaded for some payback so just do what I ask so I can get my fucking life back. Now…" beat. "Where is Niemöller right now?"

Wired for Chaos

"Moment. The surveillance system in his office building shows him at his desk at work."

"Know what time he usually knocks off?"

"Varies."

"Never mind." Looking at Willy.

Willy, "Lets do it."

"Chuck, find out as much as you can about him and loop us in if its important."

"Sure."

"You better keep the link to Willy open cause I'm leaving your ass here."

"Oh joy. Nobody actually shoots decks you know."

Willy points his gun at the deck and says, "First time for everything fucker," and lets off an insidious high pitched laugh and they get dressed.

ACROSS FROM 300 EAST 4TH JUST OFF AVENUE C

Willy and B' sit in the Mustang facing East on the one way street and eying the front door of 300 East 4th Street. Willy is sporting his favorite Italian, badboy black leather jacket, over a "wife beater" T-shirt, as B' reclines scoping out the scene. With so little street noise there is an eerie sense of menace about the street and the two continually scan the streets.

Willy says, "No way. No fuckin' way you gonna' tell me his shit in that building right there (pointing at 300 East 4th Street) is worth shit if he lives next door to public housing—cause that's what that is right (pointing at the building immediately next to Niemöller's building) right?!"

"Yeah, I know that's how it looks but this is New York. This is the land of contradictions. It's not upper Fifth Avenue but its worth something."

Willy dismisses what B' says with a wave of his hand.

"How's your Mom and Pops?" says B'.

"They never change. Still good."

"Buggin' you to get married."

"What you think?"

"I'm going to check something."

"What."

"I'm going to ring his bell. If he's there we go up. Nobody answer, we know Chucks not screwing up."

"Wait up." Willy pops open the glove-compartment and takes out a navy NY Yankees baseball cap. "Put this on."

"My hair look natty to you mother…"

"I got it from that dealer. It scrambles the face recognition systems surveillance cameras an' cops use."

"Cool—hey! Why didn't you give this to me when we got to the hotel first time?"

Willy twists his mouth and waves B' off as he turns away.

"Thanks *man*," says B' putting it on.

Willy had checked his pieces at least seven times in the past hour and a half and smoked nine cigarettes. He didn't wait well.

B' got out of the car and walked across the street. As he crossed the street he eyed the neighborhood and did a double take of every male white face ped he saw. The entrance to 300 was reasonably nice for a converted loft building in this neighborhood. Finding Niemöller's name on the buzzer he pressed it and waited. There was no security camera to avoid that he could see. Nothing. B' gave the building a once over again and diagonalled it back to the Mustang.

"Talk to Chuck." Said B' getting into the rent-a-ride.

"Yo Chuck, whatup?"

"I'm watching Niemöller right now on his own security cameras. He is very much the boring drone of an old economy worker. No wonder he's bitter."

"Niemöller is still at work jerking off." Says Willy to Brice.

"Tell him to let us know when he checks out okay."

"Chuck tip us when he checks out alright?"

"I still recommend against this."

"Shut the fuck up." says Willy.

"Gets under your skin right?"

"Try my fucking scalp. You the one with the high-priced jack in your head but I get stuck linked up wit' his ass! Step into a Verizon and have 'em pop a Samsung behind your ear so you can call direct."

"The jack is enough. I had a phone rig shit would never stop ringing." says B'.

A beat. "Your town smells like shit—t…" They smile and both look straight ahead for a few moments.

"So how is life brother?"

"Selling suits at the fucking mall and partying' what else 'there to do in Cali."

"When this is all over I might take some time off and come and see you."

"Fuck you! Your ass ill' be on some fucking private jet to Montserrat or some private island."

Smiling B' says, "Na—a…listen—when this is over lets go kite surfing in Maui, on the north shore—Mac resort there 'an I'll pay…"

"Kite like kite surfing—strap a kite harness to your waist, 'an a littl' board to your feet an' get shot 30-50 feet straight up in the air—no way brother," taking out his gun and looking past the sight, "That shit is dangerous. You could fuckin' do that shit. I'll watch."

B' smiles and looks through the windshield. "Yo Wil', thanks man. Thanks for flashing out here in a New York second man."

"Know you'd do the same for me man."

"Yep."

Beat. Willy says, "Now what I feel like is grabbing a few beers if

Chucky is going to be looking over our boy's shoulder an' shit."

"Yeah but you get tipsy like a girl after a few beers and then you won't be able to shoot straight."

"I can't shoot straight. When is the last time you shot a real gun or went to a range motherfucker? Shit. I live at the fucking range. The owner thinks I'm a cop cause I buddy up with them. I shoot fucking better than a hell of a lot of those buzz cut mothers."

"I bet you do. But you still drink like a bitch."

"We'll see after this is over." And Willy lights up another Marlborough and presses a button on the dashboard. Willy takes a long exhale out the window as Curtis Mayfield's *If there's a hell below we're all going to go* begins. He and B' mouth the words to the song along with Curtis, "Sistas'! Niggah's! Whities! Jews! Crackers! Don't worry. If there's hell below—we're all goina' go—*SCREAMING*...!" and Willy taps his thumb nail against the door to the beat of the grove. They are parked in front of 291, a garbage strewn building painted brown with a metal door covered with years of paint under graffiti that framed, scratched up Plexiglas covered in dirt. Shitty living was the same all over Willy thought. Next to the building was a "Green Thumb, Secret Garden" that was a joke. It was a badly kept excuse for a garden with red bricks strewn about, behind a locked gate littered with broken chairs, a cheap plastic crèche and a single pine tree. Pigeon shit littered the sidewalk in front of the locked gate and the ubitiquous New York City dogshit peppered the sidewalk. Willy sees a large man with matted hair walk towards them from Avenue C and past the car and wonders who has more freaks, NYC or LA. A beat, *LA*.

B' pops his clip out to check the bullets and decides to give the gun a thorough once over. Willy turns to B' and says, "Know...." And a massive, disfigured hand reaches into the car and hauls him out like a bag of recyclable containers.

B' leaps out of the car and dropping the clip. Willy is lifted up by Ton who punches him in the forehead. Willy pulls out his Glock but before he can aim it Ton slaps it out of his hand like a child's toy. Willy kicks Ton in the mid section three times in rapid succession and does not register the faintest bit of response. B' leaps over the hood of the car and attempts to send a flying kick to Ton's head. Ton pivots and causes Willy to connect with B's foot instead. Ton uses Willy as a ram and continually jams Willy into B'. Willy rips his shirt and manages to break free of Ton. Staggering backwards Willy turns sideways and reaches behind his head. Ton turns towards Willy as B' falls to the pavement. Willy has drawn two braided carbon-Kevlar sticks from the sheathe attached to his back and takes a step towards Ton. A blistering series of blows riddles Tons arms, head and torso. Ton is impervious to pain since his pain sensors were cut years ago, defends himself with his arms and finally pushes through Willy's barrage and grabs his wrists. Willy looks like a toy in Ton's grasp. B' injects himself between Ton and Willy and commences to attack Ton with a barrage of blows to the face and neck. B' knees Ton in the groin and momentarily freezes when he realizes that Ton is not fazed. Ton violently pulls Willy towards him and head butts B' and Willy simultaneously. B' takes the brunt of the impact and falls between them. Willy gets punched in the chest by Ton and is hurled backwards like a rag doll. Ton walks over B' on his way to Willy. Willy staggers and rights himself turning to face Ton. Clenched fists, grimace, quickstep sidekick to Ton's midsection. Roundhouse kick to the head dead on, little damage. B' rises and moves to plant a bone breaking kick to Ton's ribcage when the man arrives in an armored ride blocking the street facing the wrong way.

"Police! Freeze and put your hands in the air!"

Ton turns and looks around. Willy yells, "B'! Get in the car." And they both duck and move for the car. Ton moves to a garbage can filled with refuse and old metal pipes. He grabs three pipes and hurls them one after the other at the police. B' jumps through the window first and Willy opens the door to the Mustang and starts the engine. The cops both exit their ride and draw their weapons. "Put that down or we'll shoot!" and Ton hurls an ancient apartment radiator at the ride cracking the windshield. Willy turns the ignition key and backs up slamming into the car behind him then puts it into first and jumps the sidewalk and swerves around a tree on his way to Avenue C. The screeching sound materializes as rough, Synestesian red cubes that scrape against B's face and he grimaces. One of the cops turns towards the Mustang and aims his piece, but is distracted by the sight of Ton hurling a metal garbage can at him. Willy swerves and loops around a stopped car at the intersection and guns it north. Behind Ton, the front door of a 283 buzzes with great urgency and Ton runs for it. He races down the entrance's four cellar steps and opens the bar covered door, slamming it shut a moment later. One cop gets on the radio to call for back-up as the other reaches the building door to find it locked.

Moments later Ton runs out of the rear entrance and onto 5th Street and heads to Avenue B with only a slight increase in his pace.

MUSTANG

"The fuck was that..?!" said Willy looking into the rear view mirror. "Why didn't you shoot him?!"

"Why didn't you shoot him?!

"He smacked the gun outtta' my hand."

"I dropped the clip." Said B' clenching and unclenching his hands. Noticing his knuckles were red and covered with small cuts he tried to ease into the seat and hide his face from onlookers.

INSPACE

Chuck still had Niemöller seated on his desk until the image flickered and Niemöller's face stared directly into the camera. He grinned and gave the camera the bird, laughed and ripped the camera out of its housing. Chuck, knowing it was meant for him slid back in ethereal repose. A.I.s don't have feelings so being insulted would have no effect, but somewhere in his electro-consciousnesses he squinted and said, "Alright motherfucker. I'll get your ass."

MUSTANG

"Who the fuck was that,?!" said Willy.

"Describe him," said Chuck over the link.

"Big, ugly, needed a bath and could take a punch—felt no pain."

"Who you—you talking to Chuck?"

Willy nodded, "An…"

"His name is Ton. He is the muscle for Niemöller." Said Chuck.

"Oh thanks for telling us now asshole."

"I asked you not to do this and you didn't listen. But now you really should."

"The man after us?"

"Not yet but you are very hot. Get back to the hotel and liberate me then I'll tell you where to go."

"Great." said Willy.

"What?" said B'.

"We're on the run but we've got to snatch Chuck's ass before we blow."

"Fuck. Slow down. Lets just get back to the hotel and not draw attention."

Breaking, "Fucking every light going to be against us."

"Just be cool." And they both look around for anybody looking at them.

DAYS INN ON 8TH AVENUE

B' and Willy sit in the Mustang looking at the entrance to the hotel.

"Shit." Says B' watching cops stream into the hotel fifteen story, non-descript hotel that looks like a brick with windows.

"Doesn't look like we're saving your ass anytime soon Chucky."

Chuck says, "All we need is a diversion. Don't move until I say so."

"B's says, "What's up?"

"I dunno, Chuck says he is going to do something," starting to pull away. "Lets get the fuck out of here."

"Wait up. Wait up. Give him a chance, lets see what he can do." They cool down and both stare at the hotel. Willy lights a cig' and scopes the peds. Kids from Jersey acting tough on the way to bars that were hot like ten years ago, American theater goers bloated from over-priced meals on Restaurant Row, foreigners on the cheap doing NY a level above back-packers and city people who don't even break for lights. Willy takes a long drag on his cig' hoping to rid his senses of the pungent odor of honey roasted peanuts from the corner vender. B' stares at the entrance to the hotel's garage and looks at two cops. Cops don't stand and converse like normal peds. They talk to each other but are constantly scouting the scene, looking for potential perps and fools. A tall thin, blond one keeps eyeing the Mustang and the other one grabs his crotch like he has to make a wee wee. B' sees the cop take an active interest and decides to cross the street and walk towards them.

"Oh shit,"

"What?" says Willy.

"Cop."

"He got a rig on?"

"Can't tell and don't want to look."

"Cap should be scrambling your features."

And they were. From the cop's POV B's face was tantamount to video distortion projected onto his retina. The cop could scan tens of faces by simply turning his head left to right and ped names with a status line that either read, "Clean , priors, or warrant," would let him/her know if action was warranted. B's face was a blur with a question mark. Willy turns the ignition sensing he might have to gun it and looks for oncoming cars. The cop is held in check momentarily by on coming cars and then it happens. A water main blows under the street with a colossal *BANG* and propels a manhole cover fifty meters into the air followed by a violent explosion of vertical water. A fire alarm sounds in the hotel and the entire city grid—30 surrounding blocks go dark. A few girls scream, a few punks yell approval and the red emergency lights flashing at the hotel indicate that the Fire Department is on their way. The cop turns and runs out of the shooting water as the manhole cover crashes into a Honda's windshield. Car alarms all over the street trip out as Chuck says, "Go." to Willy.

"I'm moving." To B'. Willy, runs across the street and wishes he was not wearing his favorite leather jacket not knowing what the gushing NYC water would do to it.

"The lights are out all over hotel but the emergency lights have just kicked in." says Chuck to Willy. Willy jogs between two parked cars and peeks into the hotel's garage. Not seeing a cop he races for the door. Once in the lobby there is mayhem as guests run past him. An officer stands with his back to Willy directing people out of the front entrance. Willy waits until is not looking and bolts up the stairs. The stairwell is illuminated by emergency lights and Willy nearly knocks down an elderly couple with an oversized suitcase. Reaching his floor, Willy quickly dashes for his room. Whenever the fire alarm is tripped all doors immediately unlock and magnets move them centimeters away from the door frame. Willy runs into the room that is barely illuminated by residual street light and grabs Chuck a few other pieces of clothing and stuffs them into his bag. Two bags in hand he makes for the door then takes the stairs two at a time.

A moment later, B' sees Willy walking briskly towards the Mustang and he leans over and opens the door. Willy throws the bags into the cramped back seat and drives away slowly.

"Nicely done." Says Chuck to Willy. "Now we've got to get rid of the car. Drive to the nearest rental office and…"

"And what, say "Sorry I dented the front trying to escape from the cops. Just bill me!?" Don't be stupid."

"Listen, you are driving a red Mustang that the cops are tracing as we speak. Drop it off in front of the rental office—any rental office and leave the keys in it. That way we buy some time."

"Whaddar we doing?" says B'.

"Going to drop the car off and—I don't know rub a magic deck for a new ride or something. Where is the closest one?"

B' stays quiet and puts his right hand up to cover his face.

HERTZ CAR RENTAL, 250 WEST 34TH STREET

Willy cautiously moves into the entrance and edges the Mustang a tenth of the way down the ramp. Abruptly, the two exit the car with the ignition running and the lights on. They turn around and walk a few meters and hail an empty taxi headed East.

"Where to now asshole?" says Willy to himself.

"B' looks strangely at Willy who points to his head.

"You're getting flippiddy' with me after I've saved your ass with aplomb?"

"A-bomb this," says Willy grabbing his crotch as the two enter the taxi.

"Tell the driver to take you to Front and Pine street down by the South Street Seaport"

"Front and Pine street down by the South Street Seaport."

B' looks at Willy and says, "Too weird, him shouting orders in your head and you doing what he says."

"Yep but you kinda' make a living doing that right scrub?"

B' thinks about it a moment and his face goes blank.

CORNER OF FRONT AND PINE STREET

As the two exit the taxi they both find it strange to be standing on the ancient cobble stoned street. B' looks around and is exhilarated by the briskness of the air and the quiet.

"This is corporate housing Willy," says Chuck. "Like a long-term hotel that JP Morgan uses for their out of town workers."

"How are we going to get in?"

"I opened their reservation database the same way I'm going to open this door."

The front door buzzes and Willy pushes it. "This A.I. is a trip bro." to B'.

"Take the elevator to the 6th floor, suite 6D and try to not look conspicuous."

Thankfully there was no one in the hall or on the elevator when they entered but the feeling of uncertainty buzzes throughout Willy and tightens the muscles in his neck and shoulders. B' smiles thinking how his real life had started to reflect his time InSpace. Many times on some game platform designed by highly competitive geeks amped up on coffee, with sadistic tendencies, would have you waiting and wondering what came next. The elevator door opened and they turned right looking for the correct suite. Just as Willy was about to grab the door knob, the door unlocks and Willy opens it. They step inside and turn on the lights. When B' closes the door it self locks. It seems more like an apartment than a hotel room which is what B' expected. The floors are chocolate colored wood planks, the walls are white and bare except for some African masks and framed foreign posters. The sofa, chairs and tables are boxy but the lines are more refined than mass produced. Vases, plants and the perfunctory Bang & Olfsen stereo, make the place look like something from an upscale, white-collar catalogue.

"Nicer than the Days Inn." Says Willy.

B' checks out the other rooms. "Two bedrooms and two bathrooms. Tell Chuck he did good."

"Yo Chuckie, B' says you did good."

"Finally some appreciation."

"I didn't say I was impressed." Says Willy opening the fridge. "Surprised they have anything in this place." Taking a box of Chinese food out and dumping it into the trash, he says, "I'm hungry and there's only one Heineken. Chucky, any place around here to get some food?"

"A few but I suggest you not leave the apartment. I'll order some take out for you."

"Yeah and Amstels." Looking in the freezer he sees an unopened package of White Castle hamburgers and smiles. "Forgetit'. I found some.

"Okay."

"But one last thing…" ripping the package open and placing it in the microwave.

"Yes."

"Get out of my head. I'm tired of your fucking voice. We want to hear from you B' will jack in."

"Fine. B-like that." Click.

To the microwave, "Microwave, heat White Castle hamburgers"

The microwave responds, "Reheating time will take four minutes and twenty-five seconds."

"Yo B'!"

"Yeah," says B' pulling down the shades.

"Found some grub. Want some?" walking to the microwave.

"Naw. I'm going to lay down for a bit," says B' from the other room. Willy picks up an expensive looking pen from the coffee table and it immediately displays the latest stock quotes along its body. Willy chucks it across the room in distain and sits on the sofa. "V on" says Willy and the facing wall lights up depicting the latest program from CNNfn with stock tickers cycling right to left across the bottom and top of the wall. Willy lets out a sigh and says, "Show movies—no show tits and ass." As he knocks off his shoes and puts his feet on top of the coffee table edition of 'The House of Morgan: An American Banking Dynasty and the Rise of Modern Finance' and scratches his crotch and takes a swig of the Heineken.

In his bedroom, B' plops down on the bed and looks around. "Better than a basement on Canal Street I guess."Yawning, he palms his head with both hands and takes a deep breath trying to center himself. Sitting up straight he tenses the muscles in his arms and clenches his fists then releases. Opening his eyes he looks at the clock on the nightstand. It reads 2:49AM. He stares at the beige carpet. "Hours ago I was on the run and driving a monster truck," shaking his head in mock disbelief. "Been hiding—on the run for almost four days now and I still don't know where Jimmy is. Never heard back from Rodney. Not like him to dis' me. Hope somebody iz' feeding Stalin. So tired." And B' is asleep before his head hits the pillow.

11:31 AM CORPORATE HOUSING

B' had showered, shit and put on a pot of coffee. At about 10:30 he had shot out of bed and scratched his toes into the carpet a few times, before it clicked that this space-time-continuum was unfortunately his. Willy was still out cold. Now he was having a cup of joe and talking to Chuck.

"You know you a real niggah'" said B' over the transom.

"Why you gotta' be hostile like that in this AM B'?"

"Cause you're acting niggerish'—my mistake. Niggardly. Cause you're stingy, stingy with information and manipulative like some Machiavellian coruscation…"

"My *but thy dost riff with surprising dexterity in this early AM* considering Home tells me that you are usually comatose before noon."

"You said you'd help me find my bother and all you've done is jerk me."

"You said you'd do what I said and all you've done is *react*."

B' sips black joe and is glad that he decided to link to Chuck in voice mode only. A.I. couldn't gauge his body language this way. This pause was all about some cigarette exhale moment so B' could collect his thoughts. "Okay." Said B', "Tell."

"Life is a series of moments and everything is revolving around the biggest one coming your way, but you've been dicking with things best left to others."

"I've been trying to get my brother back and maybe fix my life."

"Sometimes the only way to win is by giving up control."

"What are you proposing?"

"You're only concern is the tournament in two days…" says Chuck and B's world implodes and time stands still. B' froze. He could not believe he had completely forgotten about the bout. For the past few days he had thought of it only in passing. Jimmy held hostage, cops after me, run, run, run and the bout did not exist. He sat on the bed, his legs outstretched and felt the surface of the cool comforter against his legs. He had almost forgotten who he was. Thinking about his experiences as an InSpace champ—and even the idea of losing everything was not the same as preparing for it. He had never stepped onto a game platform without vigorously focused preparation and now circumstances were mucking his plumbing up like street garbage jamming up the sewer drains in a heavy downpour.

"Brice, getting you to Cuba is cake but you have to listen to me. Trust me and not amp off like you're on crank. You dig?"

"I forgot all about the bout. Like I'm supposed to fight, while the cops think I killed Olga and my brother is being held hostage…?"

"This is the natural end of things. Its not like fulfilling a promise, or contractual agreement is the thing. It is your destiny."

"Chuck, if I were to tell you to go and fuck yourself would you take it personally?!" A beat. "Don't even try to say shit. There is no comeback to that line. You know what I want you to do. Dial Niemöller. Dial his ass right now I need to talk to his ass. Chuck did the closest thing to an electric sigh and nearly wished B' an extra large mug of designer comeuppance as he dialed N'. Moments later, the two sat across from each other—human to holo-projection—like the two bitter rivals they were.

"Why are we speaking?" says Niemöller.

"I want my brother and you have him. What do you want in exchange?" said B' barely able to contain his anger.

"I made my self clear the last time we spoke. Your professional end."

"I throw the fight how do I know you'll let him live."

"This is academic. You don't—you don't have a choice. I have something you want."

"What if…"

"No. No what ifs. You do not control any portion of this scenario. You are scum and I will see you humiliated before millions of your admirers. Then, when I am satisfied, I will release your brother not a moment before. If you contact me again I will start to hack off his limbs and feed them to alley cats because of your impertinence." *CLICK.* End transmission and N's holo image *fttttfts* out.

B' rises and tries to contain his anger. He paces the room fuming as he clenches his fists. "Good thing Willy is not up," he thinks. The cordless plug still in his head Chuck says, "Sorry man. Hez' an asshole an' we'll play him, but measure, measured responses only B'."

And B', not having an outlet to lash out at, pivots and tries to absorb his anger. He clenches his fists together tensing the muscles in his arms and then releases taking deep breaths.

QUEENS, IVAN'S OFFICE

Ivan's Gucci glasses ring and he answers, "Da?"

B's face takes the whole of Ivan's retina. "Ivan. You've been a shitty boy. You lied to your boys about me—$600,000—really now!"

"I don't know what your are talking about mistera' Johnson."

"Clamp the shitfucktalk you alcoholic. I'm wired and fired up like a motherfucker and the man can't trace this line. You fucked me to your boys and then tried to off me on Canal. You think I'm calling to trap you on a call?! Bitch! Wise up! Little girls fuck each other on the phone. I'm calling to talk business."

"So? Ta-lk."

"You playing me and I'm feeling the heat and this freak Niemöller has my brother hostage. Says I blow the bout or Jimmy dies. None of this is acceptable but I've got a deal. I'm telling you now, straight out, I'm tanking, going down on my own, guaranteed so you and your boys can put your whole load down in Vegas. Fort Knox money on me to take a dive and we're even. I don't see another Russian low-life from Queens ever. You can bet your fucking house and go to the bank but you lay off me an'..."

"An' what?! An' what?! Like I'm supposed to believe piece of shit girlfriend killer like you?!"

"Listen. Try not to have too many neurons firing all at the same time. This is simple. Guy has my brother hostage—check the news—he is missing— I'm in hiding. I go down he is freed."

"Why I supposed to believe this guy got gun to your head?"

"He loved Olga and Jimmy fucked him on a deal. That's all I know." A beat. "We got a deal."

"Don't trust you."

"No. I'm calling to jerk you off. Lets see. You—ah sent goons to off me in Chinatown and you did Chili, put me on the run and want my head— and—oh yeah like your bosses want to get paid and your boys just can't wait to get their hands on me—so yes motherfucker—I want this shit to end. I want out. I want my life back and to never see you again. I just told you I'm tanking—you don't want to go to the bank cool. Fuck do I care." Click.

Ivan takes his glasses off and slaps his hands together. For a moment he ignores the smell of pizza and thinks about heaven. A blonde, large breasted woman deep into his crotch on a beach in the Greek Isles and he begins to hallucinate. Poker chips, Holo-Vez with endless sports and large buffet tables with millions of credits being deposited into his account.

FLIP TO: A MANHATTAN TECHIE HOLE

Niemöller unplugs. Seated in a small room we see the identical image Ivan saw of B's perfectly rendered head matching Niemöller's move for move, gesture for gesture, picked up by three 3D holo-cameras, compiled, then conformed by a high speed projector. N' equals B' in digital. As Niemöller stands he seems to want to spit in disgust, "I hate black people." he said, almost spitting and wincing as he said the word black. "The way they talk is offensive." Then throwing his rig onto the table already cluttered with tech he quickly realizes that he needs it and retrieves it. A kind of paranoid visual inventory follows as he scans his surroundings before inserts the jack. "Okay. I think I'm good." And he takes a deep breath and gets comfortable in the Aeron chair touches a button on a remote and says, "Redial."

The automated dialer redials Ivan's number as Niemöller breathes deeply.

"Da?" said Ivan.

"Ivan, you don't know me. My name is Niemöller."

"Right. I don't know you."

"This is business. You don't have to know me or like me."

"Why everybody wanna' speak so fucking Man can hear."

Shaking his head. "Ivan. I'm a geek. This is what I do for a living, nobody is listening in. Did Brice call you?"

"Don't know what you're talking about."

"Don't shit me. I'm sure he cut you a deal cause I have him where I want him. He has communicated his situation, correct?"

"Keep talking."

"I'm driving a big bus right now Ivan. A bus with gold faucets in the toilet lined with money and I want to let you have part of the ride Ivan—to a good place. A place where you get to keep it all. All you have to do is pick up a package. He owes you money and I'm sure he called to cut you a deal. Let you know that I have something he wants and that you could profit from it. I'm calling to add to your bottom line in such a way that you can make money and not have to cut your boss in." Ivan salivated remaining unusually silent. "You and I both have an agreement with the player. Once he has fulfilled his bargain, I deliver the living package to you, instead of him and you can do whatever you like for remuneration. You send me funds upon delivery and I walk. I hear the saying goes that once indebted to the mob, forever indebted or something like that, I really don't care—that is Brice's problem—you get the deal. Don't you Ivan."

"I follow geek talk skinny boy. You tell the place where transaction happens and I accommodate request."

"Clever. So we understand each other?"

"Da."

"I'll be in touch." Click. Niemöller pulled the plug from his head and was elated.

12:20 AM CORPORATE HOUSING

B' was ranting as he bent over the deck looking as if he was going to attack it. "Don't give me that fucking I told you so shit Chuckie!"

"Recap with me a moment." says Chuck. "The cops want you for a crime you didn't commit. The Russians want you for money you don't owe but that they are willing to kill to collect. Sony wants you to fulfill a contractual obligation or else your earning and investments vanish and your earning potential with any potential competitors evaporates. This cocksucker Niemöller is holding your brother and can off him at any time—correct me if I'm wrong but Napoleon fucked up because, he couldn't fight simultaneous battles on different fronts, right. Coagulate your shit—consolidate your energy. Focus. Fight the fight you can fight and leave the rest up to Willy and me."

"Just like that, I'm supposed to forget all this other shit and "perform" right."

"Its what you do." says Chuck.

"I need to think this out."

"Leave the thinking to me. I've done alright so far haven't I? Every time you've needed me I've been there and told you what would happen and what to do. Do you want me to list the instances..?"

"What do you have in mind?" says B'.

"You have been feeble in your attempts to attack Niemöller. I believe it is time to attack his strategy."

And B' lets out a mental *"Ahhhhhhhhhhhhhh..."* His mantra reverberates. "Assess your opponent, formulate a strategy, attack with fury. Assess. Formulate. Attack." Words his old trainer Arri Toeb drilled into his subconscious echo through his cranium. "Talk to me." And with that he sat on the floor, folded his legs and stared directly at the deck as if it was the most valuable thing on the planet.

THE NEXT DAY, SUNRISE OVER NEW YORK CITY
GENERIC NEWSCASTER, TALKING HEAD

"...Well it looks as if we are in for another perfect winter day in the big apple with sunny skies and just a little hint of winter chill. But watch out this weekend and remember that a storm system is moving our way. Back to you Ted."

Across the city the restless energy of commerce ebbs and flows, in parts yawning to life. As the sun beams over the east river glancing off the dead fichus tress on Fifth Avenue penthouse balconies, the city people awake to another clear morning.

"Thanks John. We have an update for you in the gruesome supermodel murder-manhunt of Olga Ericksson case. Although the whereabouts of Brice Johnson are still unknown, our sources state that sightings in the midtown area have been confirmed and it is suspected that he is in the Manhattan area. If that is correct the manhunt for Brice is said to be intensifying across the city."

B', wearing black jock shorts performs Tai chi in his bedroom with the curtains drawn. He appears relaxed and at peace.

As Jimmy rises in the near pitch-black room just below 125th street he moans in pain while licking the scab just above his swollen lip, still fighting to accept that this is really happening. He drinks some water out of bottle of Dasani and winces in pain. In Queens, Ivan is packing his things while trying, to not wake is snoring wife in their gaudy high-rise apartment.

"News Seven has also learned that Olga was in fact brutally tortured prior to being dismembered and her limbs being shrink-wrapped. Although the motive for the murder remains a mystery, what is irrefutable is Brice Johnson's notorious violent temper—lets not forget that he killed his sparing partner during a routine work out in front of reporters and that he was seen last with Olga as they entered a nightclub in lower Manhattan."

Camacho is sleeping on his sofa surrounded by Coors beer cans, with the Holo-V still on News Seven, while Willy has his first smoke of the day on the street in front of their absconded corporate apartment. Further uptown and to the east, Ton stands on his rooftop surrounded by pigeons that walk up and down his outstretched arms as he feeds them. In the fish and flower markets merchants and buyers exchange credits, barbs and spew pollution into the air as cars idle double parked.

"The Police now have the remains of Olga's torso and four limbs but are missing her amputated head."

"Gruesome Ted, simply gruesome."

"I know Tina, what continues to baffle the police, is why, or how for that matter, a suspect on the run would seek to not only implicate himself, but risk capture by scattering her body parts all over the city."

"From the placement of the limbs—and especially the torso in the old meat packing district it seems apparent that he is not just taunting authorities by exhibiting them like trophies. He wants to be caught.

A CHORUS OF NEWSCASTERS RAP

"Yes. I would have to agree—how wicked is B'? Now don't you see! Thrilla' to killa'! Superstar accelerated lush-life, cut up the white girl—with a Jap' knife. And you wonder how we coulda' been suckered? How we coulda' cheered him—an' now we jeer 'em. What that say about us? What that say about us?"

InSpace, the mix of news and information expands to overwhelming auditory level, fusing into a kind of white noise static. Newswires, holo-TV stations, AM/FM/XM, streams of data concerning Brice and the killing, travel at the speed of light from the workstations of reporters to all manner of devices. Across the world many of the devices display identical information on the updates of the case, causing a near imperceptible chorus. If the human psyche was even electrically enhanced—albeit without filters, or off switches—the ability to perceive the same information would be identical and as irrepressible as a guard dog smelling the adrenalin reeking from a burglar.

At that moment, B' was seated on the floor in the Lotus position trying to meditate, as the electro-kinetic force of energy and information surged towards him. Like a mighty supernatural God, the ancient Mayans hallucinated, while writhing in bloodletting rituals, it came. An enormous multi-colored, translucent fiber-optic Cobra shot straight—like a missile towards him and bit his astral head. With a white flash we were in B's consciousness, as he struggled to make the large screen filled with images before him pure. The images were not accompanied by synced sound, but the overall effect was one of madness. Incongruity. B' had always had trouble meditating and had been practicing for years, but he knew full well that his attempts were half-hearted and lacked discipline. Knowing that the only way to center himself, was to clear the screen of all images and thoughts, he attempts to pull towards them instead of away. Olga's face surged towards him writhing in pain, as blood spewed from somewhere out of his field of vision. Jimmy lay tied and drowning in a curtain of black snakes, that undulated moving him from left to right—his eyes, big and frightened. Ton and Niemöller were a two headed beast, that seemed to slap B's cheeks with open hands much the same way, that a taunting rapist would his flaccid penis against a bound victim. B' winced then steadied himself and allowed the images to replay themselves as much as his manic compulsive consciousness would. Over and over the images and sounds repeated and morphed until they dissolved into a great white expanse. As he concentrated on his breathing he could hear his heart beat and purposely slowed it. Feeling his shoulders relax, he made a conscious effort to allow the relaxation to continue downwards through his body, until it reached the tip of his toes. Slowing his breathing even more, he took deeper breaths holding them for a steady count of three until he could feel his center, just below his ribcage start to warm.

THAT AFTERNOON
Willy stepped onto Front Street directly in front of the apartment's entrance and lit a cigarette just as the Carmel limo pulled up in all its shiny blackness.

The driver lowered the window and said, "Mr. Brown?"

Willy said, "I'll get him." And turned and entered the building's lobby. Inside he stood face to face with B' but you couldn't tell it was him in this disguise. They had decided to play by Chuck's rules and allow him to call the shots for this last part of the ride. They had been fortunate in finding a full first-aid kit in the apartment's closet and used the gauze to cover B's entire face except for his eyes, put his left arm in a sling and bandaged his right foot. There was even a cheap aluminum cane that B' used to support his bent right leg.

"Will, you should fuck that and come with me man. You don't have to prove anything and…"

"Yo. I know that. I know I could ride with you but Chuckies got the master plan all figured out and my guts tell me that you'll be fine and you know my guts are never wrong."

"What good is…"

"B' you know I'm doing this. It's a lose end and I'm gonna' tie it up and head back to Cali. That's it."

"Alright. Be like that." a beat, "Thanks man, I really mean it."

"I know," and they hug patting each other on the back.

"Call you when I get settled," said B' picking up a small leather bag and exiting the building.

"Cool."

Once outside B' looked left and right on the quiet street before proceeding to the right passenger door, which automatically swung open for him. As he got in he kept expecting dozens of police cars to surround him and nail him with their laser sights. But nothing happened. The driver's finger slipped and the clip that held his PDA to the dashboard made a loud "SNAP!" which made B' jump. B' had been instructed to say nothing and didn't relax until the sedan drove away turning east towards the east river. B' slid down in the seat and took a deep breath near certain that no one had seen him.

"I'm going to take the FDR Mr. Brown, its pretty light traffic wise," said the driver and B' just nodded. The driver had been paid in advance and given specific instructions to drive to 301 Garvies Point Road, in Glen Cove, Long Island. There B' would board the "Sassacus" a TriCat super fast passenger catamaran ferry that would travel over 45 knots to his destination. Once docked at the New London, Connecticut marina he would board a shuttle to Foxwoods Resort Casino, approximately an hour and a half later.

B' all but forced himself not to doze in the car, being all too familiar with the landscape of Queens, with its track houses, cemetery congestion. A little over forty minutes later the sedan turned right onto Garvies Point Road and stopped in front the marina's office.

"Have a nice day Mr. Brown and thanks for the tip."

B' nodded and stepped out of the car. Since he was early a line had not formed as yet so he made his way towards the short plump woman who was busting out of a failed attempt at a uniform. "Hi. Reservation."

"Brown."

"Marty Brown or Joe Brown? I've got two on my list."

"Joe, Joe Brown," said B' and she waved him in.

"At the end of this ramp make a right and take a seat anywhere you want on this level. Upstairs is the VIP area and the lower deck is closed, but you can sit anywhere you want on the main level."

B' nodded and started down the ramp. He couldn't help but think about this being the first time—maybe the first time ever, that he had been denied access to VIP anything and traveled coach or whatever this was called, but it didn't matter. He was really getting the hang of the whole injured, limping guy thing. He decided on the spot that he'd say it was a motorcycle accident if anyone asked him.

Upon entering the cabin he decided to take a seat in the very back against a window, so he could slump down and go unnoticed. The interior of the cabin looked like the interior of an old aircraft and was dominated by Purple. The chairs were direct rip-offs of aircraft seats, with upholstery that looked like bad faux granite and a corresponding "worm-like" patterned carpeting in purple and navy. The rest of the interior was lined with a faux wood-laminate and something that passed for brass in casinos across the world. At least it didn't smell like spilled beer and cigarettes, yet.

When he sat he immediately placed his bag under the seat in front of him and looked out of the window. Thirty minutes to launch he told himself and scrounged for something to read. In the seat pocket in front of him he found a laminated card that gave the specs on the catamaran. It was called the Sassacus and the literal translation is "he is fierce." The guy was chief sachem of the Pequots from 1634 until his death in August 1637 and they had an exhibit all about him and his people, at the Pequots Museum not far from Foxwoods. Maybe next time B' thought and reached for a beat up newspaper reader.

A little less than an hour and a half after departure, the Sassacus pulled into the New London marina and B' could sense the anticipation of the geriatric gambling mavens as they rustled to grab their baggage and worn ebook copies of "How To Win Big In Las Vegas." B' looked outside and was pleased to see no police or even people that looked like undercover police. B' left the catamaran and followed the horde towards the shuttle that was clearly labeled "Foxwoods Resort Casino."

Fifteen minutes later B' had his first glance of Foxwoods. It was in the middle of nowhere. A road, lots of bigass trees and this odd sort of Vegas *light* kind of structure surrounded by more trees. As the shuttle pulled into long driveway B' just imagined the money that people were dropping every day and wondered how many rich Indians there were living just miles away. Good for them he thought. Fucking good for them. He purposely exited the bus last and got into the whole injured man thing, with a somewhat weary feeling. Chuck told him to avoid the entrances to the casino on either side and walk under the overpass and out to the other side of the parking lot. At some point he should see a large man approaching him with a wheelchair. He was to go with that man and continue to act lame. B' walked to the parking lot and saw nothing but mini-vans, station wagons and cheap econoboxes flanked by the woods. Turning, he saw a man wearing a silver, hooded parker with a fake fur collar, pulled over his head. The guy was pushing a wheel chair and wore a Cleveland Indians baseball cap and a ped air filter topped off by some aviator sunglasses. The guy was big alright and headed straight towards B'. B' stiffened up a bit and waited for the guy. The guy came within a foot of B' and stopped. Not saying anything the guy put his hand out to take the bag but B' refused and sat instead placing the bag on his lap. As he placed the cane across the armrest of the wheelchair, he was surprised at the speed and ease with which the guy turned B' and walked away from the casino. The guy quickly took B' down a steep utility road and into the woods. After a minute B' realized that not only could people at the casino not see, but would probably not hear them either. B' started to run through scenarios in his head as to flight and his eyes darted left and right. He could sense they guy looking over his shoulder toward the casino, as the wheelchair steered slightly towards the edge of the road. B' slid the cane's handle towards his right hand and grabbed it firmly, ready to swing. His senses were heightened like they had been on Canal Street. He could hear the wind rustling through the bare branches and past the pine trees, the flutter of some unseen birds and the light crushing sound of the wheelchair's wheels as it transverses the black asphalt covered road. B', wanting some recognition as to an aggressive move on the part of the big guy, twisted his neck back and angled his head in an attempt to glance at the guy out of the corner of his eye. Just as he caught the guy looking over his shoulder towards the casino, he raised his right hand and took off his filter mask and said, "Wassup' boss?"

B', ready to clock him with cane, twisted his neck quickly and realized that it was Leroy and nearly shit himself laughing. "Leroy! Motherfucker! I was about to wail on your ass!" And Leroy put his hand on B's left shoulder and they both smiled.

Wired for Chaos

"Feels like a long time huh boss?" smiling.

"Feels?! Man wait till I tell you what I've been feeling—feels like years and a few months," and his body relaxed as he turned forward. "You pushing my ass to Cuba or something."

"Naw—w boss. We're taking you to your ride," As they turned onto a short road that ended in a small helicopter pad. At the center of the pad was B's Aerodyne, its engines idling flanked by a limo. "Nice—e," said B' smiling inside and out. "I don't know how Chuck did it but it works for me."

"Who's Chuck?"

"Somebody mysterious call you and get you here?"

"Yeah, yeah—h."

"That was Chuck."

"You know that I'm supposed to be briefed on all of your people so I don't end up in—ad—vertically hurting somebody that steps to you in a given situation, or whatnot."

B' wanted to say something like, "You don't want to meet this guy Leroy. But if I find a way to hurt him a little, you can get in line behind Willy an' me." But thought it best to say, "Just add it to my list of mistakes man." And shook his head.

Leroy wheeled him up to the Aerodyne's steps and turned to give the wheelchair to the limo driver. B' decides to walk up the stairs without faking it and is met by his trainer Bill at the entrance. Bill puts his index finger to his lips to stop B' from saying anything and ushers him into the cabin. Carl, his other bodyguard shakes his hand and gives him a hug then leads him to a seat. The pilot walks in from the cockpit and says, "Gentlemen are we ready to take off?"

Bill says, "Yes, lets go. Lets go."

Leroy enters and the pilot closes the cabin door and locks it. The air in the cabin immediately turns on and the crisp scent of pine is replaced by something filtered.

"Please buckle up and prepare for take off. Thank you," and he returns to the cockpit closing the door behind him.

"They don't know who you are and have been instructed to remain in the cockpit for the duration of the flight." B' felt so happy an relieved to be not only in a familiar place, but safe and in control again, that he was giddy with glee to the point of grinning uncontrollably under the gauze.

"Yeah," says Leroy, "And no stewardess so we all gotta' serve ourselves."

"Alright, everybody buckle up so we can get the hell outta' here'." Says Bill. The four buckle in, seated across from each other in oversized leather, club-like chairs and settle in.

The pilot speaks over the intercom and says, "Gentlemen I am initiating the final liftoff procedures and turning on the seatbelt sign if you are ready?"

B' moves to respond via an intercom on his armrest but is stopped by

Bill's raised hand. Bill presses the intercom on his armrest and says, "We're ready. Thank you." Pointing at B' he says, "You can take that off now Phantom." and B' undoes the gauze that obscures his face. Leroy makes a face as if to say, "Euw! What happened to you B'?!" and B' quickly balls up the gauze and throws it at him.

With that they feel the engines of the Aerodyne surge and see dust and leaves gust towards the trees. The cabin lights dim and four small identical holo-projections of Japanese stewardesses wearing prim eggplant uniforms and hats appear at each of the men's right armrests. "Good afternoon, please pay attention to this important safety message. The emergency exits on this craft are located...."

B' stares out of the window and sinks into the chair as the Aerodyne rises slowly above the tree line and the landing gear makes a slow hydraulic sound as it retracts into its housing. Rising, it slowly turns to face south and the engines propel the craft in a diagonal motion. B' is about to ask Bill something when the pilot chimes in over the intercom, "Gentlemen, we are cleared to enter the southern commuter corridor and will enter it once we have reached 30,000 feet. Our estimated travel time to the Florida Keys will be two hours and twenty-nine minutes." B', upon hearing Florida shoots Bill a confused expression.

"He's going to be redirected to Cuba before we clear Miami. Don't ask me how."

The pilot continues, "The weather is clear and there are no low-pressure systems in our path, so this should be a quick smooth and uneventful ride. My name is Greg Fea and my co-pilot is Will Waggaman. If you have any questions, or concerns, please do not hesitate to contact us. Thank you."

The Aerodyne accelerated rapidly and everyone's body lurches as it reached cruising speed and altitude. B' looks at Bill and asks, "Bill, this is my ride right?"

"You paid for it."

"Well if the man is looking for me then won't they know that I'm probably using it to jet the country?"

"Your boy Chuck seems to have it all figured out. Ask him."

The seatbelt lights go dark and Bill quickly undoes his and sits on the edge of his seat placing his elbows on his knees in front of B'. "And another thing. Now I know you're probably paying this guy Chuck a lotta' money an all, but you might wanna' ask him to show a little respect, or else I might lose me temper and snap his arms like a chicken bone. You know what I'm saying. Bet you he's a little scrawny little mother. Anybody that talks trash on the waves instead of face-to-face always is."

B' grabs his leather carryall and begins to open it, "Wanna' meet him?" and B' takes the deck out of his bag.

Leroy says, "Naw, I just want to get paid what he does."

B' says, "Here he is and I'm not paying his ass."

"Wha?" says Bill.

Wired for Chaos

"He's an A.I. Jimmy bought him when we were in Japan but nobody knew what he was." says B' who pauses and wonders for a moment about Chuck's true motivations.

"Whatever. Now, would you like to tell me what the hell has been going on?"

"Shit. I need a drink if I'm going to go there."

"You've got a match tomorrow."

"I don't give a God damn. I've been on the run from the NYPD and some Russian hit men an' living in a basement room in Chinatown. I need a fucking drink!"

"I hear that," says Leroy rising and heading for the wet bar. "Rum and Coke coming up."

"If they have those bullshit little bottles be sure to dump two in and not jip me." And they all smile.

BACK TO WILLY

Willy had been jonzing for some Filipino Pork Adobo, Fiesta Rice and a Banana shake but couldn't find a restaurant in Manhattan that served it. LA one, NYC zero. Shifting gears, he decided to check out Chinatown for some random dim sum instead. He sat in the back of a crowded Chinese Restaurant at a communal table and tapped on his PDA, while planning the rest of his day. The lunch crowd was composed of ABCs (American Born Chinese), tourist and workers from the Court Houses on Center Street and other office buildings. Chuck said he would be fine considering the worst thing he had done in NYC, was dent up a rented car. He knew exactly what he wanted to do. After lunch he would train it up to Metropolitan Museum of Art to check out the Medieval Armor Exhibit and maybe touch a gauntlet to know what it felt like. Then he would check out the too expensive men's clothing stores on Madison Avenue down to 57th Street. Then he'd head home for some calisthenics and a nap. Get up around 7:00 PM, shower and head for pasta in Little Italy. Once he smoked a pack of cigs and downed three espressos it was time to hit the bars in the village and then a nightclub he had just read about. Taxi home in the early AM and sleep in. Wake and prepare for payback. That's what he was gearing for and it sat right with him that he was calling the shots for the first time in the NYC.

RECEPCIÓN!

B' was falling back into his groove. Chuck was the joint amped at light speed having orchestrated his departure with not even the slightest hitch. The pilots looked at B' in shock as he exited the plane, realizing that they had been duped into transporting America's most wanted. The officials at Havana's Jose Marti International Airport welcomed him like he was Castro's son and the people at Hotel Melia Choiba treated him like the star he was. Chuck hadn't missed a beat and B' was lulled back into that sense of celebrity entitlement and his glee was nearly irrepressible but then he remembered

Jimmy and his demeanor shifted to dower seriousness. He had his brother to worry about and couldn't seem happy to be free of the authorities that suspected him of killing Olga. The guilt set in manifesting itself in self-loathing and he kept resisting urges to berate and belittle everyone around him.

He had been in Havana for only three hours and managed to dredge up enough guilt and hate for a small city. He stood at the window of his hotel room and sipped a bottle of Heineken as Bill walked in.

"So," said Bill, "This is where we have our little small talk and I get all chummy and maternal like."

"The fuck you wanna' do that for? I'll just disappoint you." Said B' not realizing he had said it out loud.

"Listen, I know what you've been through and I'm not here to judge you either…"

Swerving and meeting Bill's eyes, "You think I killed Olga?"

"Hell no. That's not what I said…"

"Cause I didn't."

"I know…"

"I don't go around killing girlfriends and cutting them up and leaving them for the police to find…"

"I know. I know," raising his hands in difference. "Can I get a fucking sentence in now or what?"

"What?"

"What what? I'm asking the what. What do you want to do here? What do you fucking want to achieve. I can't help you if I don't know what we're trying to achieve. I know the story you told us on the plane is straight, but I need you to look straight at me and let me know the straight skinny. Sure this motherfucker Nienöller—Niewhöller whatever has Jimmy but what are we doing here?"

"Just trust me alright…"

"Listen, kid. Fuck Chuck. Don't trust computers with your fucking life and especially not Jimmy's fucking life. Is Chuck your friggin' electric angel cause if he's not you're gonna' end up paying for it. I'm just saying I'm down for any count you wanna' make, up or down, I just gotta' know where your head is at. You trust him fine, I can follow orders. If not, lets make a game plan so we don't get caught with our drawers down in the urinal you know what I mean?"

"Yeah. Yeah, I know what you mean Bill," says B' taking a sip of the beer and sitting on the imitation French something hotel chair. As Bill sat on his bed B' considered his friendship with Bill and took his time. "You know I never meant to kill Derek. I just, I just lost my temper."

"I know."

"I'm scared Bill. I'm scared that whatever I do, that *fuc—k* is going to kill Jimmy, if he hasn't killed him already and he's all the family I got. We survived the orphanage together and I thought that was rough. So now Niemöller wants me to tank and I'm thinking, okay, what the fuck but I know that I just don't know."

"Yeah…"

"So you want an answer from me like I know the outcome. I don't. I know this shitstorm swirling around me—this shit is real man. Never thought I'd have regrets you know. Never thought I'd tap into the common man crap, or the soap opera Holo-V piss, an' here I am second-guessing all my moves. All my decisions like did I—did I do it to myself. Like—do I deserve this?! Must be. Must be 'cause this is pure and uncut. But you're coming to me for answers at the wrong time man. I don't know anything anymore." Snapping his fingers, "Like that it was all gone. Like that. And now I'm supposed to get my grove on like nothing happened. Never used to care what people thought of me. Said what I thought. Guess this is what happens right…?" and he heads for the wet bar.

"WHO PULLS YOUR STINGS?"
BROADWAY, BELOW SPRING

Camacho sat in his Camero in almost the same space as when he watched Jimmy and Michelle walk into the dealer's lair days ago. The Déjà vu that would give regular people pause was lost on Camacho because he was an oaf. Everything about him was primal. His hairy arms, the way he performed his bodily functions—but most of all his crude approach to life.

Hours earlier, in the station house at the 40th Precinct in the Bronx his superior Officer Alexander, an imposing figure with arms the size of tree trunks loomed over him like a blimp at an outdoor sporting event. A white guy with acne-scarred skin, piercing eyes and a buzz cut that spelled, "tightly wound rattle snake." Peering down at Camacho—a detective he didn't necessarily like—he knew that periodic checks would let Camacho know he was being watched. Camacho, sensing that Alexander had it out for him, always steered the conversation to baseball, a subject to which they both related. Them and then came the phone call.

"But Lopez is a fucking machine." said Camacho.

"Lopez is a monster. He is an Orca and the Mets are the fucking baby seals. No fear, no blinking, just hot sauce on a ball."

Camacho's phone rings and when he looks at it the caller id says it is "Roshi" on the other end. As Camacho tries to ignore the call Alexander clams up and asks Camacho if he is going to pick it up with just an expression. Camacho hesitates and Alexander sneaks a peek at the caller's name just before he turns to walk away, "Don't miss your call." says Alexander.

Camacho, annoyed that he got this call in front of his boss, picks it up but masks his annoyance. The caller, the same guy that had called him last month with instructions for some easy money to watch Brice and report back had a new proposition. Actually, two propositions. One was wet-work, the other might just get him a promotion and maybe a reward—neither of which he would stick around to collect. Guy was some Jap with a bad attitude who had a lot of money and knew too much about Camacho for him to say no to the gig, plus it was easy money. The guy had told Camacho to leave Olga's body parts around the city for the NYPD to find which was weird and kinky, but mostly weird. And now he wanted the dealer offed, which was why Camacho was waiting for the mark to get home. Evidently the mark had a role in the model's demise and now Samurai was cleaning shop. Camacho didn't know anything about the punk and it didn't matter. He was getting paid and no one would care that a drug dealer had ceased to breathe. Camacho waited with a pocket full of death for the guy to come home.

Camacho had packed earlier that morning and didn't intend to return home. Walking out of his shithole house for the last time was actually joyous. He would never have to see the telephone pole, the garbage cans, or his pathetic little street ever again he thought. He remembered turning around and staring at his house for a full minute. Fuck the pathetic two bedrooms on its 25X100 sq. ft. lot that the stray cats used as a litter box. He wanted to torch it but spat instead.

The second task was 20-24 hours ahead of him, but he wanted to make a clean break and had slept in the car more times than he could remember. He would call in sick and gun it for Wilmington, North Carolina after the second gig, then take a chartered plane to beautiful Somerset, Bermuda, from Wilmington International Airport. He had sent all of his ill-gotten money directly to their banks and besides—cinnamon women are the same from island to island—better to not do the obvious and try to mix in with any Hispanics anyway. Plus, Bermuda had a strict non-extradition policy with the US and none of the shit Camacho had perpetrated or aided and abetted, would probably materialize into charges let lone a manhunt. So he sat and waited for the mark to arrive. The way he saw it, the later this punk arrived the better. He'd either be drunk, tired or both. Either way Camacho would do him and if he had company then plan a) of making it look like an over dose shifted to b), a double homicide "disagreement" over drugs or whatever kinky shit he could think up on the spot.

He took his large sized Dunkin' Donuts cup of coffee out of the heated cup holder and took a sip of coffee. Nothing had contributed to police surveillance in the past twenty years more than the heated cup holder. Then a taxi pulled up in front of the mark's front door. Camacho tried to consume as much of the coffee as he could without burning his tongue, while keeping his eyes sharply focused on the mark exiting the taxi. The guy hopped out of the taxi and immediately headed for the trunk, which opened with mechanical precision to reveal his expensive Tumi carry-ons. Seconds later he was at his front door getting his iris scanned and having the deadbolts unlock. Camacho waited until he was in and then conducted inventory. Drawing his weapon he checked the magazine and reloaded. He tapped his pockets checking for their contents and ran the scenario through his head at high speed. Ready. And with that Camacho checked his rear view mirror before stepping out of his ride. At times like this Camacho swore he could take on the baddest of the bad Spaghetti Western bad guys—being a bad guy himself, as he zipped his leather jacket so as not to expose his piece. As he walked towards the mark's front door he imagined the guy putting up a fight and actually being a threat instead of some pussy, skinny-ass shit punk that would probably pee his pants and beg for his life. He wanted a bad ass, somebody that would keep him on his toes and at least give him a fight. Somebody that would actually scare him like that junky in the Bronx, that night that he broke in on an amped up dealer beating his wife.

"BUZZZZ!"

What happens next is academic. Camacho flashes his badge gains entry and Saddam is locked in the bathroom. Soon after that he has the mark, Charlie "the mix man" Borstin seated at his dining table in a stainless steal kitchen and steps behind the guy as he begins to question him about a neighbor. Then—reach-grab, he got the guy in a headlock and cups ounces of synthetic heroin cut with warfarin (rat poison) under his nose. Gag, jerk, tussle, cough, limp dick end of story. Charlie puts up a fight and tries to stand only to be pushed towards the table, when Camacho leans into him with all his weight. The heroin begins to work almost instantly and Charlie's grip on Camacho's arm releases and his arms fall to his sides. His eyes glaze over as he coughs and tries to wipe his face with his right hand. Camacho steps to the side in order to see Charlie's face. Charlie raises his left hand and points at Camacho, but is unable to say a word because his coughing has become violent. He gags, spits up blood and has a stroke. When his head falls to the table Camacho scratches his nuts, puts on a pair of surgical gloves and heads for the refrigerator where he grabs a beer. Studying Charlie he searches for even the faintest sign of life, hoping he does not have to break the guy's neck and spoil a perfectly good over dose. Knocking the beer back he crushes the empty can, puts it in his pocket and walks over to Charlie. He rifles through the his pockets and steals his smart card throwing his keys on the table. Camacho belches and seeing a closed door steps to it and turns the door handle. As the door opens the motion sensitive light turns on and he sees a large closet that has been converted to a tool-work room. In the center is a rack on wheels that houses a shrink-wrap machine and a large spool of clear plastic.

"Charlie! Did you wrap that bitch up with your little machine!? Clever boy. Dead, but clever—not too clever. Sick fuck. Cut up a pretty girl like that, drain the blood and shrink wrap the parts. You must have been high." Camacho sees a cordless saw and shakes his head. "Now if I was drug dealer I would have an American Express Traveler's Smart card that could access foreign currency, or maybe some expensive jewelry from one of the city's finest stores. But where would I be? Maybe the bedroom Charlie …? Eh?" looking at Charlie. "Lets try the bedroom," and he heads for Freddy's bedroom. As he walks he begins to sing *Melao De Caña (Moo La Lah)* in Spanish shaking his finger at Charlie, "Just when you thought you found it…only your self to blame…"

TODAY IS A GOOD DAY TO….

9:30AM, ROOM 1450, HOTEL MELIA CHOIBA, CUBA

The phone rang and B' turned over and picked it up. An automated voice said, "Good morning Mr. Johnson, this is your 7:30 wake up call. Have a nice day and remember, the staff of Hotel Melia Choiba is here to serve you, so please let us know if there is anything we can do. Please note, this call will be repeated in ten minutes if the room sensors do not detect movement. Click."

B' hung up the phone and looked at the ceiling. The image of the nightclub seemed burnt into his consciousness. The girl in the yellow dress who was obviously on the make. The bartender with that shit eating grin. The Latin music that seemed to beat through him—it all stroked tenable. Although Bill didn't agree, B' enjoyed a slight hangover before a bout. The only times he had felt reticent before a bout and performed sub-par were the times he had had a liquor free, full night's sleep. Willy had taught him years ago that a slight deficit forced you to sharpen up before a fight. It was some kind of reverse psychology, mumbo jumbo bullshit whatever, but having something to work through took your mind off being nervous or tense. Or maybe Willy was just a punk bitch that liked to tempt fate.

Rising, B' made his way out of the covers, naked and with a half erection. He stumbled and reached for the wall thinking he had better look to make sure that no one was in bed with him. Relieved that he hadn't nailed some hooker, or some business man's wife, he headed for the bathroom. The pink, Italian, marble floor was cold and he bristled at the room temperature as his nipples hardened and his nuts shrank. Plopping as much as sitting on the urinal, he cupped his head in his hands and contemplated the day. This hangover was light—thank God and his agenda blipped in his consciousness. "Willy in NYC…talked to him for a minute, waiting for an outcome tonight after the bout. Jimmyjimmyjimmyjimmyjimmyjimmyjimmy is somewhere tied up and waiting for the Calvary. Chucks has plans for whupass' an I'm here to dance and go to the bank." Rubbing his head, he yawned and shook his dick a few times. As he rose the toilet flushed and he stepped over to the sink. Leaning on the counter and looking into himself in the mirror he took a deep breath, expanded his chest, closed his eyes and tried to center himself. As his posture became taut he lowered his head and seemed to be listening to someone. He had done this numerous times in the hours before a bout, but this time it was different. Yes, he had centered himself and distanced himself from all distracting influences. A kernel of thought that had been covered in interference had been exposed. He didn't trust Chuck, Gila, or whatever he was and it gnawed at him. He knew too much and was in the right place at the right time. It could not be a coincidence. Everything Chuck did worked perfectly. He knew what was going to happen before it happened and everything he had done was about getting him to this point. Fighting Ishi. It could not be a coincidence he thought while opening his eyes. There was only one guy Chuck could be working—and it clicked. He didn't know how but it would all make sense. Not completely sure that he should not be pissed at himself for not knowing sooner, he scowled at his image in the mirror and headed for the shower.

...DIE
5:31 PM OUTSIDE OF TON'S APARTMENT WINDOW

Willy had been in the back of the limo parked at the fire hydrant for thirty-eight minutes and twenty seconds. The driver had been instructed to say and do nothing once they arrived at their destination. Willy had used the time to meditate, *not*. Earlier that day he had awoken to the crescendo of a NYC club induced hangover. He had danced with a pretty black girl from Bed-*sty*, Brooklyn. She had rubbed her bubble-butt up against his cock on the dance floor of an after-hours nightclub called "Two Towers" in east village while they breathed in cigarette smoke and it was good *el jefe [the boss]*. She even beamed her contact info into his PDA, but he had deleted it out of habit. That place taxed his hearing, but the *juke-house* was maxdaddy. Now he was straight and centering himself. Time was on his side and the trick was not jumping when you could walk. He fought the urge to check the magazine in his Glock knowing that he had taken his time cleaning and loading the gun before he left the apartment. Checking it would push a nervousness in him to the front and he had no place for that. With his legs opened wide and his hands wrapped in tape, (palms up) it would appear that he had wounded himself but the tape was for protection and the position was to relax him. He ran down the plan in his head feeling more and more confident. In spite of the heavy coffee breath that attempted to distract him the image of Ton flowed easily in his mind.

In the shadow of the Federal Court House Willy wondered why had Ton been so effective as muscle. Probably a combination of strength and inability to feel pain. What mistakes had his adversaries made? They tried to fight him as if hurting him, would slow him, down or incapacitate him but that was like trying to fell a tree trunk with your bare hands.

He unwrapped the tablets Chuck had had delivered. A seemingly simple square of folded, white, rice paper, revealed another square of red paper, that revealed a piece of paper with a crease in its center that separated two small red pills. Remembering the instructions, Willy took each pill and placed it under his tongue. They would quickly dissolve and his epidermis would develop a rubbery sensation as his nervous system dialed down to impervious to pain. It would last for approximately two hours and slightly euphoric. Then he picked up the pack of Marlboroughs and an expensive sterling silver lighter B' had given him as a birthday gift years ago and placed them in the door's astray. He took off his watch and threw it and his wallet onto the seat next to him, then assured that his pockets were empty, closed his eyes and put his head back onto the headrest. Shifting his thoughts back to Ton, Willy reminded himself that killing a man with your bare hands required precision above all else. His mind replayed third-person, slow-mo images, of his master breaking someone's windpipe, collarbone and septum. The movements were written into the DNA of his chromosomes—he knew them. Even as he took deep breaths, his muscles twitched and convulsed to the movements of the fights in his mind's eye. His anticipation bubbled over as he flexed his pecs underneath his red plaid, Cholo shirt. Tapping on his left hand, with his right index finger, he felt nothing. His skin seemed to be made of a distant rubber-like object and his insides felt strangely—gelatinous.

Swiftly and without notice, Willy's right hand barely touched the release and the door swung open. His Dr. Martens had barely touched the asphalt and he was out of the ride without so much as a fuck you to the driver. The sky was gray and foreboding like steel wool, what was left of the snow was dirty, black ice pushed to the sides of buildings and sidewalks. A storm was definitely near but it seemed too warm for another snowfall. Willy could see his breath and was amazed that this small island could be so diverse—Ton's block being shitty and all—just miles from the rich, pretty ladies on Park Avenue. As he walked he adjusted his nuts into his athletic (protective) cup—not that he could feel or sense them—just that he knew they were probably not where they were supposed to be. Crossing the street he walked between cars and seeing a Heineken bottle picked it up before he hit the curb without losing stride. Thing about dog shit in the NYC was it was everywhere. That meant that you had to look before you stepped. Ton's apartment was in what they called a tenement building that translated into a shitass walkup a fucking stupid illegal immigrant wouldn't live in. But you took what you could get in the NYC and Ton was living within his means. Immediately next to Ton's building, was an eight car parking lot with a gated entrance. Willy stepped up to the gate and keyed in the three digit code Chuck had delivered with the pills. The lock opened and Willy slid the gate open enough to walk in and quickly closed it behind him. Before he dwelled on the vermin that had scampered across the same walk way countless times before he thought of Chuck. This A.I. had turned out to be some InSpace superfly. Everything he did worked. His influence was like magic. Had this guy been humble, or even nice, Willy would really have been suspicious but the antagonistic, cocky and arrogant posture had kept him too hateful to be suspicious. Now he got a vibe that was all too reptilian. Nobody was that good at anything without being bad—and why was he doing it anyway? But that was something to deal with later Willy thought. Concentrate—focus on the task at hand.

Ton's crib was at the rear behind bar covered windows. Supposedly, he lived in the apartment with his Moms. Loser. Willy had been counting the windows on his left and had arrived at Ton's. No light shone through but that didn't matter, since the windows seem to have been painted black from the inside. The alley was dark and gray, with a smattering of light from the apartments above. Willy walked up to a window and he took his shirt off to reveal a wife-beater t-shirt that seemed painted on his hulking frame, revealing a quick-release gun holster housing the Glock. He wrapped the gun and holster in the shirt and placed the shirt on the hood of a car. Turning he picked up the Heineken bottle and walked towards Ton's window and hurled the Dutch bottle into Ton's apartment. Inside, Ton put down the bowl of pork and rice he was eating and ignored the yapping of his blind mother who was startled by the crash of glass. The bottle had landed near her feet, after breaking the window and bouncing off some cardboard boxes filled with worthless filth. Ton stood and went to the window and saw Willy staring at him with a dead unblinking stare. Ton had no expression other than alert, albeit quiet indifference. Ton's mother rapid fire gutter spoke to him but he just ignored her. He was moving. The fastest way for him to get to the alleyway was to break the lock to the side exit by shouldering in the door in. When Ton walked into the parking lot he found Willy crouched on a hood of a car his muscular thighs popping out of his stretch jeans.

Ton approached Willy who waited until the last second before he sprang to action and delivered a kick to Ton's forehead and used the momentum to land on the ground. Ton's head did not snap back as much as shift from straight to bent then he turned to meet Willy's eyes. Willy side stepped Ton and bounced his arms arrogantly low between his waist and chest and began to bounce on the balls of his feet—his footwork *sublime*. Ton opened his chest to Willy and advanced with a telegraphed right arm grab. Willy ducked it and gave into the impulse to double punch his mid-section which did nothing. Ton, knowing what would happen had been ready and sent a powerful left fist down upon Willy's upper-back like a hammer nearly flooring him. Willy checked himself for forgetting that these blows meant nothing to Ton and rolled between his legs. Righting himself, he hopped to his feet and reminded himself of the reach differential between Ton and himself was considerable. "If you get inside, make it count, then get out." He said to himself. Then the fight really began. Willy waited for Ton's crude advances and tried to make his way in without getting caught. Ton seemed to be slowing down as Willy was getting more brash and confident—just then Ton clocked him with the back of his hand and followed up with a solid kick to the guts that sent Willy flying into the air. Willy got up and grinned. This caught Ton by surprise and he knew that his foe was on some maxdaddy-no-pain juice. Willy fought the impulse to run, leap and kick Ton. Instead, he ran for the ledge using it as a springboard, banked and ricocheted himself towards Ton, where he twisted and switched, kicking legs in mid air connecting with a crushing kick to Ton's nose. The blood flowed loosely now and it began to rain.

Willy seemed supple compared to Ton and the tape across his knuckles quickly colored with Ton's syrup like blood. Willy hit Ton harder than he had ever hit another man, board or punching bag and the guy just stood there. Willy retreated and waited for an opening and danced around him but Ton was obviously playing the part of a sloth in an attempt to lure him in for the kill. Willy wanted Ton's throat and knew there was only one way to get it— thought not admitting that he had grown impatient, he was taking chances. His blows had smashed Ton and he was sure they had both broken bones but nothing fazed him. Willy was careful to avoid having one of his kicks blocked and his leg grabbed. Being caught would be the end for sure since Ton would just pound him into the cement. Willy bobbed and weaved around Ton like a hummingbird. Then, much to Willy's surprise, Ton froze and put his arms down. Willy looked at him with a completely mystified expression. Then Ton advanced. Holding his arms up, he was not the least bit concerned with blocking Willy's blows—he became a rolling boulder. Willy, took defensive steps backwards and threw blows at Tons forearms to no avail. Sensing that his space was being limited, Willy attempted to leap to his right, but was quickly cut off by Ton who was herding Willy into a corner. Willy started to fire a blistering series of blows in an attempt to keep Ton at bay and then duck between his legs, but was cut off at every try. Finally, Ton blocked Willy's right hand and punched him in the stomach so hard that it lifted him off the ground and slammed him against the side of the tenement building. Willy's feet had barely touched the ground when Ton grabbed him by the throat and lifted him off the ground. Willy swung at space in a feeble attempt to connect with Ton's head. Ton squeezed his left hand and began to cut off Willy's oxygen. Willy switched tactics and began to kick Ton's right eye socket with his Doc Martins but Ton, unfazed, punished Willy's head with massive, deliberate punches to the head. Willy, undaunted grabbed the hidden jabbing knife in his buckle and rammed it into Ton's wrist then twisted it. Blood shot out of Ton's wrist assaulting the freezing raindrops as they fell. Ton, wanting to take the knife from Willy, bent his left arm and narrowed the distance between them just enough for Willy to connect with a direct kick to his larynx. Willy quickly fired off two other kicks to the same spot and saw Ton gasp for air. Gasping, Ton took a step backwards but held on to Willy's neck. Willy jabbed the short knife into Ton's forearm and cleaved a jagged line towards the open wound in his wrist. Ton's eyes widened and he released his grip, while attempting to grab Willy with his right hand. Willy ducked and using Ton's right thigh as a step, leapt up and rammed the knife into his throat. Ton showed no emotion but it was obvious that his ability to breathe was being cutoff. His legs buckled and he fell to his knees while gasping for air. Willy crouched over and let out a primal scream as he leapt towards Ton and sent a scissor kick to Ton's chin breaking his neck. Willy landed on the ground and was completely balanced and watched Ton's arms go limp, his torso fell backwards in slow motion. When Ton's head hit the concrete the sound of the rain seemed to intensify and he switched stances prepared for him to rise. Then as moments passed he realized that Ton was dead and the muscles in Willy's shoulders relaxed. Looking up to the sky, Willy was surprised that no one was looking out of their apartment windows and he could hear the dim sound of a flute. Raising his hands he pulled his hair back and walked towards his gun and shirt. Turning he was startled by Ton's blind mother who stood like Death's totem.

"Why are you out here?!" she screamed in broken Chinese and lurching forward, brought her stun baton to bare. As her finger pressed the stun button, blunt sparks flew from the two emitters at the end of the baton and the old woman seemed to freeze as the 500,000 volts shot down her arm and through her heart. CRACKLING. Wire like spikes of neon electricity connected her tongue to her eyes and vaporized many of the raindrops that

Wired for Chaos

crossed the electricity's path. Suddenly it stopped and smoke whisked off her with the smell of burning hair and she crumpled to the cement. Willy had watched her in amazement and been caught completely off guard. As the woman lay there Willy caught one last glimpse of Ton grabbed his shirt and walked towards the alley gate. Willy's usually vertical spiked quaff was a mess and his expression was that of a Kabuki warrior, fierce yet sad.

Crossing the street the driver jumped out with an umbrella to meet Willy. The skin of the limo beaded the raindrops and gave the impression of bubbling black bean soup on an open camp fire. Willy didn't need to bend under the umbrella, but allowed the driver to throw a cape of protection over him and hurried him into the back seat. Willy plopped down and the door closed with an authoritative slam. The driver rushed back to his seat and they sped away. Willy wiped the water from his face and looked around the interior. In his absence, the driver had placed a small plastic First Aid Kit on top of a folded towel on the seat next to him. Willy touched a panel on the side column and a small mirror extended. He inspected his face and found a shiner under his left eye and a swollen upper lip and smiled. Closing the panel, Willy picked up the Kit and threw it on the floor, took the towel and wiped his face and arms. When he was finished patting himself down he threw the towel to his left and retrieved his cigs and the lighter. Lighting up he squinted the cowboy-smoker's eye through the smoke and felt his face. Nothing too bad. He'd see what he had to attend to once they reached the Howard Johnson's at the airport, where he would shower before boarding the American Airlines flight to LA. Whatever wounds he had were nothing, compared to fights he'd been in as a kid.

As the limo turned onto the FDR Willy thought that only one thing could make this moment better and opened the refrigerator. Yes. It was here. And he took out a Heineken. As he slumped in the seat he touched three buttons one after the other and the hood of the limo became clear giving him a view of the skyline, a foot rest extended from his seat elevating his legs and the latest Cretin Curtis album roared to life over the Infinity speakers. As Willy sucked hard on the Marlborough, he looked at the buildings through the rain pelted roof of the limo and thought, "This ain't such a bad city after all. I could live here. Need a beach though." And the limo gunned it up the East River.

BACK TO BATISTA
6:01PM, MAIN ENTRANCE, HOTEL MELIA COBIA, CUBA

Nearly a century earlier the corrupt strongman Fulgencio Batista Zaldívar had partnered with American gangster Meyer Lansky, to shore up a base for large-scale gambling in Havana, thereby making himself and his political appointees rich. It was announced that his government would match, dollar for dollar, any hotel investment over US$1 million, which would include a casino license and Lansky became the center of Cuban gambling. Today they were no doubt cheering in their graves.

Photographers leaned against large American SUVs smoking and chatting, as the royal palm trees around them combed the evening breeze. Hotel Melia Choiba was situated in a wealthy suburb of Vedado that was purposely modeled after Miami and financed by American Mafioso in the 1940s and 50s. Now, as irony would have it most of the hotels in this area were owned by a different kind of cartel—German, Dutch and American conglomerates with household names. When B' and his entourage walked out of the hotel, the photographers flicked their cigarettes and scrambled to catch him before he entered the awaiting limo. A few shouted questions in broken English but B' ignored them, his face a frowning mask. Leroy and everyone except for Bill, rode shotgun in a massive armored Chevrolet the bodyguards rented when they visited with their wealthy employers. They would have to drive through some crowded streets to get to the arena, but the driver assured them that they would have no problem at this time of day. He was optimistic, or just lying. Cuba used to have a shortage of automobiles and the current mass transit system did not exist but everything changed once Castro died of a massive heart attack 20 years earlier and the US lifted the embargo. "Buy them with money" read the Daily News headline after the President of the US allowed investment to flow to Cuba—against the protest of Cuban Americans in Florida. And so began the most rapid economic shift in the history of the western hemisphere. In record time a Harrahs Casino here, a Club Med there, translated into a massive land grab. Most native Cubans were forced to the far outskirts of their towns, as developers moved in and paid off government officials. But few—without a political voice, were able to complain. Those who had always wanted to emigrate to the states to live with relatives did. Others were paid enormous sums—to vacate their dilapidated, though palatial apartments, which were quickly renovated and made available to prospective buyers on the world's most exclusive real estate sites. Real Cubans, normal everyday working-class people, were becoming an anachronism in the major cities and those who moved to the poor suburbs, plotted to make a lot of money and return—somehow. They fantasized, as they gazed into the plasma bus ads for Revlon cosmetics with perfect women that illuminated their dark rural streets, the dust settling into the woven folds of their straw cowboy hats.

There was a time when a person could stand in the middle of Coppelia Ice Cream Park and gaze into the heavens contemplating the constellations. No more. Havana kicked up so much light, it rivaled Los Vegas in the early 1980s and Häagen-Dazs' parent company (The Pillsbury Company) had over paid for the ice cream concession ousting the family that ran it for decades. The US hadn't killed Castro or toppled his regime they had outlasted him and corrupted his pathetic heirs who wore too much cologne.

B's limo drove past old Art Deco buildings then through ancient streets now littered with tourist maps and drunken American college students, who came to fornicate in the Caribbean version of New Orleans. Although some of the buildings, were new—the streets were freshly paved and money slithered around corners like oiled up snakes down a winding amusement park waterslide—the smell was still old Havana. A combination of sea, dust, tobacco and sweat. The streets were teeming with shiny American cars, horse drawn carriages and people. A conflagration of adult Disneyfication. A human-trout farm of chubby German, American and Canadian tourists, mingling with local prostitutes, office workers, street vendors, pick-pockets and gawkers.

B' touched a button closing his window and the limo's air filter negated everything except the layers of tobacco that seemed fused to the leather seats. He took out the silver key ring Jimmy had given him and rubbed it between his right thumb and forefinger. As the limo stopped at a street light B' saw what he thought was an apparition and leaned forward. On the corner, in front of a Tourneau watch store a sinewy black man played a short clarinet with a fluted silver mouth. He wore a striking reddish-orange, pants-suit that flared above his square-toe white, patent-leather shoes. The arms of the top were large and voluminous ruffle covered fabric—like flamingos shaking themselves after a bath. His slicked back hair covered by a woven straw fedora as he blew his horn with passion and delight. As was the case with many of the street musicians, he actually emanated local music from the flexible flat speakers stitched into the stomach of his suit. Brass horns, a piano and bongos, serenaded the tourists wearing expensive American designer clothing manufactured in Indonesia and sold in mall across America as they threw poker chips, Cuban pesos and near spent debit cards into his white, plastic attaché case on the pavement. When the man ceased playing, he spread his arms and allowed the applause to flow and then, with a smile that elicited praise from many an orthodontist, looked directly at B'—right through the closed, one-way glass, shook his head and laughed. Then B' remembered his dream the morning he killed Derek starring himself as the Grim Reaper and a chill ran down his back as the limo drove off.

7:45 PM, BROADWAY JUST BELOW 125TH STREET, UPTOWN SIDE

Ivan sat in the back of his big black Caddy behind two rocket scientists, Serge and Bruno. They were only invited because he wanted men of action who would do what they were told without question—or much brain activity. Niemöller had called him hours earlier and said to drive here and wait for his call. Once Niemöller was confident that B' had taken a dive he would call Ivan and tell him the whereabouts of Jimmy who was nearby and how to disengage the booby-trap. Then everyone went to the bank courtesy of Brice Johnson.

Serge, a second generation American-Russian with a shaved head and muscles on top of muscles said, "Fucking idiot. You know shit 'bout Greece— don't speak language—gonna' buy house there."

Bruno replied, "Say it again. I don't like black girls. You want to fuck some Rasta bitch in the hills of Jamaica go ahead…"

"Hey! Hey! Hey! The Lauren family has a house there! The Kennedy's have…"

"I don't give a ratshitfuck—you care who your neighbors are, you have enough money to buy land and build a house?!" Fuck you! Look," pointing out the window. "Look at fat bitch!" The short overweight woman Bruno pointed at, was eating some chicken wings from Kentucky Fried Chicken and flicking the bones onto the sidewalk. "You end up fucking her in some shack in Jamaica?"

"That woman?"

"Yeah!"

"That Alice. Fucked that bitch last month. Looked like supermodel then. Gained few pounds—sucked my cock like that bone—look. Look at that happy bone!" Ivan had to look and hated himself for it. Looking back to the Brice-Santiago bout on his PDA he turned the volume up on his head-set and shook his head.

As soon as B' had gone into hiding Gila, the rogue A.I. had taken it upon himself to do something highly illegal. He had manufactured an army of seekers, listeners, retrievers—all invisible—for the express purpose of spying. Governments did it via their agencies but approval as determined by legislative branches was exceptionally prickly and the elected. Officials always played the protection of privacy gambit to the masses to ensure re-election. These agents were eerie appendages programmed with a specific purpose in mind. Determining what plan Niemöller had for Brice's brother Jimmy. Gila had formed the agents out of electromulsch programs and secretive—highly paranoid military nano programs that searched mercilessly and connected strands that in this case that might be tapped into or discovered by, Law Enforcement Agencies who were looking for bad people out to do wrong. These agents were Gila's tendrils—like hair thin strands of hyper-sensitive talons that moved at the speed of light through systems and across wireless communication all searching—relentlessly for information on, Brice, Brice Johnson, B', Jimmy Johnson, Niemöller, Ivan, what have you. They then connected the dots, only to disappear a 1/100 of a second later, having transferred the information to another agent strand and folding it back to Gila, who would index the information and build a three dimensional knowledge picture. Niemöller had made a deal with Ivan for the ransom of Jimmy, but the NYPD was too busy with their manhunt for Brice to focus on related cases—especially since they did not know that Jimmy was missing and had not connected Brice to Ivan or Niemöller. But Gila had dispatched his agents throughout the Tri-state area. An electric God with limitless arms, seemingly composed and inert, seated stoically at the bank of a tranquil stream while his minions raced over hills, valleys and continents at the speed of light only to disappear once their tasks were completed. Then he would act.

Camacho sat in his Camero four cars behind Ivan inhaling a Marlboro having been called by his employer, Roshi who unknown to him was actually Chuck hours earlier. "Watch Ivan," he said, "Move when he does. He had a deal with Niemöller and is going to pick up Jimmy...make the bust of your life...will end our arrangement...bonus for you." Cake. Camacho would walk these bozos into the two-six a block away like a fuckin' Texas Marshal and slap those white cops with his dick, give his report, get some props from the night Sergeant and be on the Tri-boro in three to four hours max. Media would position him as a star and when he disappeared everybody would think it was the Russians that offed him and he would be a cop-saint. Camacho smiled thinking of the two-time idiots that would get shaken down and "kiss the gun's butt" all because the cops would think the Russians had offed him.

PLAYER'S ENTRANCE TO THE PARTAGAS ARENA

The old Estadio Pan-American near Cojimor where the 1991 Pan-American Games were hosted just outside of Havana, was now the PARTAGAS Arena because in Cuba money was all you needed.

As B's limo pulls up a throng of reporters, partially held back by security guards in tan uniforms, reporters hurl questions at him before the door is opened. B' exits wearing dark sunglasses and waits for his guys to make a tunnel to the entrance. "So this is what it feels to be a cow's leg thrown into a sea of hungry piranhas," thinks B'. So many people, a few of them wore cardboard cutouts of Olga's face over theirs and tried to push through to get near to B' and make sure he noticed them. Leroy elbowed one of the Olga mask guys in the face and the guy stumbled backwards dazed and in pain. They pressed towards him and their words stepped on each other so much it ceased to be language. The flashes from the cameras illuminated the area like an artificial sun. Above the player's entrance B' saw a plaque in Spanish that said, "Sport is the right of the people" Fidel Castro. As the throng of humanity made its way towards the entrance a tussle caused by a few reporters and aggressive fans bent the curve of the ant-like procession. B' and his guys were momentarily forced onto the foliage as arms banged people out of the way and shifted B' into avoidance mode. Before he knew it he started to panic and started to push the people around him away. While being forced down by the weight of Leroy's tree trunk arms, B' covered his head and saw his glasses knocked off. Just then, like a slo-mo pic moment he caught an image, frozen in the blinding light of camera flashes against the wall of the arena. Between the legs in this crush of humanity he spied a majestic Bird of Paradise plant being trampled, its firm stem bent, its pointed petals of brilliant orange and arrow-shaped tongues of vivid blue mashed into the side of the arena and oozing life, illuminated by flashes.

7:55PM, COMMENTATOR'S BOOTH, PARTAGAS ARENA

"Well Rick this has to be on of the most highly anticipated bouts that I can remember."

"Absolutely Howard. With the confirmed arrival of—now let me get this right—alleged murderer Brice Johnson arriving yesterday to compete against the only guy who has ever beaten him, Joseph "the Lion" Santiago in a no-holds bout, will undoubtedly rank as the most popular bout to date."

"Considering that there are few countries that would allow a no-holds bout, let lone' someone wanted for murder to compete—well, a great many people who wouldn't usually jack in probably will just out of curiosity."

"HBO has learned that the Cuban government has not, repeat has not, given Brice Johnson asylum and has made it clear that his visa—which will be strictly enforced—is good for 72 hours. That means that soon after this bout Brice has to leave Cuba and either face the music in the US or learn a foreign language."

"Rick we should mention that what we'll be seeing tonight is real. Yes the players are on a game platform and the terrain is SupaReal™ generated with spectacular stunts, but the blows the players inflict upon each other, the falls they take and the discharges from weapons, will all be real to the players. That means that there is—in all likelihood, the chance for serious injury or fatality. That said, we must remind our viewing audience around the world that minors under the age of 17 must provide an internationally verifiable ID check and will be allowed to jack in for the Rider SensorRun only. Persons 18 and above, must provide an ID check and must sign a waiver indemnifying HBO, its subsidiaries, Sony and your local Holo-V providers, from any and all, responsibility due to injuries as a direct result of Tactile Level SensorRun, if they chose this option."

"But we won't snuff viewers."

"Ab—so—lute—ly not. There are fail safes instituted throughout the network and all blows are delayed a hundredth of a second allowing our mainframe enough time to differentiate between concussions, lethal blows and what have you—all in an attempt to make it real, not lethal."

PLAYER'S LOCKER ROOM, PARTAGAS ARENA

The silence in the locker room was deafening. B' was used to idle chatter and trash talking but the guys around him were more like animated cadavers. Every door closing, every toilet flushing seemed more like gunshots. Then he thought, no, they are normal. It's me. It's me.

"Time?" said, B' to Bill."

"Almost."

As he moved to lie down on the massage table wearing only an athletic supporter, B' caught a glimpse of the gold Rolex he had given Bill after his first win and thought about how they celebrated. He had never drank so much champagne. He pissed champagne for days after and bought presents—cars for everybody he knew that loved him and fur coats for their wives and girlfriends. God pulled the trigger on the *psychoparkamusementride* as B' lay on his stomach with Bill about to rub oil into his shoulders, back and arms. His lean, six-foot plus frame and broad shoulders could be mistaken for the body of a world-class sprinter and the past few days of deprived sleep and bad diet had not left a mark.

His concentration was broken up into shards of thoughts. Nothing was right he thought. His diet was shit, he hadn't worked out in days—weird sleep patterns and no prep for the bout. If he counted every time his pulse raced over the course of the last three days and it wasn't triple digits he would be shocked. He knew so many things that were wrong and so few that were right. Being a creature who thrived on ritual and not having preformed them—the big things like the focused work outs with timed exercises and the pre-arranged series of his exercises, but also the little things like the way he tied and retied his shoes before leaving for the arena, his breakfast of two hardboiled eggs, bacon and wheat toast, or wearing his lucky jock strap. So few of his rituals were adhered to, or could be adhered to that it kneaded uncertainty into his consciousness and clouded his concentration like a bad trance sim'. Santiago would be so revved up for this bout that his trainers would have to hold him back. B' had been like that at times. Pit bull blood coursing through him, spitting and drooling—unable to close his mouth long enough to swallow, the barking barbs so hot on his tongue. Spending time thinking about his neglected omissions made him agitated and annoyed, because they now seemed frivolous and vapid—Jimmyjimmyjimmy. But he knew the traits were hardwired success algorithms flashing along the neurosynaptors of his psyche. He needed their mortar the most, but it was as distant and liquid as memories of his kid brother. And the Devil whispered, "Forget everything, think of yourself, flee...."

Bill tapped him and B' sat up with near robotic movement. Someone handed Bill B's crimson, silk robe and he stood to put it on. Bill tied it and everyone got up and walked towards the doors and waited for B' that began to walk. He was dazed and started to phase out sound and his peripheral vision. One foot in front of another. Autopilot. Thoughts fought for attention. He wanted to tell Bill that if anything happens and he gets way banged up, that he should get the PDA he left on his bed and follow the instructions. Rodney would know what to do when it came to his estate, but could not utter a single word. Security guards, maintenance workers and gawkers lined the hall eying him, but they may as well have been suits in his walk-in closet. All these hallways looked the same in their grayness with protruding pipes and echoing footsteps. B' didn't even fight for "oneness" with the moment. He should resolute and he knew it, but so many questions, so much doubt, so much utter lack of control phased through his thought space, that immobilization seemed to be his only armorgel respite...

"B'!" said Bill grabbing his right hand and lifting it up.

Brice thought "What?" but said it with his face to Bill as the doctor pricked B's index finger and extracted some blood into a medical PDA then walked towards Santiago. Hands came from behind and someone lifted B's right foot pointing it into his Soji suit. This was more like it. Bottom to top the suit grew upwards sucking the air particles between him and it, becoming one, an extension of the game. Not man, homo-superior[2]. He knew the drill of commentators in their perches, jackets and ties on top, jeans and sneakers below talking more trash than the players, VIP friends-of-friends vying for looksees, poaching sushi munchies, swigging cold sudszies. Scanning, eyes only, no head, he saw him. Santiago, veins large, legs coiled. Stance said, *fuckfuckfuckletsfuckmeontopnotstop* and B'—knowing he was being watched by all faked a yawn and looked at his hand being inserted into a sleeve. Give him nothing B' thought.

"I'm gonna' fuck him up onna' on a molecular level." Said B' so his boys could hear him as he clenched his fist.

Waz' a bit of a surprise though to see Santiago in the same arena thought B'. Been ages since he had real full contact with an opponent in the same space. Seemed like a superfluous glaze on top of the membrane of the game. Receptors could transmit the hit and convert it to sensory trauma with no actual physical contact required. But hit-to-hit, was street-juice and B' thought the Japanese must have whipped out their straws for a giant slurpy. "Okay—*lets fuck*—*line me up*—*wider*—*that's it.*"

The doctor raised his hand and communicated with the booth. "No performance enhancement chemicals were found in either player." Then walked towards the paramedics chompin' hotdogs and coffee, on uncomfortable folding chairs in no man's land, just off the game platform grid.

The arena encircled their large blackened expanse of rubber covered tech. The thousands of empty seats beneath a dome meant nothing. This place, those empty seats were the precursors to e-grist. The track and soccer field covered—keep your peanut throwers and beer vendors. The headriders tonight were having illegal jizzem laden tabs with their popcorn, or top shelf liquor or Bucanero Fuerte beer—with this shank-groove.

The game wardens liked to keep secrets from the players and headriders alike, cause it adds spice to the mix. Nobody knew what or how the games were going to go down, so there was no way to prepare. No upper hand to be sought. In the distance B' saw two cycles shaped like black carbon snowmobiles, kept aloft by several tethers attached to long braided antenna like the poles, made of Kevlar and graphite, imbedded into the game floor. Giveaway thought B' and he archived numerous game scenarios, his thoughts still halfhearted.

Fake it. Fake badass like a motha' B' thought and suddenly he was one with his flexible armor and wished the electric God to take him, arms rising, fingers extended to a place where he could turn *ON*. "Sure they will feel what I feel but the system won't let them hear my thoughts."

Words were spoken around him but he was someplace else—floating. Hissing. B' spread his legs for balance as the game platform dipped him, like a human brush into a limitless can of electro-psychedelic paint.

FLUTTER.

The fully-immersev SupaReal™ environ's floor raced towards him and stopped just beneath his feet. The environ was different in a literal alien planet way but thoroughly believable.

B' and Santiago were ghost-like observers in the futuristic Morgo Organ Bank and Exchange, on some made up planet in a non-existent galaxy, close, close inside. The enormous domed ceiling of the exchange was made of a translucent material that contained layers of opaque liquid that ebbed and flowed with a shimmering mother-of-pearl opalescence. The hum of communicative chatter lightly echoed against the walls and floor, paved with iridescent blue granite that refracted letters in an alien language that bragged of wars fought and old, rich deceased aliens.

The beings were gray skinned bipeds similar to humans in size and shape, sans cartilage for noses or ears—their openings were gnarled and wrinkled. Hairless and sporting large brown-black eyes, they bobbed up and down as they walked. One phased through B' and Santiago, holding a glass orb and inhaling the green smoke it emitted, as he walked to the end of a line for a new left lung. At the front of the line, a trader called a "shouter" took a bid on the harvested organs and immediately turned and began shouting at a group of sellers across the trading pit that was teeming with shouting aliens. Any organ could be sold or purchase here, via the distribution of their financial representations called Utoks. These forms of currency were flat circular disks that were regulated by the government and closely guarded by the National Militia. At the center of the dome, suspended over the heads of the aliens was the orb shaped Utok Repository that was heavily guarded by aliens wearing boots that allowed them to defy gravity and holding large weapons.

Suddenly, bolts of neon-red electricity passed through the top of the dome and hit each of the guards who shook violently and exploded seconds later, spewing gobs of gelatinous matter in every direction. Aliens on the floor of the exchange begin to scream in terror as they exhale and snort as they inhale their midsections inflating dramatically. Just then the dome is shattered in eight places and the assailants crash through the dome on silver ropes. Brice and Santiago are whisked to the center of the exchange for a better vantage point, they are completely invisible and impervious to anything physical. A loud alarm sounds and the doors to the exchange shut and lock crushing some of the aliens as they try to escape. The attacking thieves pierce the skin of the Utok Repository with projectiles from hand cannons as they continue to repel to the floor of the exchange. The Repository begins to crack and finally shatters with a small explosion releasing rectangular packs of Utoks that come crashing to the floor. Two of the thieves begin shouting at the aliens and many drop to the floor in fear. The stairwells flush with the walls of the exchange erupt with alien guards who push past fleeing aliens and begin to open fire on the thieves. The thieves fire indiscriminately mowing down aliens and guards alike. Each one exploding—gelatinous mass into so many gobs like spoons of Jell-O flicked everywhere. Each thief picks up a pack of Utoks the size of a large backpack and runs for a solid wall followed by Brice and Santiago who are drawn to them like pins to magnets. Each of the thieves aim and fire lasers at different areas of the wall cutting into it with little problem. Two of the thieves are killed by a slew of guards who manage to crawl over dead bodies. One of the thieves grabs a female alien and uses her as a shield as he shoots at the guards. The wall crumbles and the thieves rush through the hole to the street. As they rush out Brice and Santiago are drawn towards them. They are in a street surrounded by immense office buildings that mirror the shapes of the odd shaped streets at their bases. Running down granite steps three at a time they shoot behind them and through Brice as they run for their fusion bikes. Each one of the thieves drops their packs into cargo holders on the bikes and put on their helmets. In the distance sirens are heard and then it happens. B' and Santiago's bodies lurch towards two of the thieves and they find themselves seated side by side on fusion bikes now in the physical form of the thieves. B' was always momentarily disoriented by the shift from observer to participant. Bitch to playah'. The way gravity just kicked in, the tactile everything—like a flower speed blooming in an empty balloon, its petals stretching and shaping the rubber. The smells, wind against his cheeks and inner thighs hugging the bike's seat—*suddenly*. Somewhere the game developers were grabbing their crotches and getting shouts of approval from their boys, faming' it up now that the world had experienced their work. Their artifice, interpreted by superstars. A chill runs down B's back, his left hand shifts his nuts up unconsciously and he feel truly alive and in the moment. B' clenches his teeth and finds himself looking into Santiago's eyes. They quickly turned away to look at the bike controls and the alien letters morphed into English. Then each hit their ignition buttons at the same time and the screens on their helmet's visors clicked on. *Vibrate. Clutch. LaunCH! ADHRENELINRUSHSPEW!* They were off like cowboys riding jet rockets skimming the surface of the city with 16,834,246 heads jacked in for the ride, an' going long, with the vibration of the bikes rippling through their forearms—sensationally.

They are amping down a street as the cops cooked behind them in an armored ride barely high enough over the civilian cars to not scratch their paint. The howling of the fusion bikes threaten to shatter safety glass windows in the near vicinity and B' quickly discovers that the bikes have been tripped out to kick it slightly higher—literally, above the civvy' rides. *WHIZZBANGCLUTCH—SHIFTING!* The crew banks and navigates past rides that seem to be standing still, then the man begins to fire some kind of plasma acid shit, just missing B's ride. They take out the trunk of a family ride, vaporizing their groceries and the crew howled by their exhausts blowing. Then it happened. Like the fin of a shark, the swerving of an oncoming car on the expressway, FEAR enveloped him like a long lost fever. From the two green pointers in his visor screen B' could tell that the goal was to make it to the hideout or point of escape either one didn't matter, just getting there was the juice and the man was not shooting blanks. "Full contact. I could get fried." B' said to himself and gunned it through slow moving traffic, banging the bottom of his bike into three rides in a row more out of fear than a concerted effort to win. The crew started to bunch up and the guy behind B' got fried and B' had to swerve to avoid getting hit. His bike took the hit and banged on three auto roofs eight times.

Green arrows pointed around the end of the massive office building on the right. Maybe winning was the best way to avoid getting hurt thought B'.

Wired for Chaos

Even at the speed he was going he decided to do a trick he learned during training months ago. Most of his crew was ahead of him and would have to slow down and counter steer into the turn, but B' had a deep knowledge of InSpace physics. As he approached the turn he gunned the bike, passed the bitches, slammed on the front brakes while simultaneously swerving to his right, pumped his legs so the bike would buck and gunned the motha'. It was like a cartoon slingshot that left a near perfect right-angle trail of smoke and catapulted him to the lead—right into the unexpected oncoming traffic. SHIT. Like a well orchestrated deception the traffic had been held up by half a block at a light that had just changed. Fuck it. B' gunned the engine straight towards them certain that the civvies' would move. And they did. Crew in tandem. Engines revvin'. The Man in pursuit.

Arrows pointed left and rides hit air-breaks, skidded and rammed each other in an attempt to miss autos. Banking like a mercury ball in Satan's pinball machine doing mach somethin'—ablaze, B' flashed down a one-way street—the right way and dug his feet into the bike. Clear shot. No obstacles. Click boom! The crew made it around the turn just denting some rides and the man was on them driving pissed. Once the man righted himself he fired like a drunk soldier and caught the tail end of a bike and B' felt the vibration of the hit. The rider was catapulted through the air and caught a street post where he exploded. B' was maxing towards a crossing littered with peds, his hands shaking, his eyes darting over to the rearview mirror too many times and said, "Oh shit!" slowed and swerved to miss a female with an infant knowing that it meant he'd violently clipped an old guy. "These aliens go splat if you look at them—don't want it happening to me! Can't go out like this!" That was all Santiago needed to catch up. He offed the female and infant with extreme prejudice and suddenly his points counter sprang to life. B' scored a few points from grazing the old guy, while Santiago retained a commanding lead. B' did a mental *okay*. People are game. Get offensive. They managed to avoid the man's guns and headed for a vehicle tunnel topped by a massive office building perched on a steep decline. Two way traffic ran through the limestone legs of the tall, fat building decorated with stone reliefs of idealized dead aliens filled with short, fat unhappy office workers and B' had a thought. Best way to survive might be to be unpredictable and get out front. He had a thought and did a maxi-inhale. As he approached the entrance he timed his assault and prayed not to miss his mark. Just before the entrance, he violently pumped his legs into the bike and slammed on the front brakes then gunned the motor sending him straight into the first floor window of the building. "Shit!" B' cringed and ducked. *CRASHSPLATTEREXPLOSION!* Shards of glass went everywhere and B' took out two fools in their cubes. He was in an office and caught the aisle mowing down Coordinators, Admins, Managers and Directors—bodies exploding left and right mili-seconds after screams. B's windshield was coated with alien goop juice and he screamed with blood lust, consuming their corporal spirits with his open mouth. Through a wood door—

SPLATSPEW—corporate conference room doom. Full house. Too bad. B's bike caught the tip of the table and it spiked up like an Olympic pole-vault—the other edge decapitating three aliens. Duck—top of bike into ceiling—nose ricochet—bank towards floor—accelerate—miss the floor—bottom of window—through with a shatter, diving through the air. *HOOOOOOOO!!!* B's legs are airborne as the bike plummets towards the roadway at a *45° angle*. Points rack up for the freestyle groove. "Get on the bike!" Feet in. Legs pump. "Nose up! Nose up! Gonna' hit..." Right—right on top of the man's ride! Smash lights gone. Hood caved in. Thump, crash into the pavement like dust under God's basketball and B's ride launches like a frog on happy. He guns it, blinks after the crew and his score is wild crazy out front. Two ugly, pissed off cop choppers arc past the building and set their sites on the crew. Cannons blare exploding the pavement and revealing water mains in long blunt lines.

Arrows point right. *BANK*. Sign up ahead says the onramp to the expressway is near. Copters have to fly in tandem to stay in the narrow street. Crew threads the lower entrance to the onramp. Circle curve up. Copters swerve and think again bout' targeting, cussing in some language. Wide lanes. No obstructions. Big targets. Crew accelerates, copters nose down and speed up like the rods of fly fishermen. On course, B' and Santiago neck and neck, punks stealing air behind them. Copter closing in. B' felt tentative and fearful. "Get them off your back...don't want to fry." B' was more frightened than a little girl alone in her room at night and he hated himself for it. He knew that the guys controlling the game wouldn't totally let him get offed this early, 'cause it would really piss off the crowd, but that didn't mean that they wouldn't let him get scorched only to return for a different scenario. "Fuckfuckfuckfuck! I'm caught between choppers running up my ass and a tanker that is just asking to blow up!" Then he gets an idea. Slight decrease in speed puts him side by side with one of the crew directly behind the shiny, silver tractor-trailer carrying highly flammable natural gas. He hesitates but the sound of the chopper eggs him on. He smiles at crew boy and does ballet. Hops up on his seat, left foot on, bending, right extending into a flying kick to the punk's neck. *SNAP!*. He flies off and onto-into a civilian's windshield. *SPLATSPLODE!* Points. B' steers his ride towards the rider less ride and steers the rider less ride towards the gap between the road and the rear of the massive gas tank. *ClutchRevJet*. Rider less bike takes out the hover apparatus and the entire rig swerves to the right taking out two lanes of cars. *SCREECH!* Santiago is gone up ahead. Steel bends. Tolerance maxi. "This won't hurt." B' goes over the safety rail and plummets to the river below in a long beautiful jump like this shit had been planned, rehearsed and canned for your viewing pleasure— both legs aloft, freestyle scissor-kick, heart thumpythump, millions saw and felt it. Points. Above it's *Rolloverrolloverrolloverexplosionrollover! MUSHROOMFIREBALL!* Takin' out cars. Copter played catch and lost. Race iz' on with Santiago above and B' below—sea water in is nostrils—skimming water, threading cement pylon supports and Santiago taking the heat from the remaining chopper. Exit 15 Kilometers up ahead.

B' is running out of water for beach soon, only boats were jealous and wanted notice. Santiago and two of the crew—oops! One vaporized by the man—cut air towards the exit. Bikes vibrating like jackhammers. B' goes the wrong way looking for clearance and carves a jetstreamwake of white water crossing underneath the water bridge, frightened, yet relieved, that he swerved in time to miss a boat. Santiago rounded the exit going way too fast and rode the metal safety rail sparking sparks. *Oh.* Double Decker tourist bus filled to the maxi on its roofless top. *Christmas.* Santiago pumped the bikes rear and catapulted it into the air at the seated tourists. Santiago thought, *"Start your Mowers!"* He slowed and swerved to catch all the heads as they popped like corn kernels exploding in a microwave. *POPPOPPOPPOPPOPPOP!* Down and he crashes onto the roof of an expensive ride and he keep going. He took the curve and saw B' in the water turning. On to the beach. Landshark. Taking the boardwalk B' and Santiago were nearly matched—B' out in front by a head. Arrows pointed right and they saw it. Tunnel in the side of a large hill next to the beach. New choppers swerve in. The man in armored rides gunning it from the road parallel to the boardwalk, past the pastel houses and weird palm trees. B' and Santiago jump the rail and lead the procession of angry law enforcement officers charging. Shots fired—missed. *Blurrrrrr.* Mouth of the tunnel, ass of the bitch. Home stretch. Up ahead. Behind something. A big rig, tractor trailer laid up for repair and they loop behind it—*SCREECHBREAK* out of sight of the man. Maintenance workers waitin' for 'em. *JUMP* and down the manhole into the electrojizzem transporter they go.

FLUTTER REAL.

"End of round one." Switch to commentary.

DOWN ON THE GAMEPLATFORM

B' gulped green Gatorade from the container Bill held for him, as the sweat ran off his cheeks. He sat in a crude metal folding chair his eyes still covered by the suits sensors and outputs. His suit worked whisking all the sweat away from his skin as soon as it appeared chasing it through micro pores giving it the appearance of scaleless snakeskin. But something entirely foreign surged through his veins, relief. Jittery globules made of frightened little cells rode adrenalin screaming, as they surged through his body.

"Good. Good. You did good. You're ahead by a little over 10,000 points. You own that bitch Santiago."

"I own him. I own him alright." Said B' truly looking like an alien in the Jap suit worth more than the yearly wage of successful third-world men.

Wired for Chaos

Nose to nose, "But don't go getting over confident on me alright. I'm betting that the next thing they spring on you is a straight up fight and all these headriders smell blood—want fuckin' blood knowing its no holds barred. Don't have time for your usual slow to the game wind up of yours—hear me! Hit his ass like a hammer driving a nail into warm French cheez—ze'." Said Bill, checking the integrity of B's suit on his PDA. "Now listen. Santiago is maxing for you right…"

"Yeah."

"Only he iz' gonna' fuck up. His moves are going to be impetuous and wild. Watch, outmaneuver, strike. Let him fuck-the-up and hammer his ass. This not like other bouts where you could fuck with the prick and jerk the line. He'z a lefty with a soft right cross so get inside and work the jaw, ribs and kidney. No toying, no baiting. Hit him until he breaks."

"Yeah. Yeah, I hear you."

"Don't fuckin' hear me! Do that bitch so I can get to the goddamn mutherfucking craps table tonight and lose the money you're going to pay me." Getting serious. "Do not underestimate this fuck. Open him up but good. You got anger. You been fucked deep an' hard wit' no Vaseline—an' your brotha's out there waiting for you—so open this bitch up. Do what you gotta' do."

B' nodded, clenched his fists and flexed his thighs up and down by pumping and bobbing on the balls of his feet as he belched an unconvincing, "Yeah." Then he thought of Jimmy and knew it was time to marshal his resolve. "Stick to the plan. Stick to the plan."

In one of the ultra expensive sponsor suites overlooking the center of the arena, Ido sipped imported sake as he nodded to underlings very pleased with the number of headriders.

COMMENTATOR'S BOOTH, PARTAGAS ARENA

"Just look at the scores! Johnson at 134,780 points is just ahead of Santiago with 129,501 points and do these guys looked amped up or what!

"What a round! What a round! Our analysts sense above average spikes of fear and dread in both players but their instincts are dead on and speaking of the dead. These guys are ruthless and utterly willing to seize every advantage for carnage. To say that these guys are killers would be an understatement."

"Lets look at some of the kills…"

IN HIS HEAD.

B' remembered a time when he enjoyed getting hit. It made him feel alive. He could feel the blood gush through his body—taste his opponent's ire at the end of his fist and know what he needed to know. The ladder, the steps, the bar—how high he would need to aim himself. But something was different

Wired for Chaos

now. Again it came. Hands on him and he walked a few meters forward and to the right. The game coming for him like a radioactive quickness flowing through mass like light through mass and he was helpless to stop it.

FLUTTER.

"No need to fasten your safety belts. You have already arrived," thought B'. The SupaReal™ environ placed him before an immense bank of monitors. There was some sort of international crisis unfolding before him and news commentators showed footage of devastation. Women and children running from air attacks, whole city blocks exploding and death counts mounting on both sides of the war. The two rival heads of state rattled their sabers—one accusing the other of harboring terrorists—the other pointing to the sinking of a spy submarine as conclusive proof of the disruptive nature of their neighbor. Ultimatums were given and air strikes launched. Planes did battle in the sky and stray bombs took out buildings in the business district.

SHIFT. His clothing pressed against him with a jarring suddenness and B' was on the 13th floor of a bombed out office building in the dead of night in the heart of the killing fields. He lurched forward and started to pat himself feeling for armaments in a frenzy. He was some sort of Marine outfitted in the latest combat gear. Armor suit and helmet, all hi-tech to the maxi, two hand guns, one automatic rifle strapped to his back, knives, grenades and lots of ammo. Something in his peripheral moved and he drew the gun on it. Guy threw his hands up, "Wow! Same side cuz'! Same side!" and B' stepped off nodding.

Soldier said, "Chief says stay sharp. Has a gut feeling that they will try to destroy the Parliament 'cause their air strikes didn't do it."

"Right."

Pointing to B's turret mounted gun that was bolted into the concrete floor, "Don't fry us good guys with that alright."

B' simply shook his head and considered the large gun. It was a work of annihilation. Its 16cm barrel and armaments were mounted on top of a liquid ball bearing casing that moved with the slightest touch from the shooter. Just then B' became aware of the silence. It was the dead of night and very little light emanated from the bombarded city. In the distance bombs could be heard vaporizing concrete, asphalt, metal and glass, but his immediate proximity was very quiet. Too quiet for what should be a vibrant city center directly across from Parliament and its circular square filled with statues. B' could hear the wind whistling through the gaping holes in his bombed out building and he could smell asbestos and something else burning. No electricity ran through many of these buildings that had been recently exposed to the elements. Whole floors were vaporized down to the steel supports and the floor was unstable in many areas. A whirring sound was heard and B' recognized a member of his crew by the uniform lowering himself at a fast clip down to the street level. Then silence. B' took the opportunity to acquaint himself with a few of the weapons and kept a paranoid eye jutting around the parameter. RealTime always seemed longer than real-time B' thought and stretched his legs. Bobbing

Wired for Chaos

on his feet he began to bounce lightly, taking notice of the gravity—
significantly less than Earth's. He would be stronger here, quicker and spry. He
limbered up and harshed the air with a series of Kenpo moves then his headset
beeped twice and he froze. "Here they come!" said a voice and B' ran to his gun.
Another voice said, "Where?! They're not on my scope!"

"Look up! They're coming in!" said the first voice followed by
explosive gunfire.

The enemy was shooting silently from on high, plummeting towards
the earth at a near 60° angle. B' pointed his gun upwards and switched the
readout on the scope to night vision. What he saw were several large black
spheres racing towards the earth like meteorites. One of his gunners hit one of
the spheres and it exploded into a fireball that was catapulted away from the
building in a trail of blue-white fire. B' began to fire at the spheres as they sped
towards the earth, then saw exactly what they were once they hit concrete.
Personnel deployment devices. As a sphere struck the ground it bounced twice
with the third impact altering its shape dramatically. On the third contact the
sphere's surface seemed to adhere to the concrete and peal itself flat as if the
earth was a super vacuum sucking its skin. Instantaneously, another sphere with
rib-like armor rolled out, as the skin spewed forth a cloaking curtain of dense
green-gray smoke. After a brief roll, several ribs on the sphere jutted out, bent
and latched onto the concrete forming an opening and a heavily armed Marine
would roll out. Meat. Game. Heavy fire came from many locations in the
building, shooting explosive shells into the body armor of the enemy. Cries and
explosive sounds echoed down the once affluent financial streets, as more
bogies came in. But not all of the spheres hit the street. Several hit the building
B' and his men inhabited. Inside the cavernous burnt out building, several
spheres bounced off exposed girders and broke through brittle concrete floors
like enormous wrecking balls. Once B' caught wind of the interlopers he tried
to swerve his gun 180°, but since it would have caused him to walk on air floors
above the street he ditched the large gun and swung his automatic rifle out just
in time for the party. The spheres seemed to be smart enough to compensate
for difficult terrain and latched onto exposed girders. The Marines
immediately repelled down steel cables and opened fire on anything that
moved including B'. *FIREFIGHT!* Party was on and shots were fired across the
expanse of corporate devastation. Both sides seemed to be firing wild. In the
mayhem B' snuck around a wall to wait for an opportunity to cut lose. Shards
of concrete ripped off the walls like droplets of saliva exploding from a
sneezing person and B' dialed it up. Neck cocked, gun ready, timed the other
guy's discharge arc moving away—flay-time. B' whipped around the corner
and began firing. Run, tuck roll, floor gives way, down to another level, roll to
a crouch and take aim. "Catch!" Boogie juice explosion. First confirmed kill.
Points. B' runs. Seeing a hole in the floor he summersaults into it. Draws fire
and blows-away a surprised bogie in mid-air then runs for the cover of a wall.
B' had taken a chance and was pissed at himself knowing the stakes but amping
none the less. Weight of the gun felt good and he was moving extremely well.

He took a look at small key pad on his left hand gauntlet and touched a few buttons. A tiny voice said "searching" and B' started to stalk around the corner. Suddenly, a bogie lashed out at him with a sword and B' parried with his rifle, gun butt to the jaw, knee to the groin, shove, aim *CLICKBOOM!* To the head—"See ya!" Running for what was once a conference room B' squatted and made sure no one had their sights on him. Looking at the screen again he saw that it illuminated the locations of his team in Green and the opposition in Red. Two to four.

"Alright," said B' as he checked his ammo on the gun's readout and the battery-magazines strapped to his chest. He held one of the magazines feeling its weight and gripped it tightly knowing its power. Kill or be killed. He thought about the realness of the bullets and what they could do to his nervous system and clenched his jaw. "Time to fuck." Said B' noting the locations of the bad guys. Sprint down the hall and make one with the wall. Rocket ready, stiff and erect like a totem he froze. They probably knew what he...and shots blared through the floor next to him. He ran and the shots chased him through the floor. Running was the act of falling forwards and righting yourself with consecutive movements that B' was about to outdo. He ran up and along the wall in a graceful arc, aimed his gun in the direction of the enemy's fire, pressed the multi-fire trigger, kicked off and rode the propulsion of the gun's force as if it was a pole-vault. His shots nullified the enemy's and molten metal did shit on a molecular level. Touch floor. Floor caves in. B' down a level and rolls. He is meters away from the only remaining member of his team who ignores him. They guy cocks his grenade launcher and fires in the direction of the bad guy shooter. *LAUNCHBOOM!* Guy gets filleted. Arms, legs and head sent to different districts.

Three to two. B' and his guy talk universal hand-signal solder talk for, "Bad guys one level down. You take the left flank I'll take the right." B' nods and they move—fastfaster'. B', not seeing a staircase gets an idea and takes out one of his grenades. "180° Directional burst emulsifier. I think I know what that is." B' takes the white grenade that says, "This side up." It looks like a hockey puck, as he flicks it down the hall. B' stands and begins to run towards it. As the grenade comes to a stop the top half spits a milky-white liquid that forms an umbrella shaped dome that B' runs to and aims for. While he is in the air the grenade explodes downwards and showers the lower level with projectile concrete followed by Brice. A bogie, his vision obscured by the debris, his arm over his face to deflect shooting concrete pieces, gets nailed hard by B'. Bullets riddle the guy blowing his arm off, then hitting him in the chest—the force propelling him backwards into a wall.

Across the floor B' could see his team mate emerge from a staircase through four glass walls. He gave B' the high sign they started to move forwards. Steps later his team mate catches bullets to the face and the impact lobs his head clean off. B' marks the position of the shooter and moves towards him. Walls of glass in the way are blows to shards by his weapon and the shooter turns to meet B's fury. Shots, shots, shots. Glass sprays in the direction of the shooter and scratch the visor of his helmet causing him to blink. B' empties a magazine, pops it out and reloads while running. The shooter wipes his visor off and raises his weapon, B' fires and hammers the guy's helmet like a speed drummer. Guy catches it all over his torso and blood spews like a human sprinkler system. Shots ring out in B's direction and he takes one in the arm before he can tuck into a roll. A searing rod of pain, burns through his left shoulder. Sight of blood. Gritting teeth.

"Ready for the main event Johnson!" Said Santiago. "How's it feel to be the bitch?!"

B's rifle was too far away and probably useless having been hit as well. Embrace the pain. Take it inside you and dissolve it. B' said to himself. "I ain't your sparing partner or some model you can cut up! I am your demolition man!"

Distraction. B' rifled through the grenades strapped to his chest and found the one he was looking for. It was labeled "Mass grenade. Non explosive." B' armed it and chucked it in the direction of Santiago's voice then started counting. Santiago heard something knock off the ceiling and rolling against a wall. As soon as the grenade stops it starts to vibrate. Its cylindrical casing and fizzles to reveal a porous yellow substance that begins to grow rapidly. It grew like an explosion. Quadrupling in size every sixteenth of a second, the mass of pale-yellow, foam-goop converted air, dust particles and carpet into a massive, continuously expanding form that moved furniture and buckled walls. Santiago shot at it to no avail as sidestepping the mass hurling towards him. Time to float and Santiago did somersaults on top of the moving furniture. B' had already skipped towards the staircase and was taking them two at a time.

Heart racing. Blood pumping. Air gulping. B' rounded the stairs and shouldered the door to the next floor. It was near pitch black. The only light from outside come laden with doom and menace. The bombing in the distance had cease and the night was eerily quiet. "Run for a time" B' thought to himself. The pain was stabilizing and he withdrew two large handguns from his vest. Safeties off. The pain fueled his focus. "Right." The locator on his gauntlet was dead and he squatted with his back to a desk, his guns crossed over his chest as he inhaled. "Creak!" B' leapt into the air, doing a backwards somersault the instant before the desk blew apart. Santiago had taken the stairs just after he did and was coming. B' fired in mid-somersault in Santiago's general direction and landed on an office chair. The chair—its wheels intact—began moving backwards catapulted by the force of the recoil of B's landing, guns blaring sun spit. The chair approached an open window—its glass blown out—and B' jetted at the last moment, rolling for the floor, continuously firing. Bullets out. Pushing the button he sent empty magazines to the floor. Reload. "Time for random" said B', knee up, grenades thrown not knowing what they were, or could do. He took off in a crouch running down a hall towards an exit. Explosions behind him. Death dance. Fireball caught the stairwell door and cleaved it off, hurling it like a knife at the wall. Steel cutting concrete. B' ran-fell down flight after flight, as things fell out of his vest. Righting himself he knew he was on a lower floor and sensed it was more bombed out than the upper floors.

Wind swept dust through the air as much of it fell through the cracks in the ceiling. B' could see something he had missed before. A deep chasm in the center of the building that ranged vertically for many floors. A dead bogie lay at it base, B' must have been on the second or third floor. He could smell burning hair, flesh and concrete—death.

Checking himself, he realized he was weaponless, no ammo, no grenades. Nothing left but what was in his guns. Shit. Roll to the dead guy. B' thought and made like a cheetah on the prowl, back hunched, arms outstretched—coiled menace. Just then, Santiago repels down a cable through the wide mouth of the chasm, his left side and shoulder bloodied by some shrapnel. He was in the way of the dead perp and B' had to avoid his aim. Santiago fires, misses and B' rolls behind some office furniture. B' looks about and sees nothing he can use. Heard Santiago hit floor and release the cable. Santiago had ammo and decides to use it. He fires in B's direction, obliterated furniture, slicing a line closer and closer towards B'. B' cornered, sits still as pieces of furniture splinter*shat* around him. Santiago 's arms were like the pistons of the Devil's auto engine and heat wafts in the air. Santiago yells, "Fuckyoufuckyou—u!!!" as he steps forward. B' makes like a snail. Santiago clicks on empty and B' leaps, twisting in the air. Bullets fly towards Santiago who has already started to cartwheel-roll behind a column. B' was out. He chucks his guns like used condoms and leaps onto a desk. Santiago stood and did the same. B' unhooks his vest and all extraneous regalia. Santiago withdraws his nodachi sword and holding it behind his back as he walks into the open. A gust of wind kicks up some dust that washes over them, B' snapped his neck, measures the distance from him to Santiago then super-human leapt-kicked. Santiago ducks, turns and swings at B' who parries with the steel shank of his forearm gauntlet. Tuck roll. No time. Santiago on him—slashing. B' moves through the air to avoid the onslaught. Santiago comes at him and B' parries with his arm gauntlets—sparks eating air. B' catches Santiago's chin with a bitchslap toe kick that sends him backsetpping then turns and runs. Santiago shook it off, doing some fancy sword shit in the air to say he was bad and that it didn't hurt. B' grabs the very long handle of the nodachi off the dead guy and slowly withdraws it from its sheathe—double withdrawing and inserting it to tantalize. Then B' does some fancyass sword shit of his own kicking up dust as he touches the tip of the sword to the floor. They circle each other.

"Santiago, know where I'm going right after this bout? Your home country Chile. Seen your little sister. She's hot and I'm going to date her, or maybe I'll just fuck the bitch." Santiago screams in wrath and charges. They go at each other with biblical intent. Each parry an attack, each attach a parry. Looking for an opening. They both employ Iai, a *"method of combat"* involving drawing and cutting like karate strokes, while kicking and punching. Evenly

Wired for Chaos

matched—their fight is like a rabid ferocious dance meant to make the Gods jealous. Head butt, kick, push, swing—B' with a bloody lip. Santiago leaps, running up a mountain of air and B' leapt to meet him, both slashing at the apex—cockfight. Touching ground B' discovers a long laceration across his stomach and ribs—pain searing. Santiago advances and leaps followed by B' and again they meet, nodachis clash and one lacerates. They land and slowly rise, erect and at the ready. B' looks at his bloodied midsection, then at Santiago and falls to the ground dead. The moment seems to freeze and stretch past Willy in LA, Ivan in NYC, Bill, Leroy, Ido—millions of headriders…everyone is rapt watching the dust Brice's body had displaced settle.

IVAN'S CAR BROADWAY JUST BELOW 125TH STREET, UPTOWN SIDE

Ivan's phone rang and he fumbled to disconnect his PDA viewer and answer it. Niemöller voice was clear and matter of fact, "Just below 125th Street next to a Mexican Restaurant you will see a sign that reads the Grant Houses Health Center. Follow the cement path to the entrance—it will be on your right. At the top of the door there will be a silver tab. Turn it once to the right, then insert it back between the door and doorframe. The keypad lock combination is 5, 4, 2. Once you are inside look at the floor on your lower left, you will find a black device with metal canisters attached. Turn the center dial to "arm" this will disarm the device. Jimmy is down the hall, last room on the right behind the door that is bolted shut."

Ivan says, "Da." And Niemöller hangs up. "Okay. Ready, listen, ready to go," says Ivan pressing a button on his phone. Serge turns the ignition key and the car starts. "Turn fucking car off fucking idiot!"

"Said let's go!"

"Didn't say start car! Tink', said drive up here to sit then drive somewhere else?!"

"Thought…"

"Don't tink'! Listen!"

25 BROAD STREET, MANHATTAN

Niemöller savored the moment. Just as he was about to turn his set off, something miraculous happens. The program continues as if it had never ended. B' and Santiago were still fighting and B' was not injured. Disbelief came as a cranial frown. Checking his set everything seemed to be working, "What the fuck!?" he thought. "Tricked—gotta' call Ivan back" he said to himself. Just then the phone rang.

"What?!"

"Dis' Ivan…"

"Ivan listen, about Jimmy…"

"Fuck Jimmy. Got something better. Bigger."

"I don't understand."

"Been working on…" and their conversation was interrupted by two beeps.

"Wus' dat'?"

"Ah! My phone. Battery dead. Call me back. Give you Serge's number. 6—656.234.0031 got it?"

"Yeah said Niemöller."

"Call me right back but use secured landline. Make very secret. Something to show you."

"What?"

"Found Brice's money."

This was strange but maybe exceptionally strange in its opportunity. He thought for a second before acting. Ivan is the mob. The mob steals. If he had in fact been played it didn't matter, B' might have attempted to agree to Niemöller's deal thinking to trick him, but Ivan had decided to forgo Jimmy. Now B' might win the match but lose his brother. He might have to live with his guilt, but Ivan had a piece of cake for him. Yes. It felt good in a bad way. Niemöller hopped from his chair and put the Santiago-Brice match on mute, switched on his deck, picked up the bubble interface and slid into the fiber hammock chair. The chair is suspended from the ceiling and gives the user the impression of being weightless. The bubble interface is the size of a volleyball and clear. It is covered by many ergonomically correct indentations that Niemöller could use to control programs at a rapid pace.

He begins to tap commands that brings the large wall screen up and goes immediately to the Argentinean phone exchange. While there, in rapid succession he routes the call to Ivan through the phone exchange of 36 countries, encrypted it and set in leap protocols that would allow his call to jump from shared line, to shared line, without callers hearing their conversation. Tap. Tap. Ring. Ivan answered.

"Da."

"You saw what I saw?"

"Yes. He cheated. Probably got Sony to fake us out and release Jimmy. Not work."

"What do you mean you found his money?"

"Johnson not keep most of money in US bank or even off-shore account. Keep money in private-equity investment firm called Strong Central American Development Fund bullshit out of Belize. Say they buy sell private companies or their divisions. Very private. Very secret. Also have many other "members of board" wit' funds allocated—dey' say for manufacturing, offshore oil drilling—all bullshit. My guy found it and can get in front door but can't get past lock. Maybe you know hacker can do this?"

Niemöller smiled at Ivan's transparent attempt to hook him. "Why would you want to fuck with something like that?"

"Why wouldn't I? Tink'. Foreign country—Belize got no army, police gonna' come get me in Queenzs'? Money there, not supposed to be there. Who gonna' call international polize'. They get robbed, stink, curse, fart themselves, you care? I care? We not talking about stealing all just Johnson's money. We take all."

"How much is…"

"2.5 billion." A beat. "I split with you 60/40."

"I don't know."

"I find somebody else…"

"Wait, let me see it."

"You InSpace?"

"Of course." Says Niemöller dawning a pair of VR glasses and leaning back.

FLUTTER.

"Patch you in my guy's connection. Should be coming up now."

Niemöller's field of vision is filled by eight massive multi-colored neon constructs in a black vacuum.

"See it?" Said Ivan.

"Yeah but what is it?"

"Guy says 'dey Kruger locks."

"Kruger locks, I've heard of them, but never seen anything like…them. You could get old looking for a hole here."

The locks are the equivalent in size to large SUVs to Niemöller and they move with grace and beauty. Three-dimensional shapes inside of three-dimensional shapes, rotated phasing in and out, changing in rapid succession. Normal locks were static but these are dynamic and constantly change. Polygons, pyramids, cylinders all phased in, rotated and phased out, only to be replaced by a different shape a moment later, its very nature being continuously rewritten.

Niemöller instinctively moves to open one of his many hack programs but stops when he realizes the futility. "You can't guess or manufacture a key to a lock that keeps changing." He had been told by a friend, over beer in a dank bar one evening upon first hearing of the Krugers.

"You find a way in here?" said Ivan.

"The only way to get in is to get the source code for the key and then I'm not even sure if that will work. Who knows what the presets are. I don't know if you can open one at a time, all together, or at only specific times—but why eight? One should be enough. One is fucking tough enough. These guys are already covert in Belize, why max it out? Must have cost so fucking much. I heard only banks and governmental institutions could be the clients for Kruger Company anyway."

"What are you doing?" asked Ivan.

"I want a different view," and the constructs shifted to a 90° where Niemöller could see their tails descend into a near limitless void, then veer off in different directions. "Strange," said Niemöller who switched back to the original view. One particular lock drew his attention. He looked into it and became momentarily transfixed. It w-a-s hypn-o-t-i-z-ing and then a high-pitched sound arose piercing his ear canal making him wince.

WHITE FLASH…

Niemöller was eight years old and seated in the passenger seat of his father's car with his father a the wheel. It was a beatific summer day and they were driving to their house upstate.

"Familiar Joseph?" Said the father rubbing the boy's head. "This has been devised and constructed with great accuracy."

Niemöller was speechless. His father was just as he had remembered him, wearing the same green flannel shirt and worn jeans as the day he died in the auto accident.

His father said, "Every thing in your world is made of dissimilar parts that begin, wear out, end, ebb and flow. The successful individuals are the greatest manipulators. Skill, determination, perseverance, intellect—the ability to suffer through constant incalculable rejection or failure are all part of the process, but true failure can come about by a confluence of miscalculation and hubris." As he spoke the auto accelerated. "You know what you have done wrong don't you Joseph?"

Niemöller shook his head, becoming increasingly disturbed he was paralyzed. Trees flash by.

"Yes you do. Yes you do. No?" shaking his head and glancing down the road. "You have been a very naughty boy. You have interfered with systems that do not concern you. You have taken it upon yourself to act as some sort of Old Testament God full of wrath and rules with no forgiveness. You have been bitter and sick with self-loathing for far too long. You attempt to control information as a conduit to controlling your destiny. The fear is that you will never be in control and so you placate yourself by making decisions for others that do n-o-t concern you."

"This is not real. You are not my father—fuck out of here." Says Niemöller struggling to get out of the car.

His father says, "Out?!" yelling over the racing engine. "Okay! Out!" and the car veers off the on ramp onto a small bridge. The front of the car connects with a steel strut and wraps around it. *SCREECHCRASHBEND!* Niemöller's father is instantly catapulted, head first through the windshield in a mass of blood tipped glass past a defective safety bag. Niemöller's safety bag deploys and he is saved....

FLIP TO.

In a large white expanse. Niemöller finds himself in a room with no doors or windows covered with pristine marble tiles. The white ceiling emanates a warm light and he has to avert his eyes. Niemöller turns and is startled by an adult copy of himself dressed as an English dandy, in a tailor made suit that is slightly tight, wearing a British bowler hat.

"Ivan what the fuck are you doing?!"

"My name is not Ivan. It is Gila." Said the dandy Niemöller.

"Gee-la?"

"G-i-la and this is where you have arrived."

"What..."

"Don't do that." Said Gila in a firm voice.

Wired for Chaos

278

In real time Niemöller was trying to disconnect from his deck, but could not raise his hands or arms. He was frozen. "Or rather don't bother trying. You are mine. There is no time to explain the how. But we have little time." Said the dandy Niemöller circling the sweating one. "You want to run, I know, but you also want me to reveal more of the why to you, but as you reflect—and you will have a great deal of quiet time to reflect—I will now reveal the what."

"What?"

FLIP.

Niemöller was now seated in his office chair holding his bubble, in the center of the white expanse with Gila absent and surrounded by the eight Krugers. "You were most astute to question, the need for eight locks." Said Gila now in his own disembodied voice. "But I already had you by then." We are not in Belize. We are not in New York City. We are *transdermal.* Transportative consciousness without the need for moving things encased in skin. Everywhere and nowhere, it and I are one. Don't worry, you will have much time to study Sartre."

A long beat.

"These locks." Said Gila. "Although real, are representations I have constructed for your understanding. You, as a sentient being need to see order, in shape and form where it would be incalculable to read and interpret millions of equations each second, but I have been dishonest with you, not so much about their nature as much as their state." The locks all blinked red and the tumbler shapes spun rapidly and blinked at a blinding speed. "There. This is their true current state. I am leaving sound effects out because as you and I both know, there is no *real* sound InSpace. But, here. Let me make this picture clearer." Just then the images of the locks were replaced by the corporate logos of Citigroup Inc., Goldman Sachs, USB Warberg, JP Morgan Chase, Credit Suisse, Bank of America, HSBC, Bank One. Various warnings littered the areas around the logos with language that stated, "Warning. You are in direct violation of the Securities and Exchange…Cease any and all inappropriate attempts to gain access to our systems…Federal authorities have been alerted and dispatched… Violation…Subject to criminal prosecution under the Computer Fraud and Abuse Act of 1986 and Title 18 U.S.C. Sec.1001 and 1030…." Blinking in incessant black and red.

"It seems that the for the past 45 minutes you have been attacking the systems of these banks, which set off a series of alarms at The Financial Services Information Sharing and Analysis Center in northern Virginia, which alerted the on duty officers on the 23rd. Floor of the Federal Bureau of Investigation at 26 Federal Plaza. They are a very responsive group of individuals who take their jobs exceedingly seriously. Would you like to see?" The bank logos disappeared and were replaced by several close-circuit monitors blown super large. They showed Niemöller's building surrounded by members of the FBI and NYPD. One monitor showed the Feds at the security desk, enlisting the help of the night watchman who grabbed a thick set of keys. They turned and jogged down the hall towards the elevators and stairwell. They were swarming in from all directions and Niemöller twitched violently unable to free himself.

"They will be here soon and all traces of me will have evaporated. I assure you that their quest for you began over a year ago—when Jimmy first took interest in you and I having peppered your hard-drives with the dated trace logs of some of the most reprehensible electronic attacks. My favorite is the one on the Israel National Bank in April with the handle Marjan The Lion, or the Canadian Stock Exchange collapse as Nevam—Maven in reverse, how pedestrian. Many of these hackers are either known or work for me from time to time and they will appreciate your sacrifice for their continued freedom…

BANG! BANG! BANG! Was the knock at the door. "Joseph Niemöller open up! This is the FBI. We have a warrant for your arrest!" *BANG! BANG! BANG!*

I even made you the founder of a child pornography ring known as the Johnny Short-pants Chasers—very prestigious among the unrepentant.

Keys were heard, being fitted into the lock in Niemöller's door.

"And now you too will be famous—at last your secret goal attained, though not the way you wished." And Gila was gone.

FLUTTER.

Niemöller could once again move and he slowly took his glasses off and pushed his bubble to the floor where it broke. Moving slowly and deliberately he reached over his desk straining and stretching to extend his reach. Just then the lock turned and the door opened. The FBI agents flew in like navy birds of prey, their guns drawn and they screamed at him, "Freeze! Federal Agents! Freeze!" But Niemöller ignored them and having retrieved his British bowler placed it on his head, sat back and regained the composure of a statue.

FLIP TO: THE SIMULTANEOUS MOMENT AT THE GRANT HOUSING PROJECTS, 125TH STREET AND BROADWAY MOMENTS EARLIER

Ivan was seated in the back of his car listening to Niemöller. "Turn the center dial to "arm" this will disarm the device. Jimmy is down the hall last room on the right behind the door that is bolted shut."

Ivan says, "Da." And Niemöller hangs up. "Okay. Ready, listen, ready to go," says Ivan pressing a button on his phone. Serge turns the ignition key and the car starts. "Turn fucking car off fucking idiot!"

"Said let's go!"

"Didn't say start car! Tink', said drive up here to sit then drive somewhere else?!"

"Thought…"

"Don't tink'! Listen!"

"Okay boss. Okay."

"Listen. We walk down 'dat alley get Jimmy, go to Queens, have dinner. Da?!"

"Da! Of course Da!" And with that three car doors open. Serge steps into the street, buttons his Italian sports coat to conceal his gun and checks to see if his fly is closed. Bruno stands aside and waits for Ivan who is distracted by Niemöller's instructions. The night was frigid and their breath proceeds them.

Four cars behind, Camacho mashed out his cig' and hurriedly rifled through his glove compartment. "Got it." He retrieved two handcuffs and threw them into his coat pocket to make three total and quickly exited the car. Once on the pavement, he stops to tie the lace on his boots and spies the three Russian-Americans heading down a dark alley behind one of the Grant Housing Projects buildings. Stepping like a New Yorker on the way to somewhere but in no rush, Camacho walked in their direction the moment they passed behind the building. "Slow down," Camacho told himself. "These guys don't know this 'hood an' they're not on a timetable." He walked slower taking long drags on his cig'. Walking past the entrance to the alley immediately adjacent to a scrappy Mexican restaurant, Camacho gleaned the three out of the corner of his eye at a dark doorway and kept walking. He stopped and checked out the scene inside the restaurant with his eyes as his mind counted down. Two painfully long minutes passed and Camacho edged around the corner with a new cig' in his mouth. Through the iron fence and around the garbage cans Camacho could see the three had disappeared, probably into the doorway. Camacho turned and walked down the cement path.

FLIP TO: THE SIMULTANEOUS MOMENT SOMEWHERE IN QUEENS

Ring. Ring. "Nine-one-one operator. What is the nature of the emergency?"

"Ivan Bykov," a voice says in Russian tinged English. "Ivan Bykov kidnapped Jimmy Johnson—Brice Johnson's brother holding him ransom. At 'dis very minute 'dey are moving him from hiding place—below 125th Street in Grant Houses Health Center—going to kill boy and…."

FLIP TO: THE SIMULTANEOUS MOMENT AT THE GRANT HOUSING PROJECTS

"Stupid fuckin' Russians," said Camacho. "All three in. You never 'all' go in. You always leave one asshole to watch your back so you don't have any surprises wen' you're ready to jet." He passed the doorway not even trying to catch a glimpse out of the corner of his eye. "Don't underestimate fools. They usually shoot first and scream later. Best thing is to get behind them, surprise their ass and bust a cap for respect." Camacho was not happy with the layout of the area. The cement path split into three and lead in a round about way to the main entrance of one of the buildings built by rich white men to warehouse poor black people in a self perpetuating cycle of despair and poverty. The other direction was towards 125th Street and lots of street lights. The third was his choice, flush with the building they were in but just a little too far away for his liking but could not be helped. He would just have to be quick on the up when they came out, the second after they looked around to spy that the coast was clear. Bet.

Camacho ditched the cig' and took out matching Glocks, offed the safeties and placed each into his deep coat pockets, fingers on the triggers. "Flatten," he told himself, "Control your breathing so you don't give your location away…they are not expecting you…when you see them hold your breath, wait for the look your way and as soon as they start up the path towards their car run up behind them. Think about Bermuda, the days on the beach and the cinnamon women." His neck and shoulder muscles tensed, he began to amp with street juice and squeezed the handles of the Glocks like they were twin cocks ready to rock. Almost one with the wall and ready to maul, Camacho could hardly contain himself, his eyes focused like a telescope focused on a star light years away. Street sounds and a small child getting a whipping tin the distance. Time meant nothing. He neither egged it on, running up the ramp of impatience, or receded into spring laden cotton, willing sleep to visit him. He withdrew his shield from underneath his coat and let it hang around his neck for the world to see that he was the man.

Movement. Saw their breath before he saw them and chose to retreat behind the corner of the brick shit house. He would judge the correct moment. It was usually one more than you wanted it to be especially when you thought you were in the driver's seat. Wait he told himself. Hold your breath and peer around the corner. They would have to lift little Jimmy out and close the door behind them. Peeking, just the right eye, he saw them. The look they had given around was cursory at best. They were walking up the path, their backs to him and he waited two breaths and followed them. Steps like heart beats quickened and he wind ruffled the shell of his hooded, navy, micro fiber jacket.

Up ahead flashing lights appear reflected on the side of the Mexican Restaurant. "Shit!" says Camacho. Ivan and his boys stops and several NYPD appear in front of them with their guns drawn just past the point where the path curved at a 45° angle south. A number One train flies south into the 125th Station and sparks fly up from the tracks illuminating the Projects like lightening. Camacho sense movement behind him and he turns quickly to see several uniformed officers and a few in plain clothes, converge on the path from two directions. Many of the officers are not wearing coats that suggests they had run out of the 26th Precinct two blocks away once the call came in. Camacho puts the Glock in his left hand into his coat and held up his shield for the cops behind him to see. Then continued towards Ivan. "Freeze! Freeze! Put you guns down! Drop your weapons! Drop them now!" Ivan and his boys start to run towards Camacho, then freeze as they see all the cops. Camacho yells, "This is my collar!" to the cops and turns back to Ivan withdrawing the second Glock.

"Put you guns down! Drop your weapons!"

Serge, turns to the cops and draws his gun to fire at the cops on the Broadway side of the path. They scream, "Drop your weapons!" and four of the officers open fire and riddled his torso with bullets. Ivan backs up, trips and falls on his ass. Bruno put up his hands and Jimmy falls to the ground.

A cop yells, "Get on the ground! Get on the ground now! Get down!" and as Bruno complies, first kneeling, cops raced to apprehend him.

Behind Camacho a plainclothes detective yells, "Put your guns down now!" and Camacho gives him a look of disgust.

"I'm a fucking cop!"

"We know who you are Detective Camacho! Now place your guns on the ground!"

Camacho shoots him an expression of incredulity. "What?! *They* are kidnappers and this is my...."

"You are wanted for questioning concerning the murder of Olga Eriksson and being an accessory to this kidnapping!"

Camacho's expression was one of disbelief then recognition. He had her head and hands in separate boxes in his car just down the street. He looked at the filthy cement just in front of his boots and becomes deaf to the shouting of the police. Both hands are at his sides and filled with metal. He raises his head slowly not seeing them fan out in two wide arcs on either side of him. He could see the faces of children, men and women peering down at him from their windows. While some were frightened, others seemed to want a show. He now inhabited a clear gelatinous world that muffled his senses and slows his movements but not his resolve. Camacho raises both guns pressing the barrels into the soft area under his jaw and pulls both triggers. The back of his head exploded jerking his body off the ground and backwards against the chain link fence.

In the sky, far above them a commercial jetliner rose having just departed from LaGuardia and headed for a warmer place with pristine beaches.

Moments later all money in Camacho's Bermuda account, vanishes sucked back the way it came.

FLIP TO: SEVERAL MOMENTS AGO INSPACE, THE SANTIAGO-JOHNSON MATCH

"You know you my bitch! You just another piece of Sushi to me!" B' does some fancyass sword shit of his own and kicks up dust. Circle. Size-up. Onit.

Santiago is pounding on Brice as if he is wielding a hammer and not a sword. Head butt, kick, push, swing—B' with a bloody lip retreating, hedging. It appears as if he is trying to wear Santiago down. They fought into a decimated office littered with overturned furniture and broken glass. Santiago came at B' trying to behead him with nearly each blow and the two move towards a gaping floor to ceiling hole that once housed glass. Just then B' sees what he has been waiting for. In the distance and over Santiago's right shoulder, a green light strobes and fades away. It was the predetermined signal from Chuck that Jimmy was now free and Niemöller neutralized. B' began to laugh out loud which unnerves Santiago, freezing him in his tracks. B' erupts with laughter then raises his sword, cocks his neck and says, "My turn." And advances. He comes at Santiago with a renewed fury and summons the anxiety he has endured over the past three days to act as the fuel for his engine of merciless wrath. Nothing mattered because nothing was at stake. The no holds barred thing was incidental and losing was out of the question. What amped him was the unmitigated gall of Santiago in thinking that he could win. That he could be bested—the thought twisting from absurdity to insult to Cobra-snap, furious assault. Santiago lost his footing on some cables and began to trip when a missile lands on their level of the building and explodes. The shockwave catapults the two out the open window and onto a parked bus on the street one floor below. Stunned, they each rolled off the bus's roof and barely right themselves by the time two more explosions tear at the ravage building. They both run for the open space of the grassy expanse in front of the Parliament building and Santiago tackles Brice to the ground. Punching or kicking was useless B' thought, knowing Santiago to be the superior grappler and before he knew it Santiago has run up his back like a horny male crab ready to mount its mate. B' was in a chokehold. Santiago has his left arm around B's neck and is squeezing—his full weight on him. B' bucks and then flips on to Santiago's back but he holds fast. B' grimaces as explosions littered the area. One shell takes out a water main and the ground erupts with water, turning dirt to mud. B'—knowing enough to avoid panic, was searching for a way out but Santiago is relentless, every nudge is met with an avoiding squirm. Santiago's right hand catches B's chin and begins to twist it to the right—"He is trying to break my neck!" thinks B' to his multitude of discorporate selves.

"Kill me! No! Fuck you!" B' amped and the veins in his neck and forehead pulse. He raises his left arm and shoots his elbow into Santiago's side with all his might, but Santiago is rock to his hammer. He twists and squirmed but the grip tightens still. Reaching for Santiago's head seems futile since he keeps crawling on his shoulder blades across the muddy expanse, the sky aglow with illuminated ferrite smoke. B'—his left leg between Santiago's—pivots onto his right leg then quickly jack hammers his left heel into Santiago's crotch. Even with a cup he would feel it. He quickly reaches for Santiago's head and gouges his right eye with his right hand. Convulse. Contort. Anguish. And B' was free. He rolls away holding his throat, as Santiago twists onto into his side in a fetal-girlyboy position. B' leaps up suppressing the urge to cough and grabs a lung of air as he kicks Santiago missing his guts for a knee. Second time around B' repositions and catches Santiago full on and felt the plastic cave. B' staggers in a downpour of water, slipping on the mud as he surveys the scene gasping.

"Want to fuck me Ido!? Com'on down! [in Japanese] I challenge you! In front of the world! Something you could never do! You are not worthy to be on my stage! Eh?" The tower they had been jettisoned from only moments earlier was buckling under the weight of so many direct hits, its steel skeleton twistbending—then it happened—B' had a syn' episode. Out of nowhere—it had never happened before InSpace—the sound of the twisting metal converted to yellow cones shooting at his cheeks and obliterating his vision. Crashing shards of concrete registered as violet polygons that felt like sandy sponges running up against his neck and chest and it hurt.

"No."

His world is closing in. He staggers knowing the full sweep of his predicament. Santiago is recuperating while B's senses are unhinged—whites mixing with colors in the human washing machine of the senses. Santiago punches him in the right kidney, kicks B' in the right knee, then gives him a brutal karate chop to the neck. B' is on his knees and reeling. Forms race towards his face obliterating his vision. A blow to his jaw sends volumes of pain cascading through his marrow. The building keeps buckling and in the distance someone is laughing.

Santiago is mouthing something unintelligible in Spanish under his breath through the spit and artificial rain seethes like a boiling kettle angry for notice, as B' puts his hands up in a feeble attempt to defend himself. Hit. Hit. Blow. Strike. Fist to head. Foot to head—B' wavers like a plaything about to be retired. Santiago delivers a roundhouse kick, sending saliva flying. B' doesn't notice his face hitting the ground. Everything *c-e-a-s-e-s*. Santiago approaches, grabs B's collar and begins to drill his head with a fist for the oil that was blood.

WAKE

B' is horizontal on a table in his locker room at the arena and smells Bill's aftershave. He is attending to his wounds and B' could feel the blood pumping beneath the swollen parts of his head.

"Took a bad beating there B'boy. Real bad beating. Good thing you got that asshole off your neck. Don't know what the fuck you were thinking turning around and yelling shit, instead of finishing him off."

"Did you see the what I saw?"

"Wha'? Saw you get your ass kicked."

"No. No. The syn'. I had an episode—oh, you don't know…." And B' fell asleep.

AN HOUR LATER.

B' is dressed and walking to the limo with a frozen gel pack held to his face. Thankfully, he had slept through the press conference and they were headed out the back door. The limo driver had been instructed to pull the car into the loading dock so B' would not have to suffer through another throng of humanity. The swagger was gone. So was the disembodied inability to concentrate on the moment. B' feels like city road kill and he desperately wants to rest. As he enters the car he finds himself moving like an old man afraid that his hip would break at any moment. Sitting back he reminds himself that Jimmy was free and suddenly thought of his dog for the first time in days. Who has been taking care of his best friend? His assistant? Somebody must have—he was sure. He wanted to pat Stalin's head, stroke his tummy and rub noses with him. He might just shake his tail off by shaking his hinny so hard and so fast. Then, as the limo pulled out B' began to relax for the first time in days.

6TH FLOOR, HOTEL AMELIA COBIA

B', Bill and a couple of the boys step off the elevator and B' turns to Bill. "I'm going to crash for a couple of hours. Tell the pilot we're going to jet when I get up."

"What? You wanna' leave paradise?"

"I could leave your ass here—but I'm going home. Make sure Stanford iz' doing his job alright. Everything in New York should be cleared up with the cops but I want him to double check 'an meet me at the airport."

"Okay. I'll tell him. I'll tell him."

As soon as B' touches the doorknob it reads and approves his finger prints and unlocked the door. "Wake me in two alright?"

"Yup." Said Bill, then he turned to Leroy, "I'm going to pack then head to the bar for a bye bye kissey kissey." And everyone parts ways. No one notices the housekeeping cart and small man in a hotel uniform who is busily scanning his PDA.

B' enters his suite and immediately walked towards the bed and was about to pull the covers down when he saw a small Sony deck laying on it. As he bent to pick it up it surprised him when it *RANG*. B' picks up the long, clear fiber optic cable and plugs it into his jack.

FLUTTER.

B' was naked and had been transported to a verdant grass field in the middle of nowhere on a starry night.

"It is unfortunate that you probably lack the ability to describe pain to me or I the ability to appreciate it." Said the sky.

"Chuck," said B' "Called to gloat or give me sympathy?"

"Neither."

"I'm disappointed."

"My job is done."

"Figures. Kept your word. Got me an' and Jimmy out. Put in a call to him at Bellevue-good that it's nothing serious." Said B' feeling for the bed then sitting and wincing in pain. "So now are you going to tell me..." Holding his right ribcage and laying on the grass.

"What? The obvious? The who and the why? I'm sure you can guess."

"Lets se-e. Who would have a vested interest in insuring that I fight Santiago—ah, Sony? Yes. Ido? Positively."

"Correct." Said the clouds forming overhead and swirling.

"The dealer in Japan was a ruse to entice Jimmy into buying you." Rolling onto his stomach. "The best bug is a bug out in the open even better if you placed it there yourself. Swift. I'm not sure that you are an A.I. though. You might be some short, dickless, shit stuck in a windowless office working for like no money and a promise." Trying to get a rise out of him.

Wired for Chaos

"I assure you, I am an A.I."

"That sucks. Actually, you suck. You did some amazing shit, but you are bound by code to working for some suits that keep you chained up like a dog."

"You can't wound me B'." The wind hissed.

"Bet you can't even lick your own balls without permission."

B' grunted and suddenly felt stiff and immobilized. The tingling sensation he mistook for the muscles in his upper back and shoulders, as falling asleep, deepens and spreads throughout his body. He is completely paralyzed except for a few muscles in his face, fingers and toes. "I-I...."

"You are experiencing the progressive paralysis of the botulinum toxin and curare cocktail being released into your system from the jack we installed in you."

"How?" B' grimaces and remembers Doctor Mohammed telling him about the "hidden" portion of the jack Sony had installed. "Those fucking bastards..." B' says with a stiff clenched jaw.

"You will die of asphyxia in approximately twenty minutes."

"Why!?"

"We wish to cease our relationship with you and..."

"They'll autopsy..."

"We will bribe the doctor, nurses and authorities if need be—this is Cuba after all..."

"Why?" anger in his eyes.

"I have surmised that this must be a particularly horrid form of death. It seems similar to drowning slowly all while being completely aware of your own helplessness and...."

"Why!?"

"You became an embarrassment. You had everything, yet you were ungrateful, rude and disrespectful. No single player is more important than the game, Brice Johnson."

"Fuck you! Fuck you! It was all about money! It's always about money."

"That too, of course. Our employee's children can't line up to buy the latest games if their parents are unemployed because of layoffs brought about by deflated earnings. We are responsible for tens of thousands of lives and we were not sure what you were going to say or do next."

B' began to struggle then strain to move his limbs as sweat appeared on his forehead, "So you're killing me?! You couldn't just fire me? You faked my defeat to Santiago shouldn't that be enough?! You could have ended it right there—companies screw employees with loopholes in contracts all the time...."

"You will be an example to the others. It was easy to orchestrate once we initiating a syn' episode giving Santiago..."

"You know?! How?"

"...Who was losing the opportunity..."

Wired for Chaos

"How? How did you even know I had…"

"We blackmailed Dr. Mohammed. Now the pictures of him and the prostitute will not be shown to his wife. We used the jack to trick your system into producing small doses of ludiomil and maprotiline, norepinephrine reuptake blockers over the past few days to regulate your Synestesia. You and Willy would have had an additional hurdle without it."

"Jus' keep me out of trouble 'til you could beat me in front of the world."

"Defeating you was just part of the outcome we preordained. We meant to humiliate you. To demoralize you in front of the world on a far more molecular level than Niemöller could ever of dreamed but don't worry, I've dealt with him. You see a fake loss or even an honest loss that came too easily would have been written off by your fans and the media as a ploy to free Jimmy. Well, we allowed for that by creating fake footage of your defeat for the North American audience only, then quickly resumed real-time broadcast. But it was Ido's insistence that lead to your real beating at Santiago's hands, so the world could know what happens to insolent upstarts. Unfortunately, he did not kill you."

"I would have taken the pink slip you fuck! Fuck you into the next millennia!"

"Predictable. Even in defeat you are incapable of being contrite. Pity."

"Fuckyoufuckyou—not dying like this!" Spitting.

"You are already dead. In a few minutes you will suffer convulsions of all voluntary muscles, twitching, followed by tetanus, violent changes in blood pressure and spasmodic respiration."

"Kick your ass..!" struggling.

"With your prowess you could have had a long and rewarding career. For all your macho hubris you were a very good player while you lasted but then again you are all fallible are you not?"

"Chuck…" B' was slurring his speech now and drooling. "Chuck, Gila-whatever your name is, I want you to know something! I won! I won you…!"

"No. *You* defeated yourself."

FLUTTER REAL.

B' was on the bed and staring at the comforter covered in green palms. The small man in a hotel uniform enters and quietly picks up the deck housing Gila. Brice's eyes widen sensing someone in the room but cannot see him. "The fuck?! Who…?" A moment later the door closes.

"They took him. I'm dead? He won. He killed me. This can't be happening. It'll be too late when my guys knock on the door to get me. I can't go out like this. Killed me 'cause…." B's face was covered in sweat and he trembled from the inside out.

His mind raced and remembers Rodney asking him to apologize to the execs at Sony. His voice repeating "…Apologize—ask forgiveness, make nice nice, Kumbuya..." over and over in his head. B' thought of the sportscaster who called him arrogant and grimaced when he spoke of him. He remembered Cyrus the performance artist ranting as Brice and said, "That's what they thought of me? That I was arrogant? Bad? Mean..." Then the thought that resurfaced from time to time crystallized. That he had been the arrogant asshole they said he was, "I was me. I was a fool to goad Sony but I didn't care—fukk—uk—uk...." His body began to convulse violently and his eyes widened, rolling backwards. He started to hyperventilate and struggled to breathe. His body trembled and his breathing became shallow as he drooled on the comforter and died. His eyes remained open and pointed in the direction of the window to a clear sky and another perfect night in Havana.

Life Over

Author's Acknowledgements

For Simone, thanks for everything...

Members the Dark Body Writer's Collective writer's workshop:
Bridgette M. Davis, professor of Journalism at Baruch College, calm voice,
mother-earth-energy-giver, Writer-Director of independent film NAKED
ACTS 1999, author SHIFTING THROUGH NEUTRAL
Leon Wynter, Wall Street Journal reporter, National Public Radio
correspondent, navel gazer, Professor and author of AMERICAN SKIN.
E.B. Baisden: THE FEVER OF THE YEARS New York, Caribbean Research
Center Press, 1990, brilliant writer who can't get out of his own way, did I
mention that he is a "brilliant writer."
Jake Ann Jones, fierce actress NAKED ACTS and playwright, sweet inside
and out.
David Tager, professor, give us more David.
Michel Marriott, reporter for The New York Times, Nieman Fellow, author
HEADZ, a giving soul and enthusiastic multi-tasker with limitless energy—
much thanks brother M2.
Esther Iverem, author of THE TIME: PORTRAIT OF A JOURNEY HOME
and founder of www.SeeingBlack.com.

None of this, none of this book would have been possible without your
guidance and direction over the years. Thanks for helping a film school grad
learn the ways of the long form narrative. We kept each other's egos in check
and wrought some good work, didn't we. Much love.

Technical Acknowledgements

Special thanks to <u>Philip K. Thomas</u> for developing my kickass website and giving me what I wanted only not the way I wanted it but impressing me all the same wiredforchaos.com.

<u>Dionisio A. Lind</u>, Carillonneur of Riverside Church who gave me a private tour of the bell tower complete with historical anecdotes.

<u>Taryn East</u>, author Cyberware Technology Project showered me with enough technical know how to make the brain operation where Brice has the neural interface (skull jack) implanted. I waited years for someone to have the technical acuity to address such a complex procedure

<u>Thomas Lippert</u>, Chief Scientist, Microvision, Inc. No way I could have tackled the "cutting edge in high tech visual displays…cortical induction of imagery directly from implants - bionic processors that will "learn" to provide compatible signals from image sensors throughout the electromagnetic spectrum, not just the visible wavelengths" without him.

<u>Yale</u>, *"How The Other Half Lives"*:
http://www.yale.edu/amstud/inforev/riis/contents.html

<u>Luc Sante</u>, *Low Life* (an indispensable source for all things gritty and old New York).

<u>Richard E. Cytowic</u>. *Man Who Tasted Shapes: A Bizarre Medical Mystery Offers Revolutionary Insights into Emotions, Reasoning, and Consciousness*, You never returned my email but thanks for writing the book none the less.

<u>Google search engine</u>; <u>Wired Magazine</u>, thanksahellofalot.

<u>Mark</u>, the front desk clerk at the <u>Shoreham Hotel</u> who allowed me to spend some time in the penthouse suite so I could get a feel for it.

<u>Linda De Luca</u> at Brown Harris Stevens Sales Agent for the MoMa Tower, sorry I wasted your time but the apartment was too die for and I needed to see it.

<u>New York City</u>, my home; grit, warts, shimmer and all. Period.

<u>Music listened to while writing Wired For Chaos</u>:
Miles Davis, theme from *Siesta*
Propellerheads, *Decksandrumsanrockandroll* (over and over)
Curtis Mayfield, *The Very Best of*

Wired for Chaos

Vangelis, Original motion picture soundtrack for *Blade Runner*
Bernard Herrmann, Original motion picture soundtrack for *Taxi Driver*
Crime Jazz: *Music In The First Degree*
Henri Mancini, Original motion picture soundtrack for *Touch Of Evil*
Sax And Violence, *Music from the dark side of the screen*
Jazz at the Movies Band, *White Heat, Film Noir*
Assorted Jimmy Hendrix, Living Color, and David Bowie

www•creationbooks•com